THE TEXAS SOLDIER'S MATCH

DEB KASTNER

&

JOLENE NAVARRO

2 Uplifting Stories

The Soldier's Sweetheart and *The Soldier's Surprise Family*

LOVE INSPIRED
INSPIRATIONAL ROMANCE

LOVE INSPIRED®

INSPIRATIONAL ROMANCE

ISBN-13: 978-1-335-43057-1

The Texas Soldier's Match

Copyright © 2022 by Harlequin Enterprises ULC

The Soldier's Sweetheart
First published in 2013. This edition published in 2022.
Copyright © 2013 by Debra Kastner

The Soldier's Surprise Family
First published in 2016. This edition published in 2022.
Copyright © 2016 by Jolene Navarro

Recycling programs
for this product may
not exist in your area.

For questions and comments about the quality of this book, please contact us at CustomerService@Harlequin.com.

Love Inspired
22 Adelaide St. West, 41st Floor
Toronto, Ontario M5H 4E3, Canada
www.LoveInspired.com

Printed in U.S.A.

CONTENTS

A *Publishers Weekly* bestselling and award-winning author of over forty novels, with almost two million books in print, **Deb Kastner** enjoys writing contemporary inspirational Western stories set in small communities. Deb lives in beautiful Colorado with her husband, miscreant mutts and curious kitties. She is blessed with three adult daughters and two grandchildren. Her favorite hobby is spoiling her grandchildren, but she also enjoys reading, watching movies, listening to music—The Texas Tenors are her favorite—singing in the church choir and exploring the Rocky Mountains on horseback.

Books by Deb Kastner

Love Inspired

Rocky Mountain Family

The Black Sheep's Salvation
Opening Her Heart
The Marine's Mission
Their Unbreakable Bond

Cowboy Country

Yuletide Baby
The Cowboy's Forever Family
The Cowboy's Surprise Baby
The Cowboy's Twins
Mistletoe Daddy
The Cowboy's Baby Blessing
And Cowboy Makes Three
A Christmas Baby for the Cowboy
Her Forgotten Cowboy

Visit the Author Profile page
at LoveInspired.com for more titles.

THE SOLDIER'S SWEETHEART

Deb Kastner

The Lord your God is with you,
the Mighty Warrior who saves.
He will take great delight in you;
in his love he will no longer rebuke you,
but will rejoice over you with singing.
—*Zephaniah* 3:17

To all the mighty warriors who daily put their lives on the line to keep our country safe.

Words are not enough to thank you for your service.

God bless you and your families.

Chapter One

Sell Sam's Grocery?

Samantha Howell snorted in outrage and crumpled the fancy-shmancy letter, written on white-linen paper, in her fist.

Over her dead body.

Her stomach tightened into uncomfortable knots, the same as it always did when she heard the name Stay-n-Shop. Didn't these people know what the word *no* meant? Just because they were a large corporation didn't mean they could walk over the little people, did it?

Actually, it kind of did. In fact, that was exactly what it meant. And unfortunately for Samantha, she was the "little people" in question.

Fury kindled in her chest as she flattened the note with her palm. As much as she wanted to toss the missive in the nearest trash can, she knew she needed to keep it. This wasn't the first time she'd heard from this giant bear of a company, but if they had their way, it would be the last. Stay-n-Shop had taken out a ninety-day option on land just inside the southern border of Serendipity. If she didn't sell to them, they'd "have no choice but to pursue permits and zoning" and begin building a store of their own. In short, the big-box store would drive Sam's Grocery out of business.

She chewed absently on her bottom lip as she reread the letter once again, her thoughts buzzing through her head like a swarm of angry wasps.

What was she going to do to save her store? What *could* she do?

"Excuse me, miss?"

The bell rang over the door and a moment later, a man's deep, unfamiliar voice registered in her ear.

"I'm sorry to disturb you. I'm looking for Samantha Howell. I was told I might find her here." His tone was as smooth as honey, with just the hint of a Texas accent.

"I'm…" she started to say, frantically sliding the crumpled letter under the nearby dry-goods inventory. Her breath hitched as she met the stranger's uncompromising brown-eyed gaze. She swallowed hard, trying to recover her composure.

"…Samantha Howell."

Having lived her whole life in the small town, it was a rare event for her to not recognize someone. Very few visitors ever came through Serendipity, Texas. The town wasn't even on the state map. She knew nearly every customer who frequented the store by name and could recount their lives down to the most current events.

Even more peculiar, she surmised the man was military, despite the fact that he was in street clothes. The severe set of his shoulders, his trim blond hair and the way he clasped his hands behind his back were dead giveaways. And his tan T-shirt was ironed, with a sharp crease lining each sleeve. Only military guys ironed their T-shirts.

She wondered which branch of the service he was in. Before leaving for Fort Benning for Basic Combat Training, her brother, Seth, had tried to enlighten her on the differences between the branches. At the time, she hadn't really been paying attention. Her brother was always talking about Army this or Army that.

To Samantha, military was military. She appreciated their service to the country, and she hung up her flag every Memorial Day and Fourth of July just like any other homegrown patriot would do, but it had all been lip service, without any truly meaningful connection to her real life.

Once Seth enlisted, that changed.

Now every newscast about the American troops, every update on the radio, was personal. It was frightening. It was family.

Seth.

In a matter of milliseconds, Samantha went from being curious about a handsome stranger to completely panicked over a brother living in consistently deadly conditions. She felt as if she'd been zapped with electricity from an open socket. All thoughts of Stay-n-Shop and her own problems instantly fled.

Was this man here about her brother?

Oh, dear Lord. Not Seth.

As the man's solemn gaze held hers, fear and adrenaline jolted her pulse. Her stomach rose into her throat in stinging, nauseating waves, then plunged back down again like a giant, out-of-control roller coaster.

The stranger's expression was grim, his mouth a thin, straight line slashing across hard, angular features. She could read nothing reassuring in his eyes and horrible scenarios spread like wildfire through her mind.

It couldn't be. Not her brother.

Seth had only entered the Army infantry last year. Immediately after his advanced training, he'd been deployed to Afghanistan, where he was working under extremely dangerous circumstances, with guns and bombs and who knew what else threatening him on a daily basis.

And now this military man had suddenly appeared, asking for her by name. Didn't the Army send a guy out when—

Oh, God, she pleaded silently, her heart pounding in her ears as she gasped for breath. *No, no, no. Dear Lord, please don't let this be about Seth. Please don't let him be wounded.*

Or worse.

Samantha gritted her teeth and shook her head. This couldn't be happening. Not to her sweet, charming baby brother, who'd always been the life of the family.

"Is Seth…?" she started to ask, her raw voice cracking under the strain and tears burning in her eyes. The man wasn't in uniform. Wasn't he supposed to be in uniform? "Where is he? Is he okay?"

Confused, the man's dark blond eyebrows dropped low over his eyes, but then his gaze suddenly widened in comprehension. His throat worked as he searched for words.

"No, ma'am. I mean, yes, ma'am. Seth is fine. That's not why I'm here at all." One side of his mouth twitched with strain as he lifted a hand and shook his head. "I'm sorry I gave you the wrong impression. I can see that I've unintentionally frightened you."

Frightened her? He'd scared her half to death with his sober expression. Her heart was pounding so hard she thought he could probably hear it from where he was standing.

"Seth is enjoying his tour of duty—or, at least, as much as a person can find pleasure in their deployment. He was born for military service, as I'm sure you're well aware. He excels in the infantry."

Relief washed over her in waves. This soldier had seen her brother, and Seth was safe and sound.

Thank You, Lord.

"Actually," the man continued, shifting from one foot to the other and clearing his throat, "Seth *is* why I'm here, although not for the reason you supposed. I assumed…" He cleared his throat again. "Although in Seth's defense, everything happened rather quickly."

Samantha's relief turned to bewilderment.

What had happened quickly? Seth could be airheaded at times, but forgetting to mention he was sending a soldier to their town defied being a card-carrying space cadet, even for him.

"I'm afraid I don't understand." A gross understatement, but a place to start. She leaned forward on her elbows and clasped her hands before her. "Obviously, I'm confused here. Can we begin again?"

The man took a step back and squared his already taut shoulders, as if she'd just invaded his personal space. Or maybe it was a figurative movement, a physical gesture indicating that he was preparing to start their encounter all over again.

"I'm Corporal—er—William Davenport. I've obviously caught you off guard with my arrival." His eyebrows lowered as he tilted his head toward her. "You don't know why I am here, nor were you aware that I was coming."

It wasn't a question, but Samantha shook her head, silently reevaluating the figure of masculinity blocking the stream of sunlight pouring in from the front glass window. "I'm afraid not, Mr. Davenport. I believe I'm at a distinct disadvantage here."

But she was quickly coming up to speed. Seth, easily diverted, had forgotten to call and let her know that his friend was coming to Serendipity to…

What?

Visit? Pass through town on his way elsewhere? Get some country air before returning to active duty?

It's too bad her parents' bed-and-breakfast wasn't up and running yet. If it was a little closer to their grand opening, this soldier might have been their first paying customer.

Now that Seth's safety wasn't an issue, she realized there was more her brother had neglected to mention—like how easy William Davenport was on the eyes. Even the scar marring his upper lip gave credence to his rough-cut masculinity. Her best friends, Alexis and Mary, would turn green with envy when she told them about her encounter with the man. If she could unobtrusively snap a picture of him with her cell phone before he left, even better. Then she'd really be able to rub it in.

"Please, call me Will," the man continued, breaking into her thoughts. "I'm recently retired from active duty—a civilian now."

Will. It was a strong name, fitting for the sturdy man before her. His voice had lowered with his brief explanation, and she had the distinct impression that he was uncomfortable with the civilian status he was declaring.

"I'm here to fill the position you have open."

"I'm sorry?" Samantha queried, so taken aback by

his statement that she jerked upright, sending both the dry-goods inventory and her briefly forgotten corporate letter flying. She watched in horror as each piece of paper floated slowly and in what felt like an intentional and deliberate way to the floor—directly in front of Will.

Her chest tightened. Maybe it was silly, but she had her pride, and she didn't like anyone reading her private business. But it had very literally landed at his feet, and there was nothing she could do about it.

It was a given that he had to go and pick up the papers off the floor. What else was there for him to do, since the Stay-n-Shop missive covered the tip of one of his meticulously shined black cowboy boots?

Samantha couldn't tell whether or not he glanced at the letter as he scooped it up. He gave nothing away in his expression and his eyes were dark and unreadable. She fought the urge to reach out and snatch the paper out of his hand, and then decided that would be too obvious a move, calling attention to the fact that she was uncomfortable with him reading the letter. Instead, she stood frozen, her hands fisted at her sides.

Without a single word, he turned and reached for the other piece of paper. Samantha quietly sighed in relief when he placed the grocery inventory over the legal missive. He spent a good deal more time looking at the dry-goods register, which made her almost as uncomfortable as the thought of him looking at the Stay-n-Shop letter.

His lips pursed briefly, his right eyebrow twitching once before his expression returned to stone. Had Samantha looked away even for a second, she would have missed the odd mix of emotions that momentarily registered on his face.

He lifted his gaze from the inventory and took a long look around the store, apparently taking stock of what Sam's Grocery carried, glancing back and forth between the products on the shelves and the list he still carried in his hand.

Was he judging the place? He gave no further indication one way or another of what he was thinking as he perused the shop.

"This is it, then? Your whole dry-goods inventory?" he asked, handing both pages back to Samantha as if they'd been his to begin with. He had a commanding air about him that Samantha didn't particularly care for. She considered herself a friendly and easygoing woman, but when it came to Sam's Grocery, she was used to being in charge, and she certainly wasn't used to being questioned about the state of her dry-goods inventory—especially by a stranger. Add to that the fact that she'd already had a long and stressful afternoon, and she was ripe for contention.

"Yes," she answered brusquely, not that it was any of his business. "So?"

"I am—I mean, I *was*—a unit supply specialist in the Army. I'm not sure how well that experience is going to segue into working for a small-town grocery, but I'll do my best. You'll find I'm quite diligent in my work habits."

"Yeah—about that." She jumped in before he had the opportunity to elaborate on why he was qualified for this job—the one he mistakenly thought was on the table for him, or worse yet, thanks to her capricious brother, believed was already a signed-and-sealed deal.

She was still a little unclear on that point. "I'm not quite sure I understand which position, exactly, you think we have open. As you observed, Serendipity is a small town, and this is a family grocery. We don't have much occasion to hire help here."

Clearing his throat, Will glanced behind him. Samantha followed his gaze and thought she saw a slight shadow flitting across the sunshine pouring in through the glass window, but she quickly brushed it off as nothing. It was probably only some animal scavenging for free treats.

"I guessed this was a family-operated business by the name on the sign outside. You're Samantha, the owner of the place and Seth's sister. That's the reason I asked specifically for you."

"Yup, that's me. My parents, Samuel and Amanda, recently retired and left the grocery to me," Samantha explained. "It's something of a legacy."

"Indeed."

Was he being condescending? Samantha's hackles rose until she met his earnest gaze—not warm, by any means, but sincere and intense.

"And do you do this all by yourself, or do you have other employees?"

"I have a woman who comes in and prepares the fresh deli products—you know, potato salad and cooked hens and the like. We sell baked goods acquired by the local café. My parents come in a couple of days a week to help out." She gestured to the rest of the store. "Other than that, you're looking at her—manager, stocker, cashier and bag-person," she said, relaxing a little. Maybe if she smiled at him he'd lose some of the somber tension from his face.

Smiles were supposed to be viral, right?

"Seth spoke of you often," Will commented in the rich, quiet manner that Samantha was beginning to realize was his normal tone of voice—not at all what she'd expect from an Army guy, based on what she knew of her brother.

"I'm sorry I can't say the same," Samantha said, regarding Will with new eyes. "Unfortunately, Seth neglected to mention you."

"He said you work too hard and never get a break, and frankly, he's worried about you. That's part of the reason I'm here—to take some of that burden from you."

As he spoke, Samantha noticed that Will's lips naturally turned down at the corners—they didn't lend themselves to an easy grin.

"Seth and I realized we could assist each other in what could possibly be an advantageous relationship for both of us," he continued. "Besides, you know your brother—once he gets something in his mind, it's hard to convince him otherwise." Will shrugged one shoulder. "So here I am."

"I see," she replied, though in truth, she didn't. The way Will was speaking, it almost sounded like he was here against his better judgment.

It was definitely against Samantha's. She wished Seth was here so she could knock him in the head. What was he thinking, sending someone who was probably a slap-happy, risk-taking adrenaline junkie to fill what was, for the most part, a repetitive and predictable position?

A *slow* job. Not that an employment opportunity really existed, but even if it did, nothing in Serendipity moved fast, nor did it change much from day to day. She couldn't imagine how Will would adapt to such sluggish surroundings.

Wasn't that part of the reason Seth had enlisted in the Army in the first place? To remove himself from a situation that would have eventually bored him to tears or sent him to the insane asylum? Samantha couldn't see how he expected that Will would fare much better. This soldier had seen combat. Working day in and day out in the grocery would be the polar opposite.

But maybe that was the point. Maybe that was exactly what Will was looking for. Someplace quiet to get away from the memories of war.

Great. *Now* how was she going to politely turn the man away? Like she didn't have enough problems already, trying to deal with the ever-increasing threat of a big-box takeover.

The bell rang over the door and her parents entered, their faces eager with anticipation. They rushed forward all at once in a gibber of exclamations, trying to be heard over each other to be the first to welcome Will to Serendipity.

Samantha reached for the Stay-n-Shop missive and tucked it under the counter.

"You must be William," her mother said, stepping forward to embrace the poor man, who looked dreadfully uncomfortable with the public show of affection. He froze at attention like a statue, his arms stiff at his sides.

Her mother, with bountiful curves and a frizzy head of blond hair, was a good foot shorter than Will. At her tallest, she didn't even reach the middle of his chest, but that didn't stop her from exclaiming loudly and squeezing him in what others might consider an excessively friendly manner.

To Samantha, it was just her mother being her usual outgoing, jovial self, not noticing how uneasy she was making Will and chattering on as if nothing was amiss. "Seth has told us all about you. We're so delighted you'll be staying with us."

Seth had told *them* about Will? And he'd be *staying* with them?

Two more shockers in a long day full of them.

Just lovely. Not only had Seth somehow arranged for Will to have a job at the grocery—apparently with her parents' knowledge and concurrence, and without a word to her—but now he'd be staying with them, whatever that meant.

Happily, whatever they were referring to, it didn't involve her, not directly anyway, since she lived in her own apartment close to the store. Her parents' house was empty most of the time, as they were working on their retirement dreams—building a bed-and-breakfast. They'd recently purchased some land along a gentle creek and were renovating several old cottages situated close to the water, but the cabins weren't yet ready for habitation. Seth's room was vacant, but surely her brother would never agree to such an arrangement. Many of his personal belongings were still in that room, untouched, souvenirs from his boyhood saved like a time capsule for when he was home on leave.

"It's good to meet you, son," her father said, extending his hand to Will.

"Thank you, sir," Will answered, clearly more comfortable with her dad's welcome than that of her over-affectionate mother.

"It's Samuel," her father corrected in his typical booming bass. "And my wife here is Amanda. The only 'sir' around these parts is my pop, Grandpa Sampson, whom you'll meet later, after you've settled in. We're glad you're here, and we're grateful to God for your help, both in the store and with our cabins. They're in dire need of repair before we can offer them to guests."

"I'm happy to be able to help you folks out and appreciate your offer of lodging, at least until I can get permanently settled."

So that's what it was, then. Room and board in exchange for his carpentry skills. Not such a bad idea, though she still wondered why no one had bothered to mention to *her* that Will was going to show up at her doorstep and demand a job.

Okay, maybe that was putting it a little harshly. Will hadn't exactly burst in and *demanded* a job. More like he'd simply assumed it was there—which, apparently, it was.

A simple "you've got a gorgeous ex-Army guy coming to work for you" would have been nice.

Samantha chuckled at her private joke. After the day she'd had, she either had to laugh or she was going to burst into tears. This was a lot to take in, and in a short time, too.

She pinched her lips, fighting the emotion surging through her chest, trying to sort out the mixed-up messages her heart was sending her brain and working not to give in to the indignant sense of betrayal she was experiencing.

Had everyone purposely kept her in the dark?

That stung more than she cared to admit. Why would her brother—never mind her parents—keep something this momentous from her? Did they not trust her? Did they think she wouldn't welcome Will with open arms?

She glanced at her parents, now speaking in soft tones with Will, and wondered if anyone would miss her if she slipped out of the store for a few minutes. She needed to vent to someone, preferably Alexis and Mary, whom she was certain would see her side of this situation.

She pulled out her cell phone and used her thumbs as she texted: *Gorgeous ex-Army guy just walked in.*

That should pique their curiosity. If she knew Alexis and Mary, they'd show up at the grocery faster in the hopes of meeting an eligible bachelor than if she'd told them it was a 911 emergency.

She gazed toward the glass door, focusing on the sunshine. The sun always reminded her of her faith and it generally gave her peace.

And it did, for a moment, until she caught the hint of movement from behind the candy aisle—and an adorable little girl appeared.

Will followed Samantha's gaze to where his four-year-old daughter, Genevieve, was peeking out from behind the candy aisle. All he could see of Genevieve from where he was standing was the thick mop of black curls that she had inherited from her mother and the large, inquisitive brown eyes that were very much a reflection of his own.

The scene would have been cute, he supposed, from virtually any other person's vantage point—a curious yet clearly shy little girl hanging back to see how the adults responded before announcing her presence.

She was a little darling, and she stole Will's heart

every time he looked at her, but the little girl's gaze also caused him a moment of sheer panic.

He was this child's *father.* She depended entirely upon him, and he hadn't given her any reassurance in this new and unfamiliar situation.

His throat closed and burned from the effort of withholding the onslaught of emotion. It was difficult to breathe, and his pulse roared in his head. Shame burned his cheeks. In all the confusion, he'd forgotten to introduce Genevieve.

She'd held back when they'd first entered, and he'd allowed her to stay near the door, thinking it would be easier for her if he served as point man. He supposed he'd expected her to come forward once he'd introduced himself to the management, so to speak.

Instead, she'd hidden in an aisle and stayed there— probably waiting for him to reassure her that everything was all right.

Which, to his chagrin, he had not done.

She was a furtive little thing—Seth's parents hadn't even seen her when they'd entered the store. But that was no excuse on his part.

This was not at all the impression he was trying to create with the Howells right off the bat, and most certainly not the way he wanted to treat his daughter. The fact that he *felt* entirely incompetent as a father was one thing. But he didn't need to display his inadequacies for the whole world to see.

Meeting Seth's older sister had really thrown him for a loop. Seth was a good-looking kid, so it should have been no surprise to him that his sister was an attractive woman. Samantha had straight, thick black hair cut in an appealing pixie style that showed off the endearing curl of her ears. She shared her brother's enormous cobalt-blue eyes, but they were breathtaking on Samantha.

Will cleared his throat and stepped over to his daughter, awkwardly placing a hand on her shoulder as he gently urged her from her hiding place.

"Folks, this is my daughter, Genevieve."

Genevieve immediately slid behind him, clutching at his legs and peering out at the unfamiliar people from behind his right knee. He crouched and picked her up in his arms. "Say hi to the nice folks."

"Hi." Genevieve said the word because her daddy had asked her to, but she didn't sound convinced that she should be speaking to strangers.

"May your daughter have a lollipop?" Samantha asked, coming out from behind the counter. He turned and met her gaze. Was this a trick question? Was he supposed to decline and ask for an apple instead? What would a *good* father do in this situation?

"I—uh," he floundered.

"She's not allergic, is she?"

"No. I mean, I don't think so." How was he supposed to keep his daughter safe if he didn't know vital things about her? He could accidentally put her in jeopardy without ever realizing he was doing so.

"Then perhaps just this once, since it's such a special occasion."

Will nodded, relief flooding through him. It was as if Samantha had somehow guessed that he hadn't known how to answer her and was filling in the blanks for him. He was grateful for her assistance.

Then again, she had put just the slightest emphasis on the words *special occasion*. He had the distinct feeling Samantha was a little miffed at him. It wasn't his fault she hadn't known he was coming. She could point that finger at her brother.

"Hey, Genevieve," Samantha said in a considerably sweeter, gentler tone of voice than she had used with Will. "Do you want to pick out a lollipop from the jar over there?"

She held out her hands, and to Will's surprise, Genevieve slid into her arms without the slightest bit of fuss. The little girl's eyes were still wide with a mixture of curiosity and hesitation, but she allowed Samantha to carry her to the candy jar. Samantha set Genevieve on the counter and lifted the lid so she could select the flavor of her choice.

Genevieve immediately picked purple. Grape. Will filed the information in his mind. Knowing Genevieve's preferences might come in handy, especially if he was ever asked to choose something in his daughter's stead—which he was beginning to realize was going come up more often than he could even imagine.

Clothes for school. Dresses. Shoes. Hair bows. What did he know about raising a little girl?

Nothing. Not a single thing.

Haley would have been able to pick out a lollipop for Genevieve. For all he knew, grape had also been Haley's favorite.

He realized to his chagrin that he didn't know *what* flavor his wife had preferred when she was alive. There were a lot of things he hadn't taken the time to find out about Haley, and now it was too late to rectify his oversights, to make right all the many ways he'd erred as a husband.

He cringed and squared his shoulders. Maybe it was too late to change the way things had gone down with

Haley, but he could still be a good father to Genevieve, and that was exactly what he was going to do—make it up to her for the years he'd been away, and never let her feel alone or unprotected again.

It was his one resolution in life—to make things right with his daughter.

"You want one?" Samantha asked, holding the candy bowl out to him. "It's on me. Free of charge."

Belatedly he realized he'd been staring at her and his composure nearly dropped. Only his many years of military training kept him from showing the apprehension that he felt in his gut.

For a moment, he'd actually considered taking the candy. He couldn't remember the last time he'd tasted a lollipop. Maybe not since early childhood. But he wasn't a kid anymore.

"No, but thank you for offering," he answered after an extended pause.

"She's a lovely little girl," Amanda Howell said. "Seth mentioned you're a single father?"

"Yes, ma'am." Will's throat felt scratchy and raw as he answered. "Genevieve's mother passed away about four months back. My daughter stayed with my in-laws until my tour of duty was up, but now I'm looking to be a full-time daddy to her."

"We'll help you as much as we can," Amanda assured him. "Isn't that right, Samantha?"

"Hmm?" Samantha was entertaining Genevieve and clearly hadn't heard her mother's declaration.

"I was just telling Will how we'd help him out with his sweet little girl," her mother repeated. "You're especially good with children. Genevieve has already taken to you."

Samantha's blue eyes widened as she looked from her mother to Genevieve and back again. Then her gaze turned to Will. "I think my mom is referring to me teaching the preschool and kindergarten Sunday school classes at church," she explained, shrugging one shoulder.

Teaching preschool and kindergarten. Those were pretty good credentials, as far as Will was concerned. As long as she didn't press Genevieve too hard on spiritual matters, she might really be the help he needed.

If she wanted to help him. Considering the way her mother appeared to be pushing him on her, Will wasn't so certain about that fact.

The bell rang over the door and everyone turned at once. Two women—one with windswept brown hair and green eyes, the other with long, straight blond hair pulled back in a ponytail—whirled into the place like a couple of dervishes on a mission.

"We came as soon as we heard," the blond said, flicking her ponytail as she made her way straight for Will. "This must be the handsome guy you texted us about. And an ex-soldier, no less. Whew!"

Will looked at Samantha. She'd texted her friends about him? Maybe she wasn't as put off by his appearance as she'd first appeared to be. In any case, she was definitely embarrassed now. Her face was bright scarlet, the poor woman, at the uncomfortable spot her friend had just placed her in.

Of course, they'd placed him in as equally tight a spot.

"My name is Alexis Granger. *Very* glad to meet you," the blonde purred, holding out a hand for him to shake. She had a firm grip, not one of those faint finger-shakes so many women were fond of. She was dusty and dressed for riding, and Will could smell what he guessed must be horses, a distinct and peculiar scent to which his nose wasn't accustomed.

It wasn't bad, exactly. Just different. And it was just one of a million and one ways he'd discovered so far today how dissimilar Serendipity was from the big-city and military lifestyle he'd known in the past.

"I'm Mary," the brunette said with shy nod. "Welcome to Serendipity." At least she didn't invade his personal space, although there was no doubt that she was eyeing him appreciatively. Between Samantha's two friends, Will was starting to feel like the candy in that jar Samantha was holding.

"I'm William Davenport," he said, shaking Mary's hand. Her grip was softer than Alexis's, more delicate. "Please call me Will."

"Will is going to be staying in Serendipity," Samantha explained. Her voice sounded high and strained to Will's ears.

Both of her friends exclaimed in delight and high-fived each other. Didn't they realize he was standing right here watching them?

Hello. Still in the room.

Mary and Alexis circled Samantha and launched into a garble of speech, but it was difficult for Will to make out what they were saying—and not because they were speaking in whispered tones.

Oh, no. Quite the opposite. They were chattering away like chickens in a henhouse, their voices high and staccato. Samantha held her hands up in protest and rolled her eyes.

Didn't these people ever have visitors in their town?

Or was it just the fact that he was a presumably single man that piqued their interest?

If that was what they were excited about, they were in for an enormous disappointment. Will wasn't the least bit interested in a relationship here in Serendipity. He was here to work, and to get to know his little girl—and that was it.

No more. No less.

He'd already messed up one woman's life with his attention—or lack thereof. He wouldn't do it again.

"We were just discussing where Will and Genevieve will be living," Amanda interjected, her voice a surprisingly reasonable, even tone compared to the younger women.

And he'd thought *she* was overly exuberant when he'd first met her.

"If he needs a place to stay, there's plenty of room on my ranch," Alexis offered with a flirtatious grin. "You could kick back with the stable hands. They've got a few extra bunks."

"I'd invite you," said Mary, her cheeks coloring a rose pink, "except that I live alone."

"You're not exactly alone with those gazillion dogs of yours," Alexis amended with a hoot.

Mary chuckled. "What about asking Pastor Shawn for assistance?"

"Ladies," Samuel said, toning down the conversation like a maestro controlling a symphony. "We've already got the details of Will's living arrangements worked out to everyone's satisfaction. He'll be staying in one of our cabins along the creek and doing cabinetry work for us in exchange for room and board. Everybody wins."

Samantha sputtered and looked like she was choking.

Her face turned beet red and her mouth moved, but no words came out. Clearly, she didn't believe *everybody* in this situation would win, but she caught herself and smiled at him.

Will clamped down on the emotions welling in his chest. She had no idea what her help meant to him. It wasn't easy for him to humble his pride and accept assistance, but this wasn't about him. It was about Genevieve, and he would do anything for his little girl.

With all he'd been through in the past months, *appreciation* didn't even begin to cover what he owed the Howells for their goodwill. He didn't know how to express it in words.

What he *could* do was pull his weight around here. He could shoulder some of the burden the grocery created. And he could get the B&B cabins into working condition and help the elder Howells realize their dreams.

"I'll get moved into the cabin tonight, and then I'm ready to start work first thing in the morning," he told Samantha.

Her eyebrows rose in surprise. "Tomorrow? Tomorrow is Sunday."

"Right," he agreed. "So?"

"So…the grocery isn't open on Sundays."

"Not at all?"

"Nope. The whole town rolls up at about six o'clock every night and all day on Sundays. You won't find much of anything open around here during the evenings and half of the weekend. Serendipity is an old-fashioned town with old-fashioned ways."

Will whistled through his teeth. "What do people do if they forget an ingredient for Sunday dinner?"

Samantha laughed. "Borrow from their neighbors or make do with what they have on hand. You'll get used to it after a while."

"I sincerely doubt that," Will muttered under his breath. As if he didn't have enough to deal with, now he was living in a town that not only *looked* like a throwback to the late 1800s but acted like it, as well.

"You're welcome to come to church with us tomorrow morning," Samantha offered. "It's a community congregation. You'll have the opportunity to meet a lot of the townspeople."

"No thanks," he said abruptly, and then realized how bad that sounded. These people had been gracious to him. He cleared his throat. "That is to say, I'm not really much of a churchgoing man. I appreciate the offer, though."

Samantha looked stunned and a little wounded, which surprised him.

"I'll be meeting most of the town folks here at the grocery, won't I?" he asked, in what he hoped was a more positive tone of voice.

"Certainly. Of course. You can meet people here at the store." Samantha smiled, though it didn't quite reach her eyes.

He hadn't meant to hurt her feelings, but surely he wasn't the only man in town who didn't believe in a feel-good deity who handed out free favors, or worse yet, an angry God who zapped people with bolts of lightning when He didn't like what they were doing.

If he was going to believe in one of those, it would surely be the latter. His life hadn't been graced with many favors.

But then again, if there was a God who punished

people for their sins, he would have been deep-fried a long time ago.

Somehow, he thought there was probably more to Samantha's request to join them at church tomorrow than just meeting folks from town. But now that he'd turned her down, he would never know.

Chapter Two

Sunday was Samantha's only real day off. As she'd informed Will, Sam's Grocery, like every other shop in town, was closed on Sundays. After she spent the morning playing the organ for the church and sharing a nice family dinner with her parents, Sunday afternoon was her time to kick back and relax, maybe read a romance novel or watch some television.

But today was a sunny day, and Samantha decided she didn't want to stay indoors. Problems were plaguing her and she desperately needed some fresh air to clear her head.

Her first inclination was to go find her friends. She was certain that Mary and Alexis had plenty to say about Will. They'd probably already started making plans for landing him a wife here in Serendipity, possibly even tossing a coin as to which one of them would have the honor.

But Samantha didn't really want to talk about Will. She didn't even want to think about him, though unfortunately, she couldn't seem to get him out of her head.

She was still mildly resentful of the fact that he'd had been thrust into her life with no notice.

Still, thinking about Will was preferable to thinking about her other issue—the letter from Stay-n-Shop. She still had no idea how she was going to handle that matter.

She sighed. One problem at a time.

Since Will was on her mind anyway, maybe she could do something nice for him and Genevieve. Take them to the park, maybe?

She raised her head and smiled, making a conscious decision to put her fears aside for the day and concentrate on her faith. This was Sunday, after all.

Despite her reservations about her new employee, she didn't have a heart of stone, and the guy had his plate full trying to take care of his little girl on his own. She had the impression he was determined to do his best despite the reticence she thought she sensed in him.

And Genevieve—the poor sweetheart, losing her mother at such a tender young age. Samantha had had a wonderful childhood with two parents who loved her and each other, and paternal grandparents who'd been married, well, forever, until her grandmother had passed away at age seventy-five last year. She couldn't imagine what losing a mother must feel like—especially for a four-year-old.

Samantha didn't know the specifics of how Genevieve's mother had died, but she knew enough to know that the little girl was both frightened and confused by her new surroundings, and by suddenly having to live with a father she hardly knew.

Yesterday at the shop, Genevieve hadn't smiled—not even when she was enticed with candy. Not even when her father picked her up in his arms. She'd barely spoken more than a word, though Samantha had encouraged her every way she knew how.

Did the child have some disability, or had recent circumstances and emotional issues just caused her to hide in her shell? She supposed only time would tell.

It didn't help that Will wasn't sure of himself as a father. Despite how strong he appeared upon first observation, she'd glimpsed the buck-in-the-headlights look when his eyes alighted on his daughter. That he loved her was evident. That he wasn't sure what to do with her was equally evident. Samantha didn't think he was as hopeless as he believed himself to be, but again, only time would tell on that count.

God had laid a lot on her plate in the past day. Will was here to stay, and somehow, she had to find a way to integrate him into her daily life. Like *that* was going to be easy. There was plenty of work to be done, and in truth Samantha was intrigued by the idea of having help, but not from the large, handsome ex-soldier.

She suspected he would be more of a hindrance than a help. Really, how could he not be? His size alone would be a hindrance—he'd be bumping into things all over the place. Besides, the store could only be described as slow and steady and the work was repetitive, with little beyond the daily routine to break up the monotony. He'd be bored one day into the job, and in her experience, bored men meant trouble.

Like her brother, for example, who couldn't keep an inventory straight to save his life, not because he couldn't count, but because he got sidetracked by every pretty girl who entered the store.

She sighed and reminded herself again that this was

not a day for problems. She didn't have the slightest idea what she was going to do with Will, but at least she had some idea of what to do with his daughter.

She walked up to the cottage door where Will and Genevieve were staying and paused a moment to collect herself. It wouldn't do for Will to see that she was still struggling with her own feelings of frustration and resentment. Those were her issues, not his.

She knew that God would want her to be generous and charitable—but knowing the truth and feeling it were two different things entirely. Sometimes a woman just had to live by faith and wait for her heart to catch up to her.

She took a deep breath and knocked.

No one answered, so after a moment, she knocked again, harder this time.

"Hello," she called. "Anybody home? It's Samantha." She thought about peering in the front window but decided it would be rude and might invade his privacy.

She'd just reached out to knock a third time when the door flew open and she nearly fell into the room. Will stood in the entrance holding Genevieve. The girl was wrapped in a green bath towel with a froggie face on the hood. Wet black curls framed her face and water dripped from her nose.

Will looked as if he'd taken a dunk. He was wearing worn blue jeans and an Army-issue tan T-shirt that was soaked with water, clinging to his chest and muscular arms. She couldn't help but take a second look.

Samantha held back a chuckle when she realized he had bath bubbles clinging to the spiked blond hair on top of his head.

"You…uh…" she said, pointing awkwardly, "have…"

Instead of finishing her sentence, she reached up on tiptoe and scooped the bubbles into her palm. With a playful grin, she held them out to him so he could see.

"A new fashion statement?" she teased.

She thought that would bring a laugh—or at the very least a smile—but instead his expression darkened.

"I was trying to give Genevieve a bath," he explained, as if it wasn't perfectly obvious. "As you can see, my mission was an epic fail."

Samantha smothered another laugh. Only an Army guy would consider giving his child a bath a *mission*. And how did one *fail* a bath, anyway?

Her gaze swept over Genevieve. "She looks clean enough to me."

Will sighed. "Maybe. But you should see the state of the bathroom." He gestured at his shirtfront. "Also, I hadn't intended to give *myself* a bath in the process."

Samantha made a final, valiant effort not to laugh at what Will clearly did not consider to be a humorous situation, but this time, a chuckle sputtered from her lips.

He looked at his shirtfront and then back at her, his twinkling chocolate-colored gaze mixing with hers. Her breath hitched.

"This is funny, isn't it?"

"Well…yeah. Pretty much. Cute, too."

"Cute?" He choked out the word, clearly appalled by the notion.

"I meant Genevieve," she assured him, though in all honesty, Will, with his wet clothes and bath bubbles in his hair, was every bit as adorable as his little girl.

Which was precisely what Samantha suspected a man's man like Will Davenport would *not* want to know about himself.

There was no doubt in Samantha's mind that every unmarried woman in Serendipity—except for her, of course—was going to be doing all she could to catch Will's eye. Will was going to have his work cut out for him.

"I came by to see if you and Genevieve might like to join me for a picnic in the park." She lofted the picnic basket she carried in her left hand. "I've got ham, turkey, fresh rolls, some fruit and cheese. I wasn't sure what you liked, so I threw in a little bit of everything."

He eyed the basket speculatively and then shook his head. "Thanks for the offer, but I think Genevieve might feel overwhelmed playing at a park with a bunch of kids she doesn't know."

"Is she normally shy around other children?"

He frowned. "I don't know."

"Well, then, there's no harm in trying, is there? If she's not enjoying herself, we can always bring her back home. But I suspect she may surprise you."

He glanced behind him, as if remembering something important he had forgotten to do. "I've still got a lot to accomplish to get us settled in before I start work in the morning."

She could hear the hesitation in his voice, but she couldn't tell if it was because he felt a duty to get his things in order, or because he didn't want to go with her and was searching for a polite way to decline her invitation.

"Oh, come on," she urged. "You have to eat."

"I'm hungry," announced Genevieve.

Will's gaze met Samantha's and they both chuckled. He tapped the tip of his daughter's nose. "Well, then, Monkey," he said, reaching to take the picnic basket from Samantha, "I guess we'd better get you dressed so Miss Howell can take us to the park."

Leaning on one elbow, Will stretched his legs out on the picnic blanket and popped a bit of a fresh whole-wheat roll into his mouth, savoring the way it melted on his tongue. The roll was perfectly baked, just the way he liked it—crispy outside and soft inside.

Samantha, Will was quickly learning, was a lot like the bread she'd brought—a little hard on the outside, at least upon first meeting, but a real softy inside.

Samantha shrieked playfully as Genevieve chased her. The little girl was, as Samantha had predicted, having a wonderful time in the park, both with the other children and with Samantha, who at first hovered protectively nearby without making Genevieve feel uncomfortable, and then flat-out joined in the games.

The kids accepted Samantha as if she was one of their own, as if it wasn't odd to see an adult crawling through their tunnels and climbing over the bars on their jungle gym. They laughed and played alongside her, even giving her a turn on the slide when she asked.

Will watched with amusement as Samantha worked up a little too much speed sliding down and, with a screech of surprise, landed on her backside, creating a cloud of dust in the sand.

Will was on his feet in an instant, offering her a hand up.

"That looked like it hurt," he commented as she brushed the sand from her jeans.

She beamed at him, her blue eyes sparkling. "The only ache is my dignity, and I don't have much of that to begin with."

Her lack of self-consciousness made Will a little jealous. He'd spent his whole life striving for decorum and honor, and yet he knew perfectly well that he had failed in every way possible to be a man. He'd never been able to please his own father. He hadn't been a good husband and father himself. He'd hurt the people he'd professed to love. Besides that, he wasn't ignorant of the fact that, with his naturally pessimistic personality, he came off as a regular old sourpuss, whereas Samantha, with seemingly effortless ease and grace, laughed at the world—and more importantly, at herself—and was a better person for it.

Though it pained him to admit it, he clearly had a lot to learn from the woman.

Genevieve ran up and tugged on the bottom of his shirt. "Swing me, swing me, Daddy," she begged, smiling up at him.

Smiling.

That hadn't happened much in the little girl's life lately. She hadn't had much to smile about.

Will's heart melted right there on the spot. What a beautiful child she was. He could see her mother in her, but what really choked him up was that he could see himself in her, as well. How had such a lovely little thing come from a soul as ugly as his?

"All right, Monkey," he agreed. "Let's go swing." He lifted her into his arms and headed for the swing set. He intended to deposit her into one of the safety swings, the ones with four sides and holes for the legs.

"No, Daddy," Genevieve protested. "I want to swing on the big-girl swing."

Will glanced at Samantha, hoping she'd give him

some much-needed direction. He didn't want to make the wrong decision and end up hurting his daughter.

"Yeah. Come on, Dad. The big-girl swing," Samantha echoed with a laugh.

Will realized that what he'd really wanted was Samantha to back him up on the decision he had already made, not agree with Genevieve. He was loath to admit that he was scared half out of his wits that his daughter would lose her balance and fall to the ground.

If she got hurt, it was all on him.

Both Samantha and Genevieve were looking at him expectantly, waiting for his decision. He didn't see any way out of it now. He was good and stuck. He set his jaw as he perched Genevieve on the *big-girl* swing, waiting until she had a good hold on the chains before giving her a gentle push.

"Higher, Daddy. Higher!"

"Honey, I don't know if that's a good idea," Will responded, once again glancing at Samantha for support, sure that she'd back him up on this one. Genevieve was so little, and the swing so high. It was a long way to fall.

Samantha laid a hand on his shoulder. "It's okay," she assured him. "Don't you remember when you were a little kid, what a thrill you got from swinging just as high as you could?"

Will cringed. He couldn't remember much from his own childhood, at least not much that he cared to recall. He knew he hadn't had a lot of playground time, not even when he was young. He'd had a strict father who believed children should be busy working for the food they ate. His father had never been happy with Will's performance, no matter how hard he'd tried.

The memory of his father's bitter voice echoed

through his head. *You can't go to church. Church is for good people. You are not good.* Will had spent all his time doing chores and studying for school and dreaming of the moment he'd be old enough to leave that house permanently.

The day he'd turned eighteen, he'd enlisted in the U.S. Army, and he hadn't ever looked back.

He wasn't going to let his daughter feel that way about *her* life.

With a whoop and a smile, he pulled Genevieve back and pushed, giving her the freedom to fly.

Chapter Three

"Yes. No. Maybe so." Genevieve repeated the words Samantha had taught her, a game she and her brother had played as a child. The little girl's high-pitched laughter pealed through the otherwise silent store, and Samantha's heartbeat rose in crescendo. She'd really grown to care for the little girl in the days since Will and Genevieve had so suddenly entered her life.

Samantha held Genevieve around the waist as the girl perched on the counter in Sam's Grocery and swung her feet in rhythm to the chant. Since it was summer, Genevieve was staying with Samantha's parents while Samantha and Will worked in the store, but the older couple had come into town to pick up some supplies from the hardware store and had dropped the girl off for a quick visit with her papa.

Samantha thought perhaps Will would join in the fun, but he just leaned his shoulder against the back wall, crossed his arms, and silently observed, his expression as unreadable as always. He was either angry about something or bored out of his skull. For all his glowering, Samantha had found Will to be a kind and soft-spoken man, so she guessed it was the latter.

Genevieve was clearly an expert at amusing herself and had quickly picked up on the game. Taking her cue from Samantha, she nodded, then shook her head and then shrugged offhandedly as she repeated the phrase over and over again, laughing all the more as her voice echoed throughout the store.

"Yes. No. Maybe so."

"Practicing to be a grown woman, Monkey?" Will asked, walking to the counter and ruffling his daughter's curly black hair affectionately.

Samantha practically did a double take. Had he cracked a joke? That would be a first. Will rarely spoke, and even when he did, he was solemn both in word and expression. Samantha sensed a golden opportunity here to draw him out of his shell a bit.

"Hey, now," she protested. "Watch it there, mister. You're in the company of a *grown woman*. You're going to get in trouble if you keep talking that way."

Will's left eyebrow darted upward. He wasn't smiling, exactly, but the corner of his mouth moved just a little. "Just sayin'."

Samantha sniffed in feigned offense. "No comment."

At least it appeared he was trying, which was enormous, not only for his own sake, but for his daughter's. Genevieve needed a father who could let go and laugh once in a while. Will wouldn't be qualifying as a stand-up comic any time soon, but his jest was more lighthearted than anything else she'd ever heard from him. It was progress.

"What have we got on our agenda today?" Will asked, his expression fading into the serious demeanor

Samantha now associated with him, the creases around his eyes and over his forehead deepening as his brows lowered.

"Not much," she answered, nodding her head toward the stockroom. "We've got a few boxes of canned vegetables to put out on the shelves. If you feel so inclined, you can give everything a good dusting before you place the product." She reached under the counter and grabbed a large ostrich-feather duster, waving it like a flag on the Fourth of July.

The look on his face was priceless, somewhere between pure surprise and utter mortification.

"You want me to dust with that?" he choked out.

"Is that a problem for you?"

"No." He answered too fast, clearly backpedaling. "It's just that…"

She raised a brow.

"I am going to look ridiculous using a feather duster. Do you want me to wear a frilly apron, as well?"

"Like a fifties housewife, you mean?"

He coughed. If it was anyone but Will, Samantha might have mistaken it for a laugh. "Yeah. Exactly like that."

She laughed, reached under the counter again and tossed a rag at him. "Better?"

"Much," he agreed, shifting from one foot to another and rustling the tips of his hair with his free hand. His lips pursed as he glanced from Samantha to Genevieve and back. She had the notion that he wanted to say something more, but he turned away without a word.

The man was already getting antsy. How on earth was she going to keep him busy? He was used to an exciting, fast-paced military lifestyle, not front-facing cans of green beans on a grocery shelf.

"I'll bring out the boxes of vegetables then." Without another word, he moved into the back room. She could hear him stacking boxes of cans onto a cart, and after a moment, he brought them to the shelves.

Samantha continued to play with Genevieve. She was glad to see the little girl coming out of her shell. School would be starting soon. The small, close-knit Serendipity classroom might be exactly what the girl needed to help her get past the trauma she'd experienced with her mother's death. Samantha hoped so, for Will's sake as well as Genevieve's.

She served the few customers who came and went, greeting each by name and asking about their lives. Often she could guess what they'd come in after without them having to say. That was what it was like living and working in Serendipity, and a big part of what Samantha loved about serving people as the grocery manager.

To her surprise, Will enjoyed speaking to the folks who'd stopped by. Though she'd expected him to be ruffled by the intimacy, the small-town dynamic didn't appear to be affecting him at all. He greeted everyone who came through the store with a friendly smile, taking the time to introduce himself and relay the brief story of how he came to be in Serendipity. Oddly, he didn't seem to mind repeating the tale over and over again.

Folks were curious, and Samantha knew that by the end of this week, if they didn't know already, most of the town would be aware she had a new employee. She was certain Mary and Alexis had already spread the word, igniting interest in the handsome, quiet, *widowed* soldier. Once the news reached Jo Spencer—the woman

who ran the local café, and the town's biggest gossip—
the blaze would turn into a wildfire. She'd have to fight
off the horde of single women who'd be lining up at the
door to the shop, making up reasons to visit the grocery
while waiting for Will to notice them. There had already
been more than a few who'd come in with nothing more
than a pack of chewing gum on their lists.

Well, maybe Will would be good for business. Samantha snorted and gave her head a quick shake. That
kind of business she really didn't need, but she supposed
beggars couldn't be choosers.

At the moment, any business was good business,
however it came about.

Thoughts of Stay-n-Shop loomed in her mind, but
Samantha pushed them back. She was still praying
about what course of action to take on that matter. She
didn't have a lot of time, but she knew better than to
act rashly without first seeking God's wisdom in the
Word and in prayer.

*What do I do, Lord? Please make Your will clear
to me.*

Those were the same words she'd silently repeated
dozens of times over the past week, and she knew she
was running out of time. *Make Your will known.*

It wasn't long before Samantha's parents stopped
by and picked up Genevieve, and the store seemed too
quiet without the little girl around. Odd, since before
Will and Genevieve, she'd often been the only one in
the grocery. She'd never noticed the silence before.

Samantha hunkered over the dry-goods inventory—
the one she hadn't finished on Saturday due to Will's
arrival—looking up only when one of her neighbors,
Delia Bowden, appeared outside the door. Delia's right

arm was laden with her newborn daughter, Faith, in an infant car seat while she managed her active toddler, James, with the other.

Delia usually brought her teenage son, Riley, to help out with the groceries, but today he was nowhere to be seen. No big surprise, Samantha supposed. The boy was getting to that age where he didn't want to be seen shopping with his mother.

Will opened the door for Delia, welcoming her into the store with a smile and procuring a cart for her so she could set Faith's car seat in the front. Samantha was still marveling at the way he turned into a different person when he was around the customers. It was odd—and unsettling—that he could turn the charm on and off like a light switch. Especially since it was usually *off* around her.

"Hey, Will?" she called, waving him forward.

He strode toward her, his smile disappearing. She was beginning to wonder if he just didn't like her. It wasn't that she thought he was purposefully trying to hurt her feelings, but she wasn't sure how she would be able to keep working with him every day if he didn't lighten up a bit. Her heart wasn't made of stone. And it *did* hurt.

"As you can see, Delia has her hands full with her kiddos," she said, gesturing to the woman and her children.

"Yeah. I noticed."

"It would be a great kindness to her if you could help her with her shopping."

"Help her?" He shook his head. "I'm not sure I understand what you're saying. I already got her a cart."

"I noticed. It was very thoughtful of you. I was thinking you could, you know, push the cart for her, retrieve groceries from the shelves, especially the high ones. Just give her a hand in general—whatever she needs."

"Wow," he said, whistling under his breath. He almost smiled at her. "Talk about customer service."

Samantha laughed. "That's how we do it in the country. Up close and personal."

"I'll say." Now he was teasing her. Honestly! The man was jerking her strings. "As I'm sure you're becoming increasingly aware, everything is more difficult with children in tow."

"Tell me about it. I can't seem to get anything done when Genevieve is with me. It's all I can do just to keep up with her."

There it was. Finally. A real half smile. He shrugged one shoulder and strode toward Delia and her children, and offered his assistance with a grin.

Samantha's breath caught in her throat. Will was quite attractive when he relaxed—which he never seemed to do around her.

"You're staring," said a high-pitched voice from beside her. Samantha started, audibly gasping and laying a hand to her racing heart as she turned.

"Where did you come from?" she asked Alexis, who was grinning like the cat who ate the canary. Mary stood beside her, a smirk on her face that said she shared Alexis's good humor—at Samantha's expense.

"Back door," Alexis replied with an offhanded wave. "Same as always."

That was the problem with back doors, Samantha decided. They could allow best friends to sneak up on her. There was no bell to announce them, although with the twitter they usually made, she was surprised she hadn't heard them coming.

"Did you ever think about knocking?" she groused.

Alexis hoisted one dark blond brow. "And why would we do that?"

She was right, of course, though Samantha was loath to admit it. There was no good reason for her friends to all of a sudden start knocking when they stopped by. They'd been visiting the shop unannounced since they were all in kindergarten together. This had to be the one and only time they hadn't made enough noise to be a circus parade—and of course it was when she'd really needed them to broadcast themselves.

This time, they'd come in on the sly and caught her staring at Will—which, of course, Alexis had announced in a none-too-quiet voice. It was unlikely that he hadn't heard her outburst.

"We've been here for a while now," Mary added. "We were eavesdropping on you and Will from the back room. That little girl Genevieve sure is a cutie. And Will is—" She broke off her statement with a sigh. "If you ask me, there's potential."

Samantha did *not* want to ask what kind of *potential* her dear friends had in mind.

"How is Sergeant Sweetheart working out for you?" Alexis asked with a loud chuckle. "Have you set a date yet?"

Will glanced in their direction, his brown eyes flickering with surprise. Samantha knew the best part of valor in this instance would be retreat.

Quickly.

"Sidebar," Samantha hissed, shaking her head. She grabbed each of her friends by an elbow and propelled them into the back room. "He was a corporal. And would you mind *not* bringing attention to him?"

"He's handsome," Mary disputed. "And single. You're single. I don't see the problem with it."

"Okay, there are a lot of problems," Samantha said, "but let me just start with three. One, he isn't single— he's a widower. Quite recently, I might add. Two, he is shy. And three, he is here to build a relationship with his daughter, not to have a romantic tryst with me, or any other woman in Serendipity, for that matter."

"Strong and silent," Alexis said, stroking her chin thoughtfully.

"What?"

"Not shy. Strong and silent. That's more poetic."

"More romantic, you mean," Samantha corrected. "And I don't like the insinuation in your tone, thank you very much."

"Will lost his wife, but that doesn't mean he has to be alone forever," Mary protested. "He deserves someone special in his life. I'm not saying you're going to marry him tomorrow or anything, but you could at least give him a chance when he's ready to move on."

"What I'm giving him," Samantha explained, thoroughly exasperated with both of them, "is space. And that's what you two ought to be doing, too. He's still grieving. Leave the poor man alone." She knew as she said it that that wasn't likely to happen.

Her friends would keep pushing and she'd balk, just like always. Whenever she'd start dating, her friends would be quick to call for further commitment, but it never happened that way. She'd find some reason or other to break things off.

She didn't know why. As cliché as it might be, it

wasn't the men, it was her. She believed marriage was God uniting two hearts in an inexplicable way. And until she found that, she saw no point in pursuing anything with anybody. Especially not with Will, who wasn't even a Christian.

"Samantha?" Will called from the front room. "Can you give me a hand? I'm having a bit of trouble with the register."

It didn't surprise her that Will couldn't pick up on the rusty machine. The cash register was older than she was, the ancient iron punch-the-dollar-sign kind that had faded out with the advent of the first computer. It fit the country feel of the grocery, though, so Samantha had kept it. She'd been using it for so many years she didn't think twice about it, but she could definitely see where Will might get confused.

"I'm going back in there to serve my customers," Samantha whispered. "And you two are going to get out of here and leave us in peace. Please, *please* promise me that you won't put Will on the spot."

"Yes. No. Maybe so," Alexis responded with a matchmaking gleam in her eye.

"So what do you do for fun around here?" Will asked as he swept dust out the front door and across the clapboard sidewalk. Samantha had just turned the sign from Open to Closed and they were cleaning up before leaving for the night. "Ride horses?"

He thought it seemed like a reasonable question. So far he'd seen a lot of trucks on the road, and at least an equal number of horses on the ranchland he passed as he walked every morning from the Howells' bed-and-breakfast to the store, and then back again each evening.

Samantha stopped wiping the front window she'd just sprayed with glass cleaner and narrowed her eyes, one hand drifting to perch on her hip. "Why would you say that?"

"I don't know. I guess because I noticed the old hitching post in front of Cup o' Jo's Café when I passed it this morning. Watering trough, too, I think. The thing looks like it's been there for a hundred years."

Samantha shrugged. "It probably has been. Folks do occasionally use it when they stop at Cup o' Jo's, if they're out riding that way. It doesn't happen very often, though. We're not quite as backward here as you might imagine."

He held up his hands. "Innocent observation. No offense meant."

"None taken." Samantha laughed. The sound was unmistakably feminine and it mixed Will's insides all up. He cast around for something to say.

"Your friend Alexis reeked of horse when I met her." As soon as he said the words he realized how awful they sounded. He was used to saying what he thought without sifting it through the filter of what was appropriate in mixed company. Being around Samantha really messed with his head.

She lifted her chin, regarding him closely, the hint of a smile playing on her lips. He turned his gaze back to the cracked wooden clapboard and swept harder. It made him uncomfortable when she looked at him that way. Tingly all over, like last year when he'd caught a bad case of the flu and had suffered a raging fever of over a hundred and two degrees.

He remembered the incident well. It had already been inconceivably hot in Afghanistan, even without his fever. Every inch of his skin had felt like it was on fire, just as it did now. His breath came shallow and ragged, and his chest hurt with every lungful of air.

Not that being with Samantha was anything like catching the flu. It was a poor analogy, but it was the best he was able to do at the moment.

He couldn't pull the wool over his own eyes. He recognized the symptoms. The *honest* symptoms.

The bottom line was, Samantha was attractive in all the right ways.

"Sorry," he apologized gruffly. "My bad."

Again, Samantha chuckled. "No need. You're just saying it like it is. I don't think Alexis would be offended by your observation. She's a rancher and spends most of her time in the saddle."

"You're not easily affronted, are you?"

Her blue eyes locked onto him, and every nerve ending in his body sparked to life. The emotions rushing through him engaged him in a way he couldn't even label. "Why would I be? If you can refrain from any more insults about women and erratic behavior, we're all good. Yes, No, Maybe So is more than a kid's game—it's a lady's prerogative. And don't you forget it."

Will chuckled. The woman was really something. She kept him on his toes. To his surprise, he found that he enjoyed working with her far more than he'd ever believed he would when Seth had first approached him with the idea.

But then again, he hadn't yet met Samantha.

"Why don't you see if you can find something to do in the back room while I tally the register?" she said, moving back to the counter and tucking the window spray and her rag underneath.

"Yes, ma'am," he answered, surprising himself with how upbeat he sounded. His heart felt lighter, too. Was he actually relaxing a little bit? Taking the edge off that gut-slicing sensation of guilt which usually burdened him?

As he entered the back room, his eyes scanned over the bins and boxes, looking for something to keep his hands and mind occupied.

There really wasn't much to do. Samantha kept her store in tip-top condition. Even her desk was spotless. Neither a paper nor a pen was misplaced.

He'd seen how hard she worked, even when she didn't have to. She was motivated by something beyond his comprehension, and everything she did, she did with a joyful heart. He'd never seen anything like it.

Will moved some of the boxes from the higher shelves onto the lower ones, making room for new product. Samantha was a tiny little pixie of a woman, five feet four at max. How had she possibly done all the heavy lifting all these years? Some of these boxes were heavier than she was, not to mention that the topmost shelves were completely out of her reach. The notion of her toting heavy boxes using only a footstool or ladder made his stomach twist in knots.

Whether she knew it or not, she would no longer be slinging heavy boxes around the back room. Not on his watch. He had just appointed himself Samantha's own personal muscle.

He scoffed at himself and shook his head.

He was here to do a job, which was the important thing. This was what he and Seth had talked about—how Will could fix Samantha's problems for her. That's all this was.

Will sorted through the inventory, organizing the boxes by category, rotating them according to date and lining them squarely over each other. He placed the older inventory within easy reach and shelved the newer products up top. It was only when he was nearly finished that he noticed that a small box of chewing-gum packages had been wedged in the far back corner against the wall. He'd missed it on his first go-round, and since the candy aisle was looking a little thin, he reached for it, thinking he'd stock the shelf with the extra bundles of gum.

He wasn't paying that much attention to what he was doing until he realized that moving the box forward revealed a file of papers wedged between the box and the wall. He couldn't conceive of how they'd gotten there. It was almost as if they'd been placed there on purpose.

Samantha must have been doing paperwork and had set the file down on the shelving unit, where it had been accidentally lodged behind the box and subsequently forgotten. It was probably nothing she couldn't live without, since obviously she wasn't tearing up the store looking for it, but he thought he should probably place it on her desk for her to deal with at her convenience.

As he set the box of gum aside, he bumped the folder and several papers fell to the ground. They were letters written on upscale paper, the fancy masthead declaring some prestigious law firm based out of New York: Bastion and Bunyan and Turner, Esquire.

The name sounded pretentious to Will, but then, he didn't care for lawyers. His only brush with them was after Haley had legally separated from him, and that had been bad news all around. In his opinion, lawyers tended to be seedy types more interested in making money than representing their clients with integrity and honesty.

But what did Samantha need with a bunch of New York lawyers?

Even with his curiosity piqued, Will had no intention of snooping, but his gaze unintentionally drifted over the first paragraph of the missive in his hands.

His breath hitched sharply as he realized what he was reading.

A threat against Sam's Grocery, written in particularly nasty legalese, on behalf of the giant corporation Stay-n-Shop. Apparently they wanted to buy out her store and replace it with one of theirs, as they had with other small groceries in the area. But they weren't asking—they were demanding. This was their third and final offer. And if she refused...

It was now a great deal more than curiosity that led him to flip through the rest of the correspondence. This was personal, engaging his warrior's heart.

These letters were menacing coercions from an adversary. And they'd been intentionally hidden. Will was sure of it. Anger stiffened his joints.

Maybe it was none of his business, but he was working for the Howells, for Samantha, and he couldn't imagine what they must be going through right now. Samantha must be frightened half out of her wits with this big corporation coming down on her the way it was.

What he *did* know for certain was that there was no way Samantha would allow herself to be coerced into selling. Not for any price. He hadn't been around the Howells for very long, but it was long enough for him to know they were a close-knit family in a close-knit community—and he'd heard dozens of stories about what life was like growing up in Serendipity from Seth.

Sam's Grocery was Samantha's legacy. She'd even been named after the store—or rather, *for* it. No *way* was Stay-n-Shop going to take it away from her. Inconceivable.

He didn't hear Samantha until she was right behind him.

"Hey, what kind of music do you like? We can change the radio station if you want. I know country music isn't everyone's cup of tea."

Will instinctively drew the letters against his stomach, as if he could hide them from her. He shook his head. "Doesn't matter to me. I don't much care for music."

"How can a person not like music?" She sounded as astonished as if he'd just declared that he was originally from Pluto.

He shrugged. "I don't *dislike* it. It just doesn't matter to me one way or the other. Country, hip-hop, pop. Whatever. It's all the same to me."

"Okay," she responded, drawing out the word in a way that indicated she either didn't believe him or else thought he was off his rocker.

Or maybe both.

Will slowly turned around. "I rearranged your shelves," he said. Her eyes landed on the folder in his hands, and she blanched.

"You did *what?*"

"I pulled all of the older stock off the top shelves to make room to store the new product that will be coming in on Monday. I also rotated everything according to date." He held up the letters.

"And I found those letters Stay-n-Shop sent you."

For a moment, she just stared at them, wide-eyed and openmouthed. Her face went from white to green around the gills to a burning-torch red in a matter of seconds.

"Give me those," she snapped, snatching them from his fist and hiding them behind her back as if her action would somehow erase them from his memory.

"Don't you think we ought to talk about it?" he prodded gently. He wanted to know what her strategy was so they could plan their next move. It didn't even occur to him that it wasn't his place to help her put this problem to rights. This was war—the more troops, the better.

"This is my *private business,*" she hissed. "Butt out."

Well, that was straightforward and to the point.

It was also wrong.

"I can help, if you'll let me," he offered, resisting the urge to reach out and touch her. The woman looked like she needed consoling and every instinct in him was screaming to do just that—and more. He suddenly pictured holding her close, wrapping his arms protectively around her, brushing his palm across the softness of her cheek.

His breath left his lungs in a rush, as if he'd been punched in the gut. He took a mental step backward. What was he thinking? He had no right to even consider acting out emotions he didn't understand himself. He couldn't—and wouldn't—hurt her as he'd done to others.

"I'm just sayin'. I work for you now—for Sam's Grocery. It's my livelihood, too, and I've got a daughter to look after. Clearly I have a vested interest in keeping this store alive and kicking."

Samantha gasped and then turned and fled the room. Will stared after her, astonished. He'd thought his explanation regarding his investment in her battle was unambiguous. Logical. Rational. So why had she run out that way? Hadn't she understood that he was saying he had her back in this fight?

Apparently not.

Chapter Four

Samantha bolted through the back door and into the country sunlight. Her chest was heaving and burning. She took big gulps of air, yet she felt as if no oxygen was reaching her lungs.

Will wanted to *help,* did he?

And for such laudable reasons, too. Not because he was concerned about her or her family, but because Sam's Grocery was his current place of employment. He was only worried about himself—but then, why wouldn't he be? He didn't know the Howells well enough to put himself out for them.

It wasn't like *he'd* have to worry about a job once Stay-n-Shop got their way and moved into town. Once they'd built their new store, Will would no doubt have his choice of any of a dozen positions, with his experience as a supply specialist in the Army. They'd be knocking down his door.

So what was *he* anxious about? *She* was the one who stood to lose everything she cared about, everything she'd worked for in this life—the intangible items that went far beyond the old clapboard building itself, like family, tradition, legacy.

And yes, she had to admit, that she was battling her pride and her deep-seated need to remain self-sufficient. She didn't like anyone in her business, especially someone she hardly knew. And yet the notion of sharing the worry that festered in her chest wouldn't let her go. The need to unburden herself was profound and powerful.

But if and when she shared her trials with someone, it most certainly wouldn't be Will Davenport.

And it wouldn't be her family. Not her father. Not her mom. Not Grandpa Sampson, who was known to spill a secret occasionally now that his mind was slowing down with age. It was out of the question. No matter how heavy a load she carried, it was vitally important that her parents not catch wind of her ongoing battle with Stay-n-Shop. She didn't want to mention it at all until they absolutely needed to know, and Samantha desperately prayed it would never reach that point.

She wasn't ready to concede. Not yet. And in the meantime, what her parents didn't know wouldn't hurt them.

Her mom and dad, inheriting the shop from her grandfather, had struggled their whole lives for their family and the small-town community, working day in and day out to build Sam's Grocery into something stable and profitable. Only recently had they been able to pursue something different, to follow their own dreams and build their cozy little bed-and-breakfast.

There was no way Samantha was going to let Stay-n-Shop—or anyone else, for that matter—ruin that for them.

She didn't need Will Davenport's help. She didn't need anybody's help.

"Samantha?" Will said quietly behind her. He was close enough for her to feel the warmth of his breath on her neck. The man was seriously invading her personal space. She stiffened.

"What part of *butt out* do you not understand?" The guy had played all strong and silent, and he was good at that game. But now he was all up in her business? Why wouldn't he leave well enough alone?

"Look," he insisted, grasping her shoulders and turning her around to face him. "I know you're scared. And I'll back off if that's what you really want. But I can help you. I know I can."

"How?" she demanded. "How are you going to help me, huh? Do you have a law degree? Are you going to take on the corporate bigwigs? Rip up their letters? Fight them off with a stick?"

She knew she was being unreasonable, but so was he. Like he could just step in and make everything right. Sir Galahad riding in on his white horse with his lance and his sword, ready for battle, determined to save the day.

Wasn't going to happen.

"You can't solve my problems for me."

"You're right," he amended. He slid his palm from her shoulder to her elbow. "I can't solve your problem for you. But I can support you, and be there if you need me."

"What?" His statement caught her off guard—almost as much as her reaction to his touch. He'd barely traced a path down her arm, yet his fingers were warm. Reassuring and oh so real.

She was the first to admit that Will was an attractive man, but her reaction to the mere brush of his hand on her skin stunned her. She'd never felt this way in her life.

She needed to get out more.

"I'm your associate," Will continued.

Precisely. Reason number one thousand, four hundred and ninety-nine why I shouldn't be noticing the minty smell of his mouthwash and the well-toned muscles threading down his arms.

And most especially because, in essence, at least, they were arguing. She wasn't supposed to be *noticing* him at all.

It must be the anxiety she was experiencing, which she'd clearly misinterpreted as something entirely different.

That's what it was. She wasn't thinking straight.

"I hope you'll also consider me your friend." One side of his lip crooked up in a half smile. "I'll help you figure out what to do about this threat—if you'll let me."

"Thank you, but I don't need your assistance. I'm fine on my own."

"Are you?"

The sharp, confrontational tone in his voice made her bristle. Guess they really were quarrelling.

"Absolutely," she snapped. "And what makes you so certain I haven't already solved this?" The challenge in her voice was unmistakable.

"You don't sound too sure of yourself."

So much for unmistakable. Was her insecurity that obvious? She straightened her shoulders, determined to ride out this conversation on her terms.

"I know what you're going through," he continued, removing his hands from her elbows and jamming them into the front pockets of his blue jeans. His gaze altered, taking on a distant quality. She hadn't wanted him to touch her in the first place, but the sudden absence of his touch was as disquieting as the distant quality of his gaze.

"How could you know that?"

"Because I've been there." He took a deep breath through his nose and released it through his mouth. "I know what it's like to be overwhelmed by circumstances in your life. I've always been independent—probably too independent. More of a curse than a blessing. But there comes a time and place where you need to let other people in, you know? Allow them to help when they offer."

Samantha moved to a grassy knoll under a sturdy oak tree and dropped to the ground, sitting cross-legged on the cool lawn. Will followed, crouching next to her.

"I hear what you're saying," she admitted as her eyes met his. "But I have my reasons for keeping this to myself. It's a family thing, you know?"

"I respect that."

She expected him to say more. Instead, he held her gaze without speaking, his brows dipping low over the unreadable depths of his eyes.

"What?" she asked when the silence grew too much for her.

"You're stronger than you know."

She stared at him for a moment, figuratively openmouthed if not literally, and then she nodded, reluctantly accepting the compliment. Will was a rough-and-ready Army guy who'd been in active combat for his country. If anyone knew strong, he did.

"Me, not so much," he continued, his deep gaze shifting to somewhere over her right shoulder.

"How do you figure?" she asked. "You were career military until your wife passed away, right?"

He quirked his lips and nodded.

"Something noble and courageous compelled you to join the military." She held up her hand to stop his argument. Fleeing his childhood was hardly the most patriotic motivation for enlisting, but that didn't matter. Anyone who spent any length of time with him could see that he was Army through and through. "You re-upped at the end of your first tour, so serving your country was obviously important to you. And yet you gave up everything to take care of your little girl. That seems pretty brave to me."

He shook his head fiercely, denying her words. "I did what I had to do. You don't know the whole story."

He paused and scrubbed his scalp with his fingers. His expression was hard, his gaze haunted and bitter.

"I'd like to know more about you," she replied. She honestly wanted to know what made the silent ex-soldier tick. He had depths to him that she had yet to understand.

"No, you don't." He scoffed, turning his face away from her. As low and gruff as his voice had become, she barely heard the ending to his statement. "I'm not the man you think I am."

Will didn't know what had come over him. He had just blurted out a bunch of personal stuff he barely acknowledged himself, much less shared with another person. But there it was.

There *she* was.

Samantha.

Brave. Fierce.

Vulnerable.

His respect for her deepened to the point where—what? Unquestionably, he felt a deep desire to protect her, especially now that he knew the enemy she was single-handedly facing. The Howells must be feeling quite overwhelmed by now, Samantha most of all.

He desperately yearned for those qualities he knew he would never possess—certainly not the way Samantha did. Honesty and integrity came naturally to her.

She wrapped her arms around her knees and looked at him with a question in her eyes, no doubt waiting for an explanation for what he'd just blurted out.

Only he didn't know how to give it.

"I wasn't a very good husband," he admitted. Regret clogged his throat, making his voice low and raspy. "And I definitely wasn't a good father to Genevieve."

"How can you say that? I've seen the way you look at her, the way you interact with her. She's your world. And you are most definitely hers."

"It wasn't always that way. I was caught up in my job. I was away from my family when they needed me most." Will sat on the ground next to her, propping one elbow on his knee.

"How is that your fault? Being away from home a lot seems like a given in your profession. Was Haley unaware that you were going to join the Army when you married her?"

"She knew. She'd always known what I was going to do with my life. We dated in high school. She knew how much I wanted to get out."

He thought she might make him backtrack, given

the open-ended statement he'd just made, but she didn't interrupt him. He was thankful. It was hard enough to dredge up these memories without bringing his father and his home life into it.

"Actually, I was already in the service when we married," he continued. "She believed she was ready to make the sacrifice and be an Army wife—at least, at first she did."

Their marriage had been a great deal more complicated than he was able to explain. But he took a deep breath and plunged forward. "I didn't give her the emotional support she needed to deal with life while I was away. As a result, she felt all alone and lonely, whether I was home or abroad. Even when I was stateside, my mind was on my next deployment."

Add to that my bouts with PTSD and it was the prescription for a rocky relationship. Who wants to sleep next to a man who wakes up screaming in the middle of the night in a full-body sweat?

He wouldn't have wished that on his enemy, much less the woman he had vowed to cherish until the day death parted them.

Will nearly groaned as he recalled the many knockdown, drag-out fights he and Haley had had. And how much silence had reigned between them when they weren't at each other's throats. "We grew apart over time, and became different people. It was awkward between us. I didn't deal with my issues very well. I closed myself off from her and wouldn't let her in, and in the end, it tore up my family. *I* tore up my family."

"What happened?" she asked. There was more than keen interest in her voice. There was compassion—and empathy.

Two emotions he absolutely did not deserve from her. From anyone. He warranted censure, not understanding. But something about her kindness compelled him to keep going.

"Haley tried her best to reach out to me and be there for me. Far more, I am ashamed to admit, than I ever did for her. But at the end of the day, she couldn't handle the constant struggle and loneliness of military life. She had difficulties making friends, since we had to move around so much. But I think the hardest thing for her was her inability to continue her education. She wanted to be a child psychologist. Transferring from college to college was a nightmare."

He paused as the sharp ache of the past settled in his mind. "We'd been married for just over six years when she separated from me. Genevieve was maybe one year old at the time. She moved back to Amarillo, where her parents still live. We were both born and raised there. I think it felt safe for her to return to what she knew, and her folks helped her make a new life—without me in it.

"*Safe*. What a cruel joke that turned out to be." He closed his eyes and gritted his teeth against the pain clenching his gut. "My own daughter never really even knew me. Not until…" His sentence drifted off into a harsh silence.

It took him a moment to collect his thoughts. Samantha remained silent and pensive, simply watching him with compassion in her gaze.

"How did Haley die?" she gently prodded. When he did not continue, she backtracked. "I'm sorry. I'm being too pushy, aren't I? My curiosity often gets the best of me and I ask too many questions. Forgive me."

"No, it's okay. I started this conversation. I don't mind telling you."

Actually, he did mind. He minded dreadfully. If he had his way, he would never speak of it again. Never *think* of it again.

Yet he didn't blame Samantha for asking. He *had* directed the conversation down this path, although for the life of him he couldn't have explained why he had done so. Hers was a legitimate question, spoken with kindness. And he knew beyond a doubt that it was her kindness that would be his undoing.

He could handle judgment, but not compassion. This was his punishment, his burden to carry—keeping fresh his knowledge of the responsibility he bore for Haley's death, keeping it at the forefront of his mind for as long as he lived.

"She was killed in a gang-related incident." *Because of me,* he thought. "I'll never know all the details, beyond what the police were able to piece together. No one was ever charged or arrested for her murder."

Remorse settled heavily in his chest. Without saying a word, Samantha nodded, sympathetic tears in her eyes. It was almost too much for Will to bear, but somehow, it moved him to keep going.

"They surmise that it started as a mugging, given that her purse was found in a Dumpster and her wallet had been torn through. Her driver's license was still there, but the cash and credit cards were gone."

He twisted his lips as he recalled the details. "She was walking home one evening from her job as a waitress at a truck stop. A *waitress,*" he repeated, the word feeling like chalk on his tongue. She'd wanted to be— *should have been*—a child psychologist working in a fancy office in a good part of town, making more than enough money. But because of him, because she'd flown from their relationship, she'd had to pinch out a living for herself and their daughter any way she could. As a waitress in a truck stop. He hadn't wanted the separation in the first place. Even afterward, he'd wanted to support Haley and Genevieve, but Haley wouldn't take a penny from him. She'd wanted to be independent. Instead, she was dead.

He swallowed his gall. "She was stopped by a group of gang members. As best as the police can tell, when they tried to nab her purse, Haley fought back. And she was stabbed to death for her effort."

"Oh, Will," Samantha said. She reached for him, covering his hand with the smooth softness of hers and rubbing the pad of her thumb across his rough skin. "I'm so sorry."

"Thank you." She was incredibly gracious, especially considering he didn't deserve her sympathy. "What bothers me most is that they never caught the guys who did it."

He pulled away from her touch and got to his feet, stepping away so she wouldn't see him clenching and unclenching his fists. His blood boiled as he mentally counted to ten. He wanted to punch something, but he didn't want to show his anger and lack of control in front of Samantha.

"I have to live with that knowledge for the rest of my life. Had it not been for me, Haley would still be alive."

He had never before admitted that aloud to another human being. He felt like he was choking. He couldn't pull in more than a gasp of air no matter how hard he tried. For once in his life, he simply wanted to *breathe*.

Despite the slight relief that grazed his heart now that he'd finally opened up to the truth, he was mortified that he'd just blurted out his culpability to his new boss, of all people. She would have every right to fire him on the spot.

Even worse than that—what must she think of him now?

"You couldn't have known she was going to be attacked," Samantha protested. "You were a continent away, fighting in a war."

"Exactly."

His heart fell. She didn't get it. Frustration made his words a bit harsher than they otherwise would have been. "I wasn't there for Haley. I wasn't the man she needed me to be. If I had been, she never would have separated from me. She wouldn't have been in that dark alley in the first place. She should never have been walking home alone at night, especially in a bad part of town. If I had stepped up—if I had been a better husband to her…"

"That sounds like a lot of ifs to me."

"Yeah." He blew out a breath and leaned his shoulder against the rough bark of the tree trunk, staring unseeingly into the distance. She was a softhearted, benevolent woman. She wouldn't be able to see how he was at fault.

They remained silent for a moment, each with their own thoughts. Will was wrestling to contain the ugly guilt spreading through him, which always happened whenever he thought about Haley and relived the details of the terrible tragedy. He had no idea what Samantha was thinking, and he wasn't sure he wanted to know.

"We got sidetracked," he forced himself to say in a

lighter tone. He should have steered this discussion back to her a long time ago. "If I'm not mistaken, we were talking about how you needed to learn how to accept help from other people."

"And I believe I told you that I didn't need any assistance."

He made a sound in his throat somewhere between a cough and a chuckle. The woman was nothing if not stubborn. She refused to let him help her and her family in this fight, but what she didn't know was that he was at least as stubborn as she was. He *would* help the Howells keep their store.

"And as *I* said, sometimes you need it. Pride can only take a person so far."

Samantha's gaze widened. "Is that what you think of me? That I'm prideful?"

"Of course not. I see the bigger picture." He crossed back to her. "Look. I know how hard it is to ask for help. But you do what you have to do. I had to depend on Haley's parents, who, despite their declining health, took care of Genevieve until I was able to be honorably discharged from the Army. I don't know what I would have done had they not been there to keep me on my feet." He gestured toward Samantha. "Once I arrived in Serendipity, you and your family stepped up to help a stranger in need. You've all shown me and Genevieve such great kindness. I can never repay you. But I do wish you'd allow me to try."

Samantha's cheeks shaded a deep, alluring rose. She scoffed. "I don't know how you could call my welcome to you a *kindness*. It was lukewarm at best, I'm ashamed to say. Not very Christ-like at all."

"Only because you didn't get a heads-up that I was

coming," Will protested. He'd been around her enough to know she wasn't usually the type of person to see the bad side of a situation or a person. She was an idealist from her head to her toes. "You've already done so much for Genevieve. She can't stop talking about you. She thinks the earth revolves around Miss Samantha."

She chuckled and her face brightened. Will heaved a great sigh of relief. Maybe the world didn't *revolve* around Samantha, but it was definitely made better by her smile.

"I like her, too," she confirmed.

Samantha's blue eyes were shining with such sincerity and vibrancy that he was almost convinced there might be hope for his world. He didn't pretend to understand the depth of her gaze, but it affected him to the very core of his being.

A frisson of awareness skittered across every nerve ending in his body. He wondered if she felt it, too.

Never mind that. He pulled his mental brakes and put a tight grip on his response to her—the adrenaline that coursed through him and the way his heart was beating overtime whenever their gazes met. He supposed he could write it off as that of a man just coming back from a tour in Afghanistan, but he knew it was more than that.

Samantha was *special*.

But whatever was between them didn't matter. It *didn't* matter, because he wasn't going to let it. There was no way he was going to put himself in the position of caring for someone again. He was hazardous material and Samantha was too good a person for him to risk wounding her. Because no matter how hard he tried to prevent it, at the end of the day, that's exactly what would happen if he didn't stop this train before it started. The last thing he wanted to do was give her the wrong impression.

She had nothing to gain, and he had nothing to offer. End of subject.

He reached out a hand and helped her to her feet, careful not to touch her any more than was absolutely necessary; careful, in fact, not to stand too close to her, because he might run the risk of inhaling the sweet floral scent of her.

He didn't doubt that he possessed the strength of will to conquer those urges, if he put his mind to it, and he had enough respect for Samantha and her family not to toy with her when he had nothing of substance to offer.

He dropped her hand as soon as he was certain she had her balance and tunneled his fingers through his hair. He'd been a loner for most of his life. It shouldn't be difficult to maintain the facade of detachment.

So why was it that he had to continually remind himself that's what he needed to do?

"Are we finished?" he asked abruptly.

"Finished with work, or finished with our conversation?" She sounded confused, possibly a little hurt. He'd obviously wounded her by pulling back the way he had. He was sorry about that, but in the long run, she'd thank him.

"Both." He forced himself to meet her gaze straight on.

Her dark brows rose into high arches. She looked as if she was going to argue, and then apparently thought better of it. "Both it is, then."

She spun on her heels and started to walk toward the shop, but she suddenly halted and turned back. Her lips twitched as she narrowed her gaze on him, watching him carefully. He squared his shoulders and met her gaze.

"Will you be coming for Sunday supper? I know my parents really enjoyed having you over last week."

Up until that moment, Will had had every intention of spending Sunday afternoon with the Howells. Having not had much of a family life growing up, he appreciated the way Samuel and Amanda Howell drew him and Genevieve into their world. He almost felt as if they had become part of the Howells' extended family.

And the food was incredible. He'd never experienced anything close to the sizable country banquet they spread every Sabbath. He thought Amanda must cook the entire week just to present the fixins she offered, extending from one end of their sideboard to the other.

But the way Samantha had asked the question, he had the distinct impression she didn't want him to come. He narrowed his eyes on her, but her gaze gave away nothing.

"Yeah, I'm coming," he said after an extended pause. "At least I was planning on it."

There. That should give her a clear way out—if she wanted to take it. She could tell him to make other plans, simple as that.

But she didn't. She just gave a clipped nod. "Well, fine, then. My parents will like that."

He had no doubt that her *parents* would like it. They longed for their son, Seth, to return safely from the war. His absence was especially felt at the dinner table, where his chair remained empty. Will didn't mind sitting in for him. And Samuel and Amanda adored Genevieve, treating her like the granddaughter they did not yet have.

"What about you?"

As much as he wanted to know the answer to that question, he hadn't realized he'd spoken aloud until he heard her abrupt intake of breath. He winced. If he hadn't previously hollowed out his own grave, he'd certainly managed to mine a wide chasm now. At the moment, burrowing into that foxhole and covering his head with his arms to protect himself from the fallout didn't sound like such a bad idea.

She raised a brow. "What *about* me?"

Will's throat worked as he searched for words, but he simply shook his head and remained silent.

Because *that* was a question he wasn't sure he wanted her to answer. Because no matter what she said, it meant trouble.

Chapter Five

Well, that was weird, Samantha thought as she laid out the Sunday dinner china on her mother's table.

Two days had gone by and Samantha still couldn't wrap her mind around everything that had happened during her conversation with Will. Yesterday she'd been thinking of confronting him, or at least picking up where they'd left off, but Saturday was always the most hectic day of the week for Sam's Grocery.

As if regular weekend grocery shoppers weren't enough to keep the store hopping, the traditional Fourth of July celebration on the town green was scheduled for the coming Tuesday and folks were planning their family picnics and loading up with extra supplies, so it had been exceptionally busy in the store. Though she and Will had spent the entire day together, they'd barely spoken, and even then only about impersonal subjects having to do with the shop. By the time the day was over, they'd both been exhausted and had parted without another word to each other.

But so far, Sunday had been a good day of worship. Samantha loved playing the organ for the service, and today had been no exception. It was her gift to the church and the congregation, and she was always happy to do it, no matter how crazy the day before had been, no matter how many problems continued to plague her. She set it all aside when it came time to offer up to the Lord the music she carried in her heart.

She was looking forward to spending the afternoon with her family, including Genevieve, who always brightened the dinner table with her sweet smiles and innocent chatter.

And, if she was being honest with herself, she wanted to see Will.

He'd said he would be there, and she knew him to be good on his word. If she could sit near him or pull him aside at some point, maybe she'd get a better handle on what had happened at the end of their conversation; although to be honest, she highly doubted it. The man was an enigma. Every time she thought she grasped what he was thinking, he turned the tables on her and went off in a different direction. Now that she'd spent more time with him, though, she was beginning to suspect it was a defense mechanism. She couldn't blame him for that—not after all he'd been through.

As soon as she'd arrived at her folks' house for Sunday dinner, her mother had put her to work laying out place settings for the meal, using their best tableware. It wasn't fancy china—not out here in the country—but it was Mom's best set, the one she used when guests were present at their table. She treated Will like a son and Genevieve like a granddaughter, but they were company just the same.

As she worked, Samantha turned over the conversation in her mind again, hesitating only for a moment when Will and Genevieve arrived and seated themselves at the table. She tried to avoid his gaze, but she couldn't help but glance at the man from time to time, nor could she help the way her heart leapt as she watched him amusing Genevieve by making animals with his fingers.

She knew the exact moment he'd shut down their conversation, the moment when she'd pushed him too far. Physically, he'd drawn away and his posture had straightened into rigid lines. His jaw had tightened until she'd been able to see the tendons straining in his neck. But most telling were his deep brown eyes, which had shaded over, fading to black. It was as if someone had dropped a dark curtain over his countenance.

She might have been distressed by his reaction had the man in question not been Will Davenport, but Will was a complicated man who often shut down when his emotions were tested.

What she found *odd* wasn't so much the fact that he'd pulled away from her but that he'd been willing to open up to her at all. Out of nowhere, he'd trusted her with sensitive information she hadn't even solicited, much less pushed him on. She knew he wasn't the kind of man to go all touchy-feely, which was just one more reason she was confused by his forthright admission.

She had to admit that it was courageous for him to speak on those difficult topics. It couldn't have been easy for him. Will was a restrained man, preferring to keep his thoughts and feelings to himself, and yet he'd shared a very personal episode of his life with her. She suspected that he didn't speak of Haley often. Her memory clearly pained him, and Samantha now knew that guilt and bitterness accompanied his tragic story.

Looking back at it now, it was easy for Samantha to see why Will had suddenly wanted to drop the sensitive subject.

The question was, where did they go from here? She now knew his history. It changed the tenor of their friendship, as did his pushing her to allow him to support her against Stay-n-Shop.

He'd said what he'd said for a reason. She'd heard his message loud and clear.

He didn't believe she ought to face her war with Stay-n-Shop on her own. He wanted her to accept the assistance he offered.

But should she accept the assistance he offered? Could she let her guard down enough to allow him to stand beside her in this fight?

The idea—no longer fighting alone, having someone guarding her back—had its own appeal. Could she trust Will enough to let him in? To make him understand why she could not and would not share this burden with her parents? Would he keep her secrets?

With a perplexed sigh, she slid into a chair on the opposite side of the table from Will, Genevieve and Grandpa Sampson. All three were quietly eyeing the food her mother was placing on the sideboard. Samantha glanced at her father, who was sitting in his usual spot at the head of the table, his rectangular blue reading glasses perched on the tip of his nose as he completed the daily crossword puzzle in the local tricounty newspaper.

"Thank you again for inviting us, Mrs. Howell," Will said, nodding his head toward her mother. "It's an honor to share your table and be a part of your family dinner."

"It's Amanda," her mother corrected gently, a speculative look on her face. "Your folks weren't the family dinner type?"

Will shook his head. "No, ma'am. Can't say that we were. We usually ate off trays in front of the television, often in separate rooms. My pop wasn't home much during the evenings, and when he was—"

His sentence dropped abruptly.

Her mom approached Will's straight-backed figure and laid a motherly hand across his shoulder. "We can't help who we grew up with, son, but we can certainly make things better when we have families of our own." She shifted down the table to where Genevieve was sitting and leaned in to plant a kiss on the top of her head.

"Yes, ma'am," Will replied. "I'm hoping to do just that." He cleared his throat. "With Genevieve."

Samantha knew how very much he wanted that to be true. When he wasn't at work at the store or helping with her parents' B&B, Will spent all his time with Genevieve, learning what it meant to be a father. Anyone with eyes could see how important the sweet little girl was to him, and if the smile on her face was any indication, he was learning quickly and succeeding brilliantly.

Her mother reached for a pitcher of sweet tea and started pouring it into their glasses. "I was a foster child, tossed around from house to house in the Dallas area." Her gaze took on a far-off quality. "I had a good deal of trouble finding my way. Were it not for the Lord and Samantha's father, I don't know where I would be right now."

Samantha's jaw dropped. In the past, her mother had only shared pieces of the story with her, and she realized there was much she didn't know about her own kin. Unlike most of the other residents of Serendipity, her mother had been born and raised elsewhere. Samantha knew she'd aged out of the government system, but her mother had never spoken much of her childhood. Samantha was ashamed to realize she'd never given much thought to how her mother had grown up.

She'd never placed herself in Amanda Blake Howell's shoes.

How could she have been so insensitive, not to have known her mother had struggled through childhood? But then again, she'd never had a reason to suspect her mother had been anything less than happy. Amanda Howell was a cheerful woman, vibrantly in love with her husband of many years and clearly content with her family life. Her rock-solid Christian faith had helped many others in Serendipity make their way through adversity. However and wherever she'd grown up, she'd turned into a beautiful person.

"Thankfully," her mother continued softly, "for the most part, I was raised in good homes with churchgoing folks who cared enough to set me right with the Lord." She paused, an unfamiliar frown marring her brow. "But over the years it was inevitable, I suppose, that I'd stay in a few rough houses—I wouldn't go so far as to call them homes—where the money my guardians received from the government for supposedly keeping me fed and clothed didn't go to necessities."

She shook her head as if to clear her mind of the unpleasant memories, and then her smile returned to her face. "I seemed to have fallen off track here. All I meant to say, my dear man," she said, nodding at Will, "is that I not only sympathize, but empathize with where you're coming from."

Her mother moved to the head of the table, where she

stood behind Samantha's father and rested her gentle hands on his arms. Her dad covered her mom's hands with his, sending a loving glance and an affectionate smile over his shoulder.

"When I met Samuel," her mother continued, "he was taking classes at a community college and I was working in the cafeteria, trying to save up for my first semester of school. He ordered a grilled-cheese sandwich with a dill pickle on the side. I took one look into his big blue eyes and I knew I was a goner for sure."

Samantha tried to swallow around the lump in her throat. Her parents had been married for thirty-five years and they still shared a special spark. It was a relationship to which Samantha could only aspire.

Maybe that was why she was so reticent to form a relationship of her own. She was waiting for the kind of love her parents shared. Only God could provide her such a soul mate. Having a husband was one of the deepest desires of her heart, but it had to be the right man at the right time. Until then, she had a business to run—or *save*, rather—and a family to enjoy.

She smiled at her parents' beaming happiness. No way was Samantha going to let anything screw that up for them.

With a contented sigh, her mother finally took a seat next to Samantha and they immediately joined hands to say grace.

As she bowed her head, Samantha's heart lay heavy with her unspoken burden. Her father prayed a simple blessing over their food and their family. Samantha's petitions were not as trouble-free. She prayed for Will, for him to find peace from all the grief that haunted him and for him to be able to bond with his little girl.

She prayed for Genevieve, who was still facing major upheaval as she settled into her new town and school. She desperately prayed that she would find patience and be able to seek the Lord's will in her life, especially for guidance and clear direction on how to deal with the situation with Stay-n-Shop. What *could* one small-town businesswoman do against a large, well-financed corporation? The situation seemed impossible, when looking at it from a human perspective.

All things are possible through Him who gives me strength.

The Scripture verse was one she'd memorized as a child. It silently entered her mind, filled her heart, and gave her new hope.

She might be one small person in the big scheme of things, but her God was mighty. With God's strength and power, she could fight Stay-n-Shop, and she would do so with every fiber of her being.

But what she wouldn't do was involve her family. As she watched her parents laughing and sharing conversation over supper, Samantha renewed her determination to win this war alone. Anyone could see how happy they were, finally being able to live out their dream without worrying about Sam's Grocery.

When her mother spoke of expanding her opportunities to serve others through their new bed-and-breakfast, her entire face lit up with joy. And Samantha knew how much her dad loved to tinker around with construction and plumbing. They'd be in paradise.

And Will? Will had his grief to work through and his daughter to get to know. He didn't need the added burden of worrying about a grocery store he'd only been employed at for a few weeks.

No—this was something Samantha needed to settle on her own.

After the main course of country-fried chicken with sides of homemade potato salad, baked beans, deviled eggs and a cheesy broccoli casserole that was her personal favorite, Samantha rose and helped her mother clear the dishes.

"Anyone for pie?" her mom asked.

Will groaned in anticipation and patted his lean stomach. "I wish I had known about the pie before I took that second helping of chicken. I'm stuffed."

"I'm sure you can find a little room left in your belly for a slice of Phoebe Hawkins's cherry pie," her grandfather commented with a satisfied grunt. "She makes the best pies in all of Texas, maybe in the whole U.S. of A."

Will chuckled and held his hands up in concession. "Okay, you got me. I'm a sucker for cherries, and this Phoebe Hawkins of yours sounds like a diamond."

Will's words immediately had Samantha bristling like a porcupine and wanting to point out that Phoebe was happily married with two children.

What is that? Jealousy? Over a woman who bakes a good pie?

Just because Samantha couldn't cook to save her life didn't mean she had nothing unique to offer the world. She played the organ for church every Sunday, and she was a crack shot with a BB gun. She could pop tin cans off a log faster than a person could number them.

Baking pies, indeed.

And what did it matter, anyway? It wasn't as if she was trying to get Will's attention—especially not after what he'd shared with her on Friday afternoon. The man was nowhere near ready to move on. He needed time to heal. That was exactly why he'd moved to Serendipity. To find peace and to spend time with his daughter. Yet more reasons for her to release whatever crazy notions that were constantly niggling at the back of her mind.

Samantha passed out thick slices of pie, stuffed to the brim with fresh-picked cherries and smothered with large dollops of whipped cream. Though in general she watched her portions, she allowed herself a small piece, seeing as it was Sunday. Sundays were special occasions. Sundays were all about dessert.

"You like your work at the store?" Grandpa Sampson queried of Will.

"Yes, sir," he answered promptly, scooping another large bite of pie onto his fork and swallowing rapidly. Apparently good pie *might* be a deciding factor in his life, Samantha thought with a little smirk at her own private joke.

"So it's going well, then," her father added. He was clearly pleased that Will had segued into daily life in Serendipity.

"Yes, sir," Will said again, directing a nod at her father. "I like serving the local folks. It's all good, except for this Stay-n-Shop nonsense. It looks like they're making good on their threat to set up competition in the area. If you ask me, they're wasting their time."

"What?" Samantha's mother screeched over the clatter of forks hitting dessert plates.

All eyes were on Will—except for Samantha's. She took in panicked glances from the people she loved most in the world, watching as their peaceful existences tumbled into a pile of rubble akin to the Tower of Babel.

She wanted to scream. She wanted to crawl under her

chair and cover her head with her hands. She wanted to pummel Will for opening his big mouth.

What had he been thinking? He had to have known this would upset them. She'd told him to leave it alone. Why would he blow her cover on purpose?

"I—I'm sorry," Will stuttered, looking from face to face with a bemused expression on his face. "I just assumed you all knew. The correspondence I read…" He cleared his throat. "The first letter was dated quite some time ago. Naturally, I thought—"

His speech came to an abrupt halt as Samantha's father stood and slammed his palms down on the table, causing the dishes to rattle with the force of his impact.

"Samantha!" he roared. "Do you care to explain yourself?"

Samantha's gaze dropped from her father's frosty stare. "I have been… There are… We received…"

How in the world was she going to explain her rationale to her family so they wouldn't be angry with her for keeping them out of the loop? Everyone was frowning at her. Even the message in her grandfather's eyes was clear and distressing: *I'm so disappointed in you.*

A mixture of conflicting emotions went off like Roman candles in her chest. Anger. Fear. Shame. Desperation.

"I didn't want to burden you with this," she murmured in a choked voice. Tears flooded her eyes. She had the distressing tendency to cry when she got angry, and she was spouting steam right now.

Her gaze narrowed on Will. *Thank you very much.*

He frowned as if to say, *How was I supposed to know?*

The answer hit her like a two-by-four. He couldn't

have known. Because she hadn't told him. She hadn't told him that she was keeping her family in the dark about the Stay-n-Shop. So he hadn't realized the fight was hers alone.

The truth was, the situation with Stay-n-Shop would have come to light eventually, Will or no Will. What had she expected? That her family would be grateful? That there would be no repercussions for keeping it a secret?

She wasn't fool enough to believe they wouldn't be upset, but if she'd already resolved the conflict, at least their distress would be short-lived. They would be proud of her for saving the day. Now she'd never hear the end of it. That she'd kept the secret out of the best intentions of her heart was no longer relevant. Not to her father, or her mother, or Grandpa Sampson, who'd owned and operated the store long before she was even born.

"Genevieve, dear," her mother finally said, "why don't you go see if you can find your little dolly Natalie to play with? I think I saw her in the toy box in the play room. Or there's a video game set up in the living room, if you'd rather play that."

Everyone at the table waited silently until the little girl was out of earshot, not wanting to upset her. But the moment she was gone, all eyes turned to Samantha.

"You didn't want to burden us with *what?*" her mother demanded in the clipped mom voice Samantha immediately recognized as censure.

Samantha cringed. She might be a full-grown adult, but her mother was still her mother. She sat back in her seat, wrapped her arms in front of her and stared at her untouched plate of pie. The cherries, which only moments before had appeared delicious and mouthwatering, now twisted her stomach. She knew she'd never be able to hold down a single bite.

She'd essentially been outed, and now she had to deal. When her family discovered the full extent of Stay-n-Shop's manipulation, and all that she was keeping from them, she might not be invited back for Sunday supper until she was ninety.

What was she supposed to say?

"Do you want me to take this?" Will asked when she didn't immediately offer an explanation.

She shrugged and glared at him for good measure. *He* was the reason she was in this position. He might as well be the one to finish the job. Her head was already on the chopping block, and he held the razor-sharp ax above her neck. All he had to do was swing it.

"Samantha has been receiving aggressive correspondence from Stay-n-Shop," Will confirmed, his mouth a hard line of disapproval. She wasn't certain whether his scowl was meant for her, because she'd kept this situation from her family, or for the dire circumstances in general.

"We're all aware that they've been buying up local grocery stores in the area," her grandfather said. "Are you sayin' they're wanting to do the same to us? Take us out and put up one of theirs?"

Will's gaze brushed over her as he nodded grimly. The room erupted as everyone expressed their outrage and disbelief, shouting over one another in order to be heard.

Confusion mounted until her father put his fingers to his lips and whistled shrilly. He raised one hand in the air to take control over the ruckus. Still murmuring their opinions, the members of her family reluctantly quieted down. Will sat rigidly, his expression neutral. Surely he wasn't entirely unaware that his words had caused all this commotion. Samantha's blood boiled.

At least the guy should feel *something* after yanking the rug out from under her world. He'd altered the Howell family dynamic, maybe permanently. He'd quite possibly destroyed her parents' trust in her. Didn't he care about how she must be feeling right now?

"So what you are saying is that Stay-n-Shop has made an offer to buy us out," her father said to Will.

"Repeatedly," Samantha replied, but no one seemed to be heeding her words. She might as well not have spoken.

"Yes, sir," Will affirmed. "They're offering for the store. But there's more."

"More?" Her mother's head snapped up, her voice a good octave higher than usual. "Like what?"

"I told them I wasn't interested in selling," Samantha inserted, seething with frustration that no one appeared to be paying attention to her. It was almost as if they were ignoring her as payback, which she was the first to admit she probably deserved. Still, she had something important to say, and she needed them to listen. She spoke louder, increasing her volume to exceed that of the other folks in the room. "Believe me when I say I firmly declined their offers."

"Offers?" her mother parroted. "Plural?"

"Then why are we having this conversation?" her father asked simultaneously.

Because Will opened his big mouth.

"Because Stay-n-Shop wouldn't take no for an answer," she clarified. "They've acquired a ninety-day option on some property on the south side of town. They indicated that they would prefer to buy us out rather than build a new store, since it would be less of a hassle for them not to have to get new permits and zoning, especially since we already own the land around the store. They plan to use the additional space to build their superstore. However, if I don't cave in to their demands, they're fully prepared to move forward with building their own store."

"Consequently driving us out of business," Will finished for her.

Samantha's eyebrows hit her hairline. There was that *us* again. Will spoke as if he were one of them, as if he had a vested interest in Sam's Grocery beyond just working there. She felt like reminding him that he'd only been employed for a few weeks, and that she had hired him under duress.

She wondered if any of the rest of the family noticed Will's inclusive wording—and what they thought if they did.

"You received repeated legal threats, and yet you didn't think this was something we should be aware of?" her father asked Samantha in a barely controlled voice. He glowered at her as only a father could do. She didn't recall ever having seen him as angry as he was right now. His face was flushed, but it was his rhythmic stroking of the white goatee at his chin that made Samantha quake in her boots. Hopefully at least a little of that fury was directed at Stay-n-Shop and not at her. Otherwise, she was in the worst imaginable trouble. She felt like she was four years old again, getting in trouble for coloring on the wall. Only these markers didn't wash off.

Samantha took a deep breath and mentally pulled

herself together. She'd always known this moment would happen—she'd only hoped it would have been *after* the issue was resolved. She'd wanted to present this as a closed case, without having to worry them with unnecessary details. But she had to accept that it was what it was.

"I kept this quiet for your sake."

"How do you figure?" her father snapped, thumping the table with his fist.

Out of the corner of her eye, she thought she saw Will wince at the gesture. But it was Will—he didn't wince. Not at anything.

"Honestly? Initially, I didn't see a reason for you to get involved," she answered. "Granted, I was a little shaken up when I got their first letter, but I thought if I declined their offer, they would go away."

"You should have told us," her mother scolded.

Samantha nodded. "I planned to tell you when everything was settled. But then those corporate lawyers came back with a second offer—more money, more pressure. They indicated their intention of securing land in the area should I not agree to their terms."

"Seems to me the tension is running a little high in this room," Grandpa Sampson declared. "Let's remember we're all family here."

"Samantha has yet to explain herself," her father said.

"She was doin' what she thought was best." Grandpa Sampson silenced her father with a look that could singe the hair off a human being. "What's done is done."

"What do you suggest we do then?" After Grandpa Sampson's admonishment, her father seemed to have calmed down a bit, though a muscle still jerked in his jaw.

"I think the first order of business is to get our hands on those papers," Grandpa Sampson suggested. He was in top form tonight, his mind clear. "We all need to read the letters to get up to speed, get a better sense of what's happening. We can't support our Samantha if we don't know exactly what we're up against. You can get them for us right away, can't you, Samantha?"

"I'll get the file when we're done talking," Will offered. "If you all can watch Genevieve a bit longer."

"Much obliged," said her father.

"It's no problem," Will insisted. "I'm glad to do it—to assist you any way that I can."

Her father nodded briskly. He understood what Will was offering, and it wasn't just running to the store to retrieve a file. He was stepping up for the family, just as he'd said he would. She didn't know whether to be relieved or feel bulldozed by his insistence on meddling in her personal business—or rather, the family business.

"Before you leave, Will, we should pray about it," her mother added. "God knows the specifics better than we ever will, with the letters or without them."

"I still have questions, Samantha," her father said. "You have yet to explain why you thought it would be better to keep us in the dark about this whole situation rather than coming to us for help," he reminded her. "We've worked our whole lives in order to bring you the security of the grocery, a legacy you could continue, should you so choose."

"Exactly my point," Samantha said. "You *have* worked your whole lives to give me Sam's Grocery, and I appreciate it more than you'll ever know. It's become my life's dream. Most all of what I want to accomplish in life is tied up in that store."

"All the more reason for you to have brought us in on this," her father argued.

"Or all the more reason for me not to bring you in at all," Samantha countered. "You finally have the opportunity to do something *you've* always wanted to do—run the bed-and-breakfast. Now I've ruined it for you, and don't say I haven't."

"How do you figure?" her father demanded, sounding a little bit wounded by her declaration. "You haven't ruined anything. It's hardly your fault corporate America is nipping at your heels. What you're saying doesn't make any sense."

"I don't think she meant any harm by withholding information," Will offered. "She really had the best intentions in mind by not telling you."

Samantha glanced at Will, surprised by his support. Did he actually understand why she'd not shared the information with her parents?

She knew she'd hurt a lot of feelings, and she wasn't sure how to repair the mess she'd made. She continued her explanation, folding and refolding her napkin in perfect lines to give her hands something to do. "I knew exactly what you would do if I told you about the situation with Stay-n-Shop. You would have set aside your own plans in order to help me until this whole mess was resolved. I mean, that's what you're going to do, isn't it?"

"You'd better believe it," her mother agreed.

"Absolutely," her father said at the same time.

"But don't you see? I didn't want you to do that. I still don't."

"Why not?" Grandpa Sampson asked. "The Good Book says that in a multitude of counselors there is safety."

Samantha threw her hands up in surrender. How was she supposed to argue with the Bible?

"I'll admit I may have made a tactical error in not bringing this to you sooner. Maybe I do need help. I'm not having any issues keeping Sam's in the black, but we don't have enough savings to hire a lawyer—definitely not the kind of lawyer we'd need to fight an enormous corporation like Stay-n-Shop."

"Then we'll have to find another way to win this battle—without a lawyer," her father stated grimly, and Will nodded in agreement. "It's up to us to find a way to fight back on our own."

Samantha felt oddly comforted now that she had other people by her side to support her. Maybe Will had been right. At the very least, she felt a little less defeated now that her family was with her. Even in their anger, she felt their love.

"I'm beginning to think I know what David must have felt like facing off against big old Goliath with nothing more than a sling and a few stones," Samantha admitted.

Will chuckled.

Chuckled.

She wanted to hurl something at him. Like her napkin. Or a brick. He just *had* to rub it in.

"Now you all are aware that I've never been to Sunday school," he said wryly. "But if I'm not mistaken, didn't David win that battle? Seems to me it all worked out well for him in the end, having God on his side and all that."

"You're exactly right, young man," Grandpa Sampson agreed with a satisfied grunt, as if he'd thought of it himself. "The Good Book says that the Lord our God is with us, the Mighty Warrior who saves. We can rest on that promise."

"I just hope we can locate vulnerability in our giant," Samantha said. "We need to find a chink in Stay-n-Shop's armor. Otherwise, we won't be slaying it with a dozen stones."

Before she realized what he intended to do, Will reached across the table and grasped her hand. Samantha was cognizant of the way the various members of her family were now staring at her with open curiosity and some amusement. But even more than that, she was ultra-aware of the gentle graze of Will's hand on hers. It was electric.

Her mother grinned like the proverbial cat who'd eaten the canary.

"It'll happen," Will assured her in his rich, firm tone. "We're going to beat these guys. You'll see."

Samantha scoffed. "And how would you know that?"

"Easy. Because I've seen your faith. And the faith of your family," he added. "If God is going to help anybody here, it's not going to be some huge, impersonal entity. It's going to be you."

"But you don't believe in Christ, do you?" she felt obligated to point out.

"I honestly don't know what I believe," Will admitted, shrugging one broad shoulder. "Being around you folks has challenged me to reevaluate. I'm still asking questions. I'm not sure. Not yet. But you are, and as far as I'm concerned, that's all I need to know."

Samantha was astounded, not only by Will's support, but by his revelation that the Lord was working on his heart. It suddenly occurred to her that maybe there was a higher purpose at work, something larger than just the fight between an enormous bear of a corporation and a tiny ant of a country store.

That *maybe* filled her heart with new hope.

"Sounds to me like this would be a good time to bow our heads in prayer," her father stated, breaking into her thoughts. The family murmured in agreement.

Will hadn't yet withdrawn his hand from hers. Their gazes met and he squeezed her fingers, one side of his mouth creeping upward.

It had taken a man of no faith to remind her of her own.

She was not alone in this fight.

She never had been.

Chapter Six

Samantha excused herself from the table just after Will. She wanted to make sure she caught him before he left for the store to retrieve the letters. She had a few things to say to him and wanted to speak to him before she lost all the steam she'd built up.

Should she be angry or relieved? She didn't know, but she was certainly eager to find out.

"Hey, Will." She caught up with him just after he'd exited the front door. "Wait up a moment. I have a question for you."

He turned to her with a frown. Nothing new there. Anyway, she was the one who had something to frown about.

But now that she was in front of him, she wasn't sure where to start.

He arched a brow. "I was under the distinct impression you never wanted to speak to me again. You wanted something?"

Yeah. An apology.

"An explanation would do, for starters."

Will dropped his gaze and shoved his hands into the front pockets of his jeans. "I guess I owe you that."

"You think?" She blurted the words out before she stopped to consider that they were a little harsh. "Sorry. I spoke in haste."

"You're not the one who should be apologizing here. I'm the one who spoke out of turn today."

"Perhaps. Why *did* you tell my family about Stay-n-Shop?"

"Why wouldn't I?" He looked up, his gaze challenging.

"Fair enough."

"I had no way of guessing you hadn't shared the information with your parents. I know now that it wasn't my story to tell."

"No," she said, her chest weighted. "It wasn't."

"I still think they have a right to know."

She swallowed her first defense. He was right, of course, which was probably what galled her most. "Be that as it may, I should have been the one to tell them."

"Yes, you should have." His gaze was compassionate rather than accusatory, which only made her feel worse.

"I'm worried about you, you know."

Her breath hitched in her throat. "Don't be. I can take care of myself."

"Why did I know that was what you were going to say?" He chuckled. "You're the most self-sufficient woman I've ever met. All I'm saying is, you don't always have to be. Your family loves you, and they want to be there for you. I want to support you, as well."

She could no longer hold his gaze. "Yes. Well, thank you for that."

He cleared his throat. "I guess I ought to get over to the store and get those papers. Your folks and your grandpa are waiting."

"Sure. Okay."

He nodded and walked away.

"Oh, Will," she called. "One more thing."

He turned back.

"I'm going over to the church to practice the organ for next week's services, and I was wondering if Genevieve could tag along. I thought she might enjoy playing around with the keys and hearing how a pipe organ sounded."

As the church organist, Samantha tried to spend at least a couple of hours practicing on the actual instrument—plus, there was something exciting about playing an instrument with that much power. She had an electric keyboard at home, and her parents owned a piano, but it wasn't the same as being surrounded by the glorious, melodic tones of the pipes.

Will hesitated for a moment. His lips twitched as if he were about to say no, but then he nodded. "I'm sure she would. How does a pipe organ sound, anyway?"

"Loud," she teased.

He was hovering, waiting for something. Samantha guessed he wanted an invitation to come along.

She hesitated. Perhaps she should invite him. It might be the right thing to do. But right or wrong, she needed space, time to process her thoughts and emotions.

"I'll have her back by five."

"All right, then." Once again he headed off toward the store. She watched until he turned the corner at the street's edge and she could see him no longer. Only then did she let out a long sigh.

She considered going back inside to spend a little time with her family before heading to the church, but she was still a little shaken up by the day's events, and she doubted anyone was going to let the Stay-n-Shop issue drop, which was all the more reason for her to make herself scarce. At least until Will came back with the letters and her parents and grandfather had time to read the corporate missives for themselves, pray over the situation, and allow their emotions to cool off a bit.

They might be angry now, but she knew that their prayers would allow them to come back to the figurative table with level heads. She didn't blame them for being incensed. Yes, they were Christians, but they were still human, and she knew she'd just disappointed them fiercely.

She made her way to the living room where she knew she'd find Genevieve, who was sitting cross-legged on the floor with a video-game controller on her lap. The television was playing and replaying a loop of music on the introductory screen of a preschool learning game. The TV was blaring a bit too loud for a song that was, in Samantha's opinion, obnoxious to begin with. Genevieve sat rocking herself in a soothing motion, staring blankly at the screen.

"Genevieve, honey, do you need help playing this game?" Samantha asked gently, sliding down on the floor next to the little girl and folding her legs in front of her.

Genevieve shook her head and continued to stare at the screen, her pink lips curling down at the corners.

"Do you want me to find a different game for you? I'm sure we have more choices around here somewhere."

Again, the little girl shook her head.

Samantha's heart sank as a realization hit her like a bullet to her chest, and made her stomach turn over in nauseating waves.

Genevieve had heard the grown-ups arguing in the other room.

The sweet girl was extra sensitive. Even if she hadn't understood the content, it wouldn't have been difficult for her to pick up on the tone.

Poor little thing. She'd been sitting here listening to the adults raising their voices at each other when they'd all assumed she was thoroughly engrossed in the playroom.

"Shall we turn off the TV and do something else?" Samantha suggested.

Genevieve nodded and turned her expressive brown eyes to Samantha. Samantha's breath caught. The little girl looked so very much like her father.

"Have you ever played a piano?"

Genevieve's gaze brightened but she shook her head. Sensing interest, Samantha had a gut feeling she was onto something. She'd noticed how intrinsically rhythmic the child was when playing with pans and spoons in the kitchen. And Genevieve often sang to herself when she thought no one was watching. Samantha suspected the little girl had a creative and artistic temperament—something with which Samantha was intimately familiar.

Music always brought Samantha peace. Maybe it would likewise benefit Genevieve.

"Well, we have a nice piano here at this house that you can play any time you want to, but at the church I've got an even better one. It's called an organ, and it makes all kinds of cool sounds. You can try it if you want."

"Yes, please." Genevieve's polite words were laced with excitement. It was touching how Will was teaching her manners.

Just one more way Will Davenport had reached Samantha's heart. How could she stay angry at a man who cared so much?

Will took a deep breath of country air. It was nice to be able to walk from the Howell's back to the cabin where he was staying, rather than having to drive everywhere as he'd had to do in Amarillo. Walking gave him time to consider all that had happened.

It was hard for Will to consider Samantha taking Genevieve somewhere without him, but he no longer felt the panic he'd experienced every time his little girl left his sight, as he had when he'd first come to Serendipity. Each day he found himself able to release her more, bit by bit, giving her the room she needed to grow into a healthy, confident child. He would have been apt to smother her to death had he not had Samantha there to temper his efforts. With her assistance, he was finding it easier to let his daughter go.

Samantha, on the other hand, was a different story. With every day that passed, he found his thoughts lingering on her more and more—and he wasn't just trying to find a solution to her problems with Stay-n-Shop.

It was Samantha herself who had his head and his heart in a regular muddle—all beautiful, generous, five feet four inches of her. He admired how, for the legacy of Sam's Grocery, she bravely stood as a buffer between her family and the big-box store, and how she'd wanted to protect everyone from pain and heartache.

He'd put her into a tight spot when he'd accidentally blurted out information he'd mistakenly believed the Howells had already known, and yet he had no doubt that the family would quickly mend their differences and pull together as a team. Samantha might have gone about it in the wrong way, but her heart had definitely been in the right place, and her family knew it.

Even with all the drama and tension, the Howells supported each other. As far as Will was concerned, this would be the day that he remembered as the first time he'd ever really understood what family was all about.

The only time Will had ever experienced anything close to that kind of solidarity had been in the military, on the ground in Afghanistan. Out there, soldiers had to have each other's backs.

What was it like to experience that kind of love and unity in a family? He was hoping to create that for his daughter. Would that he could give Genevieve the kind of strength and reassurance the Howells shared, so that she never had to fear she was alone.

Samantha was a great help in that area, offering Genevieve a good deal of stability and a friendly hand to hold. She had quickly stepped up for the girl as someone Genevieve could admire and emulate. Will found he didn't mind if Samantha wanted to add the faith element to her time with Genevieve. He knew that Samantha's relationship with God was a vital part of what made her the strong, compassionate woman she was. How could he possibly want any less for Genevieve?

Churches weren't his thing, and playing an organ didn't sound all that great to him, but he suspected Genevieve was going to love it—and Samantha had somehow instinctively known that.

As he neared his cabin located on the river's edge, he realized that being alone didn't sound all that appealing to him. The cabin would seem awfully empty without Genevieve. She filled up the room with—

Life.

Love.

He'd seen a lot of sadness and death—more than he cared to remember. Genevieve put him in a better place. She belonged with him now, by his side, with her little hand in his large one. He wondered how he'd possibly gone four years without really knowing her and being the father she deserved.

First tooth. First word. First step.

He'd missed all of that. One more regret that he would have to live with for the rest of his life.

He paused and swallowed the emotion burning in his throat. He silently vowed not to miss any more of those moments. Maybe he would take a peek in at the church and see how Genevieve was doing.

He adjusted his stride and turned left on Main Street, heading toward the steepled white chapel near the edge of town. As he approached, he noticed a sign staked to the undeveloped property across the street, and realized with a start that *that* was where Stay-n-Shop was threatening to construct their store. How ironic that the giant corporation wanted to build on that particular piece of property.

Selflessness versus greed in two blinks of an eye.

Except Will wasn't going to let that happen. He would do whatever he had to do, but he wouldn't stand there and watch the Howells' legacy go down like a sinking ship.

As he turned his attention to the church, he noticed one of the welcoming red doors of the chapel was propped open, and even at a distance he could hear deep, soulful music that threaded its way inside him, drawing him nearer.

Will had never in his whole life had an emotional reaction to music. No matter what kind of tunes were playing, they had never touched him or moved him. For him, music had been nothing more than white noise in the background.

But now it was as if the music wound around and through him, increasing in strength with every step he took, tugging him nearer.

Samantha was at the keyboard. It was fairly obvious that his daughter was there, as well, if the occasional discordant notes were any indication. He was impressed by the way Samantha played on regardless of Genevieve's help, maybe even encouraging the little girl to continue. He listened as notes poured from the instrument, seamless and beautiful as she allowed his daughter to join in the experience.

Will stopped just short of the door, feeling more awkward and reticent than ever before in his life. Marching into battle wasn't as challenging for him as walking into this church right now. Why was this so difficult for him? What was he afraid of?

Was he afraid he might discover he was wrong about God?

Church is for good people. The distant echo of his father's voice filled his mind as if he'd heard it yesterday. Will, as a youngster, watching his friends with their Bibles tucked under their arms as they made their way to Sunday school at the local chapel.

You can't go to church. You're not a good person.

This was ridiculous. It wasn't as if Jesus was going to walk up to him and charge him with all of his many failings. God's censure wouldn't be found within these four walls. God's sanctuary was far more than plaster and plywood. If Will had learned anything from his time with the Howells, it was that God was found within his people. That's who made the true difference. In his life. And in Genevieve's.

He stepped through the door and followed the sound of the organ to the sanctuary where the people of Serendipity worshipped. Deep oak-colored pews lined both sides of the room, with a wide, red-carpeted runner down the center. A large cross hung quite visibly up in the front, but his eye caught instead on a multicolored stained-glass window. The sun's bright rays were pouring through it, giving the picture of Jesus with his arms opened wide in welcome an ethereal quality that sent a frisson of awareness up Will's spine.

Unnerved, Will dropped his gaze to the white-linen-covered altar in the front. On the right wall were more pews—Will guessed for the choir—and on the left was the organ, from which came both melody and laughter.

Samantha slowed the pace of the music toward the end of the piece, finishing with a full, dramatic set of chords.

"Your daughter is quite the organ player," Samantha commented, peering around the side of the organ and waving him forward.

"I can hear that," he responded, starting in surprise. He didn't know how she could have possibly seen him enter when she was in the midst of playing what to Will sounded like a complicated piece of music. Her fingers had been flying over the keys in swift and complicated runs, up, down and then back up again. At the same time, without missing a beat, she was caring for his child—teaching her, even. The woman could definitely multitask.

"Come look," Samantha encouraged. "Genevieve knows how to find middle C."

He cracked a grin. "I assume that's an important skill in organ-hood," he quipped.

"You'd better believe it," she shot right back at him. "In piano-hood, too. The first step to a career as a concert pianist."

"That sounds good to me," he quipped.

"Daddy!" Genevieve exclaimed as he approached the organ, launching herself into Will's arms from where she'd been crouched next to Samantha on the bench. It was a good thing serving in the military had given him quick reflexes or he wouldn't have caught her. The little thing was as nimble as a chimpanzee, and every bit as quick.

Genevieve kissed his cheek and then wiped her mouth with the back of her hand.

"Yucky," she stated definitively.

Samantha chuckled, and Will joined in. "Are you trying to tell me that I taste bad?"

The little girl scowled adorably and shook her head. "No, Daddy. You have a scratchy face."

He ran a hand along his lightly stubbled jawline. He supposed he hadn't used a razor in a couple of days, maybe because he was no longer required to do so. "I guess I need to shave, then. What do you think, Miss Samantha?"

"Oh, I don't know," she said. "I kind of like the unshaven look on you. It makes me think *manly* and *rugged.*"

Will decided right then and there that he was going to keep those whiskers. He felt as if he were glowing like a fluorescent bulb. He beamed at Samantha.

"All right, Monkey," he said to Genevieve, who was, in fact, swinging on his arm as if he were a jungle gym. "Why don't you crawl on over there by Miss Samantha and show me who or what a middle C is?"

Genevieve scrambled back onto the organ bench, scooting in close to Samantha. It was an intimate and trusting move that made Will's heart warm. He stepped behind the ladies so he could better observe the process.

"Do you remember what to do?" Samantha prompted, holding up her right hand with her fingers spread wide and gesturing toward the top set of keys, only faintly indicating where the little girl's fingers should go.

"Use my thumb and not my pointer," Genevieve recited from memory.

Impressive. Samantha had had his little girl here at the church for all of, what, half an hour? And already she'd taught Genevieve to differentiate between her thumb and her index finger.

Will was definitely impressed.

"Ready? Set? Play!" Samantha exclaimed.

Genevieve's thumb came down on the key at an angle, so there was a bit of discord at the beginning, but whatever key she'd landed on, she held onto it like a pro, the note echoing deeply through the pipes.

"Way cool, honey," Will praised enthusiastically, meeting Samantha's gaze over the top of the little girl's head. He raised his brow in an unspoken question. *Right note?*

Not that it would change how he was feeling right now. His heart was filled with so much love and delight that he thought he might burst from the mere pressure of the emotions. He was so incredibly proud of his little music aficionado that it didn't matter what note she played.

"Middle C," Samantha crowed in delight, beaming as bright as the sunshine streaming in the windows. "Way to go, Genevieve!"

If Will's little girl was going to become a concert pianist, he owed it all to Samantha.

"Way to go, Genevieve!" she repeated.

He nodded in agreement, and then amended the statement slightly in his mind.

Way to go, Samantha.

Chapter Seven

William knew something was wrong the moment he heard Samantha gasp.

It was Thursday and the shop had been slow, so they'd decided to close up a little early. He'd been caught up listening to the twangy country song Samantha had been blasting from her radio as he swept the back room while Samantha counted down the till in the front, but her exclamation was audible enough for him to hear it even over the noise.

Or maybe he was just so in tune to her that he could *feel* her distress. Either way, his response was immediate.

Dropping his broom, he quickly emerged from the back room. Samantha's face was as white as a sheet. Her lips were tight and her pulse was pounding at the base of her neck.

He moved to her side, ready to suggest she pull up a chair and sit down to get her bearings when he saw the visitor standing just inside the front door. He was a tall, rangy man in a designer, pin-striped blue suit, complete with an elegantly folded white handkerchief protruding from the coat pocket and a camel-colored leather briefcase. He had a long nose and slicked-back black hair that put Will in mind of a vulture. He was one of those guys women might consider exceptionally good-looking—and he knew it. And knew how to use it, if the syrupy smile he flashed Samantha was any indication. The man reeked of overinflated ego and money.

To Will's relief, Samantha appeared to be having none of it. Her expression hardened and she tipped her chin resolutely. She looked ready to do battle. Will shifted behind her right shoulder, subtly reminding her that he had her back.

If the situation hadn't been so serious, Will would almost have felt sorry for the stranger. *Almost.* He'd been on the receiving end of Samantha's glare more than once, and he knew how uncomfortable it was, but it didn't appear to bother the spiffed-up, slicked-back fellow who still wore a confident, borderline-arrogant grin.

The guy set the hair on Will's neck on end. He was polite, charming even, but something about the situation struck Will as off.

Perhaps there was no reason to worry. It was possible that Will was misreading Samantha's signals. The blush now prettily staining her cheeks could just as well be from delight and not from distress.

But Will was a man who had long ago learned to go with his gut. His instincts had saved his hide countless times in the military. And right now every nerve in his body was screaming that they were in the midst of a minefield and he needed to protect Samantha.

Not that he had any doubt Samantha could hold her own. But it was with good reason that he'd been contending all along that a team was stronger than an individual. What was it her Grandpa Sampson had said? Something about safety in multitudes? Well, he might not be a multitude, but two was better than one. He'd learned that through his military experience and his family—and now, through the Howells. He owed them this, to be there for Samantha.

Besides, Will wouldn't be taken in by the man's easy charm or flattering looks.

The stranger laid a blue-backed document on the counter in front of Samantha and slid it her direction with the tips of his well-manicured fingers.

"My name is Cal Turner," he said with an unnaturally white-toothed grin and a hint of an English accent. "I'm here today representing the interests of Stay-n-Shop."

"I know who you are," Samantha replied, smiling politely, although Will thought—hoped—it didn't reach her eyes. "And I know who you work for. What I don't know is why you are here. I've already said my piece and it appears you don't care to hear what I have to say."

"I'm sorry?" the lawyer queried. Clearly he wasn't used to being countered. Will suspected that Cal had thought that a small-town country store owner would be easy pickings, especially a woman.

His sweet talk wouldn't work on Samantha. She was too smart for that, and Will was positive she wouldn't take it lying down. This was going to be interesting.

"Look, there's no sense running around the issues here, so let's just be blunt," Samantha countered, her voice soft but firm. "It is my understanding that you've purchased a ninety-day option on a piece of property south of town. According to your new plans, you no longer need Sam's Grocery. And even if you did, I've repeatedly declined your offers, generous as they've been. How dare you approach me again?"

Was that sarcasm? From the astonishment written in Cal's expression, the lawyer certainly thought so. Her declaration was bold and brash and completely Samantha. Call a spade a spade and force the charismatic lawyer's hand. Will's chest swelled with emotion—pride, satisfaction and an enormous sense of gratification when the slick fellow's jaw dropped. She'd clearly caught him completely off guard, which Will expected was exactly what she was trying to do in order to give herself time to think her way out of the situation. Will was happy she'd seen through Cal's manipulative tactics.

It wasn't, however, perhaps the best course of action when it came to Cal Turner. Will knew plenty of men like him—eager to do anything for the right price. He wouldn't mind bending a few rules, or ignoring them altogether, in order to get the end result he desired.

At the same time, Will understood Samantha's anger—shared it, even. And she was right. This guy was here for a reason, not a social call. If Stay-n-Shop had already settled on building a store in Serendipity, they no longer needed her or her grocery. She was, in fact, their direct competition. So why had the man presented himself here today, with legal documents to boot?

Was it possible that the Howells' prayers had already been answered? Was Stay-n-Shop pulling out of the picture?

Cal's smile disappeared and his blue eyes grew dark. He tapped his fingers against the document. "This is your lucky day. I've been authorized by Stay-n-Shop to give you one last opportunity to sign a deal with us."

"And why would I do that?"

"You might want to look over this contract before you make any decisions," he advised brusquely. "You should be grateful and know a good deal when you see one. Stay-n-Shop has upped the ante for you, although in all honesty, I can't imagine why." He took a sweeping glance around the store, a disdainful expression on his face. Clearly the country ambience that was Sam's Grocery did not appeal to Cal Turner. So much for pleasantness and charm.

Samantha sniffed. She'd seen Cal's expression, as well.

"They're offering you more than they've offered to any of the other grocers in the area. What are you waiting for?" Cal offered Samantha a black pen that was probably worth more than Will had made in a month in the Army.

"Apparently you are hard of hearing," Samantha said in a scathing tone. "I have no intention of signing your document. It's never going to happen. So why don't you just turn yourself right around and go out the way you came in. I'm sure I don't have to show you the door."

"I suggest you think before you speak, young lady," Cal snapped, looking down his nose at her. Now there was no question that he was a vulture. "Are there any lawyers in this boondock town? Because I highly recommend you get legal counsel before turning down this offer—not that I expect any lawyers around here will be knowledgeable enough to assist you in this."

Samantha merely raised an eyebrow and pointed toward the door.

"You obviously don't know what you're doing." His once-smooth voice sounded strained. "You're opposing perfectly good terms for a store that isn't worth half

what they're offering. You'd be able to buy a house."
He waved a hand in an encompassing movement. "And
what do you think all the people in your little town will
think about this? Your store is nothing compared to
what Stay-n-Shop can offer the people of Serendipity.
Variety. Discounts. *Jobs*. If they decide to build, you'll
be out of business within a year, maybe sooner. Mark
my word on that."

"Is that a threat?" Samantha asked through gritted
teeth, and Will slid a hand around her waist, curling his
thumb through one of the belt loops on her jeans. She
looked like she was about to spring at Cal like a rabid
dog. Not that the guy didn't deserve it, but choking the
life out of him wouldn't further Samantha's cause. In
fact, it might make things worse. Otherwise, Samantha
would have had to wait in line behind Will.

"Take my words any way you wish," Cal hissed.
"This proposal has a time limit on it, and the corporation is unlikely to put such terms on the table again. In
fact, I can pretty much guarantee you that this is the last
opportunity you're going to get. If I were you, I would
take it and run, before you have nothing to run with."

"Stay-n-Shop can build as big a shopping center as
they want to. They can never offer the kind of personal
customer service Sam's Grocery does. I know the names
of virtually everyone who walks in my door. I have loyal
customers who will never desert me. And if you think
they will, you don't know the first thing about family
legacies and small-town dynamics."

"Perhaps not, but I do know discounts. And I know
how fickle people are once they've had a taste of variety. And you'd be surprised how quickly your *loyal*

customers will switch to Stay-n-Shop once they realize how much they can save there."

Will could feel the tension in Samantha's back and knew how much it cost her to remain in control, yet she showed no signs of weakness. Her shoulders were squarely set in determination and her gaze never faltered from the lawyer's arrogant glower.

Will admired her strength, but he had seen and heard enough from this slick Cal fellow. He shifted so he was standing just behind Samantha's left shoulder and slid his arm from her waist to her shoulders, grasping her firmly, keeping her steady as he reached across the counter with his other arm. Leveling the lawyer with a glare, he planted his palm over the contract and pushed it back toward Cal.

"I believe the lady said she wasn't interested," he said. "I highly suggest you take your legal mumbo jumbo and get out of here."

Samantha shifted her weight so that her shoulders rested against his chest. He tightened his hold on her even more.

"This isn't the last you'll see of me," Cal warned, swiping up the contract and furiously waving it in their direction. "Next time I won't be so nice."

"You'd better hope there *is* no next time, buddy," Will warned. "You should stay away from here if you know what's good for you." If this charismatic scavenger thought he could mess with Samantha, he had another thing coming. Like Will's fist.

Cal's gaze faltered just for a moment as his eyes met Will's, and Will pressed his advantage, pointing toward the door. "I said go. Now."

Cal's gaze narrowed. "You can count on there being

a next time. We're already in the process of scheduling a town council meeting, so this is *not* the last you'll see of me," he growled. Then he spun on his heel and fled.

When the man was finally out of sight, Will realized how tightly he was grasping Samantha and loosened his hold on her. A little.

Enemy thwarted. Crisis averted.

For now.

The moment Cal Turner was gone, Samantha melted into the strength of Will's arms. She'd been holding herself so rigidly that when she took a deep breath, her head began to spin and she saw black spots before her eyes.

She had no doubt that Cal Turner would make good on his threat. He'd be back—no doubt with a legion of corporate lawyers trying to press for what they wanted. It didn't help to know they usually got exactly what they wanted.

She wished they would just leave her alone.

But what if they didn't come back? What if this was, in fact, Stay-n-Shop's last attempt to buy out Sam's Grocery? Perhaps they would simply begin construction on their own site, in which case leaving her alone was probably not for the better.

She sent up a silent prayer of thanks that Will had been there with her and had her back, both literally and figuratively, during the crisis moment. She supposed she should feel humiliated and embarrassed that he had witnessed the scene with Cal's counterfeit fawning and flattery, but she only felt gratitude toward him. She wasn't positive Cal would have left without Will's physical bulk backing her up.

Literally backing her up. She had to admit, sometimes muscle was a good thing. His broad chest had been—still was, in fact—a haven for her. She'd drawn strength from the silent power of his intensity, making it possible for her to stand up to Cal and appear strong on the outside when on the inside she was shaking.

Now that the misleadingly charming, intimidating lawyer had left and the immediate threat was gone, she was quivering with an intensity that frightened her. Even her teeth were chattering. She swiped a hand over her face, trying to steady herself.

Will tightened his hands on her shoulders and turned her around, staring intently down at her face. His gaze clouded with worry. He led her to a nearby chair, urging her to sit. "Can I get you something? A glass of water, maybe?"

"No. I'm fine," she insisted, although she felt anything but *fine*. She set her jaw, wrestling to contain her emotions.

"Just try to breathe," Will murmured, crouching before her and meeting her gaze with his intense brown eyes.

"I am breathing." She hiccupped.

"Yeah, you are," he agreed with a wry chuckle. "Breathing *fire*."

She laughed despite herself, and he grinned back at her.

"I just want to make sure you're okay."

"I'm okay, mostly thanks to you. You really helped me out today."

"You did a great job all on your own." Will nodded and reached for her hand, stroking it lightly with the pad of his thumb. "But I was glad to be there for you."

For her. Did he really mean that, or was it a slip of the tongue?

It wasn't as if she could ask him, but when his grip tightened on her hand and his gaze turned dark, words simply weren't necessary.

Leaning forward on one knee, he framed her face in his hands. They were large, rough hands—the hands of a soldier.

The hands of her hero, at least for today.

One side of his mouth curled into a half smile. His face was close enough for their breath to mingle, and yet he made no move to kiss her. He just drank her in with his eyes.

"You can always call on me," he assured her, running a finger down her forehead, over her nose and then brushing it backward across her chin. "Day or night, whatever you need. I'm here for you."

She struggled with the desire to reach forward, grab his collar and finish what he'd started. But when he rocked back on his heels, the moment was broken. For whatever reason, Will had pulled away. She didn't understand it, but she had to respect it.

Even if what she really wanted to do was fall into his arms.

Chapter Eight

"How's our handsome soldier boy?" Alexis asked Samantha as they stood in line waiting to buy sparklers and cones that sprayed fountains of sparks. The church youth group sponsored the booth on the community green, where the traditional Fourth of July picnic and fireworks display would be held later that evening.

"You haven't asked us to be bridesmaids yet. What are we to think?" Mary gave Samantha a friendly nudge with her elbow. "You couldn't possibly have imagined that we were going to forget about him, now did you?"

"I could only hope," Samantha murmured sarcastically, handing the vendor a twenty-dollar bill for the sack of sparklers and fountains she was purchasing. She glanced across the green, where Will was busy setting up lawn chairs for her parents and grandfather and spreading a red-plaid blanket for the rest of their group. He swung Genevieve around in a circle and plunked her down in the middle of the wool blanket, chuckling as she squealed with laughter.

"You could only hope what? That you'd have a ring

on your finger, or that we'd leave you alone?" Mary teased.

"Really?" Samantha rolled her eyes.

"Can we help it if we want to see our best friend settled down and living happily ever after?" Alexis gently prodded Samantha's ribs with her elbow.

"I don't know why you two are picking on me all of a sudden," Samantha grumbled. "I don't see either one of you showing off your diamond solitaires."

"That would be because our knights in army-green camouflage haven't yet ridden into our lives," Mary said with a sigh. "You are so blessed and you don't recognize what you have when it's right before your eyes. God just dropped him right into your lap."

Samantha snorted and shook her head. "I don't even know what that means. And trust me when I say that I don't even *want* to know."

"You can fool the rest of the world, but don't try to play ignorant with us. We understand you all too well. And even if we weren't besties, anyone with eyes can see the way he looks at you when he thinks nobody is watching him." Alexis's sly smile grew to epic proportions and her blue eyes sparkled with mischief. "Like right now, for instance."

"What?" Despite all her good intentions, Samantha turned to look at Will. He was seated on the blanket next to Genevieve, propped on one elbow with his legs stretched out before him, laughing at something her mother was saying to him. "He's not—"

"Ha! Made ya look," Alexis crowed. "Anyway, he *was* looking at you a second ago."

"That was so not nice," Samantha admonished, her

face warming, but she chuckled just the same. She should have known better than to fall for that old trick.

Her best friends could always tell when she was down, and surely they'd noticed something was bothering her lately. She wasn't spending as much time with Alexis and Mary as she usually did. At first they might attribute her absence to her spending extra time with Will, but it wouldn't be long before they figured out there was more going on. She hadn't yet shared with them the trials she was facing with Stay-n-Shop, but it was only a matter of time before they picked up on it—and before the entire *town* knew what the large corporation had planned.

Alexis bought her own sack full of fireworks and looped her arm through Samantha's. "Seriously, now. No progress to report to us girls?"

"I guess it would depend on what you mean by progress," Samantha countered, seeing a way to lead her erstwhile friends away from their floundering matchmaking efforts. It wouldn't take them long to figure out they were on a deliberate detour, but at least it would take the heat off Samantha, if only for a moment so she could catch her breath.

"Will is doing well at the store. Far better, actually, than I anticipated he would." Despite her best efforts, her gaze kept drifting to Will, which she knew was not lost on her friends. "He actually seems to like his work, although he's a bit of a perfectionist. He takes it seriously, in any case, and puts a great deal of effort into whatever he does."

"Was there ever a doubt?" Mary teased.

"In my mind, at least," Samantha admitted. "He's fresh from Afghanistan. He's got to be used to power and adrenaline on a daily basis. I thought he'd be bored to tears in a minute."

"Maybe the peace and quiet is just what he needs," Alexis suggested.

"Perhaps," Samantha agreed, watching Will from under her lashes. As long as he didn't look her way, she was good.

"And he's a daddy. He has a duty before the Lord to be responsible," Mary added. "That means he *has* to be all grown-up and manly and everything."

Alexis let out a low whistle. "He certainly has the manly thing going in spades."

Samantha rolled her eyes. "You guys are too much. Just leave the poor guy alone. He's my employee, for crying out loud."

"Is that *all* he is to you?" Alexis asked merrily, her blue eyes gleaming with gratification. Clearly she believed she already knew the answer to her question.

Samantha broke her gaze away from her friend's torment rather than answering the question. It might be friendly fire, but it still put her in a dangerous position.

"I thought not." Alexis's voice dropped as she pulled Samantha to a halt underneath a large, stately oak, out of hearing distance of all except Mary, who was a step behind them. "So what is the deal, really?"

Samantha sighed. It was so much easier on her when her friends weren't being serious. When they were just playing around with her, she could pretend all was right with her world. Maybe it was just a subconscious thing, but sometimes when she was laughing with her best friends, she found herself able to cling to the past, remembering her high-school days when the most taxing thing she had to worry about was whether or not her hair was working and who was going to take her to prom.

But when Alexis and Mary started asking genuine, compassionate questions—hard questions—her emotions became engaged, and she found herself very much on the verge of tears—like right now. Too much stress, she supposed, from every angle. Enough to throw any woman, even a strong one, for a loop.

But she was determined not to break down in the middle of a community event. Especially not in front of her friends—she knew them well enough to know they would worry about her incessantly and make a big deal over her problems, which was exactly what she didn't want to happen. It was more or less the same reason she hadn't brought her parents into the Stay-n-Shop fiasco.

Alexis and Mary had her well-being and best interests at heart. They were far more than mischievous matchmakers—they were the closest friends she had. They loved her, and at the end of the day, no matter how much they teased her and gave her a hard time, she loved them right back.

"How do you feel about Will?" Mary asked softly, so her voice wouldn't carry.

"I don't know," she replied, knowing they would never break a confidence. "I'm attracted to Will, obviously," she continued. She didn't need the guidance of her two friends to tell her that Will Davenport was a treat to the female eye.

"And?" Alexis prompted.

"And nothing. There's really nothing left for me to say. You want me to admit I have feelings for Will? Yeah. I do. There's definitely chemistry where he and

I are concerned. I just don't know what to do with it. I'm not sure I *should* do anything with it."

That was a gross understatement, she realized, thinking back to their near kiss just days before. She had needed his strength, and he had given it to her. She didn't harbor any misconceptions that there was more to it than that. It was the kind of special moment she'd waited her whole life to experience, but of course it had faded out as fast as it had appeared.

Will had backed away. And why wouldn't he? He was a principled man with honorable intentions, and he'd made those quite clear to her from the outset. She was just glad he'd been there when he had and that he'd had her back against Cal Turner.

"You guys definitely have sparks flying between you," Mary said, and then cocked her head and narrowed her gaze on Samantha. "Why do I feel like there's a *but* coming here?"

"Because there is," Samantha answered simply, riffling through the contents of the bag of fireworks she'd purchased so she didn't have to meet her friends' eyes. "Chemistry does not a relationship make."

"But you've got to admit it is a great start," Alexis said.

"In this case, no," Samantha denied.

"Why not?" Alexis was clearly not going to drop the subject, and even if she had, Samantha knew Mary would just pick it up again. Maybe it was better for everyone if she just set them straight on what was or, in this particular instance, was not happening between her and Will. Once and for all, and good riddance to the issue.

"Yes, that's right, but believe it or not, he told me that was the first time he's seen the inside of a church. Ever."

"Not even when he was a kid?" Mary asked, her curiosity piqued.

"Is he a member of some other religion?" Alexis queried simultaneously.

"No and no," Samantha replied. "My understanding is that Will didn't have the best family life growing up. I believe his father was a hard man, possibly an alcoholic, possibly abusive. They weren't a religious family of any persuasion."

"That's too bad." Mary's voice had softened and turned quite solemn. "Maybe the Lord will work on his heart while he's under your employ."

"I hope so," Samantha agreed, her heart welling with compassion for a man who'd suffered through so much hardship in his life without recognizing that there was a merciful God willing to see him through. "I really do."

Will had first caught sight of Samantha when he'd spread out the picnic blanket underneath a sturdy oak on the green. He might not have been looking for her, but his gaze had been magnetically drawn to hers all the same.

Okay. Maybe he *had been* looking. A little.

Which was probably why he'd been so distracted that his four-year-old genuinely beat him at several rounds of slapjack. He certainly hadn't purposefully lost the games. He had too competitive a nature for that.

Samantha was standing in a line for fireworks, speaking with her friends, whom he now knew, from knowledgeable and perhaps slightly gossipy neighbors and customers, were called the Little Chicks. As he observed the three women, he could easily see how they got that moniker—he'd never seen three ladies so animated in all of his life. Most of the men in Serendipity no doubt found that quality—and those ladies—quite appealing and attractive, which he supposed they were, but he was scared to death of women like them—outgoing, constantly invading his personal space.

Samantha most of all. She invaded his emotional space, and that was far more frightening than a woman stepping too close to him. Will knew her heart and her generosity, and for those reasons and more, he *did* find her attractive and appealing.

Better for him if he felt nothing.

Better for *her*.

"He who finds a wife finds a good thing, and obtains favor from the Lord," Grandpa Sampson remarked. He slid into a lawn chair near where Will sat watching Genevieve playing tag on the green with some of the other children.

"I'm sorry?" Will cleared his throat, attempting to erase the pure astonishment he knew was threatening to reveal itself.

"No need to hide it from me, son," Grandpa Sampson said with a hoarse chuckle. "I've seen the way you've been lookin' at her when you think no one's watching."

Will groaned inwardly. If Grandpa Sampson had noticed, others probably had, as well. His emotions were laid bare, and he'd never felt so uncomfortable, so vulnerable, in his life.

He shifted his gaze to the ground and picked at a piece of grass. "As you know, I've been married, sir. I wasn't very good at it."

"Perhaps," Grandpa Sampson remarked, "you just hadn't found the right woman. Yet."

Will couldn't let himself go there, even in his thoughts. It wouldn't be fair to Samantha.

"Just think on that, son."

Samantha was quickly approaching, and Will cleared his throat to alert Grandpa Sampson to that fact.

The old man just chuckled and leaned back in his seat.

"Check out what I just bought," Samantha said. Will moved onto the edge of the blanket to make room for her. She upended a canvas bag touting the Sam's Grocery logo, and a pile of fireworks—mostly fountains and multicolored boxes of sparklers—spread out before him in the middle of the blanket. "There will be a nice fireworks display at the end of the evening," she explained, "but folks around here like to entertain themselves while they wait."

"That doesn't sound safe." He suddenly felt like a Roman candle had gone off in his chest. "Is it?"

He'd thought they were only going to see a fireworks show put on by professionals—at a distance. And even that was going to be difficult for him. The sound of explosions, however innocent, could take him back to combat, to the war zone. Even if he was perfectly aware it might happen. Even if he tried to stop it.

Never mind *him*. If Samantha thought he was going to let his little girl play with a stick glowing with ashes, much less a fountain of sparks, then she didn't know him as well as he'd thought she did.

"Take a breath, Will," Samantha murmured, laying a warm hand on his arm. "I promise I would never do anything to put Genevieve in danger."

Will nodded and tried to even his breath, but it was difficult with his heartbeat roaring in his ears. He *did* trust Samantha. Of course she wouldn't allow anything bad to happen to Genevieve. He didn't yet trust himself as the guardian of a young one, but he could bank on the fact that Samantha would always put a child's needs ahead of her own.

"You didn't exactly answer my question," he reminded her. "Can't the grass catch on fire from the sparks?"

Samantha gazed across the park as if the thought had never occurred to her. "I suppose it *could,* but to be honest, in all of my twenty-eight years, it's never happened that I know of. Besides, the entire volunteer fire company is out here tonight with their families. Even if there was an incident—which I truly believe is highly unlikely—they'd be on top of it before anyone even knew it happened. But if it makes you feel better, we can set the fountains off along the pathway." She pointed toward the gravel path that wound through the community green.

Will swallowed hard. He knew he was about to sound like an overprotective mother hen, but he had another question to ask her. "What about burns?"

Samantha gave him a strange look. "I'm sure the occasional burn happens, but probably to reckless teenage boys who use the fireworks improperly. Surely you remember being a young, invincible risk-taker."

Will had actually never experienced fireworks as a child, or even as a teenager. His father hadn't been much for celebrating national holidays, and his mother was too timid to stand up to him. By the time he was old enough to rebel, his father had made the habit of locking him in his room.

Young and invincible had not really been part of his makeup as a teenager.

He shook his head.

"No? Well, regardless, when used correctly, I promise you fireworks are totally safe."

His gaze met hers, her blue eyes completely earnest. For a moment, there was such concern in her gaze that he suspected she guessed what was really going on.

"Trust me?" she whispered.

His gaze shifted to Genevieve, who was playing tag with a group of children near her own age. It amazed him how children naturally flocked together if given the opportunity to do so. They just found one another, and they welcomed newcomers into their midst. School hadn't even started yet and already she was making friends. He was so proud of her. And he figured he had Samantha to thank for that.

Obviously fireworks were a longstanding community tradition here, and he didn't want to give in to his desire to take his daughter and get out before he disappeared into his memories of Afghanistan. He could see the smiles, hear the laughter, smell the aroma of grilled hot dogs and hamburgers that made his mouth water. This was a full-blown party. He was the only one who appeared to be having qualms about it. Even Amanda and Samuel hadn't batted an eyelash when Samantha had dumped her load of fireworks onto the blanket.

He'd have to work to shut out the phantom sounds of gunfire and mortar blasts and remind himself that the noise and laughter around him were coming from a happy occasion.

He reached deep inside himself to find new strength. Just because he was had issues didn't mean Genevieve ought to have to suffer along with him.

He realized he would do anything for his precious little girl.

Absolutely anything. Including fireworks.

"Will?" Samantha's voice penetrated into his thoughts and he could tell from her tone that it was probably not the first time she had called his name. He suddenly realized she was touching his arm.

He tried to smile at her but knew he hadn't succeeded in the endeavor. She frowned back at him.

"Where did you go?" she asked softly.

Will considered deferring her question rather than answering it, but then she slid her hand down his arm and placed it in his, giving him a reassuring squeeze. Suddenly he found that he wanted to share the truth with her. He just wasn't sure if he could.

"It's okay if you don't want to do the fireworks," she said before he could speak. "I can give them to one of the other families. There will still be plenty for Genevieve to see, even if we don't participate ourselves."

"No. You're right. We should let Genevieve do her sparklers. I'm making a big deal over nothing."

She narrowed her eyes at him. "Don't tell me it's nothing."

He forced a laugh. "I feel that I ought to point out to you that just a few moments ago, you were arguing the opposite side of this conversation."

She tilted her head, looking thoughtful. He waited for her to say more.

She didn't.

Neither did he. So much for sharing the truth with her.

"Hey, Monkey," Will called affectionately, rolling to his feet and tousling Genevieve's hair as she came running up to greet him. "Miss Samantha bought us some sparklers. Do you want to do one?"

"Yes, please." Her big brown eyes gleamed with excitement.

"Red, green or gold?" he queried.

"Red. Red is my favorite color."

Will paused in the middle of reaching for the green box. "I thought you told me your favorite color was green." He'd been mentally filing all the useful information he'd been learning about his daughter, and he was positive she'd said green was her preferred shade. Just the other day she had insisted on wearing a poufy green skirt with a Christmas-tree green shirt and green ribbons in her hair.

"Red is my *new* favorite color," she informed him in a distinctly female tone of voice.

Apparently the entitlement of a woman to change her mind on a whim wasn't learned behavior.

"Miss Samantha's favorite color is red," Genevieve explained.

"Well," Will drawled. "That explains it, then."

Samantha giggled right along with Genevieve. The sound made Will's heart happy.

"So how do you go about lighting one of these things?" He opened the red box and slid one of the sparklers into his hand.

Samantha's surprised gaze met his. "Are you serious? You've never done a sparkler before?"

Will shook his head.

"Oh," Samantha murmured. "I'm sorry."

"For what? It's not your fault my father was an over-bearing jerk."

Samantha knelt before Genevieve, wrapping an arm around the girl's shoulder and pulling her close. She adjusted the sparkler in Will's grasp so the safe end was in his fingers and then placed Genevieve's hand over the top of his wrist. Time seemed to slow as he savored the feel of his hand, and his daughter's, enfolded in Samantha's grasp. His chest welled so tightly he thought it might burst from emotion. There was something inherently right about the three of them united in this way.

"There we are." She nodded in satisfaction and reached for the long-stemmed candle-lighter in the picnic basket. "And here we go!"

She lit the end of the sparkler. The stick glowed and then sparked brightly, popping and crackling. He didn't care for the sound, but he relaxed when he saw the glow of the firework reflected in his daughter's eyes. Her happiness was worth any price—and any amount of discomfort on his part.

Samantha was clearly enjoying the child's delight as well. She was sharing it, really. He'd never met a woman who embraced the moment the way Samantha Howell did, with such joy and vivaciousness. He envied those qualities. She absorbed the life around her, lived in the moment. He was a man who struggled to find any kind of joy or peace in his existence at all, although it was getting easier with Samantha and Genevieve in his life.

Jo Spencer, the boisterous elderly redhead who owned the local café, approached waving a lit multi-colored sparkler in one hand and a miniature American flag in the other, reminding Will of the conductor of a symphony. She was wearing a T-shirt proclaiming *Like Freedom? Kiss a Soldier.*

Will's breath caught in his throat as Samantha's gaze met his. Despite all his good intentions and resolve to keep himself away from Samantha—at least in *that* way—the T-shirt triggered a smile. If the deep rose color rising to her cheeks was any indication, she was aware of Jo's T-shirt, as well, and her mind had gone exactly where his had. There was a certain satisfaction in that.

"Isn't this absolutely the most enjoyable time of year?" Jo asked merrily.

Samantha chuckled. "You say that about every holiday."

Jo looked taken aback for a moment, but then she burst into high, melodic laughter. "I do, don't I?"

Samantha nodded and winked at Will, making his gut flip. Repeatedly.

"Well, at least this gives you all the opportunity to get out and put aside all that nonsense about the town council meeting with Stay-n-Shop. It's this coming Friday night, right?"

"What did you say?" Samantha bolted to her feet, a stricken expression on her face.

Will's adrenaline pulsed to life. He could hear his heartbeat pounding in his ears as he waited for Jo's answer. Cal had mentioned approaching the town council, but he hadn't known they'd actually scheduled a date. And neither, apparently, had Samantha.

"Oh, my dear, I'm so sorry," Jo said, raising her palms to cover her cheeks. "I let the cat out of the bag, didn't I? I didn't realize the council hadn't contacted you yet. My bad."

Will was fuming. She'd better believe it was *her bad*. He had no idea how this woman could have possibly discovered this information before the Howells even had wind of it. Didn't the town council have to contact *all* of the parties involved before they went and made a public agenda? He was steaming mad, not so much at Jo as at whatever person or entity had dropped the ball on this one.

"When's the meeting?" Samantha's jaw was set, but her voice was surprisingly steady and even.

"This Friday evening, if I'm not mistaken. I can ask Frank about it to make sure."

"Do you have any idea what their agenda is?"

Will was amazed at how well Samantha was taking the news. She was calm. Collected. Rational. *He* was the one who felt like throwing punches, like running pell-mell across the green screaming his outrage at the top of his lungs. What kind of a mixed-up, backward legal system was this?

"That I do not know," Jo said, responding to Samantha's question, and in an odd sort of way, Will's unspoken one. "I'm surprised you've had no contact with Stay-n-Shop, seeing as you'll be the competition should they decide to build here."

So much for her not knowing anything.

"I only heard there would be a meeting, nothing specific," she continued. "I'm sure you'll be contacted soon enough, dear. Oh, my, I hope I haven't gone and ruined your celebration."

"No. Of course not." Samantha managed to smile, although Will couldn't imagine how. "We appreciate you coming by."

And accidentally body-slamming us, Will added

mentally. Samantha might be able to smile through the pain, but he didn't have that much strength.

"How did she find out about this before we did?" he whispered harshly the moment Jo was out of earshot. His throat felt as dry and gravelly as the path beneath them.

"From her husband, Frank, I imagine. He's the president of the town council. Jo is a sweet lady, Will. She didn't mean anything bad by it."

Samantha turned to him, her beautiful blue eyes glistening with unshed tears. Will's heart snapped. He couldn't bear to see her in pain.

He reached for her shoulders to steady her, but she misinterpreted the gesture and stepped forward into his arms. She fit comfortably there. He could rest his cheek on her hair and inhale the floral scent of her shampoo. She was as delicate as a flower yet as strong as a rock, and she was absolutely amazing.

"It'll be all right, honey. I promise," he whispered into her hair.

She tensed for a moment, and then she leaned back to look at him, her gaze softening, baring her vulnerability. He knew how difficult it was for her, admitting she needed someone—that she needed *him*.

Something about holding Samantha close to him strengthened his own resolve. No matter what, he would not let her be hurt.

Not by Stay-n-Shop.

And most especially not by him.

Chapter Nine

The Howells called a meeting of their own, a family council right there on their red-plaid picnic blanket on the green. The fireworks show had not yet started, and most of the folks around them were celebrating with their own kin. Genevieve had wandered over to where their neighbors Ben and Vee Bishop were lighting off fountains and Vee was watching over the girl, which was just as well because Genevieve didn't need to see Samantha as worked up and angry as she was.

"We need a plan of action—*now*," Samantha announced to her family. They were hovering, looking concerned even without knowing the whole story. She crouched in the middle of the circle like a quarterback in a huddle.

"The enemy has advanced," Will murmured, a sarcastic bent to his tone.

"What do you mean? What changed?" her father asked.

"Apparently, Stay-n-Shop has already scheduled a meeting with the town council for next Friday night. Jo

Spencer mentioned it. She seemed surprised that that was the first we'd heard of it."

"Count on Jo to be the *very* first to know," her mother murmured with a chuckle that sounded half like a hiccup. Samantha knew how hard it was for her mother to contain her emotions under this set of circumstances. Samantha was feeling the same things—confusion, anger, fear, pain.

"Their calling a meeting can only mean one thing," Will ground out.

"They are proceeding forward with obtaining the zoning and permits necessary to build their store on that land they optioned," Samantha finished. "I don't think they're targeting Sam's Grocery anymore. At least not directly."

"Pardon the cliché," Grandpa Sampson offered, "but it sounds to me like we've just stepped out of the frying pan and into the fire."

Adrenaline set every one of Samantha's nerve endings alight. If it had come down to fight or flight, as it appeared to have, then they were most certainly going to fight.

"Let's take it down to the bare truth of the matter," Will suggested, his jaw clenched. "We need help. Lots of it."

"What kind of help?" Samantha was disinclined to beg, even from the town council. Their family couldn't afford a lawyer. Besides, Matthew MacPherson was the only practicing lawyer in Serendipity, and he specialized primarily in family law, not anything like this corporate fiasco.

Cal Turner had been right in that respect. This issue

was way out of Matthew MacPherson's sphere of expertise.

"We get our help from Serendipity itself," Will answered simply. "The answer is right here." He made a sweeping gesture across the green.

"What?" Samantha asked.

Will looked at her as if she was being dense and completely missing the point. Maybe she was. Or maybe she just didn't want to hear it.

"If we're going to fight this, we need to get Serendipity behind us. We need to prove that everyone supports Sam's Grocery. Stay-n-Shop can't battle the whole town. They'll most certainly see the futility of their move and go bother someone else, somewhere else."

"But what if they just go target a family like ours in another town?" Samantha asked.

Will's gaze widened and then he shook his head. "You know I didn't mean it that way. I wouldn't wish Stay-n-Shop on my worst enemy."

"Stay-n-Shop *is* my worst enemy," she mumbled.

"*Our* worst enemy," Will corrected, his gaze daring her to deny it. She glanced around at the rest of her family, who were all apparently in agreement with Will's statement.

"So what exactly are you proposing we do?" Grandpa Sampson asked, his voice gruffer than usual, bringing everyone back to the heart of the topic.

"Let's circulate a petition. Tonight. Right now, before folks get caught up in the big fireworks show. Once that gets cracking, we're going to have a harder time keeping people's attention."

"And this petition would say...?" Samantha asked.

"Something like, 'We, the undersigned, object to

the building of Stay-n-Shop within Serendipity town limits.' Then we can say a little about how everyone is supporting Sam's Grocery."

Samantha shook her head. This didn't feel right. She couldn't ask her friends and neighbors to put their necks out on the chopping block on her behalf. It wasn't fair to them. "That's putting people in quite a spot, don't you think?"

"How do you mean?"

It was Samantha's turn to gesture around the green. "I've known most of these folks all of my life." She paused, pulling in a breath that audibly hitched in her throat. "And before you ask, I will tell you that most of these people *are* regular customers at Sam's Grocery, and always have been."

"I know. I've seen them around," Will agreed. "They're good, loyal customers to the core."

"But maybe they wouldn't be, given a choice." Why was she the only one who could see it?

"What are you trying to say, Samantha?" her father demanded. He leaned forward in his chair, bracing his elbows on his knees.

"If we stick a petition in their faces, they'll feel obligated to sign it, even if privately they might be interested in the variety and discount pricing a big-box store like Stay-n-Shop would offer. It's hardly fair to make them choose between being a good neighbor and feeding their families. Besides, it's not like we can expect anyone to sign a petition without first being given the opportunity to mull it over."

"I disagree," her mother said, slapping her palms against the plastic arms of her chair. "If folks wanted big-box stores, they wouldn't live here in Serendipity.

There is a difference between free enterprise and old-fashioned family values. We're a small town with a nice country grocery. No one will want a change as big as Stay-n-Shop would bring."

"Plus, time to mull things over is a luxury we don't have," her father added bluntly.

"Honestly, I don't think the folks around here will need to give this much thought," said Will, crossing his arms over his chest, which only served to make him look more muscular and solid than he already was. And more intimidating, if that's what he was going for.

Samantha was unsettled by the thought of imposing herself on her neighbors by springing a petition on them at the Fourth of July celebration. But maybe it was the only way.

She looked at each member of her family, trying to decipher their gazes and identify their take on Will's suggestion. Everyone was watching *her,* waiting with hopeful anticipation on their faces.

Suddenly she understood. They were waiting for her to call the next play. Talk about pressure. Especially from Will, who'd come up with the idea in the first place. Didn't he realize he was pushing his agenda on her when she wasn't yet prepared to accept it?

In Will's defense, this quick tactic was in response to the fact that they *were* out of time.

She sighed. "Where are we going to find some blank sheets of paper?"

"Give me a minute," her mother said. "I think I have a few sheets of crafting paper in the trunk of my car." Her brow lowered and she pursed her lips. "I'm afraid it might be pink. I was working on a shower present for Ben and Vee's baby girl."

"Never mind the color," her father insisted with a dismissing wave of his arm. "This is an emergency. Let's go, go, go."

Her mother caught Samantha's gaze and rolled her eyes before heading off to her car. "Pink paper isn't going to look very professional," Samantha felt inclined to point out.

"Neither is the fact that we're handwriting the petition. We'll be okay, as long as it's legal. And even if it isn't, pages full of names protesting Stay-n-Shop should count for something," Will replied, tunneling his fingers through his hair. He looked like he was ready for action, ready to take on the world for Sam's Grocery. For *her*. Seeing him like that made her stomach do a little flip.

When Samantha's mother returned, she had several sheets of paper, which were, to Samantha's dismay, baby-shower pink.

"Let's make several copies of our petition, and then we can each canvass a different area of the green. That way we can get as many signatures as possible in the shortest time possible," Will suggested, his voice strong and level, and that of a man used to leading. "I'm sure folks will have a lot of questions, but we have to do the best we can and move quickly."

Samantha still wasn't sold on the idea, but in the end, she took the sheet of paper assigned to her and started her way around the outside of the green. She and Will were working clockwise, while her mother and father were moving counterclockwise, one member of the team on the outside of the green, and the other canvassing the middle. Grandpa Sampson had been charged with staying put to keep an eye on Genevieve.

Samantha approached Zach and Delia Bowden, who

were picnicking with their three children. She took a deep breath, kneeling next to Delia, before plunging in. She was fully aware that her pride was standing in the way of godly humility, but she couldn't seem to get past it. She wasn't one to put out her hand for charity, even when she needed it—as she did now.

"What are you selling?" Zach teased when he spotted the paper and pen in her hand. He cradled their sleeping six-month-old baby, Faith, against his shoulder, while his two-year-old son toddled around on the grass. "Candles? Cookies? You've caught us too late for candy. We've just had dessert." With his free hand, he patted his lean midsection.

Samantha blanched. Was she that transparent? She wasn't certain she could get a single word out. Not about Stay-n-Shop, or any other subject, for that matter.

Zach's words kept echoing through her head.

What are you selling? What are you selling?

What choice did she have? If she stayed on the road she was currently going down, what she'd be *selling* was Sam's Grocery.

Delia, a longtime friend, put her arm around Samantha's shoulders. "Don't mind Zach. He's just being a goof."

"I—I," Samantha stuttered, and then coughed. "Need your help."

"You've got it," Zach stated, before she'd even said a word to explain what it was that she needed.

"Don't you want to hear what I've got to say before you commit yourselves?"

"Sure. You tell us what it is you're asking," Zach said with a mischievous grin. "But that doesn't change the fact that we're going to do anything in our power to help you out. Whatever you need. Just name it."

Samantha gave a shortened version of the facts—Stay-n-Shop's plan to build, their option on the land, the town council meeting. She didn't see the need to mention the pressure she'd been receiving from the corporation, or the threats.

"We're circulating a petition requesting that the town council rule for Stay-n-Shop to take their business elsewhere. Of course, there are benefits intrinsic in a big-box store, especially for a large family like yours—"

Zach chuckled. "Are you trying to talk us out of signing?"

"Zach!" Delia reprimanded, reaching for the petition and the pen. "Don't give Samantha a hard time right now."

"Just teasing," Zach said, taking the petition from his wife and adding his own name to it. "You know I'm just ribbing you, right, Samantha?"

Samantha nodded and smiled in gratitude. "Thank you. This means more to me than I can say. And to my family, as well."

"You don't have to thank us," Delia responded. "We love Sam's Grocery. We would never dream of shopping anywhere else. And neither will any of your other customers. Trust me on this one, Samantha. You have nothing to worry about."

"We're all behind you one hundred percent," Zach added, gently rocking his sleeping baby. "Delia's right. You have nothing to fear. The town council will back you one hundred percent."

"I certainly hope so," Samantha agreed. She thanked them again and moved on to the next family. Maybe the Bowdens were right. Maybe all her apprehension was for nothing.

She could only hope and pray that was so.

She moved on. The next family she encountered was Chance and Phoebe Hawkins, along with Frank and Jo Spencer.

Even though it had been Jo who'd brought the council meeting to her attention, she was a little nervous approaching the Spencers. After all, Frank presided over the town council that would ultimately decide the fate of the store.

But Frank was surprisingly gracious, especially considering how gruff the old man usually appeared. He recused himself from signing the petition, of course, but wished her the best.

Frank's courtesy gave Samantha confidence to approach others on the side of the circle she'd been assigned. With each family she encountered, her spirits rose. Everyone she spoke with signed her petition and encouraged her in the endeavor. She'd been afraid she would be pressing folks to sign a petition before they were sure what they were signing, but it quickly became evident that the community not only wanted to support the store, but more importantly, wanted to champion Samantha and her family.

"How'd it go?" Will asked when they met back at their picnic site. They sat down side by side on the blanket to compare notes. Genevieve ran up and sat down on Will's lap with a squeal of pleasure.

Samantha was flushed with excitement as she displayed her hastily prepared petition. "They all signed it," she said in grateful amazement. "Every one of them. I can't believe it."

"I can," he said, showing her his own page, also brimming with signatures. "These people care about the grocery." He leaned back on his hands so his mouth was close to her ear. "And you."

A ripple of pleasure went through her. Somehow she had the impression he was speaking of more than the community's support.

"The fireworks should be starting soon," she said, observing the twilight sky. She glanced down just in time to see a dark expression flit across Will's face.

"Will? What is it?" she asked softly.

"Huh? It's nothing," he denied.

She scooted closer to him so they wouldn't be overheard. "I understand if you don't want to talk about it, but there's clearly something wrong. I'm a good listener."

He sighed. "I know you are. I just don't like to talk about it."

"The war?" she guessed. It was either that or his failed relationship with Haley, and he'd already talked to her about that.

The first firework popped in the sky, and Will flinched, despite the fact that he was clearly trying not to.

"Oh," she said, suddenly understanding why he was so reticent about the fireworks. "I'm so sorry, Will. I wasn't thinking."

"I'll live," he said through gritted teeth. "I'm one of the lucky ones. I only have a mild case of PTSD."

"Still, if you'd like to go, we could just call it an early night."

Genevieve clapped in delight. "Oh, Daddy. Look at that one. It's a red-and-green flower!"

"Your favorite colors," Will said, kissing the top of

his daughter's head. "Cool, huh?" He smiled weakly at Samantha. "I can't miss this, now, can I?"

"You're very brave," murmured Samantha, slipping her hand into his and giving it a comforting squeeze. His hands were so large, so strong, and yet for his daughter, he was exposing the cracks in his defense.

Samantha had never been more attracted to a man in her life. What was it about a man that was so incredibly appealing?

Whatever it was, Will had it in spades, and Samantha found her own defenses dropping. She leaned closer and threaded her fingers through his, lending him her strength.

He smiled tenderly down at her. His hands were no longer trembling.

Chapter Ten

Will bagged the last of Chance Hawkins's groceries with his usual care and precision. Funny—helping the folks in Serendipity with their grocery shopping needs had become his favorite part of the job.

Working as a unit supply specialist in the Army wasn't nearly as fulfilling as bagging cans of baby food and toddler treats. He'd take small-town service any day of the week. It wasn't so much stocking supplies—it was supplying people. And not just with material goods, but with a friendly countenance and a helping hand.

He was beginning to recognize most of the folks who shopped regularly at the grocery, and he had the natural gift, which Samantha had complimented him on more than once, of up-selling to his neighbors. They always walked away with a candy bar and a smile.

He couldn't imagine anything better than being here in Serendipity, working at Sam's Grocery. He'd finally found his own little spot in the world, and he and his daughter had a real home at last. He had a sense of peace he'd never experienced before, knowing that what he was doing made a difference in people's lives.

His work at the grocery. His side job doing carpentry for the Howells' soon-to-be-opening bed-and-breakfast. He enjoyed helping them out with various and sundry jobs, and he was almost as excited as they were to participate in the grand opening of their new venture.

He was especially gratified by the community's response to the Howell's petition. It was an honor just to be a part of it. As for his time with Samantha—well, all he knew was that he'd never before experienced such strong emotions for a woman. It defied words.

For once, his life was wonderful. His daughter was happy, safe and secure.

Which would last for about five seconds, if Stay-n-Shop had their way.

He hated that some large, impersonal corporation was threatening to take everything he cared about away from him. From all of them.

The town council meeting was tonight at the Grange hall, and everyone was talking about it. As Will had suspected, most everyone had been anxious to sign their petition, and from what he was hearing, the council meeting was going to be full to bursting with folks wanting to give their opinions on the issue.

The only ones who'd recused themselves were the council leaders themselves, and Will wondered if they'd formed their own judgment on the matter already. Were they weighing both sides of the issue? Was it possible that the town council felt like the Stay-n-Shop could actually be a good development for Serendipity, economically speaking?

And what about Cal? Would he be leading up the offense at the town meeting? There was no doubt that the man was compelling and enigmatic. He might be able to sway the council members. The thought made Will feel sick to his stomach.

At the end of the day, they were Serendipity residents, and had been all their lives. That had to count for something. Small-town life was the status quo. It was what they lived and believed in and had always known. Sometimes change *wasn't* the best thing. What was the old saying? If it ain't broke, don't fix it?

Sam's Grocery wasn't broken. It was a central part of folks' lives in Serendipity and had been since the town was first built. Will firmly trusted that was the reason the town council would vote in favor of keeping Stay-n-Shop as far away from Serendipity as possible.

He wished he were a praying man. Maybe now was the time to start.

"Ready for the council meeting?" Chance Hawkins asked, as if reading his thoughts. Will realized Chance could probably see the tension on his face and guess where it was coming from. Will corrected his expression. He shouldn't be frowning at customers, especially those as regular as Chance Hawkins.

"I think so."

"Looked to me like you got a lot of signatures the other night at the Fourth of July celebration."

"We did. Nearly everyone was ready and willing to sign our petition."

Chance planted his black cowboy hat on his head and lowered it over his brow. "Of course they were. We're a country town. And for Phoebe and me, and my aunt Jo, too, that's the way we want to keep it."

"I'm glad to hear it."

"We've got a babysitter lined up for tonight, so we're all planning to be there at the Grange to support you."

That was an answer to a prayer Will had never actually prayed. The more people they had there in their favor, the better off they'd be.

"And thanks for digging out those little juice boxes from the back. My toddler, Aaron, won't drink anything unless it's out of a straw."

"Glad to do it," Will said as Chance tipped his hat and headed toward the door.

He *was* glad to do it, and happy to be right where he was. He whistled as he grabbed a broom to sweep the front porch. But as he stood on the rickety wood-planked sidewalk and stared down the street at the old, clapboard-style shops and businesses, he paused and wondered if everything he had here in Serendipity was about to go away, thanks to the Stay-n-Shop.

Could he stand it if it did?

If worse came to worst, he could give up the grocery, and his job, and even where he lived.

But he couldn't give up Samantha.

He was too far gone and he knew it.

But he had no idea what he was going to do about it. The last thing a woman as remarkable as Samantha Howell needed was to be saddled with the likes of him.

Even so, he couldn't get what Grandpa Sampson had told him out of his head. His words echoed as if they'd been thrown into the depths of a canyon.

He who finds a wife finds a good thing.

A wife? When had his heart and his mind turned from just surviving day to day, to finding the permanence he was so desperately seeking? Was there even the remotest possibility that he would have another chance at life, at happiness?

...and finds favor with the Lord.

There was the rub, for if God was present in the world, and Will was beginning to think He might be, Will knew in his heart that he didn't deserve God's favor. There was no way he ever would, for he could never make things right.

Samantha could not stop pacing. She had piles of paperwork to go through, but she couldn't seem to sit still and concentrate. She was fidgeting all over the place, both in mind and body. She wouldn't have a comfortable moment until the city council formally announced their decision to turn Stay-n-Shop away with a firm *no, thank you*.

"Ready to face the dragon?" Will asked, popping his head into the back room. He was wearing a determined smile and a baseball cap that shadowed his eyes, but she was certain she saw a twinge of doubt in his gaze. Whenever he was on edge, his eyes turned very nearly black, as they were now.

She remembered how mysterious—and frankly, intimidating—he'd appeared when she first met him. She hadn't been able to figure him out back then. His stoic attitude had locked her out.

But now she could read him. She understood his body language—the way his jaw tensed or his brow creased when he was troubled. The clench of his fists that confirmed the words he could not or would not say aloud.

But there was the other side of him, too. The kind, gentle side. He didn't often display it for the world to see, but she'd caught glimpses of the man he was deep down in his heart, and the man he could become—the smile on his face whenever Genevieve kissed his cheek, the adoration in his gaze when he called her Monkey and ruffled her hair.

And sometimes, there was something special in the way he looked at her and drew her into his world. Those were the moments Samantha loved most of all.

But the expression on his face now was sheer and complete resolve. Her heart sank.

"We aren't going to win this, are we?" she murmured, laying a hand against his chest to feel the steady beat of his heart. He closed his hand over hers, pressing it to his chest.

His eyebrows rose. "Of course we are. We've talked about this. The whole town has got your back. Stay-n-Shop can't fight everyone."

"I hope you're right."

Will moved behind her and gently massaged her shoulders, rubbing his thumbs into the knots at her neck. His hands were large, warm, strong and supportive, all the things she needed right now.

Where would she be if Will had not come into her life?

He'd changed everything. He'd spurred her to action. He'd helped her make things happen. And although she was still facing her giant, she was no longer alone in her fight.

"Are we on the docket?" she asked him.

He chuckled dryly. "Honey, we *are* the docket."

Samantha frowned. "If they cleared the agenda just to talk about this one issue, they must be anticipating that it will take some time."

"If you ask me, it's just a bunch of red tape," Will responded. "They're obligated to hear what Stay-n-Shop is proposing before they can officially send them packing. Word on the street is that many of the prominent businesspeople in the community are planning to attend the meeting in person."

"That makes me even more nervous. It's going to be all I can do to keep it together while I counter the corporation's arguments, even without having half the town present to see me falter and fumble."

"They'll all be there to support you. And to watch you win."

She folded a piece of white paper into a small box and then flattened it onto the smooth oak desktop with her palm. She only wished it was as easy to crush the big-box store. "You make it sound like a sure thing."

"That's because it is, honey. It is."

That evening, the Howells gathered at Samantha's parents' house so they could all travel to the Grange hall together and enter with a united front and one purpose in mind.

Winning the war.

Samantha put on her best Sunday clothes, a soft white cotton dress dotted with a colorful variety of Texas wildflowers in purple, blue, red and yellow hues. She imagined she would look like a country bumpkin up against the slick corporate lawyers in their New York suits made by designers Samantha had neither heard of nor cared to know.

They were probably counting on that—the intimidation factor, the big-shot businessmen sanctioning their presence in the tiny country town.

What they didn't realize was that *she* was the one with the hometown advantage here. Surrounded by Serendipity folk, the Stay-n-Shop representatives wouldn't fit in. That realization made her feel a little better.

She thought of Cal Turner with his slicked-back black hair, deceitfully charming smile and forceful intimidation tactics, of how he'd tried to force her hand and make her sign papers to make her family legacy go up in smoke.

Now Cal Turner was bringing friends.

Well, she had friends, too.

She glanced once more in the mirror to check her appearance, added a brush of pink gloss to her lips and decided it was as good as it was going to get. She hurried to the living room, where Will was waiting, dressed in a white cotton shirt and black slacks. He'd even gone so far as to wear a necktie, although he kept fidgeting with it as if it was choking him.

She saw him first, and she knew without a doubt the moment he realized she was in the room. He stood abruptly, his eyes wide with admiration. His appreciative gaze took in her white summer sandals and her cotton dress.

He gave a low wolf whistle and brushed his hair back with the palm of his hand.

"Wow." It was only one word, but it was enough.

Samantha shook her head playfully, but inside her heart was pounding in response. Who needed a bathroom mirror when she could see herself so much more clearly—and honestly—in Will's appreciative gaze?

"You clean up very nicely yourself," she teased, giving him a backhanded compliment that she meant with her whole heart. "I can see you've ironed your shirt." She ran a finger down the carefully pressed crease from his shoulder to his wrist. "You know what they say about men who wear ironed clothes?"

Will arched a brow. "Enlighten me."

"Either they're in the military, or they still live at home with their mamas." She was grateful for this small snippet of conversation that didn't have anything to do with Stay-n-Shop. Will seemed to understand that she needed that brief step back, and he played along.

"I see. Really? Do *they* say that?"

"Absolutely. And seeing as you don't live at home with a woman pampering you and seeing to your every need," she continued coyly, walking slowly around him and enjoying the view of his strong jaw and broad shoulders, "you must have been in the military."

Will shook his head and chuckled again. "Well, that must have been an awfully difficult conclusion for you to arrive at, since you've known I was an ex-soldier since the very first time we met."

Samantha's heart was beyond warm. It was glowing like the glimmer in Will's eyes. He was *teasing* her. He had progressed so incredibly far from that poker-rigid man she had first met.

"Samantha," he murmured huskily, reaching for her hand and turning her toward him, stepping forward so they were face to face, so close she could feel the brush of his breath on her cheek.

"You and your theory got one thing wrong," he whispered close to her ear.

"Yeah? What was that?" she asked through the hitch in her throat, her voice suddenly unable to function beyond a whisper.

"I *am* home."

His words struck her with the force of a hurricane, yet it was everything he couldn't say—all of the emotion burning in his eyes as he continued to hold her gaze—that sealed the deal for Samantha.

He reached for her other hand, his touch all at once strong and gentle.

This man belonged in her life. And after this whole mess with Stay-n-Shop was over and their lives were back to normal—or at least the new normal—she would tell him so.

Will's forehead met hers, his luminous brown eyes glittering with unspoken promises. "Samantha, I—"

Grandpa Sampson appeared in the doorway and cleared his throat. Will jumped back, clasping his hands behind him.

"I hate to interrupt what looks to be quite the interesting moment," Grandpa Sampson said with a gruff chuckle, "but we gotta get ourselves out to the Grange hall and kill us a bunch of snakes."

Samantha looked at Will, who seemed to be as thunderstruck as she was, plus a little guilty, too.

What did he have to feel guilty about? She was the first to admit that her grandfather catching them mooning at each other like a couple of lovesick calves was a little embarrassing, but their stance hadn't exactly been compromising. They were only holding hands, not kissing or anything. And even if they were, she was twenty-eight years old, not an immature adolescent.

If she wanted to have a relationship with a man—and the word *relationship* wasn't even close to defining whatever it was she had with Will—then that's exactly what she would do. Will's support had become a cornerstone for her. She'd grown to depend on him. No—more than that. She'd grown to *care* for him. But right now they had to face the present crisis. And Grandpa Sampson was right about one thing.

It was time to kill some snakes.

Chapter Eleven

William's heart was still spinning from his brief encounter with Samantha. He felt like she'd taken him to the craggy edge of a towering cliff with white-capped surf below it and then, with a single fingertip, was about to push him over the edge.

It was a good thing Grandpa Sampson had come in and interrupted when he had. Will had—completely, inappropriately and with the worst timing ever—been right on the verge of kissing Samantha.

Where was his head? Why could he not keep his emotional distance from this woman, no matter how hard he tried?

Here they were, ready to go into the legal battle of their lifetimes, a battle that would mean all the difference in the world not only to Samantha personally but to all the Howells and to him and Genevieve, as well. This was the time for him to be putting on his mental armor, gearing up for the fight ahead, not ruminating over his sudden penchant for Texas wildflowers.

"I'm not sure exactly how we should expect this meeting to go," Samantha told her family, who'd all gathered in the living room. "I've only been to a couple of town council meetings, and they weren't about such touchy subjects or burning issues. I think the last one I attended had to do with building an official preschool in Serendipity."

"I've been to a few," Samuel remarked. "They're basic at the core, run pretty much like a board meeting at a business—Robert's Rules and all that."

Grandpa Sampson snorted. "Like any of us have the first notion about Robert and his blooming set of rules."

"It's just to keep order, Grandpa," Amanda said soothingly. "No need to get all het up about something we can't control. Anyway, I imagine it's probably not so formal as all that."

"Well, I still say they didn't give us enough time to prepare. Them corporate fools have been working on this a long time, and I'll bet *they* know Robert's Rules."

"The council is only required to give us three days notice," Samuel said. "And they gave us five. So we've nothing to complain about."

That wasn't exactly true, Will thought as he watched Samantha grimace. Had she been honest from the get-go and brought the situation with Stay-n-Shop to the family from the very first, they would have had much more time to prepare a case as a group. He knew what she was thinking. She was blaming herself. She was thinking that if anything, *she* was the one guilty of springing this on them.

Obviously, she'd never intended for the matter to go this far. He was certain that if she'd known Stay-n-Shop wouldn't take a simple no for an answer, she would have shared her problems with her family right away.

As it stood now, well, it was what it was.

"Why don't we focus on what we do know," Amanda suggested gravely.

"Right." Samantha jumped in, clearly seeing this as an opportunity to move the conversation forward. They didn't have much time before the meeting started, and they needed to talk last-minute strategy. "There are currently eight commissioners on the board. Most if not all of them are either small businesspeople who own a shop somewhere on Main Street or are kin to those who do."

"Which means, theoretically, there could be a tie vote," Will said, surprised by this new information. "Has this happened often?"

"Not often, no," answered Samuel grimly. "But it has occurred occasionally, usually in the higher-profile cases. In some cases, they've argued for a week of Sundays before coming to an agreement on an issue. On rare occasions, they've hung themselves out to dry."

"So what you're saying, then, is that we need to win five commissioners to our side," Will said.

"Yes. Precisely. That shouldn't be so hard. Should it?" Amanda started her sentence firmly, but by the time she tacked on the ending, she didn't sound quite so certain of herself.

"Stay-n-Shop is slated to present their case first," Samantha informed them. "I'm expecting them to come in ready to impress, with algorithms, statistics, presentation software and who knows what else."

"Which could work against them," Will pointed out.

Samantha met his gaze with a grateful look. "Exactly what I'm hoping will happen. Folks around here, the town council members included, might not take to all the fancy show of equipment and ideas. Perhaps they'll be more open to our simple plea, our show of integrity over industry."

"So they do their blabbing, and then Samantha, you give them the petitions with all the signatures on it and set them down the right path," her father said.

Samantha sighed. "I don't mind working with folks when I'm behind the counter at the grocery," she said. "It's easy for me to be outgoing when I'm serving people. And I know I have a reputation as a Little Chick," she continued, scoffing and shaking her head. "But in truth, public speaking is so not my thing. I'm scared out of my gourd right now."

Will reached for her hand, feeling her fingers quivering under his. He wished with all his heart he could take her place, or at least take away her nerves, but this was one battle she had to captain on her own.

"You're going to do great, honey," he murmured. "True courage isn't not being afraid. It's facing your fear and going forward anyway. And don't forget, the Lord will be with you every step of the way."

Her gaze flew once again to his, her eyes wide with surprise. "Yes, of course. Thank you."

He realized after he'd said the words that that was probably not the best advice, at least not from him. He didn't want to give her any kind of hope that he was coming around to view the world as she did. He knew she was praying for him, that he'd become a Christian, but he still didn't know where he stood with God. Certainly they weren't in good standing with each other. But he'd reminded her of the Lord because he knew it would help *her*, and ultimately, he supposed that was all that really mattered.

The Howells also looked grateful for Will's timely reminder.

"Will is right. We should pray," Samuel suggested, "and ask the Holy Spirit's covering over us as we march in to face our enemy tonight."

Will was already holding Samantha's hand. It seemed like the most natural thing in the world to thread his fingers through hers as they gathered in a circle to pray. Will bowed his head and closed his eyes with the rest of them, but his prayer was a little different than theirs.

Where Samuel prayed for peace and wisdom for the members of the town council, Will hoped Samantha would be persistent, no matter what the council's immediate impressions might be, what kind of day they might have had or what they might have consumed for breakfast. It seemed to Will that there were too many variables to lay anything as serious as this at the feet of eight different people. Better to focus their prayers on Samantha.

Samuel prayed for the grace for Samantha to find the right words, and Will hoped she'd be able to find the strength to speak so convincingly and forcefully that no one on that tiny country board had any niggling doubt of what the right decision was.

And hopefully, that would be the end of story. Happily ever after, at least for Samantha and the Howells.

He was a new man since arriving in Serendipity. Samantha had shown him his own strength and given him courage when he'd thought he had none. She made him experience emotions he hadn't even believed existed.

For him, this was only the beginning.

Samantha was shaking so hard her teeth were chattering against each other. She inhaled deeply through her nose, willing herself to calm down, although she didn't know how she was going to do that when every nerve ending in her body was screaming. The muscles in her neck and shoulders were so tight she could hardly turn her head to look at Will, who was beside her, his arm loosely draped around her shoulders as they stood outside the door to the Grange hall.

He smiled his encouragement and used his fingers to massage away some of the tension at her nape. She wondered if he could feel how tightly she was wound up or if it was just that he could see the sheer panic in her eyes. If he could see it, so could the rest of the world.

"Ready?" he whispered, leaning close to her ear.

"Not really," she said, chuckling without humor at her lame attempt at a joke. "I wish I could blink and make all this just go away."

"Me, too, honey. Me, too. But I've learned that sometimes the only way to get to the other side of something is to just muck it up and go through it. I think tonight calls for some major mucking."

"Well, I ought to be pretty good at that. I spent most of my summers visiting friends on their farms. I've mucked my share of stalls."

Will nodded and kissed her temple. "Then go to it." He gestured toward the parking lot, which was full of trucks and cars, mostly of the working variety. "Seems to me that half the town's already here, and every one of us has got your back."

"I know you do." She couldn't quite shake the sense of guilt that hovered over her like a storm cloud. If she hadn't been so proud and arrogant and believed she could handle Stay-n-Shop all on her own, things might never have escalated to this point in the first place.

Now it was time for her to fix what she'd broken. Despite everything, her family still believed in her and supported her. She desperately wanted to regain their trust. It went without saying that to do that, she needed to secure the future of Sam's Grocery.

Will was right. It was time for her to buckle up and settle this. It wasn't going to go away on its own, not with all the praying and hoping in the world. For whatever reason, God had her right here, right now, facing this particular giant, this threat to her whole way of life. She just hoped that she'd quickly learn whatever lesson it was He was trying to teach her so she could score a victory for Sam's Grocery and her family. And for Will and Genevieve.

"Here goes nothing," she muttered as she pushed the door open.

Up until that moment, Samantha had been aware of the low but distinct murmuring of the crowd inside the little Grange hall. But at the sound of the door opening, every head turned to face her and talking instantly ceased. With chairs set up in rows like the pews in a church, she felt like a bride at her wedding, except it was all the nerves without any of the joy.

She knew all these people. The ironic thing was that they *were* the folks she would invite to her wedding. Alexis and Mary were sitting in the second row on the right. When the time came, those two women would be her maids of honor—both of them—and she was grateful for their support now.

If only this was a happy occasion.

What was it Will had said? That courage wasn't lack of fear, but knowing fear and acting anyway?

At least she had Will at her side. As she walked up

the aisle in what she hoped looked like a confident manner, she continued to breathe in and out through her nose, slowly, methodically. If she held her breath, which was what she tended to do when she was nervous, she would pass out. If she breathed too quickly, she would hyperventilate and then pass out. So the only way she was going to stay cognizant, never mind focused, was to carefully monitor the air coming in and out of her lungs.

As she expected, a gaggle of Stay-n-Shop legal representatives were clustered near the front. Cal Turner, with his stylish suit and confident demeanor, was among them, though he didn't immediately glance in their direction. The other legal experts had paused briefly when Samantha and her family had entered, but now they were huddled together around a rectangular folding table on the left, covered with notes and laptops, presumably discussing strategy for the upcoming meeting. A similar table, devoid of anything, had been set up on the right for her and her family. She and Will slid into the chairs behind the table, while her family filed into the first row behind them.

Samantha looked down at the single file clutched in her hand. Even if she spread out every single page of the petition, it wouldn't even cover half of the tabletop. And she didn't even own a laptop, other than the one that belonged to the grocery. Now, however, she wished she'd had the foresight to grab it from the office. It didn't have any notes or anything on it, of course, much less a fancy presentation to share, but at least it would have looked nice and official on the bare table. This wasn't a formal courtroom, but it certainly felt like one.

Carefully avoiding the competition, her gaze swept across to the very front of the room, where, upon a small stage, the town council members sat, facing the house full of people. Samantha scanned the faces, all of them familiar to her, including old Frank Spencer—Jo's husband—the man officially presiding over the night's events.

Those sitting on the council flashed Samantha friendly smiles and her nerves settled. These were her people. Many of their kin had signed one of the petitions Samantha was holding in her hand. Surely they would bring a swift and satisfactory conclusion to this muddle created by a big-box store that had no business in a small country town.

But what if they didn't? Who could say what the outcome might be?

Samantha once again focused on her breath and reminded herself that ultimately it was God overseeing this assembly. In His mercy, He knew what was best for her, and for Sam's Grocery. She just had to trust in that.

Frank Spencer banged his gavel—which was nothing more than a regular hammer probably taken from his tool box at home—three times against the surface of the table, and waited for the ruckus to die down.

"I'm suspecting that this here is going to be a long meetin', so let's just set our policies straight from the get-go," he said. "Number one, I'm the one who was elected president of the town council, and that means I'm in charge, so you don't get to do no talkin' unless I've cleared you to."

So much for Robert's Rules of Order, Samantha thought, allowing herself the tiniest of smiles. *More like Frank's Rules.* She'd known old Frank Spencer her entire life. He was a cantankerous old goat, but he had a good heart, and he'd keep the slick corporate guys from getting too high on their horses.

"Second," Frank continued, "there will be no outbursts from the peanut gallery." He gestured to the people in the house. "That means you, folks. No cheering, booing, clapping or anything else. Got it?"

Samantha glanced back to see several people nod and murmur, but the room fell to complete silence when Frank narrowed his gaze and pointed his hammer toward them.

"Third, this meetin' will be held in an orderly fashion. First, y'all from the city get to state your case. Then," he said with a brief nod toward Samantha, "it'll be your turn to go. After that," he continued, waving his hammer in another authoritative gesture toward the house, "I'll give you folk a few minutes to voice your opinions for this council to consider."

When it remained so silent they could hear a coyote howling in the distance, Frank flashed a self-satisfied grin. "Now then, I'm going to introduce the council members one by one and allow them the chance to introduce themselves to you."

Samantha really didn't see the point in that. It wasn't like the townspeople didn't know the eight folks sitting behind the bench. She supposed it was done for the sake of the Stay-n-Shop lawyers, or maybe it was only for show. Either way, Samantha took a moment to compose her thoughts, as ready and as prepared as she could be for whatever Stay-n-Shop would throw at her. Her family was seated in the first row of chairs behind her, but Will, seated in the chair next to her, reached for her hand under the table and gave it a brief squeeze.

"Go ahead when you're ready," Frank said to the corporate lawyers as soon as introductions were complete.

Samantha shifted her attention to Cal Turner as he rose with a flourish and began to speak.

"Ladies and gentlemen," he began, directing his first remarks to the town council.

To Samantha, he sounded very much like a ringmaster at the circus. She half expected him to add *boys and girls* to the start of his speech. *Welcome to the greatest fiasco on earth!* All he needed was a top hat. She wanted to scoff. Instead, she clasped her hands together on her lap and dug her fingernails into her skin, concentrating on the pain in order to help her keep her mouth shut. She reminded herself that she'd have her turn soon.

"In consideration of all the folks here tonight," the lawyer continued, turning to address his first remarks to the house full of townspeople, "we'll keep our remarks brief and to the point. I know you all have families to go home to, and that is exactly why we're here. We at Stay-n-Shop know that you treasure your families deeply, and we're here to make a difference in all your lives."

There was an answering murmur, to which Frank put an immediate stop by threatening to pound his gavel.

"We here at Stay-n-Shop put family first. We promise you the deepest discount on the biggest variety of fresh, frozen and general-use products in the grand state of Texas."

Samantha had positioned her chair so that she might be able to see the reactions of at least some of the house, and met the gaze of Edward Emerson, who owned the hardware store. Selling general-use items would cut into Ed's business, as well. He scowled and shook his head. He wasn't any happier hearing about this than she was, and it was probably the first time he'd been fully informed.

She recognized her own failing once again of putting her pride over the genuine needs of others. She was certain she'd be hearing from Ed, and maybe others who ran businesses on Main Street, about her appalling lack of communication. Come to think of it, she was surprised she hadn't already.

She had expected the corporate lawyers to play the *family* card, but not as their leading argument. If they knew the town as well as their statistics said they did, they would know that "family and faith" ought to be their final and most significant argument. In half a minute, Cal Turner had ticked off all the reasoning Samantha had anticipated from him. At this rate, he'd have nothing left to say in a couple of minutes.

As it turned out, though, that wasn't even remotely close to the truth. She should have figured that Cal Turner would milk every statement into a variety of subpoints, and then back up each and every one of them with colorful graphs, charts and other relevant data. Samantha had to admit that their analysts had done an impressive job serving up statistics on how Stay-n-Shop had positively affected the economies of those country communities where they'd built new stores. Not only did they offer discounts, but perhaps more importantly, they provided jobs, which were valuable commodities in any small town.

Worse yet, Cal was a consummate professional when it came to speaking to both the board and the room full of townspeople. Clearly he spent a great deal of time in courtrooms in front of judges and juries, and it showed with every word that came out of his mouth. His voice was warm and rich, with the hypnotic timbre of a lullaby. His strong presence was definitely going to be a point in his favor, even without all the numbers—*dollar signs*—backing him up. He knew just when to make a gesture with his hands and what expression to wear upon his face. Through it all, he appeared affable and approachable. The bottom line was, Cal could read his audience like a book. Or rather, like a snake waiting to attack its prey. Any time he perceived interest from the townsfolk, he would press whatever issue was currently at hand right into their laps. Rather than causing them to back off, it appeared to be subtly urging them forward.

She gazed across the crowded room, noting the number of people whose expressions registered interest in what Cal was saying versus those whose body language was clearly of the opposite persuasion. Chance Hawkins, slumped in his seat with his arms crossed firmly over his chest and a scowl low on his dark brow. His wife, Phoebe, her arm draped affectionately around him, wore equal disapproval on her face. Jo Spencer was wearing a T-shirt scribbled with the words *Robert's Rules,* on which *Robert's* had a line slashed through it and had been replaced by *Country.* Now that was more like it.

But others were obviously not so quick to decide. Doubt or intrigue was written on their faces. She could hardly blame them. Cal Turner, with all his bells and whistles, was making a flashy argument, the likes of which this tiny town council had probably never seen before.

So much for an open-and-shut case.

This was going to be harder than she'd imagined.

Didn't these folks realize they were like frogs in a pot of water warming to the boiling point?

Cal began wrapping up his speech by addressing the board. "As you can see, ladies and gentlemen, Stay-n-Shop will be entirely beneficial to Serendipity and the surrounding communities. We offer any number of advantages, not to mention the jobs we will create in your economy."

He paused just long enough to slide Samantha and Will a triumphant grin. Samantha's stomach roiled when she met the man's eyes. Polished, charismatic Cal Turner thought he had her community in the bag.

Not if she could help it.

"In addition," he went on, "we at Stay-n-Shop promise to work for the good of the community. As you may know, our corporation regularly contributes to a number of nonprofit organizations, and we try to keep the money within the communities where our stores exist. We are standing here tonight ready to make a real difference in your lives and in the lives of all who reside here in Serendipity."

Cal smiled and nodded his head toward the board, taking his time meeting each and every one of the council members' gazes. He then turned to the people in the crowd, some fanning their faces with the agenda page they'd received, and spoke his last words.

"Stay-n-Shop. Discount. Variety. Charity. And employment. Thank you for your time."

Chapter Twelve

W‌ill watched in silent admiration as Samantha composed herself. She had such beauty and strength within her. He knew it wasn't easy for her to step up in front of her community and ask for assistance. She was a brave, proud woman who would rather work things out on her own than be a burden to another. A woman who protected her family at any cost, always thinking of others before herself.

She was a giver, not a taker.

But this time she needed to take all she could get.

He was rooting for her with his whole being, supporting her with every nerve ending in his body on edge. And—what?

Praying for her?

He doubted God would listen to a man with the kind of destructive past he had, but perhaps He would make an exception if Will's petition was on behalf of Samantha. At least she was a genuine believer, and strong in her faith.

He'd heard enough prayers during his time visiting the Howells to be able to mimic their style, which he assumed was the correct way of approaching the Almighty. Since he had no other example in his life, he figured he'd give it a shot.

Lord, give her the right words to say. Keep her future safe. Let her feel Your presence and give her peace.

Lightness washed over him. He was praying for Samantha, not for himself, and yet he suddenly had the strangest impression that peace was growing and flourishing in his own heart. It was the oddest sensation, one Will had never before experienced and couldn't have explained if he was asked to do so. He didn't know what to do with it. It was emotion, and yet it was something far more than that.

Rattled by the phenomenon, he did what he always did when emotion threatened to overwhelm him and overpower his thinking—he willfully tamped it down and put a block over it, pushing it into the deepest recesses of his heart, where he no longer had to deal with it.

Eventually, perhaps, he would examine those feelings. Later. Samantha needed him to have a clear mind right now.

Samantha approached Frank and handed him the file. They bent their heads together and spoke in low tones. Will couldn't make out the words, and he knew their opposition couldn't, either. She appeared to be pointing out various items to Frank, and he was nodding vigorously.

"Excuse me," Cal interrupted in a loud, authoritative voice. He stood and placed his fingertips on the table. "If there is a change in the agenda, I believe the correct procedure is for me to be advised. May I step forward and join the council?"

Frank shook his head. "No, you may not. This ain't no powwow. And it ain't a secret, either, from what I can gather." He tapped his palm against the pages of the petition. "It appears most folks are perfectly aware of what's going on here."

"What, exactly, has been presented without my knowledge?" Cal asked, raising one dark eyebrow and sounding both aggravated and exasperated at the same time.

Will had to restrain himself from cracking up at the way Frank Spencer was stringing the big-shot lawyer around. He was positive Frank was doing it on purpose, just to make a point that he was the one in charge.

Samantha turned, addressing both Cal and the crowd, gesturing to include the council members in her speech.

"Folks, you all know me and my family, and you know what I stand for. My great-grandfather was an honest-to-goodness Western pioneer, the very Samuel for which Sam's Grocery is named. Ever since the day he opened his general store to serve the community of Serendipity, our country store has strived to meet the needs of everyone who lives here."

There was a wide-ranging murmur of consensus among the crowd until Frank threatened to bang his hammer again.

Good going, Will thought. One point to Samantha for mentioning her service to the community. *Now bring it on home, sweetheart.*

"It hasn't always been easy. Just like you all, we've had our fair share of struggles. But Sam's Grocery has prevailed through the ups and downs Serendipity has experienced, and we're still here and thriving and ready to serve our community. I hope we can continue in that capacity for many years to come."

Come on, Samantha, honey, give it all you've got. Will pressed his palms into the tabletop and his heels into the floor.

"To me, Sam's Grocery is more than just a store. It's all about people, personal service, family, tradition, history and legacy." Her voice cracked and Will could see her fingers quivering. Agonizing emotion and excruciating tension were a powerful combination. When she tried to resume her speech, her words came out as half a sob.

Will was on his feet and by her side within seconds. He didn't know how these proceedings were supposed to work, whether or not others were allowed to speak at this point, nor did he care. Robert, or Frank, or whoever was leading this shindig could throw his book of rules out the window, because he had something to say.

"When I moved to Serendipity after my tour of duty in Afghanistan, Samantha and her family graciously allowed me into their hearts and their lives. They provided me with a job so I could support myself and my daughter, Genevieve—they permitted me the very great privilege of working at Sam's Grocery."

He slipped his arm around Samantha's shoulder, steadying her and hopefully reassuring her as they turned to face the council members who would ultimately make the final decision.

"I'm here to tell you what Samantha cannot. Working at Sam's Grocery has been an eye-opener for me. It has changed my perspective in more ways than I can name—and all due to Samantha Howell. You all know what to expect when you come into our store—personal service from someone who genuinely cares about your well-being, who knows you and your family by name and can anticipate your needs."

"Hear, hear," called a deep voice from the crowd. Will thought it might be Chance Hawkins, a theory that was confirmed when the man added, "They always special-order boxed juice just for my son."

Frank leveled a gaze at Chance. "We'll have no more of your outbursts. You folks will get your opportunity to talk in a minute, so zip it."

Will released a deep breath. At least Frank hadn't told *him* to sit down and shut up.

"Here's what you're going to get at Stay-n-Shop," Will continued. "The store will be sterile and sanitized and not personalized in any way, except with its fancy end-caps designed to sell you more goods. No one will personally come to your service unless you search for an associate and ask for it, and even then, it'll be a starched transaction. There won't be anyone by your side to discuss the pros and cons of red versus green grapes or to assist you when your children get unruly.

"Opening a big-box store like Stay-n-Shop will bring a whole lot of new people into town. At first glance, you might think that looks like a good thing, economically speaking. More people means more money being spent around town, at our very own businesses.

"But think about this—more people means more houses being built, more land being developed. The possibility of more large corporations setting their sights on our little town."

Will directed his gaze to each of the member of the town council. He had their attention, all right. Their rapt attention. For once, even Frank wasn't muttering under his breath.

"I ask you—where does that leave Serendipity? What happens to the small, intimate community you now call home? I brought my daughter to this town to get away from all the trappings of the city. In my opinion, it would be a shame to bring them here. We already have what we need right here, right now. A country store with tradition and values.

"I say we stand by Sam's Grocery!" Will finished, his voice rising enthusiastically for the sake of the house.

This time there was a cheer, loud and long and buoyant, most definitely rooting for the little town store. Will grinned. He'd always known they'd have the community's support.

Samantha, too, was smiling, relief and thanks in her glittering gaze. She raised a hand, quieting the crowd. "I only have one last thing to say, and I say it with all my heart. I love this town. And I love each and every one of you."

She gestured to include everyone, but her gaze was on Will alone. His breath caught. He wasn't even sure his heart was beating.

And then, when she smiled at him, his heart roared to life, beating double time at the message in her eyes. Was he imagining it, or was she targeting her remark directly at him?

Was it all in his head, or was she saying she was in love with him?

Samantha had been more relieved than she could say when Will had stepped in to speak with her. Not *for* her—*with* her, lending her his strength both physically and with his words. He'd promised her that he'd have her back, and he'd come through on that oath.

There was no doubt in her mind that the assembly agreed with Will's well-spoken conclusions on the matter, if the cheering and hooting were anything to go by.

Frank called for order and begrudgingly opened the floor for comment. One by one, members of the community stood and shared what Sam's Grocery meant to them. Some shared personal stories about various times Samantha or her parents had been there to meet specific needs in their lives. Others spoke of the quality of the goods and the personal dose of customer service that went along with it.

Every observation was encouraging and in Samantha's favor. Frank didn't even try to stop that steamboat once it had pulled away from the dock. The entire council sat quietly, listening to the testimonies, sometimes grunting or nodding but saying little else.

"I call for a quorum," Cal demanded when he had apparently heard enough.

Frank turned his crusty frown upon Cal. Anyone else would have cringed, but Cal merely lifted his chin. "You can't call for a quorum. You aren't a member of this council."

"Then you do it," Cal challenged brutally.

Frank would have none of that, staring the overbearing lawyer down until he looked away. "I'll call for a quorum when I'm good and ready to call for a quorum, and not a moment before. Now sit yourself down there and be quiet."

Shaking his head and snorting at the implied insult, Cal reluctantly seated himself and started talking quietly among his cohorts. Samantha didn't even want to know what Cal was saying to his associates.

"I am, in fact, going to call for a private conference before I call for a vote," Frank said. "I believe this issue needs more discussion. The other council members and I are going to make use of that sweet Texas twilight so we can talk among ourselves and come to some kind of consensus on the matter. You all stay put until we get back." He leveled Cal with one last glare just for good measure.

The council members filed from the room, their expressions solemn. The knot in Samantha's belly tightened. These eight men and women were prominent members of the community, and all, like Frank, had auspicious and voluble opinions. It wasn't like them to be so quiet. Even Frank wasn't saying a word.

Maybe they had nothing to talk about. If it was already decided between them, at least in their own minds, then the end of this meeting would be quick and painless, at least for Samantha and her family. She'd be so incredibly relieved when the positive verdict came back and she could put this whole ugly part of her life behind her.

But what if they hadn't decided in her favor? What if Cal's presentation about economic development had won them over?

Friends and neighbors gathered around Samantha and her family, congratulating her on her speech and wishing her well. Alexis and Mary huddled close to her, loudly offering their forthright and not-so-nice opinions of Stay-n-Shop and Cal Turner and bubbling over with their love for her. Through it all, Will stood next to her, his arm still protectively draped over her shoulder as he spoke to Chance and Jo about how they thought the meeting had gone. Samantha knew that eventually she'd have to contend with her best friends' teasing remarks about her relationship with Will, but for the time being, she had no inclination to move away from the encouragement and strength he silently offered her.

Samantha looked around her at all the folks milling about and listened to the hum of their support. Her heart warmed as she realized how truly blessed she was to have a sympathetic community behind her. Her friends. Her family.

Will.

Had he understood the message in her gaze? Did he know how she felt about him?

"That went well, don't you think?" Will whispered, bending his head close to her ear. His breath was warm on her temple. "Take a look around. Everyone here is raring to go, to start celebrating our victory."

It did rather look like the folks of Serendipity were gearing up for a party, all smiles and laughter in every direction. Apparently no one thought Cal Turner and Stay-n-Shop stood a chance. Samantha's chest filled with gratitude and appreciation for everyone who'd taken precious time away from their families to come to her defense.

"Thank You, Lord," she murmured.

"What was that?" Will asked, leaning closer.

"Oh, nothing. I was just thanking God for His good gifts."

Will looked surprised. "But you haven't even heard what the council has to say yet."

She chuckled. "Don't you see? It's not about that." She gestured to the many people surrounding her. Supporting her. Loving her. "It's about this."

Will nodded, though he never took his eyes off Samantha. "Yeah," he agreed softly, his voice taking on a husky quality. "I think I do understand."

Cal Turner and his associates had taken the opportunity to pack up while they waited. Cal caught Samantha's gaze, his eyes still smug, still proclaiming the victory that he believed was his. He straightened his tie and grinned at her, and it sent a shiver down her spine, as if a diamondback rattlesnake had slithered over her shoe. She had the distinct impression from his black gaze that he enjoyed what he did, wrecking small-town dreams and messing with people's futures.

Samantha made sure her smile was secure. As the minutes rolled on and there was still no sign of the council, Samantha started to worry.

The knot in her belly that had been there since before she'd walked into the room now started roiling with pierced, jagged edges. She felt a little shaky and wondered if maybe she'd accidentally been hyperventilating as her nerves increased. Only Will's firm arm around her shoulder kept her grounded as she leaned into him and consciously slowed her breathing.

"You okay, honey?" Will queried, his brow creasing.

"What do you suppose is taking them so long?" It felt good to get the words out, to share her apprehension with him.

The family gathered around the table and the folks from the community started returning to their seats. Surely a ruling was coming soon.

"Aw, it's nothing to worry about," Grandpa Sampson assured everyone. "Old Frank is probably jawing away about nothing out there. You know how he gets, especially if he thinks he's in charge of the operation."

"He kind of is," Samantha pointed out. *In charge of our future.*

"Well, then, that's a good thing for us, isn't it?" Her father's tone was firm and encouraging, but Samantha could still hear the sliver of doubt in his voice. "Frank would never dare vote opposite his wife or he'd never hear the end of it, and we all know which side Jo is on."

That much was true. When it was finally her turn to talk, Jo had taken the floor like a pro. She'd made no apologies when she ripped Stay-n-Shop all to shreds. She was like a mama tiger protecting her cubs, and in this case, the cubs in question were the Howells.

"All we can do is wait," Will said, giving Samantha's shoulder a squeeze. "There's no sense fretting until we know what we're going to be up against. But this may very well be the end of our fight."

"Or just the beginning," Samantha groaned. She wasn't sure her heart was going to be able to take it if she had to wait much longer. She thought her chest might explode from all the anxiety rocketing through her.

Just then, the council members started filing in the door and taking their seats behind the front table. Samantha tried to read their expressions, but none of them were giving anything away. Not *one* of them. And that's what was scary.

No smiles. No relaxed postures. Instead, they sat as still as statues and just as straight. The room was absolutely silent until Frank banged his hammer-gavel against the surface of the table. Samantha had no idea why Frank thought he needed to do that. He already had everyone's attention. Even the corporate lawyers seemed to be waiting with bated breath for the council's decision.

"I'm callin' this meeting back to order," Frank announced in his usual gruff tone. She tensed, waiting for the anvil to plunge down on her.

Will slid his arm from her shoulders to her waist and pulled her more tightly against him. Hip to hip. Shoulder to shoulder. She was not facing this moment alone.

"I'm sure everyone here knows just how important a decision this is," Frank began.

The crowd murmured in agreement.

"Our decision will affect not only the Howell family, but the community of Serendipity in general."

He paused and took a sharp breath of air before continuing. "As you must have surmised, the town council members here have carefully deliberated on the subject."

The hum of voices in the room dropped abruptly into silence, with Frank ready to make the life-changing announcement. *Pronouncement,* as far as Samantha was concerned. She could almost hear the collective intake of the crowd's breath. She was most certainly holding hers.

"What we've concluded," Frank continued, "is that it won't be fair to either party if we make a rash decision based on a few minutes of discussion. This is an extremely weighty matter. We are giving ourselves one week to think on it and deliberate some more. When we've come to a consensus, we'll directly contact the persons involved with our ruling."

Anger was the first of Samantha's emotions to set in, and adrenaline jolted into her system, bringing her nerve endings alive. She shook her head in protest. Stay-n-Shop wasn't a person. It was an entity. An unfeeling, impersonal entity with lethal steel-trapped jaws that were about to eat her alive.

"Just like all of the rest of you, we on the town council have known the Howells most all of our lives, so we understand just how sensitive this matter is. Naturally, it's difficult for us to be unbiased in our thinking, which is why we're taking a step back. Sam's Grocery has held a key position in Serendipity for a long time, and we're conscious of that.

"But allowing Stay-n-Shop to build their store in our area also offers folks some benefits we've not seen before within this township. We might not like it personally, but we've all acknowledged that there are both pros and cons to this scenario, and it's our duty to weigh them carefully and rule in the best interests of the majority. It ain't as cut-and-dried as all that, and like I said, we need more time to think on it. That's all I've got to say on it for now. Meeting adjourned."

There was a roar as the folks who'd showed up to support the Howells echoed their feelings of distress and outrage. They were clearly not happy with the outcome of the proceedings.

From across the room, Cal met Samantha's gaze and gave her a cold smile. As far as he was concerned, he'd won.

In a sense, he had. If the folks on the council had to think about it, that meant they were divided on the issue. And if they were uncertain, if there was even the tiniest sliver of doubt in their minds, Cal Turner would find some way to push his point home and urge the vote to his favor.

Samantha felt like someone had kicked her hard in the gut. Just when she'd started to believe that having the folks in the community behind her would sway the decision, she'd had the rug pulled right out from under her and had landed straight on her head.

And here she'd thought Stay-n-Shop might finally go away and leave them alone so they could move forward with their lives.

She was despondent and absolutely livid that her reality had come to this. Economics versus legacy. Money talked. It screamed. The almighty dollar was twisting the life out of what was left of her heritage.

Discounts. Variety. Employment. Economic development. And what they had the nerve to call *charity*.

Really—who could fight with that?

She'd certainly put forth her best effort, but to no avail. Will had tried, as well, adding his own words to hers, standing up to the corporation and trying to show the people of Serendipity all they would lose should Stay-n-Shop enter their town.

The crowd had gotten the message, but the council, not so much. Had they even heard Will's argument against bringing a host of new residents to town? Or had they turned that reasoning on its head?

Samantha groaned and slipped out of Will's grasp. She was breathing so heavily she was seeing spots. She made a beeline for the door, desperately needing fresh air and a moment alone so she could pull herself together. She needed to see the stars in the sky to remind her of the Lord's presence and feel the soil below her to ground her to the earth.

She peered upward, trying to pray, but the twinkling of the night sky was not enough. Because it appeared to Samantha that God had abandoned her in her hour of greatest need.

Chapter Thirteen

Will watched Samantha make a mad dash for the nearest exit, but despite the fact that he desperately wanted to follow her, he did not immediately spring up out of his seat. He'd seen her expression just before she'd turned away. She was struggling frantically not to lose it—at least not in front of other people. He well knew what it was like to need a little space to regroup, and he respected Samantha enough to allow her to gather herself before he came after her.

But it wasn't easy to sit and wait when she'd just been blasted by a life-changing emotional mortar, and all he wanted to do was find her and attempt to console her as best he could. He couldn't even begin to imagine what she was feeling right now, being told her legacy wasn't worth immediately upholding, and knowing nothing except that she'd have to wait longer to know for certain the direction her life was going to take.

He knew how *he* felt about it.

Actually, he didn't. Or at least he couldn't put words to the whirlwind in his chest that was causing his blood to roar in his ears. Flabbergasted might be close to describing what was going on. He had no idea how the town council could possibly see any true good coming out of soliciting big business. Did they not realize the ramifications of allowing Stay-n-Shop to build their store in Serendipity? How could they not have considered the many testimonies given by the folks who had come to support Samantha and the Howells, who felt Sam's Grocery was a vital part of their community?

Will decided he couldn't wait another second to find Samantha and take her in his arms and assure her that all would be well. That it would all work out in the end. With a determined set of his chin, he strode out the door. He had to find her and remind her that she was not alone.

It didn't take him long to discover where she'd gone. He found her slumped on the ground behind the Grange hall, away from the main doors and the parking lot where everyone else was heading. She sat with her back against the wall and her arms around her knees. Her head was resting within the crook of her elbow and her shoulders were quivering.

Was she crying?

Will's heart felt like someone was holding it in his fist and squeezing it. He didn't think for a moment that Samantha's tears showed any kind of weakness, but he didn't know what to do with a sobbing woman, how to make things better for her. It was killing him that there was nothing he *could* do for her to make things right in her world.

And there was the rub. As desperately as he wanted to, he couldn't help her. There was nothing he could do to make things better for her.

He crouched before her and tentatively laid a hand on her shoulder.

"I'm here, honey. Talk to me," he murmured.

Samantha didn't say a word. Instead, she rolled forward, wrapping her arms around his neck and burying her head in his chest. Her movement was so intense and unexpected that he nearly lost his balance. He caught himself and rocked forward onto his knees, cradling Samantha against him and allowing her to sob on his shoulder.

His heart ached for her. He desperately wanted to take away her pain, yet all he could do for her was hold her close, brushing his palm against the softness of her hair and soothing her with quiet words spoken lower than a whisper.

After a few minutes she stilled in his arms, no longer sobbing, but gasping heavily with a hitch in each breath.

He faltered for words. What could he say that would console her? What if he said the wrong thing, as he'd often done with Haley? What if he managed to screw things up, to make Samantha feel worse and not better?

"The answer isn't exactly *no*," he finally stated softly.

Samantha used her palms on his chest to push back and meet his gaze. Her glorious blue eyes were shimmering with tears. Her mascara had run, leaving little streaks down her face and black smudges underneath her eyes. He rubbed them away with the pads of his thumbs. As he looked at her, he realized that Samantha was always beautiful to him, inside and out, no matter what. The thought thunderstruck him.

"It might as well be no," she countered. "You saw the look on Cal Turner's face when Frank announced that they were going to table the motion. If the council has to think about it, then it's not the open-and-shut case we had hoped it would be. And if it's not as straightforward as all that, the corporation has made their point. They'll only push harder now that they know they have some leverage."

"We made our point, too, honey."

"Apparently not well enough. Do you think that all the talk about bringing in jobs and building up the town worked against us?"

Will felt like a crane's iron ball had swung around and knocked him in the head. *Had* his argument been turned on him?

"We still have to hold out hope," he responded firmly. "We have to believe that the council members will do the right thing. They are all longtime residents of our town. I'm certain that as they think it over, they'll see Stay-n-Shop for what it is—a threat to our small-town way of life."

"What if they don't? How do we know they aren't going to focus on the *benefits* of the big-box store? What if they see it glowing in marquee lights?"

Will sighed and shrugged. "I suppose we can't know for sure. But I do know who you can depend on completely."

Samantha looked at him expectantly. Will wanted to tell her that she could depend on him completely, but he knew better than to promise her any such thing. Haley had depended on him, and look what had happened there. No. There was One far greater and more reliable than he was.

"Old Frank?" she guessed, thinking he was talking about the council members.

"I expect Jo will keep him in line, but I was actually referring to someone else."

"And that would be…?"

"God, of course. Ultimately He is the one in control, don't you think? He's going to bless you and take care of you no matter what the council decides."

Samantha remained silent, looking pensive.

"You've got your family," he reminded her. His voice turned raspy when he added, "And so far as I am able, you've got me."

She pulled him tighter, as if she was proving to herself that he was really here. She was practically choking him, but he didn't mind. He couldn't really breathe anyway, not when he was so aware of the moonlight softly caressing her face.

He *was* here. And he would be. Like he'd said—as much as he was able.

"Don't forget—tonight most of the community spoke up against allowing Stay-n-Shop to build."

"No. I won't ever forget what happened tonight. I'm forever grateful that all those folks cared enough to fight for Sam's Grocery."

Will chuckled dryly. "They weren't fighting for Sam's Grocery, honey. They were fighting for *you*." His heart welled with his own feelings for her. He cared so much that it scared him. "They were there for you and your family, and for our whole way of life in Serendipity."

"Our soon-to-be-changing way of life," she reminded him grimly.

"Maybe," he admitted, his voice deepening. "Or perhaps it won't make any difference at all, no matter what they build or don't build. You saw how many people came out for you tonight. Who's to say they'd even patronize Stay-n-Shop? Just because it might exist doesn't mean the residents of Serendipity will have to shop there."

"Not at first, maybe."

"Not at all," he assured her. "I imagine most folks are going to keep shopping where it's familiar and friendly, with the townspeople they've known all their lives—Sam's Grocery." He was determined to make her see his point, but she seemed equally determined to ignore it.

"Until they need something on a Sunday afternoon and they realize they can run over to Stay-n-Shop to get it. Don't you see? We can't compete in their arena. Once folks try it, they're bound to go back. Maybe not a lot at first, but as time goes on, our customers will start migrating toward the convenience of the big-box store, and my business—*our* business," she corrected herself, "will dry up and eventually blow away like dust in the wind."

"You can't think like that or you've already lost the war," Will insisted.

"Maybe I have. Maybe I should just concede now and cut my losses."

"What?" Will's voice rose both in tone and volume. That didn't sound like Samantha—like the never-give-up, never-give-in woman determined to protect her family and her town from Stay-n-Shop's bad influence. This was a woman who felt the obligation to take the whole world's problems on her shoulders just to keep others from having to suffer.

"It's just—"

"It's just *nothing*," Will interrupted her before she could finish her pessimistic statement. He cupped her face in his palms, forcing her to look him directly in the eye. "Don't you give up. Do you hear me? Don't you even think about it."

One lone tear rolled down her cheek.

"Look to God for your strength," he reminded her softly.

She sighed, leaning her cheek into his palm. "I know you're right. It's just the waiting I can't stand. I need a decision, one way or another, so I can move on with my life."

Her eyes gleamed so blue. Her skin was soft under the roughness of his hands. The floral scent of her shampoo was playing havoc with his senses, wafting around him and drawing him closer.

Her gaze was begging him to put an end to her misery. She needed something to remind her that there was so much good in Serendipity, so much good in her life.

She needed…

He needed…

"Will," she whispered, holding perfectly still as he closed the small distance between them. "I—"

He brushed a finger over her lips. "Shush. Don't say anything."

He slid his hand over her hair and cradled the nape of her neck, adjusting his arms around her until they fit perfectly together. His blood surged through his chest like a waterfall in a tropical paradise and he cherished the moment as his lips hovered over hers, their breaths mingling warmly together.

In the back of his mind, he was still aware of his guilt. He shouldn't be here. It wasn't right. He couldn't be the man that Samantha needed him to be.

Tomorrow that might be true, but at this moment, he couldn't be anything *but* what she needed him to be. He sighed and gave in to the inevitable, despite how long and hard he'd fought against it. He could no more stop himself from kissing Samantha than he could stop the stars from twinkling in the sky.

Her eyes were like those stars—glittering, luminescent. "Samantha, honey," he whispered against her lips. It was his last conscious thought. Her soft mouth yielded to his, her lips giving and receiving. He wanted her to know his support. He wanted her to feel his love.

His grip tightened as he deepened the kiss, putting his whole heart into showing what he could not say, and knowing it was what she most wanted to hear.

I love you. And you are not alone.

Samantha ran a hand over Will's strong shoulder and sighed. Her other palm rested against the graze of whiskers on his jaw. It was wonderful to be in his arms. She hadn't realized until now just how long she'd been waiting for this moment—maybe from the first time he'd walked in the door of Sam's Grocery.

His kiss was at once gentle and demanding, soft yet intense. His arms surrounded her like a fortress, his shoulders a stronghold against everything bad and difficult in the outside world. Nothing existed except Will—the solid strength of him, the enticing musk of his aftershave, the way he'd whispered her name in the passion of the moment.

He made her feel beautiful. Safe. *Loved.*

The unspoken, invisible bond between them was unlike anything she'd ever experienced before. Their embrace wasn't just a meeting of lips but the union of two hearts. She'd prayed about this moment from the time she was old enough to understand the nature of love, and she savored it with all that was in her being, because now she recognized those emotions tugging at her heart.

She was in love with Will.

Her heart was soaring. Will cared for her, too. She realized, looking back, that he'd been silently communicating his feelings to her for quite some time—protecting her from nearly the moment he'd first walked into her life. She'd simply misread the signals.

But now he was showing her how very much she meant to him in a way that was beyond misinterpretation.

He had to know she felt the same way about him. She put just as much meaning into their kiss as he did. But where Will preferred to convey his emotions through deeds and actions, Samantha needed to say the words. Out loud.

"Will," she murmured as he tenderly leaned his forehead against hers. "I want you to know that I—"

He seemed to freeze suddenly, and then bolted to his feet and backed away. The movement was so abrupt, so harsh, that Samantha, completely shocked, hardly knew what to do.

"Don't," he rasped, the single word a direct order. "Don't say it, Samantha."

"What?" she asked in bewilderment. Her mind was still muddled and cloudy from the kiss and her heart was still pounding in her ears. She felt like she was being plunged back into mental chaos after having a moment of pure, beautiful clarity.

Maybe she hadn't heard him right. That had to be it. She hadn't understood what he was saying.

"What's wrong, Will?"

"I think we ought to stop right here, before anything else happens."

"Are you kidding me right now?" she demanded.

He tunneled his fingers through his hair, leaving it pointed and disheveled, a mirror image of the way her emotions felt right now.

"We got caught up in the moment," he explained, his voice grim, a far cry from how soft and loving it had sounded just moments before. "We were both upset. It happens. Let's leave it at that."

"It *happens?*" she repeated as her heart was pierced by the sharp edges of Will's words. "It happens. That's all you are going to say about it?"

She felt like a puppet. Will had jerked her strings and she had blindly danced to his music. And then in the next instant, he'd dropped her, leaving her in a mixed-up heap of parts on the floor.

Maybe Will was right. Maybe they *had* gotten caught up in the moment. Her stress level was through the roof, after all. Her entire life was falling apart. But in her case, the pressure had only forced her to admit what she'd already known deep down—that she had feelings for Will.

That she *loved* him.

He, on the other hand, was brushing those emotions off as if they were nothing. And yet he'd been the one who'd reminded her of all her blessings, who had encouraged her to lean on God during the tough times when she was beginning to believe she had nothing and no one.

For some crazy, wonderful and now absolutely mortifying reason, she had thought, at least for a moment, that she had Will.

What a fool she had been.

"So, what was that, then?" she hissed. "You were just stealing a kiss because I'm vulnerable right now?"

His eyebrows lowered over his smoldering eyes, which had turned almost black, as they always did when he was experiencing great emotion.

"Don't do that."

"Don't do *what?*"

"Don't belittle what we shared. It meant a lot to me."

She ignored his admission. He was just yanking her chain again, and she would have none of it.

"It seems to me that you're the one belittling what we shared. It also seems to me you're doing an awful lot of ordering here. You aren't in the Army anymore, Will, so don't tell me what I can and can't do."

"Please," he pleaded. "Don't diminish what happened here tonight. I care for you. I really do. But for reasons I can't explain, I can't go there with you."

"Can't? Or won't?" Maybe she was being unfair, pushing him further than he was ready to go, but she had to know the truth. He couldn't just kiss her like that—like he was ready to give her the world—and then step back and tell her he couldn't *go there*.

"Honey, I can't give you what you're asking me to give to you."

She felt like Will was taking a chain saw to her heart, methodically cutting it into smaller and smaller pieces until there was nothing left. "If that's true, Will, then why did you just kiss me like that?"

He looked at her for what felt like an eternity with those heart-stoppingly beautiful brown eyes that for once she was able to read clearly. She saw love in his eyes—she was sure of it. But she also saw fear, and uncertainty.

"I promised you that I'll be there for you," he said, his voice hard, even cold, "and you can bank on that promise. No matter what happens with Stay-n-Shop, I'll be by your side."

"Is that all this is to you, Will? Is this just about the Stay-n-Shop?"

"That's all it can be, Samantha. Trust me on this. Let's just focus on the Stay-n-Shop and leave the rest alone."

He turned and headed back into the Grange hall, leaving her right where he'd found her before he'd changed her world with a single kiss.

At the moment, she didn't give a fig about Stay-n-Shop. She wanted Will. She wanted *all* of Will, especially the one thing he apparently refused to give.

His heart.

"Hey, Monkey," he said as he scooped Genevieve into his arms, squeezing her extra tight and running his hand across her black curls. Holding his little girl in his arms was his anchor to reality right now. It was all he had.

"Thanks, Delia," he said to the woman hovering in the doorway. "I appreciate you watching Genevieve tonight."

"Anytime," Delia said pleasantly. "How did the meeting go?"

Will's mind immediately flashed to those moments after the meeting, when he held Samantha secure in his embrace. The most wonderful minutes of his life. And his biggest mistake of all.

"The Grange was filled to bursting with folks coming out to support Samantha and her family. I think it went well."

"I heard Stay-n-Shop brought in a whole legal team."

"They did. Hopefully the council will see through their arguments and keep Sam's Grocery safe."

"Tell the Howells I'm praying for them."

"I suppose that's the best thing we can do for them at this point."

"Daddy, you're holding me too tight," Genevieve exclaimed, wiggling.

"Sorry, Monkey," he said, bending to place her on the ground.

"Your daddy just loves you so much he wants to squeeze you like a stuffed animal," Delia said with a chuckle.

Well, that was true. And more. Genevieve was all he had. He didn't want to screw that up.

"Thanks again," he called over his shoulder as he buckled Genevieve into the car seat. Delia waved and closed the door.

"Are we going to see Miss Samantha?"

It was an innocent question, but it pierced Will's heart like a knife.

"No, sweetheart. It's late. Miss Samantha might already be sleeping." He knew she wouldn't be. Not tonight. Not after what he'd pulled with her. She was probably stomping around her house, mulling over his demise.

And rightly so.

"Miss Samantha promised to show me how to play the piano," Genevieve said.

Will's throat burned. "You really like Miss Samantha, don't you?"

"She's nice to me. And she's so pretty. You like her, too, don't you, Daddy?"

Will hadn't shed a tear since he was five years old and his father threatened to hit him if he didn't stop bawling like a baby, but at Genevieve's words, his eyes burned, and it took every bit of strength within him not to give into the urge to let go. It hurt that much.

He had to clear his throat twice to answer. "Yeah, Monkey. I like her, too."

Chapter Fourteen

Will hadn't seen Samantha in three days, and he hadn't slept in nearly that long, either. There was no doubt in his mind that she was avoiding him, and he supposed he really couldn't blame her. He'd hurt her—deeply—which was the last thing he'd ever meant to do. But now it was too late to take back what he'd said—or what he'd done.

On Saturday, Samantha's parents had asked him to take a day off from the store to finish building a wrap-around porch for one of the cabins near the river. There was a certain satisfaction in building things up instead of tearing them down. As he set the planks, he'd listened to the gentle swoosh of the river gliding over large, pointed rocks, and to the birds singing what Will imagined to be praise songs from the trees. A rare black squirrel had even approached him when he got too close to the animal's home. He'd been impressed by the squirrel's angry chattering and apologized for disturbing him.

It was a peaceful scene, but Will had felt no tranquility in his heart. Not while things were so completely unresolved between him and Samantha.

He'd declined to attend church on Sunday. He was too confused and confounded to come up with a reasonable excuse for why he wasn't going, especially since he'd only just started attending at all, but fortunately, the Howells didn't ask. They merely wished him a good day and left him to his own devices.

He'd hoped giving Samantha a couple of days to cool off and pray would give her new perspective, but it didn't take him long to realize he was wrong on that count.

Sometime during the night on Sunday, Samantha had left an envelope taped to his door, which contained a key to the store and brief, scribbled instructions for him to go ahead and open the shop Monday morning on his own. He'd thought maybe she was running errands and intended to arrive late, but as the hours slowly passed, he came to the distressing realization that it was unlikely that she was going to put in an appearance at all.

He was able to handle the store on his own with no problem, even with all the extra customers coming out in droves to support Sam's Grocery and bolster Samantha's spirits. He wished she could have been there to see the day's business, and thank the community that was well and truly behind the Howell family legacy.

Whether or not Stay-n-Shop was allowed to build on that land, Will firmly believed that Samantha's heritage was safe in the hands of the wonderful, faithful folks of Serendipity.

As the day ended and there was still no sign of Samantha, Will closed up, cleaned up and found himself reaching for his cell phone. He dialed Samantha's mother.

"Hello? This is Amanda."

"Hey, Amanda. It's me, Will."

"Hi, Will. I just fed Genevieve a bowl of macaroni and cheese. She said she was hungry and I like to spoil her a little bit when I can. She's like a granddaughter to me. I hope you don't mind."

"No, not at all." He was happy to hear the pleasure in Amanda's voice when she spoke of Genevieve. Samantha's mother and his young daughter had a special bond. They were good for each other, much in the same way that Genevieve and Samantha were good for each other. He pushed the thought out of his mind. "Actually," he continued, "Genevieve is the reason I'm calling. Or—er—part of the reason, anyway."

"Sure, Will," she said, sounding intrigued. "What can I do for you?"

"Have you seen Samantha recently?"

"I saw her yesterday. She played the organ for church, but she left right afterward. Why? Did she not show up for work this morning?"

"No. She left me the key to open with, so I figured she was going to be late, but she never came in at all. I thought maybe she was spending the day with you all. I guess she needed some time alone."

"That's odd."

Will sighed. "No, not really. I'm fairly certain she's avoiding me. She's not picking up her phone, either. Do you have any idea where she might have gone if she was upset?"

To her credit, Amanda did not ask what Will had done to upset her daughter, even though he'd pretty much admitted that was exactly what he had done.

"You really care for her, don't you?" she asked softly.

Everything in him burned—his eyes, his throat, his heart. He wasn't sure he could speak, but Amanda was waiting for an answer.

"Yes, ma'am, I do."

"So? What are you waiting for? Writing in the clouds?"

Will chuckled. "That would be nice."

"Indeed it would, but love is never that simple, or that tidy. We're all a mess inside, you know. Every one of us carries baggage. But when God unites two hearts, they can lift each other up, carry their loads together."

"But I—"

"Love my daughter. Go get her. Try the church. Ever since she started learning music as a little girl, the church has been kind of like her refuge. Playing the organ seems to help her organize her thoughts and work through her feelings about whatever is bothering her."

Which would be me.

"And before you ask, I'm happy to watch Genevieve for you for as long as you need me to."

"Thank you, ma'am," he said, gratitude welling in his heart. Once again, he was astounded by the Howells' continued generosity toward him. They just gave and gave without a second thought.

He could see where Samantha got her heart from.

"It's my pleasure," Amanda insisted. "That's what family does. We step in and help each other."

Will's throat clogged with emotion. He ended the call and then just stood staring at his cell phone.

Had she just referred to him as *family?*

He didn't know how that had come about, but it made him want to stay in Serendipity more than ever. It would be such a shame if he had to walk away from the best thing he'd ever known. If only he could make Samantha understand that no matter how much he loved her—and he did love her—he would not risk hurting her the way he had hurt Haley.

It was *because* he loved her, because he'd never experienced anything remotely close to the bond he had with Samantha, that he had to back away from the relationship. If he had to, he would even go so far as to leave Serendipity, but he hoped with all this heart that it wouldn't come to that.

Amanda had reminded him that everyone carried scars, perhaps even regrets, and that if he could get past his troubles, Samantha might be waiting at the end. But he felt so weighed down by his past. Could he ever let it go?

He heard the organ long before he actually entered the sanctuary of the church. Samantha was playing a dark, brutal piece of music that immediately reached into his soul and tore pieces away, leaving every last nerve vibrating with tension.

If her selection was anything to go by, she wasn't even remotely close to getting over being angry with him for starting what he couldn't finish, not that he'd expected her to be.

Now it was time to explain.

The last majestic chord of the piece set him off balance and he had to shake his head to try to regain his mental focus.

"'Toccata in D Minor,'" she said as she slid from the organ bench and approached him. "It's Bach."

"It's chilling is what it is," he countered. He didn't

know who this Bach guy was, but he sure wrote unsettling music.

She leveled him with a glare. "It *is* a little cold in here."

Well, at least she was honest—and she wasn't talking about the music or the air-conditioning. It was a place to start.

"I came to apologize," he said bluntly.

Her expression didn't change, yet Will felt her shift in emotion just as clearly as if she had burst into tears.

"I'm not here to apologize for kissing you, so let's get that clear right off the mark."

Her shoulders sagged, but Will didn't know whether it was from relief or dejection.

"Kissing you was the best moment of my life."

"Me, too, Will," she said, crossing her arms as if she needed to protect herself from him somehow.

"Along with the day Genevieve was born, of course," he added.

"Of course," she agreed, the sad smile on her face showing him that she knew exactly how important his daughter was to him.

She understood. She *got* him.

And he was going to walk away from all that? His brow furrowed. He considered himself a strong and powerful man, but did he have the fortitude it would take to do what was best for Samantha, even if it wasn't best for him?

She reached out and brushed a hand along his shoulder, bringing him back to the present.

"What are you not telling me?"

"I've told you everything. I can't ever be in a relationship with you. I won't. I'll hurt you, and I never want to do that. Don't you see?"

She frowned and shook her head. "See what, Will? What is it that you think is going to happen if you let yourself be with me?"

"I'm dangerous, Samantha. It's my fault Haley is dead. If anything were ever to happen to you because of me, there's no telling what I'd do." He took a deep breath, and finally let the rest spill out. "I don't deserve you, or your love."

Samantha took a step back, stunned not only by the words Will had uttered, but by how vehement his tone had been. His eyes were dark and reproachful—he was condemning himself.

Criminal, judge and jury. Guilty as charged.

But how could he say that, much less believe it?

Samantha stayed very still, as if Will would disappear if she made the wrong move. She ignored the very strong urge she had to wrap her arms around him and tell him what an amazing man he was. "Will, it's not your fault she's dead."

He leveled her with his gaze, cold and accusing. "Isn't it?"

"No, it isn't. You can't blame yourself for what happened in a dark alley a continent away from where you were at the time."

"Haley wouldn't have been in Amarillo working as a waitress in a truck stop if we hadn't been separated. If I had been a better husband to her, she would never even have been in that dark alley. So you see, it is my fault." His words held such agony that Samantha felt her heart ripping into shreds, her eyes pricking with tears.

"I see no such thing, Will Davenport," she retorted.

She could stand it no longer—she took his face in her hands, trying to make him look at her, to see the truth in her eyes.

He groaned and tried to pull away, but she wouldn't let him.

"Do you want to know what I see when I look at you?"

He couldn't answer her. She could practically see the battle that was being fought within him, and she realized that now it was her turn to stand by him, to offer her support, to help him win his war.

"I see a strong man. An honorable man. A man who puts his whole heart into everything he does. A man who puts his daughter's needs above his own. A man who is brave and unselfish."

"I'm not any of those things," he rasped.

"You are in my eyes." She was going to make him hear her, even if she had to put her own heart on the line. She gathered her courage and finished what she'd started to say the other night outside the Grange. "I love you, Will Davenport."

He took a harsh, deep breath, as if someone had punched him in the stomach.

"Samantha, you can't. You shouldn't. I'm not—"

"Why can't you forgive yourself?" she asked before he could finish telling her all the reasons why he was undeserving of love. "God forgives you."

"How can God forgive me?" He shook his head, unwilling to believe it, yet Samantha could see the hope gleaming in his eyes. He wanted to believe. He just didn't know how yet.

"How can God forgive any of us, Will? We've all

sinned. No human is worthy of what God gives us. Jesus died so we could have forgiveness. So we could find love."

"Even me?" The hope in his eyes had turned to understanding. She could see the fear receding, replaced by strength and courage. She could see the man she loved coming back to her.

She leaned her forehead against his and reveled in the moment when two hearts became one.

"Even you, Will. Even you."

He framed her face with his large, strong hands, and caressed her cheek with his thumb. "God must have blessed me, if I'm here with you."

He brushed his lips softly against hers, once, and then again.

"Likewise, I'm sure," she whispered against his mouth.

He kissed her again, pulling her close. She could feel the strength of his embrace, yet his touch was infinitely gentle for all that. Tough, yet tender.

When he lifted his head, she had a brief moment of panic. Was he turning away from her again?

But, no. His gaze caught hers, and his mouth moved as if he were going to speak, but no words came. Not at first.

"You know I'm not a man of words," he said softly, "but these words need to be said. Over and over again. Every day, for the rest of our lives." His eyes glimmered with emotion.

"I love you, Samantha Howell. I want to cherish you. Protect you. And show you every day that I love you."

His smile was radiant. That was the only word Samantha could think to describe it. And it matched the glow of her heart perfectly.

"I love you," he said again, stronger and louder this time. "I love you." The sound echoed through the sanctuary, and he laughed.

He tucked her head against his chest, his cheek resting against her hair. "I love you."

Chapter Fifteen

It was so quiet in the Grange hall that Samantha could have heard a pin drop. It wasn't because the hall was empty. On the contrary, it was full-to-brimming-over with town folks, once again out to support the Howells and Sam's Grocery.

Samantha had taken her place at the front right table, where she'd sat just a week before, facing off against Cal Turner and the Stay-n-Shop legal team. Will sat beside her, his fingers laced with hers. She took a deep, calming breath, and Will squeezed her hand, adding his silent encouragement.

There was no more arguing to be done. The town council had called together this assembly to render their decision. Samantha just hoped she could hear and accept it with strength and dignity. Whatever the outcome, she had Will, her family, her friends and the townsfolk whom she held so dear.

Frank banged his gavel, although why he thought he had to do that was beyond Samantha. No one was speaking. Everyone's attention was already trained on the council.

"I'll come right to the point," Frank said without preamble. "No sense dragging this thing out."

Samantha's heart dropped into the pit of her stomach. If Frank and the council didn't want to draw out the news, it must be bad.

"After much discussion and a thorough review of the issues, we've come to a resolution."

Samantha couldn't help herself. She glanced across the way. Cal grinned and winked, like he was flirting with her. Or rubbing her nose in her pain and loss.

"...Sam's Grocery."

Samantha had been so caught up in Cal's unbelievably callous behavior that she'd missed Frank's pronouncement, but she didn't need him to repeat it.

The crowd cheered. Will stood, pulling her with him as he whooped and turned her around.

"You did it." He kissed her cheek and slid his arm around her shoulders as he turned her to face her exultant family.

"No, Will," she protested, tightening her grip on his waist and meeting his adoring gaze. "*We* did it."

"Hey, you two," Samantha called as Will and Genevieve came in the front door of the store. For some reason she was reminded of the first day Will had walked into her life, hoping he had a job and a place to stay. She knew he hadn't been looking for love—quite the opposite, in fact. But love had found him.

And she was never going to let him go.

"The week is almost up," Will reminded her as he sent Genevieve out back to play with some of the neighborhood children.

His eyes sparkled, and it was then that she realized

he was holding something behind his back. His expression didn't reflect his usual serious demeanor. It was light, merry—almost boyish in its enthusiasm.

She smiled. She could get used to this side of Will.

"All right, there, mister. Give it up. What do you have behind your back?"

Why *did* he look that way? What *was* behind his back?

"Wouldn't you like to know?" he teased.

She waited for him to reveal his prize, trying very hard not to imagine the diamond solitaire that Alexis and Mary would have wished for her ring finger. There was time enough for that later. She and Will hadn't even talked through many of the serious issues couples discussed— they were too busy enjoying each other's company for that.

She darted around the counter and made a play for his hand, but he danced back out of her reach.

"Uh-uh. You've got to give me something first."

She reached for the lollipop tub on the counter. "Sucker? I believe I offered you one the first day we met."

He chuckled. "You know that's not what I want. Plant one, right here." He pointed to his cheek. Samantha stood on tiptoe to oblige, but at the last moment turned so her lips landed squarely on his.

"Now then," he continued cheerfully, "I've got something special for you. Something I think you're really going to like."

"Are you going to keep tormenting me, or are you going to show me?"

"I'll show you," he said, bringing his hand out from behind his back.

It wasn't a ring box.

Of course it wasn't a ring box. She was being silly. But she was surprised by the small moment of disappointment that flashed through her. Hopefully it didn't show on her face. The last thing she wanted to do was make Will feel like he'd somehow disappointed her when in fact he just kept exceeding her expectations at every turn. She loved him so much she sometimes thought her heart might burst from it.

She looked closely at what he was holding. It was a small scroll of paper, tied with a red ribbon.

"Let me guess. Is it a Dear John rejection letter? Is it from you?"

"No, it is not," Will denied. "On both counts. And I even tied it with red ribbon because I knew that was your favorite color."

"It was last week," she said with a grin.

"Oh, you ladies. So unpredictable."

"I'll show you unpredictable if you don't give me that paper."

He slipped it into her hand and then crossed his arms, watching with glowing eyes as she pulled the ribbon and rolled the page down flat. She scanned the contents and then squealed in exhilaration and leaped into Will's arms, wrapping her arms around his neck and her legs around his knees.

"It's official!"

"Yes, ma'am. Stay-n-Shop is pulling out of town, and the council is saying good riddance."

Tears pricked at her eyes as joy welled in her heart. Seeing the decision on paper made it final. Certified. *Over.*

"I'm going to have to bring you good news more often if I'm going to get thanked liked that," he added, setting her to the floor.

"Just your presence is enough," she assured him.

"Still," he said, "there might be one more surprise for you…"

She narrowed her eyes on him. As far as she could tell, his hands were empty, but his gaze was not. It was full of all the love in the world, and she knew it reflected her own. "One more thing what?" she prompted.

"Well," Will said, reaching into the front pocket of his jeans, "if you insist, I might give you this."

He held up a ring. There was no box, but it was the most beautiful thing she had ever seen.

Or rather, it was the most beautiful moment in the world when Will knelt before her and smiled up at her. He took her hand in his, and she could feel his fingers trembling.

"I want to do this right, Samantha. Starting from this moment." He paused and his lips quirked. "Samantha Howell, will you be my wife?"

She stared first at him, and then at the ring. She would have pinched herself to see if this was real, except the gleam in the depths of Will's brown eyes told her it was true. The diamond solitaire, surrounded by tiny rubies and emeralds, sparkled in the sunshine that poured through the front window.

"Green and red, just in case you change your mind about the color," he teased.

"Oh, you," she exclaimed, holding out her left hand. "Now put that on me."

He stood and wrapped his arms around her waist, then kissed her thoroughly. "I want you to know I love you," he said, his voice deepening with emotion. "I need you with me always. And I promise I'll always have your back."

* * * * *

A seventh-generation Texan, **Jolene Navarro** fills her life with family, faith and life's beautiful messiness. She knows that as much as the world changes, people stay the same: vow-keepers and heartbreakers. Jolene married a vow-keeper who shows her holding hands never gets old. When not writing, Jolene teaches art to inner-city teens and hangs out with her own four almost-grown kids. Find Jolene on Facebook or her blog, jolenenavarrowriter.com.

Books by Jolene Navarro

Love Inspired

Cowboys of Diamondback Ranch

The Texan's Secret Daughter
The Texan's Surprise Return
The Texan's Promise
The Texan's Unexpected Holiday
The Texan's Truth
Her Holiday Secret

Lone Star Legacy

Texas Daddy
The Texan's Twins
Lone Star Christmas

Lone Star Holiday
Lone Star Hero
A Texas Christmas Wish
The Soldier's Surprise Family

Visit the Author Profile page
at LoveInspired.com for more titles.

THE SOLDIER'S
SURPRISE FAMILY

Jolene Navarro

Consider now, for the Lord has chosen you to build
a house for the sanctuary; be courageous and act.
—*1 Chronicles* 28:10

This story is dedicated to the military families
that support, serve and protect our nation.
Especially Baron Von Guinther for talking with me
until the wee hours of the morning in San Diego,
brainstorming this story and helping me
get to know the hero, Garrett Kincaid.

Chapter One

Texas state trooper Garrett Kincaid scanned the yard, hoping to find it empty. The afternoon sun had gone into hiding as the breeze carried the aroma from the overabundance of flowering plants. When he arrived home from a long shift, sleep was the only action item on his agenda. Ha, he was funny.

His garage apartment offered sweet seclusion a few steps away. He might actually avoid a conversation or another offer of a meal from his energetic landlady, Anjelica Ortega-Garza. She threatened his resolve to stay out of relationships. There was too much to like about her. He even liked the way she said her name with the Spanish pronunciation. It rolled off his tongue so smooth. He shook his head and made himself stop playing with her name. It was just a name.

It took so much effort to tell her no. He had to admit he'd never eaten so well. According to his mother, pushing buttons on a microwave counted as a home-cooked meal. And during their short marriage, Viviana's favorite dinner came in a to-go bag.

Another scent mixed with the flowers and he knew

coffee and bacon were close. The lady could cook. She seemed to have an overdeveloped need to feed the entire population of Real County and every resident within a hundred-mile radius.

"Stop right there. Don't even think about it!"

Firm and sharp, the command stopped Garrett mid-motion. He turned to find the lady who had just been in his thoughts. Standing with her hands planted on her hips. Petite and lovely, she looked in charge. A purple scarf got caught up in the wind before she tucked it back into place.

He groaned. His resolve not to think of her in a personal way took a hit every time he saw her. So much for avoiding her.

Her normally friendly smile was gone, replaced with a glare, but not at him. A few feet away from her, a silky mop of a dog lay on its belly. Big brown eyes darted between Anjelica and a small herd of colorful chickens. Maybe they were a flock. *What do you call a group of chickens?*

He'd grown up in the city surrounded by noise, not hills and odd farm animals. A month ago he would have told anyone who asked that he was a city boy. But living fifteen miles from a town that was in the middle of nowhere, Texas, he discovered a new side of himself. And a new plan, to build a home of his own where people wouldn't bother him, especially an overly friendly landlady.

The one-room cabin would sit on the edge of the Frio River. He could see the waters running so clear it washed all the grime away from life.

He sighed. After his disastrous marriage, the biggest part of his plan was to stay single, no ties and no family. There was a sign over Anjelica that screamed Hero Needed and he vowed to never play that game again.

A small whine sounded from the silky mop with a pink bow. Maybe he could still make it up the stairs to the apartment over her garage. He glanced to the door, estimating how long it would take to—

"Officer Kincaid!"

He dropped his head before turning to face her. The woman made him nervous with her whimsical smile and dancing movements. Fragile and naive, someone else who needed to be protected from the real world.

Her golden-brown eyes found him, bright and eager. The commander of a moment ago vanished as she made her way toward him. The fluff of a dog that Garrett had never seen before followed, deciding to chase her flowing skirts instead of the chickens. "How was work? I always pray nothing happens." Her eyes slipped to the gun he had holstered at his hip. "Uneventful night in your line of work is a good thing, right?"

"Yes, ma'am."

"I saved a couple of extra soft tacos. Egg and bacon along with fresh coffee. I can bring them to you."

"I—" Before he could find a good excuse, Sheriff Torres's patrol vehicle pulled into the drive and parked behind his SUV. An unexpected visit from the local sheriff usually brought bad news.

Anjelica's smile vanished. She clutched her scarf with one hand as the other held her stomach. She displayed all the signs of someone who knew to expect bad news. In a few steps he closed the gap between them.

A woman in a fitted business suit and low heels got out of the passenger side. She was tall, with her dark blond hair forming a neat bun. In his cowboy hat, Sheriff Torres approached with the woman close behind.

"Morning, Anjelica. Kincaid." He nodded to each of them and shook their hands.

Garrett watched as Anjelica took a deep breath, in and out.

"Kincaid, this is Sharon Gibson. She's with CPS."

Child Protective Services. Relief loosened the muscles he hadn't even noticed had tightened. So it was work related and they were here for him, not her. He gave Anjelica a reassuring smile. Her shoulders dropped a notch and her smile returned. She moved to the woman and shook her hand.

The woman turned to him, offering a greeting. In her free hand, she carried a couple of folders. "Nice to meet you, Officer Kincaid."

"Likewise. So, what can I do for you?" The one thing he dreaded the most was domestic situations involving kids. He turned to Torres. The sheriff shook his head. Garrett's brows crunched inward. Now he was confused.

Sharon Gibson cleared her throat. "We're here because of your son in Kerrville."

"Excuse me?" There was no way he'd heard that right. He glanced at the sheriff's grim face. "I don't have any children. I've never even lived in Kerrville."

"You were married to Viviana Barrera Kincaid while in Houston, correct?"

"For a short time."

She tilted her head. "Are you saying her son is not yours or that you are unaware of the boy, Garrett River Kincaid Jr.?"

The world stopped spinning. Where had his blood

gone? Glancing down, he noted that his body looked intact. Muscles pricked as if drained.

The woman looked around. "Is there somewhere we can sit and talk?"

His mind had gone blank. Sit? She wanted somewhere to sit? Behind an invisible wall, he watched Anjelica pick up her dog. Words were exchanged.

She walked to her porch and disappeared into the house. The woman, Sharon Gibson with CPS, followed her onto the porch and sat on a rocking chair.

Commands from his brain went unheard by his body. Nothing worked. Frozen. Viviana had found a way to pull him into her drama all over again.

Torres stopped next to him, placing a firm hand on his upper arm. "I take it you didn't know about the boy. No one likes being blindsided." The sheriff patted Garrett's tense shoulder. "Come on—we'll get this worked out."

A son, no way. There had to be a mistake. Viviana, for all her faults, would have told him about a child. It had to be Ed's, her boyfriend she kept going back to. How could they know for sure that the boy was his? He was going to be sick. Deep breaths.

He followed Torres up the steps, not seeing anything but the folders on the low table between the chairs.

Anjelica pushed open the screen door. The hinges needed to be oiled. She sat a tray on the small table. "I have sugar and cream. Does anyone need something else, like water?"

Sharon smiled. "This is perfect, thank you." She poured cream into her cup.

Garrett stared at the swirls of the white getting lost in the black liquid.

"Garrett?" Anjelica's voice brought him back to the present. The warmth and smile were gone. Now he got the same glare the chicken-chasing dog earned. He was a dog.

He shook his head. If he tried to drink or eat anything, it wouldn't stay down.

At the end of the porch, across from Sharon, Sheriff Torres sat on the swing and took a drink from his cup. "Sure you don't want coffee? Maybe some water?"

"I'll get you some water." Anjelica disappeared into the house.

Sharon took a sip before she looked at him, a soft smile on her face. "So you were married to Viviana Barrera?"

Breathe, Garrett. You have to breathe. He nodded. His throat too dry to make a coherent sound.

"Her son's name is Garrett River Kincaid Jr. You're listed as the father on his birth certificate. Family members also say you're the father."

"Are you sure?" What kind of man didn't know he had a kid? Even his loser of a father stuck around for the first few years. "I didn't know." His jaw hurt, but he made sure to keep his face calm. A clear mind and facts, that was what he needed to sort this out.

"This is an emergency situation. You can challenge with a DNA test if you want to, but the state uses the name on the birth certificate and acknowledges you as the legal father."

Garrett looked at the curve of the rocker resting on the worn boards of the porch. What had Viviana done now? He cleared his throat, the need to explain, to make them understand, burning his gut.

He heard the creak of the screen door again and

looked up. Anjelica handed him a water bottle. Fighting the urge to press the cold bottle against his neck, he rolled it between his palms. His landlady vanished inside the house again. "Why are you the one telling me this? Are they in trouble?" If CPS was involved, something had to be wrong.

Sheriff Torres leaned his elbows on his knees and Sharon took a deep breath. He wanted to yell at them to stop messing with him, but he sat and waited. He pressed his right thumb into the center of his left palm. He could hear the chickens in the yard and music playing somewhere in the house. None of it seemed real.

"There's a history of domestic violence with her current boyfriend."

Viviana's life was a history of domestic violence, from the time she was born. The need to save her had eaten him for years.

"Yesterday a neighbor called to report shouting and gunshots. Two bodies were found. It looks as if he shot her, then turned the gun on himself. It's under investigation. The officers found the boy, Garrett, his baby sister and a dog hiding in the backyard."

All the blood left his body. If Sharon kept talking, he didn't hear it. Viviana was dead. Grief and regret swamped him. She was dead and she had left children behind. Not just the one boy named Garrett Kincaid, but a daughter, too. *Oh, Viviana.*

He ran his hands through his hair. "More than one?" He didn't understand. "How many children did she have? Are they Ed's?" This couldn't be real. "I can't imagine he allowed her to put my name as the father. This isn't making sense."

The caseworker's brow drew closer and she gave him

a questioning look. "Ed? I don't know who that is. The current boyfriend was James Barrow. He is the father of the little girl. She's ten months old. He was an auto mechanic and had a job in Kerrville until about a month ago. His family lives in Houston."

He rubbed his face. "She moved on to someone worse?" Trying to figure out Viviana's love life wasn't important right now. Her children were now orphaned. What a mess, a living nightmare.

He took in one long breath, counting to seven. "Tell me what you know." He looked Sharon in the face. If what she said was correct, the boy wasn't an orphan. Garrett's stomach rolled.

No, the boy had a father, and that would be him. Maybe. Just because Viviana put his name on the birth certificate didn't mean the boy was his, but he couldn't just leave them, either. From the first time he met her at the age of ten, he had been desperate to rescue Viviana from her life. Taking her children would be a way to do that, since she never allowed him to help her.

"The boy, Garrett River, just turned five. Pilar is the girl—she's ten months old. With the birth certificate, letters from the mother and other family members' statements, we have enough evidence to immediately place them with you if you're willing. It doesn't mean you're taking permanent custody of the girl. There will be a hearing for temporary placement that needs to happen rather fast. The courts will decide on that first, then permanent in six months."

Custody and court dates? Garrett leaned back and closed his eyes. "I gave her an ultimatum. Viviana picked Ed. I left Houston, blocked her from my phone and filed for divorce." He jolted from the rocking chair and paced along the edge of the porch. His muscles jumped under his skin, restless and tight.

Oh man, what if she'd tried to call and tell him about the pregnancy? He covered his eyes with his hands, pressing the palms hard against his eye sockets. He had been so set on not allowing her to use him again. His stubbornness could mean he had left a son behind. "What do I need to do now?"

"We need you to take immediate custody of the children." She took a sip of her coffee. "Because you're a state trooper, a veteran and the state-acknowledged biological father of the first child, we could place Pilar with you if you're willing to take her. We would still have to go to court, but my hope is you agree to be the temporary solution. We still need to follow up with home inspections and parenting classes."

Looking at the horizon, Garrett cleared all thoughts and concentrated on breathing.

Torres cleared his throat. "So he doesn't need a DNA test to claim the boy? Where are they now?"

"No, as far as we're concerned, he's the father. He'll only need the DNA test if he wants to challenge the birth certificate. Right now the kids are in an emergency shelter in Kerrville. We'd like to get them out of there as soon as possible. It's not designed for the care of infants and small children. There's no one that's capable of caring for the children on the mother's side of the family, and the father's side refuses to take them."

"So you want me to take both of them."

"We do prefer keeping them together whenever possible."

He nodded. A baby needed a crib and a car seat… Well, he wasn't even sure what all a baby needed. The boy was only five. Did he need special equipment? "What timeline are you looking at for me to take the kids?"

"So you're willing to take both of the children?"

He nodded. He didn't see any other choice. If that was his son and his son had a sister, he'd keep them together. Even if the boy wasn't his son, he was Viviana's and no kid deserved to start off life that way.

Everyone was looking at him. Glancing away from their intense gazes, Garrett turned to the horizon. This was not how he imagined fatherhood entering his life. A strong urge to pray plagued him, but he didn't even know where to start.

Sharon gave him a big smile. "Good. I know this is a shock, but the faster we can get these little ones settled with you, the better. Can you pick them up tomorrow? We'll set up a house inspection afterward."

"Tomorrow." A flash of panic constricted his lungs. Garrett turned to Torres. He was the closest thing to a friend he had in this town, but their only connections were the Marines and state law enforcement. Could he help with the kids?

No, not *the* kids, *his* kids. Hoping the sick feeling in his gut didn't show on his face, he forced a smile for Sharon.

With a warm glow in her eyes, she leaned forward and touched his hand, offering him two plain-looking folders. These folders would change his life forever. Was he ready? Could he do this? Parenting two babies who'd suffered a major trauma. He had his own issues to deal with. Nodding, he took the folders from her. "Thank you." His fingers dropped them on the tabletop as if they had burned him.

He had been so careless and Viviana…oh, Viviana. He thought of the girl he had loved. His love had not been enough. Would he be enough for her children? The children were caught in a horrific trap and it looked as if he was their best hope. That didn't say much for the poor kids. He had to be stronger than his nightmares. Another wave of nausea rolled over his stomach.

This had to be made right. They needed a safe place, a home. He was all they had left. Maybe his mother could take some time off work.

Anjelica opened the door. "Do you need anything? More water? Something to eat?"

"I didn't even think to ask. I got custody of two small children, a small boy and a baby girl. Can I move them into the apartment with me?"

"Two? Not just the son?" Her mouth open, she blinked a few times before turning to the CPS worker. "Without a doubt, they'll be welcomed here. Anything they need."

Sheriff Torres nodded and turned to Garrett. "I'll talk to Pastor John. The church will make sure you have what you need. Don't hesitate to ask for help on this. Check to see if you can take some days off work to get them settled." He looked at Sharon. "He'll have the support of the community. We'll make sure he has all the bases covered."

Garrett rubbed the back of his neck. All the bases would mean childcare with his crazy schedule and appropriate gear for the kids. Food that kids ate. Did a ten-month-old baby even eat? Was she still on a bottle? *Oh man, they need psychotherapy.* He jerked his head to the caseworker, who now stood next to him. "Did they witness the incident?"

Pursing her lips, she gave him a slight nod. "We believe the boy did. Everything's in the report. Like I said, they found them in the backyard. At first the dog made it difficult to get to them. We're not sure if they crawled out before or after the incident."

And there it just went. Had he really thought things couldn't get worse?

Anjelica moved closer to the edge of the porch. "Sharon, you don't need to worry." Tenderness softened her eyes to a golden honey as she looked at Sheriff Torres. "These kids won't be alone. We can all lend a hand."

Without even knowing what had happened, she stepped up and offered her service. He hated the thought of her reaction to the fact he had a son he didn't know existed.

Asking for help went against everything he'd ever taught himself. But if he and these poor kids were going to have a chance at surviving this ordeal, that was going to have to change.

A dry throat was hard to talk around. He swallowed and managed a simple "Thank you."

Sharon smiled. "I have given you some shocking information, Officer Kincaid. In the folders you'll find my number if you need to reach me. You'll be appointed a new caseworker." She smiled at Anjelica. "Thanks for helping."

"It's the least I can do." She looked at Garrett, her wide smile tighter than usual. The new coldness burned in her usually warm eyes.

Gathering her bag, Sharon turned away from them. She stopped at the last step. "You'll make a big difference in their lives. You're doing the right thing, Officer Kincaid."

Then why did it feel like he was making the worst mistake in his life? He turned to Anjelica. "I have to go to the apartment and see what I can do to make it kid ready."

Nodding, she followed him off the porch. "You're going to need stuff for a baby. Crib, changing table, bottles, car seat, probably clothes and shoes for both of them."

The lifeline that tethered him to Earth disappeared. It was as if he was floating away from everything he knew and had no way to get back. How was he going to make this work? Halfway up the steps, he realized Anjelica was still following him. He raised an eyebrow when he turned to look at her. "What are you doing?"

"I'm going with you. We'll need to make a list. I probably have most of what you need."

"I appreciate the offer, but you were heading into town. You don't need to change your plans for me."

She tilted her chin and looked him straight in the eye. "I'm not doing it for you. I'm doing it for those two little ones…" Lips pulled tight, she closed her eyes for a moment. "If they came to find you on a Saturday, it's an emergency situation. With me, kids always come first." Her normally open expression had a bit of steel in it as she narrowed her gaze.

Garrett sighed. "I have no doubt about that."

"I have a grandmother, a mother, sisters and cousins that will help."

He couldn't imagine that kind of large family. Of course, this morning he couldn't imagine being a father, either. Unfortunately, they didn't have any other options. Innocents couldn't be allowed to suffer because of his mistakes.

"Besides, you forgot these." She held up the two folders. Folders that he was sure told an ugly story.

He had to make this right. As much as he wanted to keep his distance from Little Miss Sunshine, he had a feeling he needed her more than he'd ever wanted, or needed, another person. He glanced behind her, scanning the fanciful farm. Especially a delicate female who seemed to live in another world altogether.

Anjelica kept her gaze hard and firm as she looked back up at Garrett. He sighed and turned his back to her, his hand resting on the wood rail. The muscles in his neck coiled. What kind of man didn't know he had a family?

Her cousin Yolanda said good looks spoiled a man. She would have argued that Garrett Kincaid was a solid man, a bit standoffish and a loner, but good. Now she wasn't so sure.

His jaw flexed as he unlocked the door. She gritted her teeth. How could men be so...so careless?

They entered the apartment in silence. He had a son and a baby daughter he didn't know about. She pulled her gaze away from his jawline and studied her hands. How could she have mistaken him as a man of honor?

Anjelica, judging Officer Kincaid won't solve any of the problems. You don't know the whole story. She knew when it came to children she had to be careful of filtering thoughts through a haze of resentment.

Holding her daughter happened only in dreams. Esperanza would have been five next month. Tomorrow's date was burned into her brain, the day she'd lost her precious baby girl. During this time, between Esperanza's death and due date, her emotions were always closer to the surface. A twist of the silver charms on her wrist helped her calm the negative thoughts.

Garrett moved to the kitchen counter that ran against the back wall. Redirecting her thoughts, she focused on him as he put the gun in a safe.

At the counter, he turned and leaned, arms crossed. His uniform stretched over broad shoulders. "Okay, enough of the silent treatment. You're bound to have questions."

"It's really none of my business." She scanned the bare room. Did he dismiss the dangers of his job the way Steve had waved off her worries of his joining the Marines? "Well, other than you're moving two children into my very small garage apartment. There's no real kitchen. And you have a very dangerous job."

The urge to scowl at him needed to be tempered. Her family lived by the rule of speaking your mind if it was helpful, kind and true. She wasn't doing a good job of it. There was always something helpful and encouraging to say, and if she tried hard enough, the right words would find their way to her lips. "What you're doing is a good thing. You stepping up and taking the kids, even if it is a little late." She bit her lip. That did not count as kind, it wasn't helpful and it might not be true. Her thoughts were going crazy.

Garrett stood across the room and stared at her, a tight, closed look on his hard face. "Do you have any questions or just observations?"

"Sorry." Okay, she needed to come straight out and ask. "You have a young son and baby daughter that you didn't know about? How does that happen?"

Leaning back against the counter again, his masculine knuckles turned white as he gripped the edge. "I'm not sure. Right now I'm feeling a bit blindsided." With his head down, he seemed to be studying his boots. "It seems the boy's mine. The girl has another father." He raised his head and looked her in the eye. "There's no excuse for abandoning a child, but I… I left town hoping to leave all my ex-wife's drama behind. I didn't know I was leaving behind a son to deal with the mess."

She didn't understand the blow to her emotions from hearing he had been married. Why would that even bother her?

With a heavy sigh, he stalked to the table and sat in one of the two chairs. Playing with the empty saltshaker, he never looked up. Anjelica moved to the other chair and waited.

"I met Viviana in the fifth grade. She was my best friend. By the time our freshman year came around, I was in love. I spent those four years rescuing her. When I left for Afghanistan, we stayed in touch. According to her letters, she'd made better choices and gotten out of her father's house. He was not a nice man." He looked up briefly, but with a sigh he lowered his head again.

"She said she was waiting for me to return home. We met at the airport and I asked her to marry me right there." His focus moved from the simple saltshaker to the balcony door. "Looking back, I realize I had made her into a woman of my dreams. I imagined us with a home and family that even included a dog. While reading her letters, I created a life in my head that wasn't real."

Wrapping her hands over her upper arms, she tried to stave off the cold that crept into her veins. All of the letters Steve wrote her during his tour in the Middle East had been about home, too. He talked about the long hours of doing nothing. Telling her how he reread her letters over and over to get a piece of normal. He would draw pictures of the farm and the projects he planned to start when he got home. There were pages where he wrote of their daughter's future and all the kids they would raise. Her heart twisted. *Don't go there, Anjelica.*

She packed thoughts of her husband away and fixed her attention on Garrett. "How old were you when you joined?"

"Eighteen. I had just graduated and didn't have many options." He blew a hard puff of air. "The Marines were a blessing. They gave me focus and a sense of belonging, but it wasn't always easy." Standing, he rubbed the back of his neck. "I thought we were ready for the next phase of our life. I wanted to feel normal." He gave a harsh laugh. "That didn't work out so well."

Garrett walked to the French doors and opened one of them. The breeze released some of the tension that had weighed down the room. Four saxophone cases lined the wall. They were the only personal items other than a small stack of mail in his living quarters. The quietness lingered.

He reached for one of the cases. She'd heard him play several times, usually at night when he came in from work. Sometimes it was slow and soothing, other times energetic and raw, but it was always good. The music would wrap around her while she worked with the clay. She didn't feel so alone when he played.

Dropping the strap, he stared off through the French door. With a sigh, he joined her at the table. "It's hard allowing the old nightmare to resurface. A few weeks after we were married, Ed, one of her boyfriends she forgot to mention, started calling. Viviana ran to him, until he beat her—then she'd come home and I would patch her up. That had always been my job. After several attempts of trying to report him, I had to get out. At one point she threatened to tell the police I had hurt her. My career was on the line. I left. Changed my number. Deleted hers so I wouldn't be tempted to check on her. I made a clean break. I made sure she had no way to get in touch with me. If I had just left her one way to contact me..." With his elbow on the table, he pressed his forehead into his palm.

She heard resentment in each word. If his ex-wife had hidden the boy from him, he had every right to be angry. "Why are you taking the girl, too? It sounds like there's a chance the boy is not even yours. Why did they come to you for placement?"

"I guess we were still married when she gave birth, so my name is on the birth certificate and there's no one else." He shrugged. "As a little girl, she had dreams of living in the county with lots of animals." He snorted. "I promised her I'd make her dreams come true. Maybe I can make good on the promise with her children. Also, I'd guess there is a fifty-fifty chance the boy is mine. I couldn't take one without the other—she's his baby sister. Can you imagine how much he would hate me if I didn't bring his sister home with him?" He scanned the room and blew out a hard puff of air.

She still struggled with the idea of not knowing about a child and then taking in two. "Where's their mother now? Why have they been taken from her?"

His jaw did the tick thing again and he nodded to the two folders she had set on the table. "Everything about them and their mother is in the folders." He shook his head.

Picking up one of the folders, she flipped it open. "You haven't seen the children?" It was the baby girl. Her heart melted at the big eyes, perfect tiny lips and tons of tight curls that surrounded the sweetest face. "Oh, Garrett, she's adorable. Look at her."

As if wearing a neck brace, he turned and gave the eight-by-ten photo a quick glance. With his attention back on the door on the opposite wall, he nodded. "She looks like her mother." He moved away. "For now, I should clean out the office so it can become their room."

"What happened? How'd she lose the kids? What about the fath…?" She flipped to the next photo. Shocked by the scene, her stomach heaved. The folder fell from her grasp. She leaned over and braced herself. "I'm gonna be sick."

Garrett rushed to her side. He muttered under his breath as he pulled her hair back. "Do you need the restroom?"

Forcing in deep breaths, eyes closed, she shook her head. "No, I'm fine now."

"I should have warned you the crime-scene photos might be in there." He went to the mini refrigerator and pulled out a bottle of water. "Here." He pressed the cold plastic into her hand.

Sitting up, she leaned her head back. She adjusted her scarf. Knowing horrible things happened was one thing; seeing them in pictures was a completely different story. How was she going to get that out of her head? "Oh, Garrett, those poor babies. We have to help them."

Garrett pulled the other chair next to her and placed his hand on her shoulder at the base of her neck. "I'm sorry. I should've looked through them before letting you see the folders. I was…just avoiding."

"Were they in the room? Did they see what happened to their mother?"

"The boy might've been." He was so close she could hear his breathing. "Pilar is a baby and, hopefully, won't have any memory." Leaning back, he pushed his hair away from his forehead.

With the folder in hand, she was careful not to look at the bloody photos, instead focusing on the picture of the little girl and her information sheet. "Her name is Pilar Rose. She just turned ten months old." Making sure to breathe, she reached for the second folder.

Hand flat on the folder, he spread his long fingers over it as if to protect her from the contents. "I just want to see him." She held her hand out for the deceptively plain folder Garrett covered. "I'm prepared now. I was caught off guard. Let me see them."

Instead of handing over his son's file, he opened it.

She kept her gaze on Garrett's face as he stared at the top photo of the little boy. He blinked several times and his throat worked up and down. Not able to resist, she peeked over his arm and saw a serious little boy with Garrett's green-gray eyes staring back at them. He was a little darker with a mop of curly hair, but other than that, she was looking at a young version of the man sitting next to her. Garrett pressed his hand over his eyes.

She moved back, wanting to give him space to collect himself. Two breaths in, one hard breath out. Counting the steady rhythm gave her something to focus on instead of asking questions. He was breathing with his whole body. A broken heart was nothing new to her, but to watch such a controlled man fighting to hold it together made her want to wrap him in her arms.

The hard muscle along his jaw popped. This time,

instead of wanting to scowl at him, she wanted to comfort him. Fisting her hand in her lap to keep from running her fingers along the tense muscle, she fought the urge to sooth him.

After a long while, he slid his hand down his face and covered his mouth, looking up at the ceiling. She saw moisture on his eyelashes. He handed her the photo, paper-clipped to an information sheet. Scanning the sheet gave her somewhere safe to look. "Garrett River Kincaid Jr. He has your name."

"And apparently everything else, too. No DNA test needed. It's like looking at an old picture of me as a kid." He stood but didn't go anywhere. The silence grew tense.

She didn't know what to say, so she tossed a few words around. "He has curly hair." *Well, that was a stupid thing to say.*

"I had curly hair as a kid, too. When I went to school, my dad shaved it off so I wouldn't look like a girl. It came back straighter." He lifted one hand and ran it through his own thick hair.

The neat cut was now unruly, but she still couldn't imagine him with curls. "The kids in my family all start off with ringlets, too, but around five or six they lose them."

"I don't know how to do this, being a father."

"We can make it work." She blurted it out. Thinking of what happened to those two small children, she knew they needed a home full of love and good memories. Tears started burning her eyes. "We have to make this right for them. We have to bring them to a real home."

He took his eyes off the bare walls and looked at her. "We?"

"I won't let you *not* let me help." She hugged the folders.

The obstinate man lifted an eyebrow at her.

She gritted her teeth and pressed the folders closer to her chest. With one deep breath, Anjelica looked back at him. "Okay, so I didn't word that very well, but you get my meaning. They need more than food and a bed to sleep in. They need consistency, a home filled with love, and you need help."

"Right now they need a safe place." He disappeared into the smaller room he was using as an office.

She hadn't been up here since he moved into the garage apartment. There was nothing on the walls. The bookshelf remained empty. A brown sofa and a small round table with two chairs had been provided in the rental. He hadn't added anything of his own, not even a TV. The only personal items were the saxophone cases. Not a single picture of his family or friends.

Garrett came back into the living area and sat a laptop on the table. "He's five and she's ten months old. What am I gonna need? Maybe I should make the smaller room my bedroom and put them in the bigger room." He looked up at her. "Or does a ten-month-old need to be in a room with an adult…a parent? I work nights sometimes and if there's an emergency…"

The color left his face.

"Garrett, you'll need someone to watch them when you're at work."

"I'm going to call my mother. If she could move here, that could work. I can sleep on the sofa. I've had worse."

She had a bad feeling he was going to be stubborn about taking help. "I have some baby stuff. It's all unused. I have a crib, high chair, changing table, rocker and the smaller stuff like blankets."

He rubbed his eyes and stared at the screen.

"You need some sleep."

He checked his watch. "I'm fine."

She reached over and pushed the top down on his computer. "Get some sleep. I'll have the things they need by the time you wake up."

She took a deep breath and smiled. Could she do it? Could she hand over all of Esperanza's furniture? She closed her eyes and felt the peace wash over her. Garrett's baby girl needed a room full of love, and Esperanza didn't.

It was time. She opened her eyes and smiled at Garrett. "God provides."

He sighed. "Not sure about God, but I'm not your problem to fix. I do need some sleep, but I don't have a lot of time to waste to get everything ready for…"

"You have enough time to sleep. I'm telling you, almost everything you need is close. Okay? When you wake up, come over to the house."

Yes, it felt right. Maybe this was why she hadn't cleaned out her baby girl's room yet. God knew Garrett would need it.

Chapter Two

An explosion rattled the walls. Garrett jerked straight up from sleep. No, not an explosion, just another nightmare. He threw back the heavy blanket and sat on the edge of the bed. Avoiding the frayed braided rug, he made sure to plant his bare feet on the cold tile floor. Taking several deep breaths, he anchored himself in Clear Water, Texas. In the present. Sand blew against the roof. Grinding his back molars, he buried his fingers in his hair. Not sand. Afghanistan belonged in his past. The thin glass in his window shuddered under the force of the violent wind outside.

The sound that had woken him penetrated the room again. Not in his head, but outside. A hefty storm was making a fuss and building power. Barefoot, he left the bedroom and walked across the apartment. The security light keeping it from being too dark to see. Opening the French doors, he stood at the threshold of the small balcony. Tiny bits of hail had collected on the deck. A few minuscule chunks pelted him. His thin T-shirt offered little protection from their sting.

He blinked, confused by a cloth flapping in the desert wind, twisting around a group of kids playing soccer. His fingers closed around the iron railing. It was cold, hard…real. He inhaled, pushing his lungs to their limit. With eyes shut, Garrett fought to get his mind back to the here and now. *I am standing on my balcony in Clear Water, Texas.*

It had been a while since he'd had this type of episode. Maybe the news he'd gotten today was part of this mixed-up nightmare. He was taking full responsibility of two kids. He knew firsthand no matter what you did, bad things still happened. Another boy's smiling face and bright dark eyes came to mind. Counting breaths, he shook his head.

His mind latched on to the present, and he opened his eyes again. This time, he made sure he saw Anjelica's backyard. Even in the dark he could still make out the miniature farm surrounded by ranches that gave the illusion of endless hills and trees. A cry came from the area of her large garden.

A bedsheet? Okay, that was real. Why was that crazy woman chasing a bedsheet across her yard in the middle of a storm? He didn't even have a sense of time. He glanced inside and saw the clock, which read 10:33 p.m. He had slept longer than he'd planned.

Shaking his head, he grabbed his trench coat and slipped on his boots. With his hat firmly planted on his head, he made his way down the stairs of the garage apartment. He knew she was a bit on the fanciful side, but this was strange behavior even for her. She had no business being outside with hail and lightning. Did she have a death wish?

By the time he walked through the gate, she was balanced halfway up the deer-proof fence, attempting to untangle the sheet from the eight-foot corner post. Her bare feet were precariously poised on the tie bar between the huge cedar post and the stay. Her new fluffball pet leaped about and barked.

"Bumper! Stop it!" She tugged at the sheet. Anjelica's long dark hair was plastered to her like a second skin, making her look more like an elf. Even standing on the tie bar, she couldn't reach the top of the corner post. Did she notice the hail? Cutoff sweatpants exposed her golden-brown skin to the elements. He shook his head as he cut across the tilled garden.

The dog finally caught the edge of the white sheet between its teeth. "Bumper! No! Bad girl! Let go!" As she tried to pull the sheet away from the Yorkie, Little Miss Sunshine lost her balance.

Garrett rushed to catch her. She landed in his arms with an "Oomph." Lightning streaked across the sky as he ran for her covered back porch. He counted the seconds between seeing the flash and hearing the thunder. Five seconds. Too close for comfort. His arms tightened their hold when she started wiggling. "Hold still or I'll drop you." She might be small, but she struggled against him with toned muscles.

He leaped up the three steps and under the eclectic collection of ceramic wind chimes that lined her porch. Their musical notes sounded angry tonight.

"No! No, I have to cover the bush! The hail's gonna destroy it."

"You don't have any shoes on, and even small hail can be dangerous." Once he had her bare feet on the boards, he looked into her large eyes to check their dilation for signs of a concussion. Her irises were so dark he couldn't see her pupils in the dim light.

Maybe she already had brain damage. Another bright light flashed, and for a split second he could see everything as if it was high noon. He saw a thick heavy scar that ran across the base of her neck. The soft edge disappeared into her hairline by her cheek. Then he was blinded again just as quickly. Was that why she always wore a scarf?

She tried to push past him. "I've got to cover my plant before it's destroyed."

The ceramic chimes thrashed in a sudden gust of wind, and it was hard to hear over all the noise. "No, stay here." He made a gesture to her head and feet, hoping she understood. "I'll cover the plant."

Pulling his hat low, he ran back into the storm and crossed the yard to retrieve the sheet. The dog followed, leaping and barking like they were playing a game.

"Bumper, get back here," Anjelica yelled from the top step. The undisciplined dog ignored her.

With one hard yank, he had the sheet down. The two-foot bush had already lost some of its early growth. Small leaves dotted the ground. Using the wind to help, he threw the sheet over the top of the plant. Then Garrett looked around for something to anchor it.

"Here, use these." Anjelica ran past him to pick up some red bricks lining the bottom of the fence. At least she had mud boots and a hat on this time, along with a bright orange scarf wrapped around her neck.

The pelts of hail grew harder. He tucked his head and drew his shoulders higher. He was apparently as crazy as his landlady.

The dog pulled on the sheet, tossing her head back and forth with a growl. The furball could fit in his pocket but fought with the fierceness of a lion. The pink bow did nothing to soften her attitude.

"I've got this!" Garrett pointed toward her porch, hoping she would follow his command. She shook her head and moved to the base of the bush with a brick.

"Bumper! Stop!" The dog darted away from Anjelica and grabbed another corner.

Garrett scooped the bit of fluff up in one hand, holding the pup out of the way while he tucked the heavy sheet around a brick with the other, making sure it was under the bush and tight enough to stay in place.

On the opposite side of the shrub, his tiny landlady crawled out from under the plant and put her hands on her hips. "I think that'll do it," she yelled before finally running back to the safety of the deep porch.

He followed. One step behind her, he tried to shield her from the worst of the storm.

Once on the porch, she threw her beat-up hat on a bench, then sat on a worn rocking chair and pulled off a boot. She wore two left rubber boots. One of them had colorful stripes, but the other one was purple with white flowers all over it. Yep, she lived in another world altogether.

"Glad you found proper footwear."

Waving a delicate hand toward her yard, she said, "This wasn't in the weather report. I couldn't find my boots when I realized it was starting to hail." She pulled off the purple boot and dumped water out of it. "My only thought was to get to my Esperanza. It just started sprouting spring leaves."

She never made eye contact as she flipped her hair over her shoulder. Wet, it looked black. Instead of the usual colorful blouse, she wore an oversize faded purple

T-shirt with Fighting Angoras Football printed across the front. "I know it sounds irrational, but I just wanted to cover my plant." With a deep sigh, she stood. "Thank you so much for coming to the rescue, but I guess that's what you do. Rush into danger like a good soldier." She stood and took Bumper from him. The little dog started licking her face. "You know, now that you're a father, you'll have to be more careful."

His eyebrow lifted high as he stared at her. "Did you really just call me out for being in this storm? I wouldn't be out in the storm if you had stayed inside."

She blushed and looked away. "Sorry. I'm not feeling very rational right now." With the back of her free hand, she wiped at her eyes.

Oh, please don't cry. He scanned her cluster of outbuildings and enclosed pens behind the garden area, a mismatched collection of painted structures that housed chickens, rabbits and goats. She was the mayor of a miniature village for all the misfit farm animals in the county, and now he was adding two children to the mix. He shouldn't be surprised she had easily agreed to him moving the kids into the garage apartment. She collected damaged goods. "Looks like everyone else is safe from the storm." That should make her happy.

She rewarded him with a smile. Nodding, she kissed the top of the silky mop's head. "My dad bragged he built those to withstand a tornado."

The hail was larger now, dime-sized nuggets zinging off the tin roof like ricocheting bullets, putting his nerves on edge. He took a deep breath. He was in Clear Water, Texas. Far from war.

At least tornadoes were rare in the Hill Country. He took off his own hat and slapped it against his leg.

Chips of ice clattered to the wood flooring. Calling the weather in Texas unpredictable was the definition of understatement.

It wouldn't surprise him if he found a few bruises in the morning. He pushed his hair back. The little frou-frou dog ran over to him and put a paw on his muddy boot. The clipped tail wagged so hard its whole body squirmed. "Bumper?"

Anjelica smiled at the wet rat. "I found her just the other day on Bumper Gate Road. I put an ad in the local paper, but no one's come to claim her."

Standing in front of him, she moved in for a hug before he realized what she had planned. "Thank you for saving my plant. I do think you'll do a fine job as a father."

His jaw clenched. He had never been a touchy hugging kind of guy, but he'd been hugged more times in the few months since he'd moved to Clearwater than he had his entire life. He remained still, not wanting to offend her by pulling away.

Kids liked hugs, too. He remembered wanting to be in his mother's lap, but she had always been too tired or too busy. He managed to lift an arm and give her a pat on the shoulder, hopefully not too stiff. She shivered in his arms. They were both cold and wet. "You need to go inside and change."

She backed up and grinned at him as if she'd made a new friend. "Thank you, Officer Kincaid. Um, now that you're a father, you might think of a less dangerous job?"

He frowned. "I like my job."

Another flash of lightning. He counted again, one Mississippi, two Mississippi, three Mississippi. A golf ball of solid ice landed at his feet. He narrowed his eyes and then looked at the path back to his apartment. The trip back to the garage wasn't far, but with that last bolt of lightning, he doubted it was wise to run across the yard again. He looked at his watch. It had taken him a couple of hours to go to sleep, but he had been out for seven hours.

"Officer Kincaid—"

"Call me Garrett."

"Oh!" She grabbed his arm. "Now is as good a time as any to show you the baby equipment."

She leaned in closer, and the smell of vanilla and earth intrigued his nose. The lyrical sound of her voice tickled his ear. "Promise not to tell my parents I was outside in this weather. My mom would have a fit and Papa would tell me to move back home, again. They wouldn't like that I'd go that far for a simple shrub."

He had a feeling there was nothing simple about the shrub.

"Come on." She turned and opened the screen door.

Garrett followed her and crossed over the well-trodden threshold. In his line of work, he'd been in about every kind of housing, but this was straight out of a children's picture book. Alice's rabbit hole had nothing on this girl.

It was everything his apartment wasn't. The old farmhouse had a huge kitchen. A family of ten could easily sit at the table.

Even though the cabinets were painted white, splashes of color touched everything. More ceramic creatures hung from strings, while others lined the windows and cabinets.

"Sorry about the mess. I made a big batch of tortilla

soup earlier tonight to share with my grandparents and a few other people in town. Then an idea struck, and I ended up in my ceramic studio before I cleaned. Have you eaten since lunch? Here, let me get you some." Without waiting for his reply, she loaded a ceramic bowl with the aromatic soup. Fresh herbs and spices filled the kitchen. His stomach grumbled in anticipation.

She pulled a spoon out of the dishwasher and moved to the table. "Here, sit down and eat. I'll slice an avocado and heat you up a corn tortilla. What do you want to drink? I have milk, sweet tea and water."

"Water's fine." Before he got the first spoonful of soup to his lips, she had a small plate with avocados and thin corn chips on the table next to him. Another trip and she handed him a warm tortilla and a tall glass of ice water.

"I'll put some in a container for you to take to the apartment for later." She set a blue bowl on the counter, then dug around in the cabinets. "I'm the only person that lives here, and I still can't find a lid." Pulling out a red one, she held it up and smiled at him. "Found one." She snapped the red lid onto the blue bowl.

Of course she did. Why start matching now? "Please sit and eat with me."

With the dog bouncing about her feet, she sat down across from him. She slid the plastic bowl his way.

"Thanks." He dunked the tortilla into the warm soup. He didn't want to waste time with forming more words. He had fallen in love. He closed his eyes and savored the rich flavors on his tongue.

"I'm the one that's grateful. Thank you for braving the storm and helping me cover Esperanza."

He opened his eyes. He really shouldn't have been surprised by anything she said. "You name your plants?"

She smiled again, but this time it was a little tighter, not as bright. "It's an Esperanza plant, the same name as my daughter. I planted it as a memorial for her."

Great going, Garrett. "Well, it's a beautiful plant. And a beautiful name. It means hope, right?" He cleared his suddenly dry throat. "Looks like we covered it in time."

Maybe he should leave…instead of staring at her like an idiot. Obviously, she no longer had her daughter. The baby stuff she said she had, it must have been… another reminder that children couldn't always be protected from bad things. And now he was responsible for two who already had a tragic backstory. He took a deep breath and set the spoon down, his appetite gone. "Thanks for the soup."

"I'm glad I had it here for you. Are you finished?"

A nod was all he managed. She took everything to the sink. The lights flickered as the thunder rolled through the house. She tilted her head toward the ceiling. "Doesn't sound like it's letting up." The lights wavered again. "Follow me—I'll show you the baby stuff I have ready for you and Pilar." She walked through an archway that took them into a living room. Several mix-and-match sofas and chairs made for a welcoming room. He was surprised by the white sofa. The red floral sofa he expected, but the white one? How did she keep it clean? He didn't know anyone who actually dared to have white furniture. Red, white and blue pillows and blankets were everywhere. Yellow flowers were tucked into odd containers all over the room. It looked well lived-in, the site of years of family events and memories.

"I've been wanting to tell you how much I appreciate you playing the sax on the balcony. When I'm working in the studio, I open my door to listen. You should come to church with me one Sunday. Pastor John is really into music. Did you ever play in a band?"

He nodded and followed her around the furniture that looked as if they'd been salvaged from an old barn. "All through school, and when I joined the Marines, I played for them, too."

"Wow." She stopped in front of a floor-to-ceiling bookcase and looked up at him, making him feel taller than his six-one. "I would have taken you for a football player, you know, the warrior type. I don't think of soldiers as musicians. Do you play any other instruments?" She tilted her head as if trying to recalibrate what she knew about him.

"I was a total band geek, marching and jazz. I play some strings, too, but I prefer the sax. I didn't get any size on me until later in high school—I wasn't a jock." He cleared his throat. She looked as if she wanted to add him to her collection of odd animals now.

He glanced at the shelf behind her, and a wooden display with a folded flag caught his eye. The flag sat above some medals and a picture of a young Hispanic male in dress blues. Next to that was a wedding picture. A very young Anjelica in a white wedding dress standing in the arms of the same soldier. Letters were etched into the wood: Estevan Diego Garza.

She turned and looked behind her. "Oh, that's my husband, Steve."

"He was a marine, too." *Way to go and state the obvious, Garrett.*

"Yes, one of the heroes that didn't come home." Graceful fingers touched the picture. "Being a hero was his life's dream. He planned to become a firefighter or EMT when he got home." A bright flash flooded the room in blinding light. Then everything went dark and silent.

He reached out to touch her arm, but the lights were on again and she had her happy face back in place. "I'm sorry. I'm going on and on. You're here to see the baby stuff." A few steps and she opened a white painted door.

Nerves started crawling again. Garrett's skin became too tight for his body. The urge to escape and go back to his simple rooms had him feeling edgy. There was nothing wrong with beige. Beige was calming, very calming. A peaceful color for kids who needed a quiet place to heal. He liked quiet places.

Concern in her eyes, Anjelica placed a gentle touch on his arm. "Are you okay?"

She was the one who'd lost her soldier and a baby, but she was worried about him?

"I'm good. We need to get this settled so I can figure out the next steps I need to take to make this right."

"Garrett, it's not your fault the way things played out."

A corner of his mouth twitched. She actually had him smiling. "I don't think that's what you were thinking earlier."

"Guilty. Sometimes we dive headfirst into conclusions and judge too fast. Sorry. So are you ready to see the stuff?"

"Lead the way."

* * *

Anjelica stood at her daughter's door. She had put so much planning and time into decorating this space. Each step had been documented and sent to Steve, along with images of her growing belly.

Five years ago, she spent hours in that rocking chair, crying until every part of her body ached. After a while, she was able to visit the room without crying. The sadness was still there, but softer. The last few months, she kept telling herself to call her mom and sisters so they could help her pack it up.

Now she knew God had another plan for this room. "Garrett, most of what Pilar will need is here." She turned on the overhead light and waited for him to join her.

In the middle of the room, she stopped and took a deep breath before she turned back to him. "This would have been Esperanza's room. Nothing has ever been used."

Garrett stood in the doorway and scanned the room with a slow steady movement. "I can't take your stuff from here."

"Why not? I was to the point of packing it up. It was made for a little girl. Everything your daughter needs is waiting for her."

His head jerked up. "She's not my daughter." Both hands dug into his hair, interlocking the fingers at his neck. With his head back, he closed his eyes and blew out a slow waft of air. "I guess by tomorrow she'll be my daughter." He closed his eyes, his jaw working twice as fast as before.

She wanted to put her arms around him and soothe the pain. Instead she stepped away and placed her hand on the quilt draped over the rocking chair. Buela had made the blanket. "Garrett, you can do this. I think God brings people into our world that need us and vice versa. It's been heavy on my heart that all the stuff was being wasted." She walked to the white crib that was tucked into a colorfully painted cove that had once been a closet. Pink and green triangle flags hung over the bed. "Please let me give it to Pilar and your son."

Confusion marred his strong face as he watched her. "Why are you doing this? What do you get out of helping us?"

Adjusting the blankets they had picked out so long ago, she smiled at his cynicism. "I can't save every child out there, but I can help you save these two." If she wasn't careful, she was going to cry. She feared he would misunderstand and this could all fall apart. She stiffened her spine as she turned and glared at him, making sure not to show any weakness. "Stop being so suspicious and say thank you."

He walked around the room. Touching the rocking chair, setting it in motion. He saw the bags full of new supplies and clothes. "What's this?"

"While you were sleeping, I called a few of my family members and ladies from the church. They gathered some stuff you'll need for the children."

In front of the chest of drawers, he stopped and looked at the wall.

She had painted *Esperanza* across the upper part of the wall, surrounded by stars and butterflies. The whole room was decorated with flowers and friendly critters, a little secret garden.

With a frown, he stared at the wall. "You painted this?"

A nod was all she managed.

He moved to the window and held the wispy sheer curtain to the side so he could look out into the storm. Wind slammed the rain against the window.

"I called my mother."

Disappointment should not have been her first reaction, but it was. She had started thinking of them as a team when it came to these two kids she hadn't even met yet. "Oh, so she's coming to help? You don't need me, then."

He rubbed his face. "No." He looked away, staring at the mural. "She hasn't returned my calls. It looks like I'll need someone to watch the kids. A temporary fix for now. Until I can get a place of my own and make permanent arrangements." He turned back to her. "Is there anyone in your family you recommend?"

"Me." Before he could form any words to argue against her idea, she rushed on to explain. "I've been thinking about this all day. I'm a sub at the school and I volunteer with the group home. I know what these babies have been through, so you wouldn't have to explain that to someone new. I can stop taking sub jobs and you can pay me the same daily fee, but I would be available day or night."

He looked back out the window. Lightning flashed. She forced herself to breathe and waited for him to process the options.

Well, she tried to wait. "I also had another idea. Please, listen and think about it before you respond. I think you and the kids should move into the house. It's bigger and I can live in the apartment."

She chewed on the inside of her cheek while waiting for his response.

"No." He crossed his arms. "I'm not kicking you out of your family home."

"You're not." Hands planted on her hips, she tilted her head. "The garage is part of my family home and I actually lived there as a teenager once."

"No. We'll stay in the apartment. It's fine. I'm not moving into your house."

"Okay. Then what about hiring me as your baby-sitter?" She smiled. "I do think it's important to have someone that can watch them with your crazy hours. I can be right there at a moment's notice. The next best thing to a live-in nanny. I always wanted to be Mary Poppins."

He didn't say anything. He stared at her with the muscles flexing in his arms.

She broke eye contact first and rearranged some of the pillows. "You don't have to worry about taking the kids anywhere or waiting for someone to get here. It's perfect, right?"

"I don't like asking for help."

A giant eye-roll threatened to pop from her head. *Stubborn men.* "You didn't have to ask for help. I'm of-fering. My heart is hurting for these babies. I'm so sorry your mother isn't coming, but I think this will work out well for the children."

He sighed. "It's funny if you think about it." He leaned across the crib, picking up a stuffed ladybug. "This morning I didn't even have a girlfriend. Now I'm talking about baby furniture and hiring a nanny. Seems I skipped a few steps from bachelorhood to fatherhood."

The sadness in his eyes ate at her heart. "God has placed these kids with you. It's going to be okay."

He sighed. "Are you sure you want to take us on full-time? I have a feeling these will not be well-adjusted kids." He gave her a lazy, lopsided grin. "I know I'm not well-adjusted—I'm barely housebroken. I don't even know what a normal family should look like."

"Well, the one thing I'm an expert on is family, and first let me tell you, there is no such thing as normal. Believe me, I know." She could not hold back any longer; she walked over and hugged him. His frame tightened as if in fight-or-flight mode. She held him gently until he relaxed and gave her a stiff pat on her shoulder. "Garrett, I want to help those sweet kids."

The muscles in his forearms bulged. Head down, he backed away from her. "They might not be so sweet." Then he nodded, his face relaxing. "Okay, so I have a stocked nursery and a nanny. This might work." He looked up. "Thank you, Anjelica." Halfway to the door, he stopped. "What about the boy? I need to get him a bed, too."

"I can call around, but if nothing comes up, we have a couple of bunk beds upstairs." She brushed past him to cross the living room but paused in the doorway. The smell of earth after a rainstorm crossed her senses. Closing her eyes, she absorbed the scent. It was rich and dark.

"Anjelica?"

Jerked out of her own head, she jumped forward and bumped into him. Large hands steadied her. "Are you okay?"

Looking up, she saw the concern in his eyes. He looked that way a great deal when around her. He probably thought she was a complete flake and maybe he was right.

"I'm fine. We can move all the stuff in the morning." She rushed past him. She needed some distance. That was it. Other than her family, and the one date she'd had with Jake Torres, she hadn't been this close to a man in a long time. She'd forgotten how good they smelled, and how different they were compared to her.

"Can I use your restroom?" he asked.

"Sure—right through that door." She pointed to the right of the staircase.

Standing in the middle of the living room, she lost her purpose. What was she doing?

Anjelica went back into the kitchen. Bumper barked, demanding attention. The little Yorkie looked like a rat just rescued from a flooded river. Anjelica grabbed a towel and rubbed down the little dog. Garrett and Steve seemed to have a great deal in common. Why did some men want to rush into danger?

Buela and Mom were always on her about getting back into the dating scene. She knew it was time. But not with Garrett. He had too much on his plate already.

The biggest problem was his job. He was a lawman and she didn't see that changing anytime soon.

Talking to the dog, she made her way to the studio off her kitchen. "Just because I married one soldier doesn't mean I want another one in my life. No thank you." She held Bumper up so they were face-to-face. "Next time around, I want a man with a nice safe job. Maybe I should warn Garrett about the matchmaking duo. Now that he's a single father, I'm sure they have bumped him up on their list." She chuckled. This might be fun to watch, because it was not going to be her. Nope, his job was too dangerous for her peace of mind. But she was ready to date again.

In a few months, she'd be twenty-five. On her wedding day, she had imagined life with Steve in five and ten years. He'd be back home full-time, and they'd have two or three kids. She rubbed the little dog's head and sighed.

Si Dios quiere. Her parents had taught her that saying for her whole life, to trust in God's will. Sometimes it was easier to say she trusted in God's will than live like it. The wind rushed against the wall and slammed the screen door. Hail hit the roof harder and the storm whirled around the old house.

Loud banging made her jump. The wind played games with her outdoor furniture. She rushed to the door.

Garrett gently caught her by the arm. His hard face looked even sterner. "You can't go out there." His voice sounded like a growl. "It's even more dangerous than before. It's late anyway—you should go to bed."

She narrowed her eyes and pulled her arm out of his light grip. With her hands on her hips, she lifted her chin. "I outgrew a bedtime a few years back. What about you?"

The wind manhandled the hundred-year-old oak trees around her yard. The sound sent chills up her spine. She sucked in a large volume of air as she looked out the window. The force of the storm pelted the hail into the passageway. The rain came in at such a slant, looking as if it could slice through skin.

With muttered words under his breath, Garrett pushed her farther into the kitchen. "Is there a room without so many windows?"

"My studio." Bumper barked and jumped around her feet. "There's just the garden doors, but I have shutters over them. It's in there." She pointed to the door on the other side of her table. "But my animals. What—"

"They have shelter." He opened the door, flipped on the light and peered in. "This is good." He took her hand and pulled her inside the studio space and closed the door.

Sitting on the wooden bench her grandfather had carved, she patted the empty spot next to her. His big frame took up the rest of the space, long legs stretched out in front of him.

Total chaos reigned outside. She often thought of the wind as a gentle lullaby at night, but not now. It expressed itself like a two-year-old in a full-blown temper tantrum, a giant two-year-old. It sounded as if trees were being tossed around.

Bumper buried her head under Anjelica's arm. Her heart slammed against her sternum. "Dear God, please keep everyone safe." Thunder rolled, but in the studio they couldn't see the flashes of lightning. The walls rattled. The lights went out, plunging them into darkness. "Oh no, I left candles in the kitchen."

"We'll be fine. It shouldn't last long. We're safer in here in case any furniture or branches get tossed into one of your windows."

Another clap of thunder was followed by a loud crash. This time the whole earth shook. An explosion sounded too close. Had something hit the house? Blood rushed to her ears. "What was that? Oh, my babies have to be scared."

His long fingers found her hand and took hold. "It's okay. Good thing about Texas is the storms never last long. So this is your grandparents' house?" His voice reached out to her, low and soothing.

She knew he was distracting her and she let him. "My great-grandparents had the property and a small house. My grandparents started this house and added on and updated as the family grew. They wanted to move into town and have a smaller place, so they sold it to Steve and me."

As quickly as the wind had started, it was gone, the silence heavy. Anjelica held her breath and waited, but she couldn't even hear the rain anymore. "Is the storm over?"

He squeezed her hand. "Stay here while I check the damage." He stood. He flipped the switch, but the room stayed dark.

"I'm going with you."

He frowned and opened his mouth, then shook his head. "Stay close to me. There could be lines down. We don't want to rush out and make things worse. Trees and structures could still fall."

Bumper squirmed in her arms. "Let me put her in the washroom and get the flashlights."

As they exited the back door, she gasped. Her world had been turned upside down. She prayed she'd find everyone safe and sound.

Garrett's warmth and solidness comforted her. Looking around, she found most of the rocking chairs and some of her wind chimes were missing. Broken pieces of ceramic projects littered the ground. Frantically scanning for the piece celebrating her wedding and then pregnancy, she didn't find it. It was her favorite, whimsical shapes and swirls with sunflowers, frogs and butterflies in an asymmetrical layout.

She gasped. Large pieces of it were scattered across the porch. She found one of the frogs on the bottom step. She picked it up and ran her thumb along the jagged edge where the leg had been.

Garrett rushed to her side. "What is it? Are you okay?"

She nodded. "Sorry. It's one of my wind chimes. I started this one when we bought the house. Each section was tied to a memory." She made sure to smile at him. "It's just an object, right? The memories are in my heart. Let's make sure everyone's all right. That's the important thing. Not broken pieces of clay."

"Are you sure?" He looked back at the porch. "Was it the one with the big sunflower and bugs?"

She had to laugh. "Yes, butterflies, ladybugs and frogs. Steve loved frogs. He always had a pet one growing up. He wanted to put a pond for frogs on the property. I didn't want the cleanup or risk to children. I was going to decorate the nursery with frogs if we had a boy." She closed her eyes and gathered her thoughts. "I'm sorry—this doesn't matter."

"Do you want to gather it up?"

"No, it… We need to take care of my poor babies."

The beams of their flashlights scanned the area. Debris, both natural and man-made, cluttered the yard. As they walked past the empty garden, she let out her breath with a sigh of relief. Her pens and outbuildings all stood strong. He followed her to each shed and helped her check the huddled groups of animals. Everyone was safe and accounted for. Her father would be proud of his work.

Garrett's phone went off. Glancing down, he pulled his lips tight. "I need to go. We have low water crossings that need to be barricaded." He glanced at her little farm. "Everyone is safe for now. You stay inside until we can get someone out here to look deeper at the damage."

He turned to the garage and stopped. There on the roof they found the reason for the loud crash.

The old hackberry tree had moved into his bedroom. Thinking of the possibilities, she felt her heart skip. "I'm so glad you came to my house."

He gave a dry laugh and shook his head. "There has to be irony in this somehow. I just inherited two homeless kids and now it looks like I'm homeless, too." He rubbed the back of his neck.

"No, you're not. I think when you said no to my offer of the house, God wanted you to say yes."

"You're joking, right?" He looked down at her.

She shrugged and gave a halfhearted laugh. "Maybe. But you have to admit my plan is sounding better now."

"I'm still not kicking you out of your own house. Where would you live?"

"I can move into town. You could have a fully furnished house. We don't even have to move anything."

"No. I couldn't live in your house while you live somewhere else. I'll call Sharon and tell her I need more time before I pick up the kids."

"We can't let those babies stay in emergency care. If you refuse to live in my house, I could call my family and have the roof fixed in less than twenty-four hours. You know there aren't a great deal of rental options in Clear Water." She tucked her hand into the bend in his arm and leaned in close. *"Si Dios quiere."*

"Did you just say he wants God?"

"No. It's a saying that means to trust in God's will. My grandmother and mother say it all the time. It's drilled into my brain. *Si Dios quiere.* It's how I try to live my life. The worse things get, the more I lean on that trust."

"I don't trust easily." He was looking straight ahead. The muscle in his jaw popped. "My son probably doesn't trust men at all. Will you go with me? I'm sure they have issues, too, and men would be on the top of the list. You, being the nanny, might help them feel safer."

"I would love to."

He nodded and patted her hand. "Okay. Don't worry about the roof." He waved to the apartment. "I'll take care of it after I get off work."

"*You* don't worry about this." She made a bigger wave. "You worry about rescuing the good people of the county and I'll take care of my property. You are about to discover the power of the Ortega army. Be very happy we are on your side." She gave him her best wicked laugh. "My father and brothers will have all this cleaned up and fixed before you can drive your patrol car around the county three times."

He looked at her one more time. "Are you sure you're okay?"

"Yes, I'm stronger than I look. I promise." She'd learned the hard way how strong she could be. Now she hoped she was strong enough to make the right choices for her heart. She wasn't sure how much more it could take.

Si Dios quiere. I'm trusting You, God.

Chapter Three

Anjelica looked at her hands clasped tightly around the handle of the bag she had packed for the two little ones they were about to take home. Garrett pulled his truck into the empty parking lot of a nondescript brick building. It didn't even have windows on the front, just one glass door.

During the forty-five-minute trip to town, she told her heart not to get too engaged. These were his children. His family, not hers. She was just the nanny. But still, the pictures of those innocent faces embedded themselves in her head. She had a feeling that in the end, her heart would be broken again. She was never the kind of person who could keep an emotional distance. With her, it was always all in or not. How did someone teach their heart portion control?

Garrett cut the engine. He leaned over the steering wheel and looked at the sky. "I can't believe how fast this has happened."

"You made it easy for her to move the kids from an emergency shelter to a home. I'm sure she wishes all her cases were this easy." She checked her watch again. "We're early."

With a glance to the backseat, he opened the top button of his starched blue shirt. His black cowboy hat and jeans looked sharp. "Well, I guess it's time to fill those car seats." He cleared his throat. "Thank you for all you've done so far."

"How could I not help?" Waiting for him to move out of the truck, she sat in silence. Her attention went to her watch again.

Thirty minutes early. If he needed to sit out in the parking lot, she could do that, but she really wanted to see the kids.

"Okay." With one hand on the door, he turned to her. "Are you ready?"

She bit back a laugh and just nodded. He was a mess. She imagined a first-time dad might react the same way with the birth of his child. But for him, skipping those first few years probably made it harder.

The heat off the black asphalt threatened to melt her makeup. Garrett held the glass door open for her as he pulled on his collar. "It's unusually warm for March."

Nodding, she entered a sterile and empty lobby. Green vinyl chairs lined a paneled wall. Above them were posters depicting women and children, along with warning signs of abuse or neglect. A narrow corridor led to rows of more doors.

Without any hesitation, Garrett started down the hallway. At the far end, Sharon and an older man stepped out from one of the rooms. "Oh, Officer Kincaid, you're early. Good. The children are here. This is Joe Ackerman. He's your new caseworker."

The men shook hands and everyone else was introduced. Half of the wall behind Garrett was glass, so they could clearly see inside what looked like a conference room.

The man stepped back through the door and spoke with a woman who stood inside holding an infant car seat. A little boy sat in an oversize chair, his feet dangling above the floor as his small hand hung over the side of the yellow blanket covering the baby.

Anjelica touched Garrett's arm. Looking down, he raised his eyebrows at her. She pointed to the brother and sister. "There they are." Not sure why she was whispering, Anjelica shifted her gaze between the man standing next to her and the little boy who looked so much like him.

His forearm tensed under her hand. He stopped talking and became still. Nothing moved.

Sharon broke the silence. "Are you ready to meet them?" She turned to look at the kids.

Garrett took in a deep breath. He licked his lips and his throat worked as if he were trying to swallow. Anjelica wanted to wrap him in her arms.

Sharon continued talking, apparently oblivious to his struggles. "He attended the Head Start program. We know he can speak Spanish and English, but he hasn't spoken since they've been in custody. They documented that his oral development is behind, but that isn't unusual for a dual-language child. Pilar is physically behind. She's not sitting up on her own yet. There are small developmental delays, but they look to be more environmental." She sighed and looked back at the kids. "He's protective of his sister and gets very upset if he can't see her. There are several signs of general neglect."

"Such as?" Garrett asked without taking his eyes off the children.

"He knows how to make her bottle and dress them both, and he can work a microwave. We have found him changing her diaper. For a five-year-old, that indicates to us that he was the caregiver."

Had she just heard him growl?

Anjelica's fingers tightened around his arm. Garrett's other hand came up and covered hers.

"He's been appointed a child psychologist. He's experienced a traumatic event and will need time to heal and feel safe. You'll need patience in large supplies." She looked at Garrett and smiled. "I'm so relieved you're letting us place Pilar with you. I'm not sure Rio would survive being separated from his sister."

Garrett nodded. "Rio?"

"At Head Start they called him Garrett, but we've discovered his grandmother called him Rio. The rest of the family called him River. What do you want to call him?" Sharon looked through the window at the kids.

Garrett shrugged. "We could ask him what he wants to be called. If he wants Garrett, I'll go by something else. Can we go in now?"

Oh no. I'm not gonna cry. Anjelica let go of Garrett and squeezed her fingers together in front of her. With a count to five, she steadied her heartbeat.

He paused with his hand on the door. "What do I say?"

Sharon gave him a soft smile. "Keep it simple. I'll introduce you. But still tell him who you are and what's going to happen in small steps. Don't lie or make promises you can't keep."

With a nod, he walked through the door. Anjelica

followed but hung back, staying close to the wall. She needed to proceed slowly. This was his time to bond with the kids. As much as she wanted to hold that baby girl, she was only a temporary babysitter. The hired help.

The mini Garrett tucked his feet under himself and hovered over his sister. His curly dark hair hung in his face, hiding his eyes. The baby appeared to be asleep. She looked too small for a ten-month-old.

Anjelica watched as Sharon and Garrett approached the little boy. The small body froze, becoming unnaturally still. He didn't look at them directly but from the corner of his eye.

Anjelica held her breath. She couldn't even imagine what either were thinking. Would the boy trust Garrett? Would he be healed from this ordeal, or was he permanently wounded?

Garrett went on his haunches so he was eye level with his son as Sharon introduced them. After a brief smile the young women handed him the car seat with the baby inside, but he couldn't take his eyes off Rio.

He studied the features of the little boy. Wayward curls framed the small face. Each feature perfect and delicate. He was so tiny. His own father's words buzzed across his brain for a moment. Telling him he looked more like a pretty little girl than a boy. His father would laugh in front of his football-watching buddies and say the dog made a better son. He narrowed his eyes. No, he wasn't going there and *his* son would never be shamed like that.

Body locked in place, Garrett didn't make a move, not even daring to breathe as he looked at the miracle that sat before him. A boy who looked like him, a boy who was part of him. How could he not have known?

So much time already lost. How could this wounded little guy who didn't know him ever trust him? All his son knew was that a man now calling himself his father had abandoned him, had left him behind.

The boy continued to ignore him.

"Hi there. My name is Garrett River Kincaid, just like yours. I knew your mother. We went to school together." Nothing. "I'm your father and I'm here to take you home."

Mini Garrett made a whimpering sound and moved closer to his sister. Garrett sat in a chair and pulled the blanket back from the sleeping baby. "It's gonna be okay. Your sister is coming, too." Garrett had no idea what to do. He looked at Anjelica. Back against the door, she was still standing on the other side of the room.

He looked at the boy, who was fiercely trying to cover his sister. The easiest and fastest action would be to pick them up and put them in the truck, but he remembered being a kid and not understanding what was going on around him. It had been terrifying.

Pulling a chair closer to his son, he looked to Anjelica. "Why don't you join us?" As she slowly moved to them, he turned back to his son. "I want to introduce you to the woman that is going to help take care of you and your sister, but I don't know what name you want to use." The boy didn't acknowledge anyone in the room but kept his gaze on his sister.

"Your mom called you River? She always loved my middle name. Did you know there was an actor she liked with the same name?" The boy's lips stayed taut as he focused on his sister. "What about Garrett?"

A heated glare briefly made contact with Garrett under the dark curly hair that hung across the boy's forehead. Garrett fought the urge to brush it back. He was pretty certain that the boy wouldn't be comfortable being touched. "Okay, I'll take that as a no. I'm told your grandmother called you Rio. That's clever, using the Spanish name for *river*. Do you like Rio?" No response.

Frustrated, he looked to Anjelica for help. She shrugged and leaned forward to look at the infant. No longer sleeping, the baby girl blinked at them. *"¿Puedo recoger, Pilar?"* Without taking her gaze off the little boy, she patted Garrett's shoulder. "I asked if I could hold his sister."

Garrett grinned. "Yeah, I speak *poquito* Spanish." He measured about an inch between his thumb and index finger. In simple Spanish, he reassured his son that Anjelica was a nice lady who loved babies. "She has an *abuelita*, too."

For the first time, Rio looked away from his sister and glanced between them, acknowledging their presence with a scowl.

She smiled at Garrett. "I recognize that look." Turning back to the little boy, she smiled. *"¿Rio, Puedo recoger, Pilar. Por favor?"*

The big brother nodded and pulled the blanket off his sister. Anjelica reached down and unbuckled the strap, then gently picked the baby up. Pilar was too tiny and fragile to be healthy. As she cradled the infant in her arms, a look of total bliss covered her face. Garrett's breathing slowed. He knew, without a doubt, she would love these kids in ways he couldn't.

A tiny hand reached out and took the edge of the yellow scarf Anjelica wore today. "Hey there, sweet girl. Are you ready to see your new home?"

Home. He would be taking them home. He looked around for some water. His throat had gone unbearably dry.

A touch on his shoulder caused him to jump. Sharon stood there. He'd been so absorbed with the kids and Anjelica that he'd forgotten Sharon was in the room. Not good. They needed him to be on top of his game. He couldn't afford to get distracted.

"I have a few papers for you."

He placed the empty carrier on the floor and rolled his neck. "Sure. I have some questions about the dates for our court hearings." He looked down at the little boy, who had all his attention on Anjelica. "Rio, I'm going to talk with Ms. Sharon. Anjelica will stay here with you and Pilar. Then we'll take y'all to your new home."

After a moment of being ignored, Garrett joined Sharon at the other end of the long table. As she explained the process and timelines again, he kept glancing over at the little family he was about to take home. They were his responsibility now.

Anjelica sat at the table next to Rio. She was softly singing to them, gently brushing the baby's face and playing with her small fingers. He tried to figure out what he was feeling, but he got nothing. How had he ended up here? *God, I hope You have a plan because I got nothing.*

Anjelica looked up and caught him staring at her. If there was a picture of perfect motherhood, it would be there, Anjelica. He almost snorted when he realized God had already answered his question. Yes, there was a plan and He had put Anjelica smack in his path. Okay, so maybe he was going to look a little deeper into trusting God.

"Garrett?" Sharon closed the folder. "Do you have any questions?"

"So after a few months, I can apply to adopt Pilar?"

"Well, yes, but you don't have to rush into anything permanent."

He had to admit he was surprised by the feeling of protectiveness he already had for the girl, and he hadn't even held her yet. "She doesn't have anywhere else to go, and I'm pretty sure the best way to make my son hate me forever would be to separate him from his sister."

She chuckled. "Yes. For now, let's take the first step. Get the three of you settled. The first court date will have to happen fast because of the emergency situation."

"Speaking of getting us settled, what happened to the dog that was with the kids in the backyard?"

Rio looked up, his face becoming animated as his gaze darted between the adults. That had gotten his attention.

"She was taken to the pound."

"What do we need to do to pick her up?" He looked at Rio. "Do you want to get your dog?"

His son didn't answer but jumped from the chair and pulled the diaper bag off the table.

"I'm not sure you—"

"It's my son's dog. We can pick her up on our way home. The dog helped protect the kids." It should have been him standing between his son and the violent mess of Viviana's life. "We're not leaving her in the pound."

With the strap over Rio's shoulder, the bag dragged

on the floor as he headed to the door. He stopped and stared at them. An expression too stern for a five-year-old hardened his face.

"I'll call the shelter and let them know you'll be claiming the dog."

"Thank you." Joining Rio, Garrett reached for the bag. "I'll take this. We have new car seats for you both in my truck."

Anjelica adjusted Pilar on her left hip and held her free hand out to Rio. His son glared at her and pressed his back against the wall.

"Rio, walk with us. *Por favor.*" She kept her hand out and waited with a smile on her face.

Garrett held the door open. "If you want to come with us to get the dog, you'll need to hold her hand." After a silent moment, the small hand slipped into Anjelica's. With a heavy rock in the pit of his stomach, Garrett followed his new family to his truck.

Surreal was the only word he could think of as Anjelica smiled at him over her shoulder. She carried his daughter on one hip while holding his son's hand. His children. What was he going to do now?

Chapter Four

Garrett checked his rearview mirror again. They were still there, secure in their seats. He couldn't see Pilar. Her car seat faced backward, right behind him. With the blanket Anjelica had packed over his head, Rio sat on the opposite side of the truck. Seeing himself in the boy was still a bit bizarre, and the kid had some strange behaviors.

He chuckled. There were times he wanted to hide under a superhero blanket, too.

Between the car seats, a big spotted Catahoula cow dog stretched out. Her head rested on Rio's arm. Her white coat with large black spots was covered in gray and brown smaller specks. She was a beautiful dog.

The unrestrained joy at the reunion between boy and dog tugged at his heart. Even now, the big dog hardly took her focus off her boy. Engraved on her dog tags was the name Selena.

Memories of Viviana and him listening to the late artist flooded his mind. It had been one of their go-to albums whenever life got too hard. Viviana would dance and sing along to "Bidi Bidi Bom Bom" until he laughed.

She would sing in Spanish at the top of her lungs, trying to get him to sing along. They would finish by slow dancing to "I Could Fall in Love."

Had she chosen that name because of the connection to him, or was he reading too much into a dog's name?

Now the dog eyed him with a suspicious glare, but then again, he might have been reading his own insecurities in the mixed blue and brown eyes.

It was clear she would hold out judgment on him. He could hear her say she'd trust him for now, but mess with her little humans and his life was over. He owed this Selena an extra treat. Life had gotten harder for his son than it had ever been for him. He'd had a charmed childhood compared to his son's.

Instinct told him he had a son who suffered from PTSD. If a preschooler could suffer from post-traumatic stress, he would think seeing your mother killed would do it. No telling how many fights he had witnessed or heard. The real question was, could he provide the kid with the help he needed so he wouldn't be scarred for life?

"So are you going to share?" Anjelica crossed her arms and raised an eyebrow.

His eyebrows knotted. "Share what?"

"I want to know what you found funny. I could use a chuckle, too, but you're all grim and serious again. So I guess it's over."

With a nod to the backseat, he turned onto the country road that would take them to Anjelica's home. His home. "Just thinking that disappearing under a superhero blanket sounds like a good coping strategy to me."

Garrett hit the brakes harder than planned, pitching everyone forward. Rio's blanket fell. As the little boy grabbed it with one arm, he reached for his sister with the other.

Cars, trucks and a church van filled every area a vehicle could park around Anjelica's house. He saw Pastor John and a couple of teen boys carrying a soggy mattress from the side of the garage. Two baby goats played with a couple of laughing kids along the side of the house.

He slowly pulled up to the gate. The De La Cruz twins, Adrian and George, waved at him from a truck loaded with debris that now carried his bed, too. The quiet property he had started to think of as home had been invaded. Music played somewhere in the backyard.

Yesterday, while he helped with a couple of water rescues, only Anjelica's father, a couple of brothers, Adrian and George, along with Pastor John, had shown up to help repair the roof. As the sun started to peek over the hills, they'd all shown up again, plus Sheriff Torres. Now it looked as if the whole county was hanging out on Anjelica's little farm.

The plan had been to move the kid's furniture into his apartment while they went to pick up Rio and Pilar.

"Oh, Garrett. I'm so sorry. I knew my dad and brothers had called in a few friends to help with the apartment, but I didn't know they would invite the whole town."

"What's going on?" Scanning the property, he frowned. He wasn't sure he understood what had occurred since he left.

"Well, I called Mom about getting some of the things you needed that I didn't have, and, well…that means she called Aunt Maggie, who in turn called the family and church members."

She looked at him with apprehension on her face. "They want to help. Between getting the kids here, cleaning out the apartment and setting up for them, we didn't have time to get it all done. I wanted to have everything ready. So…um, I called."

"She called church members?" His stomach flopped a bit. While he was in Kerrville picking up his new family, the whole town had learned what a screw-up he was. "I'm not much into people knowing my business."

Her eyes softened. Leaning across the console, she touched his arm. Warmth seeped through his shirtsleeve. "It's not like that. They really want to help. I mean, don't get me wrong." A soft chuckle broke the tension in the cab. "In Clear Water, the story is across the county before you finish telling it." She patted him on the arm. "But this way, we tell them what we want them to know and they're not making up crazy stories."

Knuckles tight on the steering wheel, he watched people come and go between the house and garage. "The story is crazy."

His jaw popped a couple of times. With a shift of his gaze, he looked at the backseat. Rio had pulled the blanket back over his head and the dog rested on his leg.

"I don't want people looking at the kids as if something is wrong with them."

What he really wanted to do was hit something. He needed to do something physical, to shake this restlessness off his skin.

One call and she had a whole town at her doorstep. Anjelica's family, most of whom he didn't know, were helping without asking why. His mother hadn't even returned his calls yet.

Envy was not a pretty emotion. He glanced at the people moving around the house.

He wasn't sure why he wanted to talk to his mother so badly, anyway. Gina would remind him of all the ways he'd messed up again. If she refused to help him, he would have to rely on Anjelica and her family even more. Acid burned his stomach.

Some of the women standing on the porch waved when they noticed them parked on the road outside the gate. He didn't have a great deal of experience with families other than Viviana's. Hers always involved drama. He hated drama.

Yeah, he really needed to go for a run before he exploded, but he didn't have time. The days of going for a long run whenever he wanted no longer existed.

He hadn't been this edgy since he first returned from Afghanistan. He rubbed his palm over his eyes. "I can't keep using you and your family to help me with my problems."

With a cute tilt to her head, she smiled. "Are we back to that? At the very least, this will give you enough time to find the perfect place to make into your permanent home, if that is still what you want." She glanced behind them and checked the sleeping Pilar.

Lowering her voice, Anjelica kept her focus on the baby. "Garrett, you don't want to be moving the kids from house to house, just making do. They need stability."

As he eased the truck into the driveway, his jaw started to hurt from biting down. With a deep breath, he forced each muscle to relax.

His instinct yelled not to take their help, or maybe it was pride. Sometimes the difference between the two was hard to find. Pride might come at too high a price if it cost the kids' well-being.

A soft touch pulled him out of his thoughts and brought his full attention back to her. The warmth of her touch went through his shirtsleeve.

With one click of a button, she rolled down the window. The sun's reflection exposed gold-red splashes in her hair he hadn't noticed before now.

He turned away from Anjelica and scanned the green valley surrounded by hills coming alive with spring growth. In her world, family always helped when needed.

"I'm sorry," she said again.

He snorted. "For your family or my mistakes? Not your problem, but your family is here to help. You're right. We couldn't have gotten it all accomplished in such a short time. The faster I can have the kids settled in the apartment, the better. We need to thank them for their help."

"Garrett, it's not your mistake the way things played out."

With the Tahoe in Park, he gritted his teeth. He hated crowds. They couldn't be comfortable for the kids, either. Adrian De La Cruz waved at them as he drove his work truck full of debris off the property.

"I appreciate the help, but I'm thinking this will be overwhelming for the kids, especially Rio."

"You're right." She glanced at the backseat again. "I'll have Mom clear out the house and send everyone that's not working on the apartment home. I know they want to welcome your new little ones. We're just used to hanging out with each other." She leaned in and squeezed his hand. "Everything gets turned into a party with them, but they'll understand."

He wished someone could explain it to him because he sure didn't understand any of this.

Checking on the kids again, he saw a small hand poking out from the blanket. Rio patted the dog, even though he hid. Wanting to hide from the world, he understood.

How was he supposed to help these kids when he was on the verge of losing it himself? The cabin in the woods overlooking the river would have kept everyone away, but now the world knocked on his door in the form of two innocent babes.

Garrett rotated his grip around the steering wheel, twisting the braided leather.

"Garrett, are you ready?"

No, but there wasn't much choice. "Yeah, you get Rio. He seems more at ease with you. I'll carry Pilar."

"I can go ahead while you wait in the truck and clear them out."

"No, the kids need normal, and for you this is normal. We need to thank them for everything they've done for us." Normal? He would follow her lead because he had no clue. He did know it wasn't normal to scan for snipers or explosive traps. He had to tell himself that these were the Ortegas, and they weren't going to harm the kids.

Pushing his lungs to their limit, he stepped out of his SUV and onto the unsteady ground of a new world.

"Do they show up unannounced often?" He moved to the passenger door behind him and opened it. In his truck, a baby who now belonged to him slept.

From the open door on the opposite side, standing next to the covered Rio, Anjelica smiled at him. "To them, family just shows up when needed. They do seem to have adopted you." She grinned. "Really, I'm so sorry. The concept of personal space is foreign to them, especially when they have a mission."

"Mission?" With a gentle unsure touch, he removed the straps of the car seat.

"Oh, Garrett, I'm sorry to tell you, but you and your new family just became mission number one."

His head came up fast and he hit his head on the edge of the door frame. He closed his eyes and pinched the bridge of his nose. Spots danced behind his eyelids.

"Are you okay?"

He nodded. "Great, now I'll have a headache."

"Relax." She winked at him. "I promise most of the time they're harmless. They'll clear out fast." She nodded to the little boy, who was pretending to disappear. She tugged at the blanket. "Rio, this is your new home. There are some people that want to welcome you, but they won't be staying. They just want to say hi." The blanket hung over her shoulder, but Rio kept his eyes closed. He had Selena's long leash in a tight grip.

A crowd had gathered on the front porch. Everyone had huge smiles on their faces as they waited.

He looked at Anjelica as she made her way to his side. With her free hand, she squeezed his arm. "Are you sure you don't want me to go in and ask them to leave?

"It's going to be okay." Maybe if he said it enough, he would believe it.

With a sigh, he picked up the sleeping Pilar. The strangeness of holding her was already giving way to a peaceful wonder. Her lax body molded to his hard frame, her soft cheek pressed against his shoulder.

Trust and love given without asking. He took in the smell of baby shampoo in the thick curls of her dark hair.

The easy acceptance that made her feel safe enough in his arms to sleep scared him a bit. Picking up the diaper bag from the floorboard, he glanced at his son. The now-familiar glare worried him. How was he going to make this work if his own son hated him? Had he scowled at his father the same way?

He tried to pretend they were not being watched by a bunch of people he didn't know.

With his free hand, he reached for his son to reassure him they were in this together.

Rio jerked his shoulder out of Garrett's touch and turned his head away from him.

Anjelica patted Rio's back. "Come on—let's go check out your new room. My mom and Buela, along with a bunch of cousins and friends, are waiting to say hi."

The little boy leaned back and took in all the people standing on the porch. He narrowed his eyes and then looked back at Anjelica. She gave him an encouraging smile, then turned it on Garrett. "You'll both be fine, and Rio will learn to trust you. Just give him time."

The not trusting was a survival skill his son had unfortunately had to develop. The kid had a great deal to get over before he would trust Garrett.

"I know you have an *abuelita*. I have one, too. We call her Buela." She nodded. "She wants to meet you and Pilar. My mom and cousins, too. Everyone here is very nice."

He pulled back and made a whimpering sound. The dog gave a low rumble of a growl.

"This is too much for him." Maybe he should tell everyone to leave now.

The front door opened, and the screen door banged shut. From the side of the house, Bumper came running, followed by leaping and kicking baby goats. She started barking and dancing around Anjelica. A cold sweat coated Garrett's skin and his breathing became labored. At the end of the leash, the Catahoula's hair stood along her spine as a low growl rumbled from her throat.

"Bumper! Stop it." Anjelica picked up Rio and balanced him on her hip, then scooped up the energetic dog with her free arm. "Shh, be nice. Rio, this is Bumper." Bumper stretched her neck out and licked Rio's car. The little boy giggled. Selena reared up on her back legs with her front paws on Rio's leg. She pushed her nose between her boy and the fluffball of a dog.

Tension tightened Garrett's muscles. A dogfight could break out with Rio and Anjelica stuck in the middle, and he had Pilar in his arms. He wouldn't be able to react fast enough if he needed to.

Bumper barked and Selena's tail wagged as Anjelica patted her on the head. She chuckled. "Look, Rio, they're already friends." She made eye contact with Garrett. Her eyes gleamed. "This is a good sign. Everything's going to be all right." She smiled at Rio. "Ready to see your new home?"

He leaned over and checked out the people on the porch again. Looking up at Anjelica, he gave her a solemn look and a slight nod. Garrett had not been able to get any response from the boy—well, unless glares counted.

God, I know I haven't talked to You much, but it seems I really need some guidance with this little guy.

With Rio on one hip, Anjelica released Bumper to the ground and took Selena's leash from Rio.

This is it. Garrett followed her again. She waved at the women on the porch. That seemed to be the permission they needed to swarm. Before he blinked, they were surrounded.

He couldn't keep an eye on all of them at once. Someone touched his shoulder from behind. He jerked around. Pilar lifted her head and gave a soft cry.

Breathe, Garrett. Breathe nice and easy. No one here is trying to harm the kids. You are in Anjelica's front yard.

Anjelica's mother led the pack. "We hear congratulations are in order. What a shock, right? So we are throwing you a surprise baby shower and home-warming party all at once." All the women laughed.

He worked to keep the panic off his face; he could play it cool. Something must have slipped, though, because Anjelica looked at him with concern. He tried to smile and reassure her he was fine, but it felt a little forced.

"Mom, I'm sure all he wants right now is to get the kids familiar with their rooms and settled."

A small herd of children ran through the yard, disappearing into the house.

He couldn't do this.

Anjelica wanted to protect Garrett from the wave of people, but she learned long ago to go with the tide. It went much smoother that way and you got out faster. She knew they meant well, but they didn't seem to understand someone not wanting them in his life.

She glanced at Garrett. This had to be a bit alarming for a man who sought solitude. Less than a day and his world had been turned upside down. Her heart went out to him as he tried to take it all in stride.

"Officer Kincaid! *Como esta?* How are you?" Buela cupped his jaw and kissed the cheek opposite the sleeping child. "They have worked very hard and the apartment is almost done! Praise God, in time for your new family."

"Como esta, Buela?" Anjelica greeted her grandmother.

"Muy bien. Good, good." She went to her granddaughter and cupped Rio's face. "So tell me who this fine boy is."

"Rio, this is my Buela and my mother." She shared a smile with the older women. "This is Garrett River Kincaid Jr., Garrett's son and Pilar's very brave brother. He goes by Rio."

He tucked his head against her shoulder, closed his eyes and started sucking his thumb.

"Hello, Rio. We heard how very brave you were to save your sister. This will be a great home for both of you and your dog. Big dogs love living in the country."

Her mother hugged Garrett, then placed a hand on Pilar's back, her hand going up and down on the small rib cage. "Oh, *mijo*, your daughter is precious."

"Mamma, this is very nice that everyone's here to greet us, but I think it might be overwhelming for the kids." Rio had tried to pull the blanket back over his face but just managed the corner. She refrained from pointing out that Garrett had gained a slight green tint to his skin.

Anjelica couldn't help but think she should get Garrett his own superhero blanket.

"Mija, they are almost done with the apartment.

While everyone is clearing out, let's visit the playroom we set up for the children while they are with you."

Taking Garrett by the hand, Anjelica led him through the sea of women. He muttered a few thank-yous as they crossed the yard.

The other women backed up, making a clear path to the front door.

"Oh, we're so sorry." Aunt Maggie was standing on the steps. "We wanted your children to feel welcomed."

"We didn't even think about all the newness of this for the poor lambs." Yolanda joined her mother.

Words swirled around them. She noticed Garrett taking deep breaths through his nose. Pilar stiffened and started fussing again. He patted her back.

With Rio still on her hip, she led Garrett up the steps and to her house. Vickie held open the door.

"Thank you." She turned to Garrett. "This is Vickie. She's married to Sheriff Torres."

With a nod to the woman, he followed Anjelica and Rio into the living room. The smell of fresh cinnamon rolls from the oven filled the air. Garrett adjusted Pilar and whispered to her.

With the door closed to the chaos outside, there was an unobtrusive peace in the house. The baby reached for his nose and smiled at him. Her heart melted as Pilar made the sweetest gurgling, and Garrett smiled. Some of the color returned to his face.

The door opened. Pulling the baby close, he turned to face the intruder. It was her mother, her sisters and Buela. Her tiny grandmother clasped her hands together. "Come on. Before we check out the apartment, we can show Rio the playroom in my house.

Eyes closed, Rio had gone into stealth mode.

"Garrett, these three are my younger sisters, Mercedes, Esmi and Jewel," Anjelica said.

He nodded to each of them as his large hand supported the back of Pilar's head. He moved next to Anjelica. "We'll just have to show Pilar the playroom, since we can't find Rio."

Anjelica smoothed the boy's soft curls. "I hope he likes trains and basketball." She leaned forward and kissed his forehead. "If not, he'll need to let me know what he likes. I hear he has a bed that looks like a car."

Her mother placed her hand on Rio's back. "It's been a long day for everyone. Let's get everyone out of the yard, then we can show you your new room in your dad's apartment." She leaned in close to Garrett. "All the women are cleaning up and clearing out."

"Thank you, Mamma. We can give Pilar a tour of the house. Buela said the apartment was almost finished. Will it be ready for them to sleep in tonight? I could fix a room upstairs."

"They'll be ready tonight. Just the final touches."

Buela waved her hands toward the kitchen. "Dinner is warming in the apartment oven."

"We thought about setting it up here, since this house was meant for a family, but the babies' main home will be in the apartment with Officer Kincaid, right? You should have switched houses." Her mother gave her a pointed stare.

"Mother."

Garrett's gaze met hers across the room. The panic seemed to be climbing back into the mist of his green-gray eyes.

She wasn't sure who needed comforting more, Rio or Garrett. Well, Garrett was a grown man. A man she didn't want to be attracted to. She couldn't let his vulnerability convince her heart to look at him as anything other than her boss. The screen door opened, and her youngest brother, Philip, popped his head in "I was sent to tell you that they will be ready upstairs in another fifteen minutes."

Chapter Five

"Good, we have time to see the playroom." Buela had apparently had enough talking and marched out of the room, not even questioning if her troops would fall in line. Like a good private, Garrett followed her.

Adjusting Rio to her other hip, Anjelica moved next to him and leaned in close. He had to tilt his head to focus on her soft voice and not the scent of vanilla and spice.

"I'm so sorry. She looks all sweet, but she is kind of a bully. She tends to take over." She looked up at him and smiled.

He decided not to point out she was always trying to feed him and had even jumped in to rearrange his life without his asking for the help.

Jewel laughed. "Yes, a tiny bully with good intentions, but a bully nevertheless."

Crossing the living room to the nursery, they passed four kids sitting around the coffee table, coloring. Bumper was curled up between two of the girls, her short tail thumping when she saw him. Selena had not left Anjelica and Rio's side.

With a deep breath, he trailed the women. There had

to be something for him to do, something to move or fix. He'd have joined the men working, but it didn't seem right to leave the kids with Anjelica so soon.

Six women crowded the room, staring at a man on a ladder. Tiny clothes covered every surface.

"Look at this one." The sheriff's wife, Vickie, held up a mini dress in pink camo print, drawing everyone's attention. Daddy's Girl was printed across the front. "Isn't it the cutest?"

The knot in his stomach pulled tighter.

Maggie Shultz, one of the aunts, was opening packages of little towels and putting them in a basket. "We were just organizing the chaos before leaving. Most of these things will be moved to the kids' room in your apartment. We decided to stick with the secret-garden theme. Is that okay?"

Was she really asking his opinion? "Sure." He couldn't imagine a baby would even notice.

The man with paint in his hair started down the ladder. "It's done." He stepped down and reached a hand out to Garrett. "Hi. I'm Gary, a friend of Pastor John's. I was asked to add *Credo* and *Amor* along with *Pilar* and *Rio* to the wall. Anjelica said she wanted *Faith* and *Love* along with *Hope*. I did some work upstairs first so it would be dry by the time they moved in." He nodded to the baby on Garrett's shoulder. "We cut it pretty close."

Yolanda put a stack of clothes she had been folding in a dresser and hugged Anjelica. "It's beautiful. How are you doing with all the changes?"

"I'm good. It's time." After one more nod and a tight hug, Yolanda turned to him. "This must be a jolt to the system. From bachelor to suddenly having two children in one weekend."

Understatement of the year. "Yes, ma'am."

"Please, call me Yolanda. I don't understand how a woman could not tell a man about his children." She patted his arm. "Anjelica told us about your mother not being able to help."

He shot a glare at his nanny. Was she going to be telling them everything?

She looked worried. "I told them she was working and couldn't get off with such short notice."

"It's understandable. I'm sure she'll come as soon as she can." Buela stood in front of the newly painted wall. "Gary, you're truly gifted." She turned back to the group. "Now, Officer Kincaid, you must have no worries. You have us. If there is one thing Ortegas are good at, it's taking care of kids. Had eight myself and raised twelve." She moved to Rio. "No worries for you, either. Pilar will have many sweet dreams in her new room upstairs."

The artist gathered up his paints and said his good-byes.

Garrett watched him leave with longing. "Maybe I should check on the apartment before we take Rio and Pilar up there?"

"Let's put a blanket on the floor so Pilar can stretch and play. She's been in the car seat all day. And you can see what the men are doing." Leaning down, Anjelica put Rio in front of a large basket full of toys. "Rio, pick some toys for your sister." With a job to do, Rio started digging through the basket.

The little girl blinked a few times and looked around the strange room. Her arms tightened around his neck when Anjelica went to remove her from his arms. His heart twisted and he placed his free hand on her back. "It's okay. I've got her."

Anjelica nodded and petted the back of the soft curls. "She already trusts you. That's good, but she needs floor time to build her strength."

He moved to the blanket on the floor and laid Pilar on her tummy, but she fussed a bit. "I can take her with me."

Yolanda had a strange seat-looking thing. "This will help her sit up." The women took over, gently pushing him back. Rio gave her toys.

Garrett stood at the door for a while and watched as Pilar smiled at her brother. The women encouraged the brother and sister with their praise.

Hesitant to leave, he backed into the living room. Glancing out the front window, he noticed most of the cars were gone. The house did seem quiet…quieter than it had been when he arrived. The little dog sat on the pillows as if waiting to be served. As he walked past her, she jumped down and followed him.

Moving to the back door, he found the sheriff, Jake Torres, and Pastor John in the kitchen.

The pastor held out his hand. "The apartment looks great. My guess would be better than before with the De La Cruz twins on the job. Couldn't help but notice a nice collection of saxophones. I take it you play?"

"Yes, sir."

"We have a solid band at the church, and the family likes to play. You'll have to join us sometime."

"Thank you for helping with the repairs."

"Hey, Kincaid." Torres shook his hand and then pulled him into a shoulder bump, finishing it off with a couple of hard pats before he stepped back. "The apartment looks great. You're staying here and Anjelica's watching the kids. Sounds like a perfect fit."

"I think it'll work for now. Thanks for helping." The sheriff had grown up in Clear Water. He would know more about Anjelica's husband. "Torres, did you know Steve Garza?"

Tight-lipped, he gave a sharp nod. "Anjelica's husband? Sure. He was a few grades behind me in school. Good kid, a bit reckless sometimes, but he never meant any harm. They got married the week after graduation. He enlisted and was killed his first tour in Afghanistan." Torres gave him the look. "She's special to us."

The pastor nodded. "She has a tendency to give and not allow others to help her." He cleared his throat. "We're a close community and would hate to see her taken advantage of by someone she's helping."

Garrett gave the men a quick affirmation. "Duly noted, but she is a bit forceful in her offer of assistance. She really hasn't given me much choice."

Both men chuckled. The pastor grinned. "She's an Ortega. I'm married to one and know them well." He patted him on the shoulder. "Sorry—they will come in and try to take over your life. But their plans are all for good."

"Two kids and a storm already messed up any plans I had managed to make."

Jake Torres nodded. "You know what they say about plans."

Garrett raised an eyebrow. He really had no clue.

Torres put a hand on his shoulder. "You make plans and God laughs."

"Yeah, well God's having a grand old time with me, then."

Anjelica's grandmother joined them. "You gentlemen look up to no good."

Pastor John hugged her. "Officer Kincaid was just saying how impressed he was with the Ortegas' fast-moving organization." With an arm around the small woman, Pastor John turned back to Garrett. "You have to thank the little general here." He nodded to the matriarch of the Ortega family. "When she mobilizes the Ortega army, anything can get done." He winked at the blushing grandmother. "She's a great friend to have on your side." He turned back to Garrett. "I'm going to gather up the boys I brought and take them for the pizza I promised. We'll be praying for your new family."

"Thank you."

Jake gave him another hug. "You're doing a good thing here, keeping the kids together. Don't hesitate to call." Jake stood back and stared him straight in the eye.

Garrett nodded and tried not to break eye contact. He was afraid that as a fellow marine, Jake saw too much. Jake narrowed his eyes. "Call for any reason, even if you just need to talk. I also know a man who works at the VA named Reeves. He's been there. Easy to talk to. Don't try to do this alone."

Garrett smiled and nodded. "Got it. Thanks for all the help today."

"Not a problem."

Vickie came into the kitchen with the now-small group of women. She wrapped an arm around her husband. "Hey, missed you." She gave him a quick kiss. The town sheriff and former marine laughed. "Missed you, too."

Anjelica, her mother and a couple of other women giggled. Someone muttered, "Newlyweds."

Everyone started talking at once. Garrett couldn't

keep track of the conversation, but they didn't seem to have a problem.

Man, how did people keep their sanity with big families?

He focused on Anjelica. She was talking to her mother. "I am more than capable of making dinner for a small family. I cook large dinners all the time." Frustration replaced her usual cheerful smile.

Some of the ladies agreed with her, while others started arguing.

Buela held her hands up. "Ladies, please. You're giving poor Officer Kincaid a headache."

"What about me?" the sheriff asked.

"Oh, Jake, you're used to us!"

"And on that note, I'm out of here. Call at any time, Kincaid."

"Now, *mija*," the tiny grandmother said, taking charge, "we know you are more than capable of fixing dinner for a whole mess of people. But there will be two scared babies under your care and a brand-new father. They need your full attention, so let everyone pitch in and help Officer Kincaid by providing dinners for the first week he has the children. Everyone wants to help. You should let them."

Anjelica's face softened. "You're right, as always, Buela." She kissed her grandmother's cheek. "Okay, Mamma, sign people up."

Maria Ortega turned to him. "Do you have any preference or anything you don't eat?"

He shook his head. "You really don't have—" Her glare cut off any argument he might have thought he had. "No, ma'am. I eat whatever you put in front of me."

She smiled and nodded. "Good. Your mother did

well. Okay, we are out of here. You both get some rest. You're going to need it."

And with that, they were all gone. "Let's get the kids from Jewel and take them to their new home."

He followed her back to the playroom. His pulse picked up as Pilar lifted her hands to him. Her grin did him in. This was why he'd sacrificed his serene one-man existence. Now he needed to prove he deserved her trust.

"I think she wants you."

Rio crossed his arms and glared again.

"Hey, little man, the look's getting old. Come on— get Selena and let's go upstairs." If he kept after it and stayed the course, Rio would open to him.

Anjelica took his son's hand, and Garrett led his new family home.

The apartment looked brand-new. Not only had his roof been fixed, but there was new carpet. Someone had hung artwork on the walls, framed pictures featuring the American and Texas flags. There were a couple of paintings of mounted Texas Rangers. It actually looked as if someone lived there.

The old sofa was gone and in its place was a large sectional, wide with pillows stacked high and a soft cozy blanket on the back. The old table was still there, but it now had three chairs and a wooden high chair.

Anjelica turned in a slow circle. "Wow. This looks great." She looked at Rio. "Let's go see your and Pilar's room."

Garrett followed, along with both dogs.

After a very brief tour of the new room, they moved to the table.

"They left a macaroni casserole and baked chicken in the oven." She pulled out plates and set the table.

"Pilar, I'm going to put you in the high chair so we can eat." He explained everything step by step as he strapped her into her seat. He made sure to include Rio in his one-sided conversation.

Anjelica handed him a small bowl of cheesy pasta. "Here, feed the baby."

The big brother watched Garrett's every move. "Does your sister eat solid food?"

Rio looked over to Anjelica and nodded. The kid was still refusing to acknowledge him.

She gave him a hesitant smile. "It seems she does."

"Are these safe to give her?" He blew on the hot noodle.

"Does she have teeth?"

Garrett tried to look in her mouth. Sticking his fingers inside didn't seem like a good idea. She smiled at him, showing off a few tiny white teeth. He handed her one curved pasta. Love and adoration radiated from her face. He sat on the chair closest to her and handed her one piece at a time.

"You need to eat, too." Anjelica set a full plate in front of him. She helped Rio into his booster chair.

"I should have thanked them for having this ready for us." Garrett kept his attention on Pilar, making sure she didn't choke.

"They understand that there's times when help is not asked for but needed. Please, don't worry. You thanked them several times, plus you aid the community as a whole. Everyone appreciates your service."

The short silky tail wagged as Bumper sat up on her hind legs. Rio laughed and the little dog jumped up onto his lap.

"Bumper, no. Get down."

Not to be left out, Selena tried to nose her way into Rio's lap, also. The Yorkie jumped onto the table. With a lunge, Selena tried to jump up, but her heavy paws landed on the edge of the plate, flipping it and tossing food through the air.

"Down." Garrett's firm command was instantly obeyed; the dog went to the floor and rolled halfway over, her eyes apologetic. Rio jumped from his chair and covered Selena with his small body.

Garrett's heart twisted. He slowly lowered himself to the floor next to Rio and Selena. With a deep sigh, he placed his hand on Rio's back.

The muscles along the bony spine tensed. "Rio, I'm not going to hit Selena. I just wanted her to sit." Garrett relaxed his jaw.

Anjelica put the little dog in the kitchen and told her to stay. She joined them with a broom in hand and picked up the plate.

He looked at her for help. She offered him a sweet expression of understanding. His attention went back to the boy. "Rio, I'm not mad. I don't want her jumping on the table or begging for food while we eat. It's a bad habit." The Catahoula licked Rio's face. Garrett petted her behind her ears. "She's a good dog. I'm sorry I yelled. Next time I'll make sure to be calm when I give her a command."

Anjelica had scooped some of the food up. "Here, Rio, help me clean. Sometimes accidents happen and we have to take care of the mess."

"She's right. The dogs can learn to stay in a certain area while we eat. Do you think you could teach Selena to mind her manners?"

Rio sat up and nodded. Garrett went to the kitchen

and called Selena to him. With her head lowered, she followed.

Anjelica smiled. "It looks as if she's decided to trust your dad." She ruffled Rio's curls.

With a huff, Selena lay on the kitchen mat and watched every movement he made. Bumper sat next to her.

Everyone went back to eating.

Garrett glanced around the table. Family, his family. Time and experience proved he was no family man—he had no clue how to be part of a real family.

What if he let these kids down, like his father had done? Or worse, not take care of them in a world that was unstable. The one time he'd needed to protect a kid, he hadn't been able to. And the result had been devastating. Garrett locked his jaw. He was not going back there, couldn't afford to. That was Afghanistan.

His son needed him. He wouldn't let this kid down, too. He didn't know how, but he was going to be a better father than the man who'd left him.

Kenneth R. Kincaid had taught him one thing: a real father never walked away from the people who were counting on him. Garrett had messed up the first few years of his son's life, but he was here now and nothing was going to get between him and these two kids who needed him. Nothing.

Anjelica gathered the plates off the table.

"So what do we do now?" Sitting between his new son and daughter, Garrett looked as lost as Rio.

"Well, you can have some family time in the living room. Pilar can play on a blanket to build up her strength. I think they would enjoy listening to your music."

"I read online that young kids should be in bed by eight or eight thirty. Then another site said they have internal clocks and know when they need sleep, so a parent shouldn't force a bedtime. What do you think?"

She smiled, biting back the urge to laugh at his uncertain expression. He seemed so vulnerable. "You're the parent. How do you want to set up expectations?"

He picked up Pilar. "Growing up, I didn't have a bedtime."

Pilar closed her eyes and snuggled deeper into Garrett's neck. He rested his cheek against the top of her head. "One of the things I loved about the military was the routine. An eight-thirty bedtime? What about it, Rio?" He laid his hand on top of his son's head.

The little boy crossed his arms and pulled away, looking in the opposite direction.

Her heart twisted at the injured look on Garrett's face. "Eight thirty would be a good time. You'll be fine. All parents struggle trying to figure this out."

Garrett patted the baby's back, his large hands making her look small. "What about baths? She seems too little to put in a tub."

"I could help you give them baths tonight. There's a seat to use in the bath for her. You set up a routine, and they'll start counting on it."

Garrett nodded. "Routines are good. When I'm at work, they'll have the same schedule with you, right?"

"That's the idea." Drying her hands, she turned to face the table. As she leaned against the counter, her heart reeled at the matching expressions on father and son.

Backs straight, they had the same stern look. She knew right then that she was in danger.

"Come on, guys—Rio and Pilar have a new room to explore. Let's go check it out."

They spent the next twenty minutes trying to get him to play in their room. Garrett even read a couple of books with Pilar in his lap as he sat cross-legged on the floor. Oh yeah, she was in trouble.

Falling in love with the children was a risk she was willing to take, but Garrett was not on her list of eligible men. Not only did he risk his life every time he went to work, but he was an alpha male and seemed to be antisocial.

A true loner. He didn't come close to the type of man she wanted to marry. Falling for him would be disastrous to her sanity.

The kids needed her focus. They went through bath time, and with one story, Pilar was sound asleep in her new bed, the crib Anjelica had bought for her daughter. Rio was a little harder, but he snuggled in, and with Selena at the foot of the bed, Garrett and Anjelica eased out of the room.

Whimsical lights danced on the ceiling from the night-light.

They stood in the living room looking at each other. It had been such an eventful day—weekend, actually. Anjelica wasn't sure what to do with this newfound intimacy. Especially with a man who seemed to want none of it—this man she could not, would not love.

Chapter Six

Anjelica walked over to his saxophones. "You did it. Day one in the bag, including dinner, bath and story time."

"Not me, we. Couldn't have done it without you." He wanted to do something for her. Crossing the living space, he went to the freezer. "They stocked my kitchen, including ice cream. I think we deserve a treat."

She joined him in the tiny area. "Sounds like a perfect ending to this day. What can I do to help?"

"Make yourself comfortable on the new sofa. Let me feed you for once. Of course, I'm not actually cooking anything, but it's just as good…almost." He set a bowl on the coffee table in front of her. Neither spoke as they concentrated on eating. Finishing his dessert, he leaned back on a stuffed pillow and savored the silence. The tension he had been holding all day slipped away.

She gathered the bowls and took them to the sink.

"Hey, I'm supposed to do that."

She laughed. "I beat you to it." After washing the simple dishes, she turned to face him. "So what else do you need done? I can stay and talk through anything you're not sure about."

With a grin, he laid his arm across the back of his new sofa. "That would take more hours than we have available. Anyway, you and your Ortega army moved fast. I think your family did everything that needed to be done." He still wasn't sure about all the changes. Was it normal to feel so detached from your own life?

"After seeing those pictures, I had to do something. Your world turned upside down on you. At the same time, duty called, and you had to go out helping others across the county after the storm. The least I could do was make some phone calls. I'm sorry if I overstepped, but we didn't have much time."

"It's as if everything fell into place while I wasn't looking. Thank you." He nodded, not sure what else to say.

"Is there anything else you need?"

He had to snort. That was a loaded question. He didn't know much about kids; there would be things he didn't even know existed. "Not that I can think of for now. I'm a little too wired to go to sleep. I'll play the sax for a while. You can stay if you want."

"That sounds lovely."

With his favorite sax in hand, he went to the balcony. It would soften the noise, and the weather was nice. As his fingers moved over the keys, the music consumed him, releasing the anxiety of the day. *God, thank You for this gift.* He didn't know how to pray. But he could have a conversation with God through notes of his song.

Without it, he was sure he would have lost control of his mental status long ago. As it was, he felt as if a thin string held everything together.

Over an hour had slipped by when he noticed Anjel-ica standing.

"It's getting late and your little ones will probably be up early. Feel free to call at any time."

He put the sax in its case and followed her to the door. "Thank you. I can't imagine how I would have handled it or gotten any of it done without you."

"God provides before we even know to ask. I'm grateful to help." She reached over and patted his arm.

Her family did that a lot, touched and hugged. For the last three months, he had been trying to avoid her because she would be a complication to his plans. But she ended up being the one to pull everything together and had gotten him through an overwhelming situa-tion. He stepped back before he gave in to the urge to pull her close.

This was not a date. She worked for him. Thoughts of kissing had no business being in his head and needed to be locked down.

She looked so fragile. It just didn't mesh with the warrior she became for his children. A woman who had lost her own child and husband. He had no right to ask more of her.

She smiled one last time, then left, closing the door behind her.

Restless, he put the clean dishes away and went to stand on the balcony. It felt like a lifetime ago that he stood in this exact spot and saw her running through the storm.

Now he needed rescuing. Before heading to the shower, he secured all the doors and windows. Check-ing on the children, he just stood in the doorway and watched them. They'd probably be up early and he needed to be alert, but sleep seemed dangerous. He hated letting down his guard for any amount of time.

After one of the shortest showers in his life, he checked on the kids one more time. He couldn't shake the unease that kept his skin tight when the children were out of his sight.

He was going to learn to cope, or he'd never get any sleep and drive them all crazy.

Selena had moved from Rio's bed to the rug in front of the crib. She raised her head and watched as Garrett made his way to see Pilar.

Arms out wide, she was still sound asleep. He petted Selena and turned to check on Rio. The small race-car bed was empty.

His heart jumped to his throat. He couldn't be in the restroom. Had he run away? No, he wouldn't leave Pilar.

Rushing into the living area, he found a chair in front of the pantry and crackers missing. Doing a quick sweep of the apartment, he found all the windows and doors still locked, so Rio had to be in the apartment somewhere. "Rio." He kept his voice low and calm.

Scanning under the beds, he saw just boxes. The first night and he'd lost his son already?

Breathe, Garrett. He's here somewhere. What if he'd hurt himself and couldn't call out? All the horrific scenarios that could happen to a five-year-old flashed through his mind. He shouldn't have left him alone.

He grabbed his phone and hit Anjelica's number. She picked up in one ring. "Garrett, what's wrong?"

"Rio's not in his bed. He took crackers out of the pantry and is hiding somewhere. I can't find him."

"I'm coming up."

He searched the apartment until he heard her at the door. "Thanks." He was saying that a lot lately.

"Not a problem. My guess is that he's close to Pilar."

"That's what I thought, too, but I can't find him."

She got down on the floor. "Rio, come here, *por favor*." Twisting around, she faced Garrett and pointed under Pilar's crib.

Going to his hands and knees, he scanned the area again, this time slower. That was when he noticed the boxes of diapers had been moved away from the wall.

"What do I do?" Going in and pulling Rio out by his legs didn't seem like the best thing to do to a kid who already had issues.

Selena crawled closer to the edge of the crib next to Anjelica. Her tail thumped against the floor. "Rio, you have a really cool hiding place, but you scared your dad."

Silence. Anjelica reached in and slid a box to the side. There sat Rio, curled up with his superhero blanket.

Garrett got a pillow and comforter from the bed. He joined Anjelica and Selena on the floor. "Hey, little man. If you're going to be sleeping under your sister's crib, you need to make a bed. We also have a food rule I didn't tell you about. If you're hungry, it's okay to get it from the pantry, but you have to eat at the table. No food in the bedroom."

The box of crackers slid out to him. "Okay, thanks. Anjelica is going back to her house for the night. I'll be in the bedroom next door if you need anything."

He looked over at the first woman he had spent any time with since his marriage. "I think he's sleeping there. I used to sleep in my closet. Small spaces can feel safer."

She nodded. "Good night, Rio. Remember, we care

about you and need to know where you are when we call your name."

Garrett walked her to the door. "*Thank you* is getting old, but I don't know what else to say."

She laughed. "It works, and it never gets old. I'll have breakfast ready in the morning, including bacon. See you then."

Once again he closed and locked the door behind her. Standing at the window, he watched until she made it into her house and waited until the lights went out before going to his own bed, where he would toss all night.

Anjelica stood at the kitchen door, cup of coffee in her hand as the sun's early-morning light caressed the landscape. She had fed all her fur babies, gathered the eggs and turned the chickens out. Now a debate battled in her head, pinging back and forth.

Should she go upstairs and help Garrett or wait here? The little ones were Garrett's responsibility, but he had hired her to help. The question was, how much? She knew her family could be a bit forceful in their attempts to help, and she carried the same gene.

During her grief counseling, they'd explored all her weaknesses and strengths, which ironically were the same. Portion control was the key to a happy heart.

What if Garrett was overwhelmed but afraid to ask for help? Taking a sip of coffee, she batted down the urge to run upstairs. It was still early.

The side door of the garage opened and Rio was the first out. He had his hand on Selena's collar. Behind them, Garrett had Pilar wrapped in a blanket. Her heart did a funny flip-flop at the sight of the Texas trooper and his family.

No, no, no. It was a job.

Seeing her at the door, Rio leaped across the sidewalk and ran to her. Garrett looked like he'd gotten even less sleep than she had. And she didn't recall ever seeing him with scruff along his jawline. If she refused to acknowledge his masculine beauty, would it stop enticing the dangerous thoughts that stirred in her brain?

Last swallow of coffee for fortification—then she leaned down to greet Rio.

Garrett gave her a sheepish grin. "We're here. Who knew getting two such small people up and ready would be so complicated."

Hugging Rio, she lifted him as she stood. "I can help in the mornings if you want. That is why I'm here. Once you go back to work, we can set a schedule. With these guys, we need to be ready for a full-court press."

He strapped Pilar into her high chair and headed straight to the coffeepot.

"Not sure I have the energy for a full-court press. I've never needed coffee the way I need it this morning." He actually moaned as the hot liquid slid down his throat.

"I have fresh eggs, bacon and sliced tomatoes. Here, sit down and eat. Do you want orange juice or skim milk?" She offered Rio a small cup of each. He held the mug of milk with both hands like Garrett and took a deep drink, then gave his own little moan. Twinges warmed her heart.

She glanced at Garrett to see his reaction, but he had his head buried in his hands. The timer went off. "How about cinnamon rolls? They were made yesterday."

"I could hang out in your kitchen just for the aromas." He fed Pilar a couple bites of egg before eating the tomato on his plate.

"You know, you hired me to run interference whenever you need it." She gave each of the guys a two-inch-tall cinnamon roll. Licking the gooey goodness off her fingers, she sat down at the table.

"My brain is rubbish this morning, but have you made two sport references in the last two minutes?"

She shrugged and winked at him. "In Clear Water, everyone is a Friday-night-lights fan. Plus I was a total tomboy. I actually had a basketball scholarship but got married instead." Sitting across from him, she grabbed a pear out of the fruit bowl. "Don't let the girlie clothes fool you. On the court, I'm a fierce Mayan warrior. It's the Ortega blood."

Shaking his head, he grinned. "I assumed you were the artsy type that protested violence of any kind."

Changing the subject would be good. "Do you want more bacon?"

"You don't have to feed me. I've managed several years on my own."

"You're not on your own anymore." She nodded and took a bite from the pear.

He cleared his throat. "For some reason, that scares me even more."

Reaching across the table, she touched the back of his hand. "We've got this. You've been given a tremendous gift and it can be consuming, but we'll do this." She glanced at the kids. Pilar played with her eggs and Rio stared at them. It looked as if more of the sugar glaze had gotten on his face and shirt than in his stomach. "We'll set a daily routine and everyone will know what to expect."

* * *

Garrett shot straight up in his bed. Breathing as if he had just sprinted two hundred yards. Cries echoed in his head. Swinging his body to the edge of the bed, he planted his feet on the cool surface of the wood floors. Slowing his breathing, he closed his eyes and focused on the present in Clear Water, but the cry came again.

Pilar.

In the next room, Pilar cried. He checked his phone. Three in the morning. In the last two weeks, she had settled into a routine. She was off schedule.

Concerned, he went into the room and found her standing against the railing of the crib, her face red and damp from the tears. Rio was holding a bottle to her, but she slapped it away. The little boy turned and glared at him.

"It's okay, Rio." He crossed the room. She stretched her arms up to him, wanting him to pick her up. Without hesitation, he complied.

Lowering his voice, he started singing "Twinkle, Twinkle, Little Star." With one hand on her bottom, he realized it was a little damp, so he took her to the changing table. "Hey, pretty girl, what's the problem? We're going to get you a fresh diaper, all right?"

Another cry ripped the room as her back arched. This wasn't usual for her. She liked talking and cooing while he changed her.

Rio had pulled up a box and stood at the end of the changing table. He touched her face. It didn't soothe her.

Once she was clean, Garrett lifted her and held her against his shoulder. The soft curls brushed against his stubble as he sang softly against her ear. He'd seen

Anjelica do that as she rocked the baby to sleep. Her crying went to a few sniffles and hard hiccups.

Taking a deep breath, Garrett relaxed. He could do this. With another pat on her back, he leaned over the crib to put her back to bed. As soon as he moved her away from him, she started crying again.

Bringing her back to his chest, he started singing. This time it seemed to irritate her. The tiny body stiffened. Rio crossed his arms and glared at him. Even the dog glared.

"It'd help if you could tell me what's wrong. If at least one of you would talk. I can't fix the problem if I don't know what it is." He cradled her in his arms and started swaying. He offered her the bottle again. That didn't help. It seemed to make it worse.

He lifted her back to his shoulder. "You know, when you think of being a father, it's all about playing ball, Christmas mornings and the first bike rides." He massaged her back. His voice low and soft, he walked. "You don't imagine the odd hours or how obsessed you become with the bodily functions of another person."

Pacing back and forth, he tried another song. Maybe he'd done something wrong when he changed her diaper. He laid her down, then took off the onesie and the clean diaper. "Baby girl, I'm trying to fix it." Her skin was smooth, not a mark or blemish.

After what seemed like an hour of Pilar fussing, nodding off, then crying again while Rio and the dog glared at him, he wanted to cry himself. Rio turned his back and marched out the door, Selena on his heels.

"Rio!" A sigh didn't even begin to express his level of frustration as he followed his son.

At the front door, Rio reached up and unlocked it.

Okay, he needed to place the lock higher. "It's four in the morning. We are not going outside." The duo headed down the stairs. *Anjelica.* He was going to Anjelica for help.

Okay, so my son is smarter than me. Or maybe the little guy just had better parenting skills.

Whispering soft nonsense words to Pilar, he passed Rio and walked across the driveway to the kitchen door. Pilar's cries had turned to sniffles. "Hang on, baby girl. We're getting help."

Standing in front of the old wood door, he noticed areas had peeled off, showing years of different paint colors. Pilar nuzzled her nose against his neck. Maybe she had gone back to sleep. He took a step back, about to turn and head back to his living quarters.

Pilar opened her mouth and let out a yell as if he had pinched her. The door opened and Anjelica stood there in an oversize T-shirt and sweats. She glanced down at Rio and Selena, then brought her gaze back to him and Pilar.

"What's up with the family field trip?" She laid a hand on the baby's back.

"I can't settle her down. I've changed her twice, tried to feed her and walked or rocked until… I just don't know what else to do. Rio thought you might be able to help." Okay, so why had he just ratted out his son? "I agreed. So here we are."

She took Pilar. "You and Rio had a conversation about this?"

"Well, no. He walked down the stairs and I followed. Sorry—I know you're not officially on duty, and I hate bothering you, but I don't know what to do to make her all right."

"Have you taken her temp? She feels slightly warm."

He hadn't even thought about her being sick. "No. How do I take her temperature?" He dug his fingers into his hair.

"My aunt left a kit for you that includes an ear thermometer."

"I have to poke something in her ear? That doesn't sound safe."

Pilar reached for him, her lashes wet from tears. "I think she wants you."

"Why? I haven't been able to help her at all." Garrett's hands engulfed her little chubby body. "Should we give her something for the fever?" As he cradled her, she grabbed his thumb and started gnawing on it. Eyes closed, she slobbered all over his hand as her gums went back and forth. "She's trying to eat me."

Anjelica laughed. "I think we might have our answer to what's wrong." Moving around him, she took Rio's hand and headed up the stairs to the apartment. "If she is cutting teeth, it can be painful. Can you feel anything on her gums?"

"But she already has teeth."

"Yes, and she will get more, a whole mouthful."

Pausing, Garrett watch the look of bliss transform the little face as he rubbed a calloused thumb over the swollen gum. "I think I feel something right under the surface." Eyebrows pulled, he looked at her. "How do I fix it so it stops hurting her?"

"Let's take her temp, then go from there, okay?" Anjelica made her way to the nursery and opened the top drawer of the light green dresser. With a weird-looking gun-shaped instrument, she moved to stand in front of him.

Instinctively, he pulled Pilar closer to him. "What are you going to do with that? It looks like it might hurt."

A tiny fist hit Anjelica's thigh. A scowl that mirrored Garrett's was planted on his small face.

"Rio!" Garrett's voice came a little sharper than he intended, causing everyone to jump. Pilar started fussing again. "Shh…baby girl, I'm sorry. It's okay." He turned to his son and took a knee. "I didn't mean to scare you, but you can't hit. You have to use your words."

The small boy reached over and touched his sister's face.

"I want her to be better, too. But I can't allow you to hit people. In this house, we talk. I promise not to hit Pilar, Anjelica or you. I might yell, but I'll never hit you, and I expect the same from you. We'll fix problems by talking, using our words. Do you understand?"

Rio nodded, then looked up at Anjelica. He licked his lips.

Anjelica dropped to Rio's level also, placing her hand on his shoulder. "Your father asked if this will hurt her. Are you worried about that, too?"

Arms crossed over his middle, he glanced at Garrett.

"Go ahead—use your words."

Thick eyelashes blinked a few times and the only sound in the room was the slurping of Pilar chewing on Garrett's thumb. She fell back to being content in the midst of tension.

"Yes, ma'am."

He spoke! He shot his gaze to Anjelica. *Oh no.* For a moment, Garrett thought Anjelica would start crying. What if that made Rio think he had done something wrong?

He smiled at the boy and patted him on the shoulder. "Good job, Rio."

Anjelica pushed some loose strands of hair back and cleared her throat. "Yes, nice job. I love hearing your voice. Now, about the ear thermometer. What if I show you how it is done? I can use it on your dad first."

Rio shook his head. "Me. Try on me."

"Okay. Ready?" She leaned in closer and showed him the gun, pointing out the details. "I'm going to put it in your ear and push the button. You won't feel a thing." A moment later she showed the screen to Rio. "It says you have a temp of ninety-eight. That's perfect. Now that you know it won't hurt her, let's get Pilar's temp."

Garrett stayed on his knee, with Rio holding Pilar's hand as Anjelica did her thing. "She has a slight fever. I would hate giving her anything at this point. Let the fever do its job." She looked at Garrett and grinned. "Chewing on you seems to help. I do believe you're the biggest chew toy I've ever seen."

"But how do I get any sleep?" He glanced at the clock. "I have to be at work in four hours."

"We can try some numbing cream for her gums and—" she moved to the basket of toys "—let's see if there's a toy to replace your thumb."

"They make cream for cutting teeth and we have some?"

"Yes, thanks to my family. I'm sure it was Aunt Maggie. She thinks of everything. Since it's so late, or early, depending on how you look at it, let's go ahead and settle them into bed. I'll stay with the kids and you can get a little sleep before going to work, and you won't have to wake them up to bring them to me."

"Are you sure?"

"It's best for everyone."

How would he have survived without her? How had his mother done it all without help? He'd never realized how tired she must have been all the time.

She knew how hard it was to raise two kids alone. One message was the only contact he had had with her in the last two weeks. She was loud and clear about her thoughts of Viviana and told him to let the state take care of them until he knew for sure Rio was his. His mother had never been a fan of his ex-wife.

He stood at the door and watched as Anjelica helped Rio organize the bed he had created under the crib. When she turned and found him staring, she raised her eyebrows.

"Go on with you. We've got this covered, and you need to get your sleep so I don't have to worry about you tomorrow."

"Yes, ma'am." He needed to leave before he started thinking about her being here permanently and how it felt to be worried over. "Thank you." The words sounded low and rough.

In order to break the invisible chain that held him to the spot, Garrett closed his eyes and spun away from Anjelica and the children.

Creating a fantasy life around a woman had never worked out and now he had a son paying the price. He had one mission and that was to stay focused on Rio and Pilar.

Chapter Seven

The early-morning sun had yet to make an appearance as he pulled into the drive. Today marked one month since Rio and Pilar arrived in his life. House inspections and parenting classes had become the new normal. They were one step closer to official family status.

Before getting the kids from Anjelica, he should go upstairs, lock away his gun and change out of his uniform. He tried to keep his weapons out of Anjelica's sight, knowing how she felt about them, but tonight he needed to see the kids. He needed to touch them and know they were safe before he could go to sleep.

Nothing like an ugly accident on 83 to turn a normal shift into a nightmare. Dealing with death always left him feeling a little hollow.

Home had never looked so good.

Home. Coffee. Sleep.

Maybe he should skip the coffee. In a couple of hours, the kids would be up.

Garrett stifled a yawn as he used his key to open the door into Anjelica's dark house. Normally, he would have left them here and joined them later for breakfast, but there was nothing about tonight. He should have been home hours ago, before their bedtime.

He hoped Anjelica didn't have anything planned for the day. Oh man, he didn't pay her enough. She deserved a big bonus.

Today was officially her day off, but the accident had his shift going seven hours over and he wasn't sure he could function enough to be responsible for the kids.

Easing across the living room, he made sure to sidestep a toy truck. He gave a prayer of thanks for his own mother.

There had been so many long hours of two or three jobs, but she had managed to keep them in a safe home with food in the kitchen. He hadn't appreciated her efforts at the time. All he had known was his mom was always gone.

She hadn't had a supernanny like Anjelica or people like the Ortegas to help her when the nights were too long.

He'd call her tomorrow and thank her. She deserved this time to herself and not to be pulled into his drama.

He first checked in Pilar's room and found it empty. His heart jumped and he made sure to control his breathing. All the worst scenarios popped in his head.

The door connecting the nursery to Anjelica's room stood open. With hesitation, he entered, finding it empty, also.

Breathe, Garrett. Breathe. They're here somewhere. He quickly scanned the house and found it empty.

Maybe she had taken them up to the apartment when he had called about being late. He couldn't move fast enough as he leaped the stairs three at a time.

His living room was empty. He rushed to the nursery.

A sigh of relief emptied his tense muscles.

All three people of his little family slept safely in the room. Pilar was sprawled on her back with her arms wide, not a care in the world. On the little car bed, Rio lay curled up in Anjelica's lap. She leaned against the wall. They still wore their day clothes.

He smiled at her soft snores. He would have never guessed that she was a snorer—or that he would find it endearing. It made her human.

His family had tried to wait up for him.

Without one of her brightly colored scarves, the soft T-shirt she wore revealed a scar that ran across her collarbone and up her neck. The tip faded into her hairline.

The need to heal Anjelica always lingered, but now it was hard to ignore. She had suffered so much loss and pain. Somehow she still faced life with such openness and willingness to help others.

As gently as possible, he picked up Rio, moving him to the side, and tucked him under his hero blanket. This might be the first time he actually slept in his own bed.

Anjelica shifted to her side and scooted down to the pillow, the soft sounds from her throat stopping. Taking the quilt off the foot of the bed, he covered his pint-size heroine.

She turned her face to him as he tucked the blanket around her. "Garrett, you're home?"

The sleeping edge of her whisper did things to his gut.

"Yes, ma'am." The fresh scent of vanilla and flowers filled his senses. He leaned in closer.

Her hand came up and she threaded her fingers through his hair before they fell to the base of his neck.

"Good. We were worried. I listened to the scanner for a bit, but I couldn't…"

His heart expanded in his chest. Emotions that scared him clogged his throat. "Don't waste your time worrying about me."

Her eyes opened, clouded with sleep. She gave him the softest smile.

He couldn't resist any longer. He leaned forward until his lips pressed against the tiny scar next to her ear. The perfect skin marked with the evidence of the strength she hid under all her softness. He rested there until his breaths synchronized with the pull of her lungs.

Her hand moved back up and smoothed his hair. He wanted to stay there forever. Their pulses dancing to the same rhythm.

Swallowing back the need for real contact, a complete kiss, he forced himself to move and press his lips to her forehead instead. Staring at her, he lingered as long as he dared.

She wanted and deserved a permanent relationship that included a family of her own without mounds of issues.

Pushed past normal limits, his brain cells were not connecting.

Closing his eyes, he stood. She rolled to the other side and tucked her hands under her cheek, snuggling under the quilt.

With slow steps backward, he eased out of the room. As tired as he was, sleep lingered out of his reach. He got a bottle of water, then sat on the sofa.

Anjelica had made it clear from the beginning that she didn't want to get involved with a law enforcer.

He understood her need for security and stability.

His job didn't offer either. There were so many guys in his line of work who were divorced, and he was one of them. Restless, he flipped to his side.

A reflection of light caught his attention. The security light outside had hit the glass of a patriotic poster one of the Ortegas had hung in his apartment. She belonged to a fallen brother and deserved his protection. She needed someone with a safe job and no baggage.

As tired as his body was, his brain wouldn't shut down. He closed his eyes and took slow deep breaths. He needed to go to his own bed, but right now he didn't have the energy to get up.

Down! Down! Cover! He pulled someone's arm to protect them from the explosion.

He had to react faster this time or they were going to die.

"Garrett." Soft fingers pressed against his jaw.

He opened his eyes and found his hand gripping Anjelica's wrist. Hard. She lay next to the sofa awkwardly.

He let go and jumped to his feet. Holding his hand out to help her up, he tried to stop shaking. Or at least hide it. *Five...four...three. Breathe.*

"I'm so sorry." He scanned her for any injuries, not able to bring himself to look her in the eye.

She took his hand and rose up in front of him. "I'm not hurt. You were trying to protect me. You said, 'I got you. I got you.' You pulled me down as if to shield me." Cupping her hand around his jaw, she forced his face toward her. "Really, you weren't trying to hurt me." Stepping closer, she put both hands on his face and made him look at her, in the eye. "Next time I'll be more careful when I wake you up."

"You shouldn't have to be careful." He moved out of her reach.

"Garrett." She used the voice she used when Rio was upset. "You lived in and survived a war zone. I would have to be clueless to not be aware of PTSD."

"I've been home for over five years. I don't have PTSD. It was just a bad dream."

"Have you talked to someone about these bad dreams? Do they happen often? Maybe Jake can help you. He was a marine and—"

"I don't need to talk to anyone. Now you sound like Torres. This is the problem living with people. They want to know all your business and ask questions."

"You've talked about this with Jake?"

"No."

She sighed, a deep heavy one of frustration. "I'm only asking because I care about those kids in the next room." She crossed her arms and glared at him, the sweet concerned expression gone.

Blood left his face and limbs. "What if it had been Rio? Or what if he saw me pulling you to the ground? It would've terrified him to see me attack you like that." He had become a danger to the ones he should be protecting.

"Garrett, it's all good. You didn't attack me. Rio is fine." She moved toward him with her hand out. He did a side step around the sofa. "I need to go for a run." He looked back to the door to the room where she and the kids slept last night. He needed to get out of the house, to push his physical limits in order to get out of his own head. "Can you watch the kids for a little bit longer?"

"Of course I'll watch the kids. You've had less than two hours of sleep. So take your run, take a shower, then get some real sleep. We'll be fine. I have some shopping to do in Uvalde—I'll take the kids with me. It's good for them to get out of the house. Later today the family's coming over to make piñatas and confetti eggs, *cascarones*, for Easter. We'll be outside. So you can stay in your room and sleep."

"Easter? Isn't it a little early?"

"With my family's crazy schedule? No this is the only time we can all get together, and it's a big family event. We don't want anyone left out."

He nodded like he understood while keeping the sofa between them. His eyes went to the scarf she had on, but he knew how soft she was under the bright blue material. Kissing her on the scar had been a huge mistake. Now he had a hard time getting the thought of a real kiss out of his head. He really needed that run.

With Garrett stalking out of the room, Anjelica flopped back on the sofa. She picked up the pillow Garrett had been using when she went to wake him up. From the kids' room, she'd heard Garrett having a nightmare. Her plan had been to wake him up and tell him to go to bed while she stayed and made breakfast.

The pillow in her lap smelled like the soap he used. With a heavy sigh, she stood. Rio and Pilar would be getting up soon. She needed to get them fed and out of the apartment by the time Garrett finished his run. He probably needed sleep. He also needed to talk to someone, but that was out of her control.

Later she'd do some research on PTSD. It seemed

they were living with two males who had an overzealous need to protect the people in their lives.

Garrett needed psychotherapy as much as his son did. Maybe he hadn't been suffering from PTSD, but with the upheaval in his life, it might have kicked in for the first time or returned. She needed to find out if that was possible.

As she started working in the kitchen, Garrett came out with his Marines T-shirt and sweats. Selena sat still as he put on her leash.

He gave her a sheepish grin. "Are you sure it's all right if I go for a run? I can keep it short."

"No. Go for as long as you need. I'm going to make breakfast. If we're gone when you get back, I'll leave you a plate in the oven."

"Thanks, you don't ha—"

Her stare stopped him cold. "Don't you dare say what I think you are about to say. I don't do anything I don't want to do. We'll be in Uvalde most of the day. Even when my family gets here, you can ignore them. I'll explain you were at the accident site all night. They'll understand. Of course, anytime you want to, you can join us."

"Okay." Walking past her, he leaned in and gave her a light kiss.

They both jumped back as if reacting to an electrical shock. Her heart lodged in her throat. She blinked. It hadn't been a dream. Last night he had kissed her.

Not a normal kiss, but next to her ear. He had kissed the edge of her scar. Her hand pressed against the spot, heat radiating from her skin. His gaze darted around the room. "I'm sorry. I just…"

Anjelica couldn't read the emotions on his face. He turned toward the front room, then back to her.

He ran his fingers through his hair, leaving it standing in the cutest way. A very dangerous adorable helpless look settled on his face.

"It's okay, Garrett. Go for your run."

With a nod, he was gone.

Standing alone at the screen door, she touched her fingers to her lips.

Chapter Eight

Garrett flipped onto his back. Interlocking his fingers over his chest, he lay still and focused on the sounds of Anjelica's family having fun. If he strained, he could hear talking and laughing with music in the background. A few times kids' voices erupted in squeals, only to fade away quickly.

He worried about Rio wanting to hide instead of running and laughing with the other children. Maybe he should go check on him.

Anjelica would be there, and after last night—and then the accidental kiss this morning—he didn't know what to say to her.

To get his mind off his emotional battles, he imagined Pilar having a great time being passed around while Rio hovered and stressed over all the strange people. Music came through the walls, not from speakers but live strings and a trumpet.

He stood and walked to the balcony. Pulling the heavy drapes back, he saw a yard full of color, people, animals and tables. The big garden in the middle of it all had started to turn green. As he scanned the area, the size of the crowd surprised him. A group of men had guitars, basses and the trumpet he heard. Anjelica ran over and talked to them. Her hands flew as the yellow scarf she wore fluttered around her, tangled in her dark hair.

Glancing at the clock, he calculated he had slept eight hours straight without interruptions. That was the longest stretch of sleep he'd had since becoming a father.

After a quick wash and shave, he changed and headed to the door. But before his hand touched the knob, there came a faint knock. The hinges creaked as it slowly opened. Rio poked his head in the small opening.

Garrett crouched down. Rio's eyes widened before he gave his dad a tentative smile.

"Hey, little man. Everything all right?"

Rio nodded, his curls falling into his eyes. His small hand pushed his hair back, allowing him to scan the room. Garrett froze midaction as he realized he was making the exact same gesture. "Were you looking for me?"

Another small nod. Then he looked down at his shoes.

"Rio, you have to use your words. This is a safe place to talk." He refrained from reaching out to stroke the boy's hair. This was the first time his son sought him out. He didn't want to do anything to startle him. Slowing his breathing, he held still and waited.

"Anjelica said you were sleeping." Rio rubbed his thumb against his palm. "Are you awake now?"

A lightness lifted the corners of his mouth. "Yeah, I'm awake. Thank you for letting me sleep and coming to check on me." He wanted to reach out and hug his son.

"Rio?" Anjelica's voice drifted from the bottom of the stairs. "Your dad is sleeping."

Standing, Garrett opened the door all the way. "I was up and about to come out when Rio came in to check on me." He gently squeezed the little shoulder. "We were just talking."

Anjelica's eyes widened a bit before she gave him an understanding look. "Well, as long as everyone's good, I'll head back to the party. We've dried the eggs for the *cascarones* and are stuffing them with confetti. Then we'll start adding the paper and glue to the piñatas." She clasped her hands in front of her waist. "So does this mean father and son will be joining the festivities?"

"Come on, son, let's go make a piñata." Okay, that was not something he'd ever dreamed of saying, but it felt right.

As they stepped through the back door of the garage, most of the crowd stopped and stared at them. Rio ducked behind his legs.

Anjelica clapped. "Now that Garrett's awake, we don't have to stay quiet. Tío Guillermo, you can start the music again." She laughed as children of all ages dashed to the table she had covered in large canvas sheets. "I'll be at the piñata table. Join me when you're ready."

Celeste, just a year or so older than Rio, ran over to his son. "Hey, Rio, I was looking for you. Do you want to come help make the piñata? It's really messy and fun."

Rio blinked at Pastor John's daughter a few times but didn't make an effort to move away from Garrett. "Rio doesn't talk much."

She smiled at him, then back at Rio. "That's okay. Daddy says I talk enough for a whole pack of people."

She held out her hand. "You don't have to talk if you don't wanna."

Eyes so much like his own looked up at him. Garrett went to his knee. "Do you want me to go with you?"

Rio nodded and slipped his hand into Garrett's as the little high-energy blonde grasped the other and started skipping to the table. "You'll love it. We make two, a giant one for the bigger kids and a smaller one for, well, the smaller kids." She laughed as she looked back at Rio. His son just nodded and watched her in complete fascination.

Maybe being led around by pretty girls started early for the Kincaid males.

On the table, two bamboo-framed structures were being covered in strips of newspaper and white paste. It looked messy. Adults and kids laughed as they criss-crossed the strips. Glue covered everything. Rio looked up at Garrett, doubt in his expression.

Garrett sighed. He had his own doubts about this adventure. Celeste laughed and pulled Rio into the middle of the crowd. People shifted and gave them room.

The enthusiastic daughter of the pastor plunged her hands into the bucket full of the glue mix, then pointed to a stack of torn paper. "Rio, hand me the paper and I'll coat it in glue. Then we can put them on the donkey. It's the donkey that carried Jesus into town before he was arrested."

Doing what he was told, Rio glanced up at him with a bit of panic in his eyes. Garrett came in close to him. "Do you know the Easter story of Jesus?"

He shook his head. Celeste gasped. "I thought everyone knew the Easter story." On her knees, she twisted around and yelled, "Daddy!"

Rio turned the opposite direction as if looking for an escape route. Picking him up, Garrett placed him on his lap. "It's okay. Not everyone knows the story."

Pastor John came over carrying the guitar he had been playing. "What's wrong, Celeste?"

"He doesn't know about the donkey that carried Jesus or the Crucifixion or the Resurrection. Can you tell him the story of Jesus and Easter?"

Some other people came over and Pastor John pulled up a chair to the end of the table. "My favorite story to tell from the Bible is the Resurrection of Jesus. Rio, do you want to hear it?"

With a nod, he started scanning the crowd. Garrett assumed he searched for Anjelica. She had Pilar and was walking across the yard, heading straight to the table, which had collected a crowd. Garrett made sure to sit still, not fidget or scan the crowd for threats. This was a happy family event.

One of the older kids complained about it not being Easter yet, so why did they have to hear the story again?

Anjelica stopped to stand next to them. "I would love to hear the story, Pastor John. It's a story we should hear often all through the year. I even have some Resurrection eggs. Rio can show everyone as you tell it." She handed Pilar to him.

Garrett settled her on one leg as he balanced Rio on the other. "It's been a long time since I heard the story. Pilar's never heard it, either."

A few others joined them at the table. With a couple of strums of his strings, Pastor John's soothing voice started recounting the days that led up to the ultimate sacrifice.

Anjelica handed an egg to Rio at each turn of the

story. He carefully looked inside to discover something that had to do with the journey. The other men who had been playing now gave the story a soft musical background.

Garrett had never been so moved. He sat with his children and listened to the story of how he'd gained the undeserved path to forgiveness. This was the reason he'd given up life as a solitary bachelor. These moments made every sacrifice worth it.

"Why did he do it?" Rio whispered, surprising everyone who had never heard him speak. Garrett had no clue how to respond.

Pastor John set the guitar down and leaned forward. "That's a great question. The Bible tells us that God so loved the world that He gave His only son. He loved us so much He didn't want to be separated from us. We are His children and He wants to be with us forever, even past this life."

Rio's expression turned even more serious as he processed the new information. He had to have questions about his mom and the way she died.

Celeste handed Rio a strip of newspaper. "My mommy's in heaven like yours." Rio scooted off Garrett's leg and stood closer to Celeste in order to smear the glue-coated paper over the soon-to-be Easter donkey.

Needing to stretch his legs, Garrett stood. He made a face at his daughter. Pilar laughed and grabbed his nose. A sunny yellow headband gathered her dark curls away from her face. He realized he would have no idea how to fix her hair if he was alone. Something else for his ever-growing list of things he'd thought he would never need to know.

As she made sounds, he talked back to her. She had to be the happiest baby ever.

In the early years, Viviana planned and dreamed about the kids they would have one day, a boy and a girl. "If your mamma was here, she'd play with you and love you." He lifted her up and rubbed her tummy with his nose. The giggles would cure anyone's sour mood. His own smile felt good as he continued to play with her.

"She's looking so much healthier since you brought her home." Buela stood next to him, wiping her hands on her green-and-pink apron. "Can I hold this precious girl? Anjelica is looking for you."

His daughter laughed and reached for the tiny grandmother.

"Where is she?" He scanned the backyard, which had turned into an impromptu fiesta. Kids played chase with the baby goats around the outside of the garden.

Next to the yellow blooming Esperanza with a small group of women stood one of the most beautiful women he had ever met. Anjelica threw her head back. A hearty laugh with no apologies consumed her whole body.

Her face lit up when he joined the group. "Garrett, I was just telling them that you play several instruments."

"She said you played in the military band." An older man spoke, one of Anjelica's uncles, but Garrett couldn't remember which one. "Why don't you join us?"

That was all it took. Before he knew what happened, Garrett was playing with them and being invited by Pastor John to join the church band. Music had always been the thing that grounded him.

It was another gift God had given him that he took for granted. What had he done to deserve all the gifts that now made his life worth living? Rio, Pilar and Anjelica.

Maybe he should give something back. One thing his mom taught him was to always be grateful when others did something kind for you. She made sure he showed his appreciation.

He didn't have much to offer, but he had his music. His music was about the only thing worth giving.

Anjelica turned her face into the gentle breeze that wove its way through the backyard. It danced with the trees, adding its own music to the gathering. Rio sat in her lap as he watched his sister. Pilar played on the blanket next to the Esperanza that Garrett had helped her save. She played with Rio's soft curls. Her daughter would have been just a little younger than Rio. She bit the inside of her cheek.

Pilar laughed and threw one of her teething toys. So much stronger than a month ago, and she had a smile for everyone. Rio, not so much, but at least he was not scowling at everyone who walked by. Just the ones who talked to him.

The brightly colored piñatas were hanging in the tree drying, and the hollowed-out eggs were filled with confetti. Now everyone sat around listening to the music her uncles, Pastor John and Garrett played.

This was living. She closed her eyes and thanked God for His many blessings. She couldn't resist kissing Garrett's son on the top of his head. He turned and looked at her.

"I was just thanking God for the perfect day with so many people that love each other. Look how strong Pilar is getting. She pulled herself up to sit."

Celeste sat on the edge of the baby blanket and started talking to her. Rio eased down from Anjelica's lap and sat next to his sister. Anjelica wasn't sure if he was being protective or saw Celeste as a new friend.

Glancing over at Garrett, she saw that he was watching, too. They made eye contact and he raised his eyebrow in question. Shrugging, she gave him a smile and sat back. Watching him play was pure pleasure.

Her grandmother joined her. "Something about a man playing music just stirs your heart, doesn't it, *mija*? I saw your *buelito* play at a friend's party and I fell in love."

"Buela, please don't start."

"You need to open your heart or the years will slip by and you'll be alone."

"Being alone is not the end of the world. The wrong man would make it worse. I'd rather be alone than miserable."

"Oh, *mija*, he's a good man."

The only way to get out of this argument was to stop talking. Eyes closed, Garrett had lost himself in his music. Why couldn't he be an auto mechanic or a banker who played the saxophone? Why did he have to make a living by putting himself in direct danger?

Behind the garden, her brothers had started a bonfire with the pruned limbs from her pecan trees. She loved the smell of pecan wood burning. Soon it would be too hot and dry to light a fire.

Her grandmother was right about her heart wanting to love again. Her wayward thoughts of Mr. Hero Man apparently proved she was ready to try a new relationship. Maybe she should join a singles' group in Kerrville.

There was no way she was going to hand her heart over to another save-the-world kind of man. She sighed. Pilar pulled at Rio's hair. The children laughed.

These two already had her heart, but she had to draw the line at their father.

She glanced at the object of her denial. His eyes were closed as he absorbed the music. She had to figure something out because she knew, without a doubt, she was already walking across dangerous ground.

"Tía Anjelica, there's a man at the door that's looking for Officer Kincaid." Her nephew Jordan looked concerned. "He looks official. He's in a suit." He glanced at her charges on the blanket, then leaned in close to her. "I think he might be here about the kids."

She patted him on the back. "It's okay. Will you watch the children for me while I see what he wants?" She tried to tell herself there was no reason to worry. It was late Saturday. Maybe they were just his last visit for the day.

"Thank you, Jordan. I'll be right back."

"Yes, ma'am." The lanky teen plopped down next to the blanket.

Should she get Garrett or see who it was first?

Before she could decide, Garrett had noticed her standing and staring at him. He raised an eyebrow in question. She gave him a slight nod. Without hesitation, he put down the sax and walked over to her.

"What is it? Is something wrong?" He turned from her and scanned the yard.

"There's a visitor at the front door. No one I know uses the front door. A man in a suit. It might not be CPS, and I was debating if I should tell you now or after I knew for sure."

"We knew he could be stopping by to see how the kids were doing." He smiled. "This is good. Look at Pilar sitting up. Rio is hanging with other people without a blanket over his head, and he's started talking to us. I think this is good timing."

"You're right. Not sure why I feel all jittery." As she turned to go into the house, Garrett followed, placing his hand on the small of her back. She relaxed. *"Si Dios quiere." We will trust in God's will.*

"Si Dios quiere," he repeated in his Texas drawl. The warmth of his breath tickled her neck as he leaned in close to her ear. The solid weight of his touch created a warm, safe feeling. She hurried ahead through the kitchen, forcing him to drop his hand.

She clenched her fist. His touch was no different than that of her father or brothers. No different, no different.

For her next day off, she was determined to look into the singles' group at the church in Kerrville. A teacher would be nice. She could date a teacher.

"Officer Kincaid. Mrs. Ortega-Garza. How are you doing?" John Ackerman held out his hand to Garrett, then her.

"We're good. Is this an official visit? Was there another house inspection that needed to be done?" Garrett smiled at the man, looking completely at ease.

She remembered her manners and greeted the man, too. "Nice to see you again. Would you like something to drink or eat?"

A shake of his head had her jumping ahead to why he might be here. "The kids are doing great. Pilar is sitting up and Rio has started talking to Garrett. Both of them are outside with my family. They're so happy." *Breathe.*

Anjelica, breathe. Garrett reached over and took her hand. She didn't look at him. She couldn't.

"That sounds great, but I'm actually here to give you some bad news. Well, maybe you'll like it. I know the placement was an emergency and you had not been aware of your son."

Now he squeezed her hand a little tight. "But he's mine now, right? Both are doing well here. Is there a problem?"

"Are you still wanting to adopt the girl?"

"Pilar." Garrett nodded.

She realized she had stopped breathing. With a deep breath, she relaxed her muscles and tried to calm her rolling stomach.

"The paternal grandmother has changed her mind and has petitioned the courts for full guardianship. So if you had doubts about taking a child that's not your biological daughter, then this is good. But if you're serious about being a parent to both? Well, not so good."

Garrett's fingers tightened, then relaxed around her hand. He repeated the motion, but when she looked at his face, he seemed unfazed by the news.

"What are her chances of getting custody? Since I'm his father, they can't take Rio from me." His gaze stayed focused on the CPS worker.

"No, no. Rio's yours. Do you want to fight for custody of the girl?"

He glanced at her. The panic buried in the depth of his eyes tore her heart.

She returned the grip on his hand before turning to Mr. Ackerman. "But the court would want to keep the kids together, right? I don't understand—we were led to believe there was no one that wanted Pilar."

Mr. Ackerman pushed his glasses up and nodded. "When we arrived on the scene, they were our first contacts. At the time, they made it clear they didn't want the children. Now that things have settled, Cecilia Barrow, the deceased father's mother, claims to have changed her mind."

Garrett stepped away with a low growl. "Viviana would have wanted me to have both of them. They need to stay together." He ran his fingers through his hair before turning back to them, his stone face back in place. "What do I need to do to secure Pilar as my daughter?"

"Well, go forward with your petition, stating that you want to keep your son and his sister together. The kids have an appointed lawyer. But the final decisions will be with the judge. She tends to go with blood, but for this case, that's hard. On one hand her brother, on the other her grandmother. There's just no way of knowing." He looked around the house. "How are the children settling?"

Anjelica jumped in before Garrett could say anything. "Rio still prefers sleeping close to his sister. They're very close, and the doctor that Rio is seeing says that it will help him if he can choose where to sleep. It gives him some control in a limited way."

Mr. Ackerman smiled and nodded. "Yes, I'm aware of the recommendations."

"Oh. Okay. Do you want to see the kids? They really are thriving here with Garrett." She needed to stop talking.

"That sounds great."

Planting a sweet smile on her face, she led them through the house. The three of them stopped on the porch.

"This is a great house. Do you plan to stay long-term, Officer Kincaid?"

"Call me Garrett. The kids are by the garden." He went stiff. It was subtle, but she saw the shift in his stance. He was on guard.

She scanned the yard to see what had upset him. Her family was in different groups, most split between the music and building up the bonfire. A few were playing horseshoes. She glanced to her yellow-flowered bush.

She stopped breathing. They were gone. Celeste, Rio and Pilar were not on the blanket. Even the blanket had vanished. They had to be around somewhere.

She looked for Jordan. He had joined the group at the fire pit. Oh no. The fire was dancing about four feet into the air. Where were the kids?

Chapter Nine

A buzz vibrated Garrett's skull. The popping of the burning wood amplified across the yard. Something in the corner of his eyesight flashed. He cleared the steps and was in front of Jordan before a complete thought formed in his head. The teen had been in charge of his missing children. A dog barked.

The pressure on his chest tightened. He needed to say something to Jordan, but he couldn't speak. An explosion went off and he turned, ready to dive in and get the kids out.

He had lost the kids. Sounds and movements blurred. He tried to focus on his hands. They were shaking.

He was in Anjelica's backyard. A warm body brushed against his leg as a cool nose pressed against his hand. Cool nose? He looked down and saw Selena, her one blue eye and one brown eye looking up at him. If she was here, the kids were close. They were okay.

Jordan took a step back.

"Garrett?" A hand touched his arm.

Taking a deep breath, he forced each muscle to release the tension. To lose control now would be the worst timing. Half the community stood around watching, along with the caseworker.

His hand dug into the soft coat of the big cattle dog, and he made a point to look Anjelica in the eyes. He needed an anchor and he needed it fast. He'd be useless to the kids if he wasted time battling phantom enemies from the past.

She leaned in close. "Garrett, they're inside the garden. Under my beanpoles."

The edge of Rio's favorite blanket poked out from under the wooden pole structure built for the bean vines. It was in the shape of a tepee.

Jordan's gaze darted between Garrett and the kids. "Oh, *Tia*, I'm sorry. They were just playing. Celeste and Rio were pulling her around on the blanket. I thought they'd be fine. I didn't realize…"

Garrett nodded and moved that way. He had to get his children. Rio had gone into his hiding mode again. Which meant he was frightened.

As they got closer, he heard sweet giggling. For the first time since he noticed them missing, he breathed.

Don't let them see you upset. The CPS worker was right behind him. He could *not* show any weaknesses, not with his guardianship of Pilar at risk.

If they thought he was unstable in any way, they might take Rio, too.

Selena barked and ran to the garden gate. She sat next to the poles. Getting as close to the kids as she could, she looked back at Garrett, her big tail thumping the ground.

A miniature goat with long gray hair and a black face had gotten into the garden and climbed the steep edge of the slanted poles. Head down, ready to butt anyone who got close to the kids.

Anjelica gathered the goat into her arms. Going down on her heels, she peeked under the superhero tent.

"Hey, guys, you worried us." The corner of the blanket was pulled out of her hand. At the same time Celeste popped up from the other side, laughing.

"Rio took Pilar for a ride on her blanket. She laughed the whole way. This is the coolest garden and it's not even full of plants yet." She looked under the blanket, than back to Anjelica and Garrett. "Did we do something wrong? We were just playing."

"Sweetheart, you can't take a baby for a ride away from the adults."

"But they can still see us. Daddy says not to get out of eyesight." Her smile was gone. "Oh, that's the rule for me because I'm a big girl. I guess a baby has to stay put. I'm sorry."

Garrett moved to the other side of the structure and got down to Rio's level. Not that the boy would notice. He had his head tucked down and knees pulled up. He couldn't have made himself any smaller. Pilar looked at him and smiled when Garrett reached to pull her into his arms. "Rio, I'm going to give Pilar to Anjelica."

His son had his hand on his sister's arm. He tried to pull her closer.

As gently as he could, Garrett removed Rio's death grip and lifted the baby off the ground. Tucking her into his arms, he touched her tiny chin and smiled at her. "Your big brother took you for a ride?" His heart was in a knot. Now the grandmother wanted to take Pilar from them.

Her son had killed Viviana. The woman had turned

her back on them and now wanted to claim her. It wasn't right. Everything tilted out of control.

He glanced at the CPS worker. The man observed every move they made, every word that was spoken. Had he noticed how close to the edge Garrett was when he found the children missing?

Anjelica moved in next to him. "Here, let me take her and you talk to Rio. I think both of us leaving his sight with all of the people, and then the caseworker showing up, was too much for him."

Garrett nodded. "You're right. One of us should have stayed with him and explained what was going on." He handed over Pilar. He moved closer and, in a low voice, whispered in Anjelica's ear, "What do we say about the grandmother?"

She peeked down at Pilar, then gave him a half-hearted smile. "I wish I knew. Let's just get him calm and in the house. Then we'll deal with what we tell him."

Warm fingertips touched his face. He wanted to capture her warmth. He was proud of himself for not grabbing her hand and pressing it against his lips. How had life gotten so complicated that he needed his crazy landlady to save him?

"I'll tell my mom that we have to deal with the children's case. She'll take care of everyone here. If I take Pilar inside, I'm pretty sure you can get your little man to follow without a fuss." Her hand went back to tending the baby.

What would she do if he leaned in and kissed her? Her deep golden eyes darted away from him, glancing over his shoulder. Ugh, Mr. Ackerman watched.

Garrett stepped back and nodded. "Go ahead and

talk to your mom. Rio and I will meet you and Pilar in the house." He made sure to say it loud enough for Rio to hear. "Celeste, you go with Ms. Anjelica."

"Yes, sir. Sorry about taking the baby for a ride."

The woman who was becoming indispensable to him and his family walked away. He wanted to call her back, to run after her. She stopped and spoke briefly with Mr. Ackerman.

The heavy weight on Garrett's shoulders stayed in place as he dropped to the ground. After waiting for a bit, he picked up the corner of the superhero blanket. Rio had his head up.

"Your sister's fine. She's in the house with Anjelica. I plan on joining them as soon as you're ready. I'm not going to leave you, Rio. Even if you can't see me, I'm here."

The boy wiped at his face and glanced at Garrett. "He's not taking us away?"

Garrett's gut twisted. "No, little man, you're mine. No one is taking you away from me."

"What about Pilar?" He scooted closer to Garrett. The edge of the blanket fell away.

How much should he tell him without causing more damage? "Pilar does have a grandmother that wants to see her. Do you know Cecilia Barrow?"

He nodded. "Grandma CeCe. She was nice." He had scooted all the way over to Garrett and wedged himself next to his leg. A couple of the small goats had wandered back into the garden, nosing around. They looked exhausted from all the running earlier. The white one made himself comfortable next to Garrett. Rio gave a soft giggle as the gray one started chewing on his ear or hair. Garrett couldn't figure out which, but he was pretty sure he needed to stop it.

Garrett had to smile. How had he found himself sitting in a country garden with a son and a goat on either side of him?

"So, little man, are you ready to go inside? I promise I'll tell you if anything is going to change for our family." He brushed back the one dark curl that flopped over Rio's eye. "That's what we are now. I didn't know you were with your mom, but now I have you and I'm not going to let anyone hurt you. You also have to tell me if you're worried or scared. Together we'll fix it. You're not alone, Rio. Do you understand?"

With a sigh carrying a hundred years of burdens, his son stood. He might be five, but he had the eyes of an old war-weary vet.

Garrett stood, dusting off his pants. With one hand he picked up the discarded blankets, and the other he held out for Rio to take. "Let's put these goats up before they eat Ms. Anjelica's new plants."

The small fingers reached for his as they put the goats up for the night. He swung Rio up, and they made their way across the yard full of people and into the house, where Mr. Ackerman waited. Garrett had to find a way to keep his family together.

Anjelica imagined Garrett wanted to hide from the world tonight. Mr. Ackerman had finished his inspection and told them everything he knew of the grandmother's claim. After he left, she and Rio had joined the family for a while and watched the bonfire burn down. Garrett sat on the porch swing holding Pilar, wrapped in a blanket.

As Anjelica climbed the steps, he opened the blanket and invited her to hide with them. Rio sat with Celeste, roasting marshmallows as her family sang songs. Settling in next to father and daughter, she bowed her head for a small prayer. *Lord, these babies deserve a place of love and peace to heal their wounds. Please let it be here, if that is Your will.*

Her heart and mind could not imagine anyone taking Pilar from her family, from Garrett.

Family by family, everyone left. Now the four of them unwound from the day's hectic activity and bad news in her art studio while Garrett played soft jazz.

As his fingers played random melodies that relaxed them, her hands shaped the wet clay as it spun on the wheel. Anjelica blocked out all the worries and focused on shaping a new vase. The sweet sounds of Garrett's saxophone floated around the room as he stood in the open doorway. Rio had his own slab of clay, and Pilar bounced in her colorful bouncer.

She stopped the pottery wheel and looked at the round wide bowl her vase had turned into.

Rio yawned as he formed what looked like a bear. Gently setting his sax to the side, Garrett smiled at his son.

"I'm not finished making Selena. I want to make Bumper, too."

"I'll put them in a plastic bag for you so you can work on them later."

Anjelica wanted to wrap all three of them in love and make the real world go away, just like they had under the family quilt. She had no power over what happened outside this home, or even the hurt and doubt inside Garrett's heart. No matter how much she wanted to.

Instead she gave him her best smile. "Can we play a little longer? They can stay here tonight. We can camp out in the playroom."

Rio's eyes went wide and he nodded. "Please."

With his troubled eyes, Garrett forced a smile. "Sounds like a plan." He lifted Pilar and she snuggled into his neck.

Anjelica worried that he didn't get enough sleep.

The landline rang. Her heart jumped. She'd forgotten about that phone. It never rang. "The answering machine'll pick it up. If it's important, I'll call back. Probably a sales call."

"Hey! Anj. It's me, Jewel. You didn't answer your cell and we need to talk." The voice on the machine belonged to one of her middle sisters. "Call me back when you get a chance. I have a gift for you." Laughter bounced out of the phone. "You are going to love me more than you do now."

Before the voice cut off, a knock on the door startled her. She glanced at Garrett. "Okay, this is getting weird. No one ever comes out here except for family." She was grateful he was here. "And they never knock. It's too late for the UPS man, and CPS has already been here."

With a nod, Garrett stood, putting his hand on the place he normally wore his gun. He shook his head and winked. "I'm sure it's fine. Stay here with the kids and I'll check it out." He turned to the dogs. "Stay."

Selena sat up straight next to Rio and watched as Garrett walked through the door. Bumper ignored the command and ran for the front door.

The barking got louder and faster before Anjelica heard the door open. Then there was a high-pitched "Coco!" followed by silence.

She heard another deep male voice join Garrett's.

"Anjelica." Garrett came to the door. "They say that they're here for their dog. Appears Bumper's real name is Coco."

Now? It had been over a month. She had started to think of Bumper as hers. Rio moved to stand next to her. With a tight smile, she took his hand and headed to meet Bumper's family.

Picking up Pilar, she stepped into the living room to find a red-haired little boy rolling on the floor with an overly excited Bumper. The little boy had the most electric-blue eyes she had ever seen.

A man kneeled next to them. He looked up at her and stood, holding out his hand. Now she had seen that shade of blue twice. The young boy had to be his son.

"Hello, I'm Dane Valdez, the new athletic director at Clear Water ISD. I met your sister at Garner State Park. She told me you had found Coco. Sorry it's so late. I had planned to come tomorrow after church, but Alex was too excited to get her back, he talked me into coming tonight." He gave them an embarrassed grin. "We thought we lost her in Dallas, but she must have slipped out of her crate when we were looking at houses last month."

The boy was now sitting up and the little dog was licking his face. "Daddy, I told you we'd find her. We can take her to our new home."

Garrett looked behind her. "Where's Rio?" He moved to the doorway. "Rio?" He looked back at her, concern in his eyes. "I don't see him or Selena."

"He was just with me."

Coach Valdez looked at her. "Does your son hide often? Alex went through a hiding phase."

"Oh, I'm the nanny. Garrett's their father."

Garrett's jaw flexed. "What if he ran—"

She didn't give him time to finish. Putting Pilar in his arms stopped him. "Here, take her. I have an idea where he's gone." She headed to the kitchen.

Garrett turned to the stranger in their house. "It's been a rough day." He gently bounced Pilar as she started fussing. "Shh. It's okay, baby girl." He followed Anjelica to the kitchen.

The father and son were close behind him.

"What's a nanny?" the boy asked his father.

"Someone that helps take care of kids in their house when the parents are working." The new coach put a hand in his pocket. "Have we come at a bad time? Jewel said she would call you and let you know." He put his free hand on his son's shoulder. "We can leave. I'll call about Coco tomorrow."

"Daddy, no! I want to take Coco home now."

Anjelica found Rio in the washroom, trying to get into the dryer for his blanket, which was almost done drying. "Rio, it's okay. Bumper is their dog and they're very happy to find her."

Rio turned and looped his arms around Selena, burying his face in her fur.

Anjelica went to her knees. "Sweetheart, they aren't taking Selena. She's yours, but Coco was just here waiting—" her throat starting burning; she could cry later, not now, not in front of Rio "—for her family to come get her. Just like your dad came and got you."

She looked out into the kitchen and smiled at Garrett's stern face. "He tried to get his blanket so he could hide Selena."

The little boy holding Bumper… Coco…stepped closer. "Rio? That's a cool name. I'm sorry we scared you. My mom gave me Coco before she died. I had promised to take care of her, but she runs away a lot. Thank you for taking care of her."

Rio walked out of the washroom, his hand tight around Selena's collar. He looked at the boy, who was a few years older than him. With several slow steps, he stood in front of Alex and patted the silky mop of a dog. "My mom gave me Selena, too. She is named after a famous singer my dad likes."

"Is your mom dead, too?"

Rio nodded.

Anjelica swallowed. "So you're moving to the area? We'll have to set up a playdate for the dogs."

Alex looked at his dad. Dane smiled. "Sounds like a great idea. Someone in the family should be dating." He chuckled at his own joke.

Steve would do that, say something lame, then laugh because he thought it was funny. The action was such a man thing to do that she had to smile at him.

"So have you moved into town yet?"

"Yep, I rented one of the Val Verde townhomes. I start at the school next week. Since you're a nanny, do you have anyone you could recommend to pick Alex up from school? In Houston they had an after-school program, but here all they offer is a Wednesday program at the church. Which is great, but I need other days, too."

"Dad, I can hang out at the gym with you."

"Alex, we've talked about this. It's not safe."

She glanced at Garrett and found a stony expression that told her nothing. She faced the coach. "Let me think about it."

Dane glanced around the room. "Do you have paper so I can write down my number?"

"Pilar has fallen asleep. I need to go get ready for work, so I'll take her to bed." He held out a free hand to Dane. "I'm the local Texas state trooper. Nice to meet you, Coach. Hope you have a winning season."

"Thanks. And thanks for keeping our dog."

"Oh, that's all Anjelica." He held out his hand for his son. "It's bedtime. Say good-night for now. It sounds like you'll be seeing them again."

Anjelica held it together long enough to see Coco out to the car with her family. With a big smile and a wave, she sent them off into the night.

Chapter Ten

Standing on the edge of the porch, Anjelica watched as the taillights disappeared. A little boy had been reunited with his dog, and she would even see them again. Happy endings were good. There was no reason for the emptiness in her heart.

She would not cry. There was no reason to cry. Heading back into the house, she went straight to Esperanza's room. At the threshold she stopped. It wasn't her daughter's room anymore. It was a playroom for two children she took care of for someone else.

Garrett rocked Pilar, his voice carrying the words to "I Will Always Love You." Rio had fallen asleep on the area rug. Selena lay next to him.

Anjelica stood there and made herself breathe. It wasn't working. Her chest pulled tight, so she bit hard on the inside of her cheek.

Garrett looked up. "So Coco is off with her family." He kissed the sweet forehead of his little girl, the little girl she might lose.

No, not hers. Pilar was not hers to lose. She belonged to Garrett. Everything she loved belonged to someone else.

A sob broke her steady breathing and she forced it back down. Rule number one, never cry in front of people; it made them feel uncomfortable.

She knew she was just a temporary caregiver of the dog and the little girl. They were never hers to begin with.

Garrett must have put Pilar down, because he was suddenly there. In the door frame with her. His large, strong hand on her arm.

"Are you all right?" He ducked his head down, trying to get her to make eye contact.

She couldn't. With a nod, she turned. Her room was too far away. She needed to get behind a closed door so she could fall apart in peace. That was how she got over Steve and Esperanza. She'd survive this, too. It was nothing compared to her other losses. *God, I'm so tired of just surviving.*

He caught her arm and gently turned her to face him. *No. No. No. Don't be nice to me. Don't talk to me.* "Don't" was all she managed. She didn't have the strength to pull away from the comfort he offered.

"Anjelica, it's okay." One tug and he had his arms wrapped around her. She was cocooned against his warmth.

That was it—the fight was over. Her right hand went under his arm and flattened against his shirt. Under the material, hard muscles covered his ribs, which protected the heart she could feel beating. Her other hand balled into a fist and pressed against his upper chest. The pain and fear that had been buried for the last few hours boiled up and poured over her well-tended walls. Poor Garrett. She sobbed.

One arm held her close, his hand soothing her hair.

The other covered her angry fist and held it close to his chest. He whispered something, but she couldn't hear it over her own heart breaking.

Her greatest fear had happened. She broke down sobbing and couldn't stop. Her whole body went numb. Without Garrett holding her up, she'd have been a puddle on the rug.

Her feet went out from under her. Garrett, with one free arm, swept her up and carried her to the giant red overstuffed rocking chair.

Unaware of how long they sat there, Anjelica calmed down to hiccups. She sat up and wiped at his Marines T-shirt. It was so saturated with her tears that she had no chance of getting it dry.

"Sorry." The single word crawled up her raw throat. Her eyes ached. Her whole body felt beaten and bruised. "Sorry" was all she managed.

"Stop. You have nothing to be sorry for." His thumb wiped her cheeks. "Truthfully? You held me together as much as I held you." In the moonlit room, the sharp edges of his profile were highlighted as his head went back. He drove out a long heavy sigh.

"I didn't want to put Pilar in her bed. I didn't want to let her out of my arms. The thought that they might take her away…" He closed his eyes. "It's eating at me. Then Mr. America shows up to take your dog. Rio freaks. If you hadn't come in, I would've stayed in the rocker all night holding her."

He caressed her hair, his fingers moving in a soothing rhythm. She looked up at him and found his eyes still closed. If it weren't for the steady movement of his hands, she would have thought he had gone to sleep. Her grief had been so consuming she hadn't really thought about his worries. He was so fiercely protective that she should have realized he would want to fix her heart-aches.

She touched the firm pulse on the base of his neck with the tips of her finger. A soft sorrow of loss burned at the edges of her chest. Would this bring on his night-mares?

Her gaze took in the beautiful outline of his strong features. "I'm really sorry."

A growl rumbled from his throat. "Don't say you're sorry. Then I'd have to say it, and right now I'm too angry for a sincere apology."

Okay, so maybe it was time to change the topic. "Did you just call Coach Valdez Mr. America?"

His lips pulled into a lopsided smirk. "I guess I could have called him Mr. Football or All-American."

She sat up, away from his warmth, and pushed her palm against his chest. "Are you jealous?"

"He took your dog and tried to steal my nanny." He sounded like a three-year-old.

Was he serious? "You're messing with me, aren't you?"

"Maybe." A grin told her she'd been played.

"Well, I am more of the strong-silent-music-man kind of girl." She settled back down against his shoulder. Here the world felt right.

"He worked hard to get your number. Was all slick about it, too. It's all about the dogs and kids, really? Did you fall for that?"

A strong hand with long fingers, a musician's hand, turned her face to him. The pulse in his neck picked up a faster beat. She watched, holding her breath as he lowered his head.

A tentative touch at first. His lips touched hers, asking for permission. Leaning in, she gave it.

The kiss washed over her. Even though his lips stayed on her lips with a gentle pressure, her skin tightened. Sensations buried long ago came back to life.

From her bottom lip to the corner of her mouth, he explored every nuance of a kiss. She missed feeling cherished. But this was wrong. She pulled back. He let her go. Her traitorous heart grumbled that he didn't even try to stop her. On uncertain legs, she stood.

"It's been a rough day. It's also been a long time since I was kissed and I… I just…" She what? Didn't remember it being so all-consuming? That didn't seem fair to Steve's memory. Her skin tightened with goose bumps. Shivering, she wrapped her arms around her waist. Arms that had just been around Garrett.

He was not her type. She put more distance between them.

He stood and ran his fingers through his hair. "You're right. I need to get to work and put this day behind me. We need to focus on the children."

She nodded.

"I think it would be better for the kids to stay in their room tonight."

Another nod was all she could manage.

He gathered the children and Selena, and paused in the kitchen.

"Night, Anjelica."

She followed him to the door and watched as he went up the stairs. Was Garrett right in his opinion that the new coach had been trying to get a real date with her? If she was smart, she would call Dane Valdez, but now the thought of going out with another man seemed wrong.

Garrett was a lawman. One day he might not come home. There would be no saving her heart again.

Being alone was not a new feeling, but tonight, after being in Garrett's arms, it left her empty. Like those nights after she lost Steve and Esperanza. She'd been so empty with no one to hold.

Her phone vibrated. Looking at the screen, she saw it was Jewel. She had missed three calls already. She needed the distraction.

"Hi, Jewel. Sorry I missed your calls. What's up?"

"You just need to say thank you. I sent the most gorgeous guy your way. He's new in town, so you don't have to worry that we're related to him." Her closest sister laughed. "He also lost his wife, so you don't have to worry about the awkward dead-spouse talk."

Anjelica shook her head and grinned. One of the things she always loved about Jewel: she didn't tiptoe around the elephant in the room. Some people thought she was too blunt, but it was nice being with someone who just said what she was thinking.

"Yes, I met him. He came over tonight to pick up Bum... Coco."

"Oh no! He said he would drive over on Sunday! How did you look? Isn't he yummy and so sweet? He has already volunteered to work with the Christian Athletic Fellowship. And that boy of his is too cute. Did you hit it off? Did you trade numbers? I was hoping to give you a heads-up so you'd make sure to look good, not that you could ever look bad. I mean, on your worst days, you still outshine the rest of us. He said he needed someone to watch his son after school."

"Breathe, girl." As much as all the matchmaking

upset her, she couldn't help but smile. Her sister had the best intentions, like everyone else in her life.

"Oh, sorry. So, did it go well?"

"He just came to pick up the dog. His son wouldn't let up until they stopped by. Rio got upset and hid, but we worked it out and plan on setting up a playdate so we can visit Coco."

"Wow, one meeting and you already have a date. I knew y'all would be perfect for each other."

"It's not a date."

"Um…let me see. Prearranged time and place to meet with a man. Sounds like a date to me. I'd take it."

"Then take it. Listen, I'm not sure about a man who waited so long to find his dog. I mean, it's been over a month. They just now started looking for her?" She put the phone on speaker and started braiding her hair. It was nice talking to someone she didn't have to over-analyze every feeling with.

Jewel continued. "They were down here looking for property to buy. You know, he's a new athletic direc-tor for next year. They thought Bumper, or Coco, was asleep in her crate."

One quick breath and she was still talking. "They thought they had lost her for good. But when they actu-ally got down here, he did some more digging. Being a single dad and relocating can't be easy. And you know that dog is crazy. So, I would say it's not his fault."

"Garrett didn't even know he had kids a month ago and he still remembered to get their dog."

"Oh, so that's how it is. Garrett's a better dad. I thought you were never going to date another man in uniform with a gun strapped to him, no matter how good-looking. And I quote."

"That's not how quotes work and I'm pretty sure I didn't even say that." Now she was starting to get a headache. "Anyway, I'm not interested in Garrett that way. His kids need full-time attention, and that's all I have time for right now."

"You might officially be a lost cause. You're surrounded by great-looking men that love their children and you don't have the time. I give up. You're the one that says trust God's will. Not sure you really believe that."

Anjelica flopped back on her pillow. "You might be right, but I won't rush anything."

"I'm not saying to start planning a wedding or even kissing—I'm saying you could go on a date. No kids or dogs or any other animal, just you and an adult male."

Anjelica groaned, thinking of the kiss she should *not* have been thinking about.

"Anjelica Ortega-Garza! You've been kissing someone. It has to be that gorgeous state trooper."

"It was an accident. We both agreed not to go there again."

"Accidental kiss? How does that happen? You fell and your lips landed on his? I know you. The only man you had ever locked lips with was Steve. So what happened, when and how was it?"

"All that matters is that it's never happening again. I'm not strong enough to live with the uncertainty of his job."

"He kissed you tonight? After you met the hot new coach? What a man thing to do."

Anjelica closed her eyes and sighed. "I tell you what I'm worried about and all you heard was your theory of why he kissed me? I've got to get some sleep. I'll see you Sunday."

"I'm sorry, sis. You know we all love you, right?"

"Yeah, I do. Love you. Night."

Anjelica put her phone on the nightstand and pulled the comforter down. No one got it. They all thought she was strong. They didn't see her real self. She was one small heartbreak away from a total meltdown.

What she didn't know was whether it would come from Garrett or his kids.

Chapter Eleven

Garrett stood on the balcony. Moonlight dusted his sanctuary. Two nights ago, he had experienced the most nerve-racking kiss in his life, and now they were pretending it had never happened.

He needed to start looking for a new place to live. Peace was more important now than ever. Living so close to her was not calming in any way. How much longer would he be able to stay here, anyway? Rio and Pilar would need more room as they grew.

Leaning on the rail, he took another sip of coffee. The light of her studio shone past her porch. She enjoyed listening to his music while she worked. He stepped inside to pick up a sax. The act of creating arrangements used to calm him; when did it become about her?

Before he could produce one note, a cry came from the nursery.

Picking the fussy baby up, he pressed his lips to Pilar's forehead. An unnatural warmth came off her skin. She had a fever. Heat came off her little body.

He felt better equipped this time. Between the parenting classes and Anjelica, he knew he could take care of her tonight. Taking her temperature, he found it too high and gave her the liquid medicine like Anjelica had shown him.

In the rocking chair, she settled across his chest. That worked for a while, but she started crying again. She was dry and didn't want her bottle. It wasn't her teeth this time.

What if she was really sick? Should he take her to the emergency room, or would that be overreacting? Rio stayed by his side. His son somehow got wedged between Garrett's leg and the edge of the chair. He was sound asleep. Pilar whimpered on his shoulder.

There was no way he would be able to move if he needed to get up. She kept coughing, and her breathing didn't sound natural.

He leaned his head all the way back and looked at the ceiling.

Pilar coughed again. Now it sounded like there was something in her chest. She lifted her head and started whimpering again. Restless, she squirmed until she had wiggled out of his hold. It was hard to keep a gentle grip.

Pilar took hold of the bottle like she was starving when he offered it to her. They were supposed to stay on a feeding schedule, but if it would make her stop crying, he was all for it.

After a couple of pulls, she screamed and threw the bottle across the room. Rio woke up and went after it without hesitation. Rubbing his sleepy eyes with one hand, he offered her the bottle with the other. She slapped it, bowed her back and cried louder.

Garrett glanced at the door. Anjelica was just a staircase away. She would know what to do, but she wasn't working now and he needed to learn how to do this on his own.

He tried to ease out of the rocker so he could get his phone, but Pilar threw herself back so hard he almost dropped her.

He held her with both arms, stroking her wild curls. "Shh...baby girl. We'll figure out what's wrong and take care of it."

Rio followed him to the living room and watched as he called the nurse hotline Pilar's doctor had given him. Maybe the boy was starting to trust him; he hadn't run to Anjelica yet.

After he went through all the symptoms with the nurse, she recommended that he take her to a small bathroom and fill it with steam. She was having a hard time breathing, and now he knew to feel for the rattling in her chest.

The nurse also made him an appointment for the morning.

Sitting on the edge of the tub, he almost fell asleep. Rio put a hand on Garrett's arm. The concern and old wisdom in the young eyes brought a wave of guilt.

Garrett forced a smile. "I'm fine, little man, just a little tired. The important thing is to get your sister comfortable so she can get some sleep. Tomorrow we'll take her to the doctor to see if she needs any medicine."

Rio nodded. A soft knock on the front door had them both turning.

"Garrett? Rio? Is everything okay?" Anjelica had come up the stairs to them. "I thought I heard Pilar crying."

The tension keeping his muscles coiled tight relaxed. Anjelica would know what to do. "We're all in the bathroom. Pilar couldn't breathe well, so I'm making steam." He adjusted Pilar to his other arm. She was relaxing and her breathing was already easier. "Come on in."

Anjelica eased into the small space. She smiled at Rio. "Selena is standing guard at the door." She sat on the other side of the small tub. "Why didn't you call me?"

"It's your night off, and after all the extra time you put in the last few days, I wanted to prove I could do this myself."

The steam in the room had Anjelica's hair hanging in loose curls. "I didn't do very well and ended up calling the nurse helpline. I'm not sure I'll ever get this parenting thing down."

With a soft laugh, she shook her head. "That's what good parents do—they call for help when they need it."

He nodded. If he kept looking at Anjelica, he would start thinking about that kiss again. It had been so long since he spent this much time with a woman. It had him off-kilter.

"I've got a doctor appointment for her in the morning. I need to call and get someone to take my shift."

"I can take her."

"No, I'm the one responsible for her. I'll—"

"Garrett, no one expects you to do this all by yourself. That's why I'm here. My family means it when they say to call them and ask for help. They know kids." She reached for him. Tender fingers stroked his wrist before she wrapped her hand around his. "They probably knew about this steam shower trick. You have a whole team and these babies deserve that. Don't deny them or yourself out of stubbornness or pride."

"There are single moms that do this all the time. My mom somehow managed to raise me and my sister without any help."

"That's not how it should be, though. Everyone should have a mighty Ortega army." She let go of him and moved to touch Pilar's forehead. "Look, I think it worked. She's fallen asleep and her skin feels normal."

He adjusted her on his shoulder, pressing his palm against her back. "No rattling. We did it, Rio. We helped her feel better." He sighed and stood.

Rio, leaning against Anjelica, smiled up at him.

"Come on, little man—let's put y'all back to bed."

As they headed to the nursery, Pilar gave a soft snore, followed by a hiccup from her crying. His heart twisted, and there was a horrible burning in his throat. It would be so easy to fail at parenting, and the stakes were too high. How could he be responsible for not only their well-being but their full development into adult life?

Laying her in the crib, he pressed his lips to her forehead. His hands looked so big as he tucked her in and said a little prayer. After making sure she would stay asleep, he picked up the rejected bottle and headed to the kitchen.

Anjelica poured milk into a pan. "I thought some warm milk would help us all get back to sleep. Rio, do you want chocolate in yours?"

With an energetic nod, his curls bounced around his face.

Garrett laughed. "Would the chocolate override the benefits of the warm milk? Rio, use your words."

"Yes, please."

Anjelica grunted with a smirk as she opened the pantry door. "Would you stir the milk?" she asked as she dug through the selves.

After checking the milk, Garrett turned his back to them and rinsed out Pilar's bottle. Working with Anjelica made everything better. There was no way he could have tackled fatherhood without her.

A loud crash and a child's cry had him spinning around to face the source of such a sound. He lunged at the small boy standing too close to the threat.

Arms wrapped, holding the warm body to his chest, he rolled up against the wall. The boy's clothes were wet. Blood? Oh no! He was too late again.

"Garrett?"

Focus, Garrett. To keep everyone safe, you have to stay aware. The boy was crying. He was alive. Opening his eyes, he studied the boy. His son, Rio. Alive. Not... He blinked to clear his mind of the child he'd failed to protect in Afghanistan.

Garrett blinked. "Rio? Why does he have blood on him?"

"Garrett. It's just milk. There's no blood. Let me check him to make sure he didn't get burned."

Slowly getting to his feet, he checked Rio. "Did I hurt you?" He gently pulled the wet shirt off his son as he checked for any marks on the tender skin. "I don't think the milk had gotten hot yet." He ran his hand along the thin arms. "I'm so sorry, Rio. I didn't mean to scare you. I thought you were in danger."

Anjelica knelt beside them with a towel in her hand. "Come here, Rio. I'll dry you off. Your dad has a hero complex and is always ready to jump in and save us. Even from a pan of spilled milk." She looked the boy straight in the eyes. "Now, I do have a rule you need to follow so your dad doesn't go all ninja on us anymore. Stay away from the stove and don't ever reach up there and touch a pot, even if you're trying to help. When you are tall enough, I'll teach you how to handle the pots. Do you understand?"

Garrett closed his eyes. "I left the pot handle facing out." He reached for his son and pushed the damp curls back. "I'm sorry about that, Rio. I'll be more careful in the future."

Big gray eyes blinked. "You're not going to hit me?"

Anjelica stopped a soft gasp midway and covered her mouth.

"Rio, look at me. I will never hit you. If you do something wrong, we'll talk about it and figure out the consequence." How could a grown man treat a small child that way?

He stood and ran both hands through his hair. His heart and gut got so twisted he couldn't think. "Anjelica, do you mind washing him off and putting him to bed? The consequence tonight is no hot chocolate for any of us. I didn't put the handle in the right place, and Rio messed with something on the stove."

Anjelica looked at him with her bottom lip stuck out. "I wanted hot chocolate." She winked at him, and then her mouth eased into a smile.

Rio stood with his head down. "I'm sorry, Anjelica."

"We want you to be safe, Rio. No more touching anything on the stove or in the oven, okay?"

"Yes, ma'am."

"I'll wash him off and tuck him into bed." With a tenderness and understanding he did not deserve, Anjelica nodded at him while she herded Rio to the small bathroom.

He went to the sink and splashed cool water on his face. With a drink in hand, he slid into a chair at the small table. The juice vibrated as he raised it to his lips. He set the glass back down and pressed his forehead into his palms. His elbows dug hard into the tabletop, trying to stop the shaking.

He couldn't do this. Reality slipped too easily from his mind. The kids were already too fragile. They needed someone they could rely on, and it wasn't him.

Anjelica helped Rio settle into his makeshift bed under Pilar's crib. Leaving, she paused in the door frame.

The whispered notes of Garrett's saxophone floated through the air. Eyes closed, she allowed the music to wrap around her.

God, give me the words to help heal all the hurts and confusion I know Garrett is trying to fight alone. Let him know You have him.

Moving all the way into the room, she listened. The pain and love moved from him through the sax and into the night. He stopped, setting the instrument back in its case, his profile highlighted by the moon.

"Sorry. When I don't know what else to do, I play."

"Don't apologize—it was beautiful. I do the same with my art. Getting my fingers in the clay helps me focus. Some of my best conversations with God happen in my studio."

He nodded. There had to be a way to reach him but still keep her distance. After that kiss, she needed to move carefully.

"Are you okay? You had another episode. Was it the noise of the pot that set it off?"

His jaw went stone hard as he stared out into the night. That was not the response she hoped for. "Garrett."

"I don't think I can do this. Maybe she would be better off with her grandmother. We don't know her. She might be perfect for Pilar."

Anger surged through her veins. "Now you're being an idiot."

That got his attention. Tonight his eyes looked more gray than green as they narrowed at her. "That's your pep talk?"

"It's one in the morning. Being a parent is tough and you *will* make mistakes. You apologize, make it better and move on. You don't give up on them, or yourself."

She crossed her arms over her chest. The need to touch him, to soothe him, would only get her in trouble. *God, I need You to lead this.* "You know her place is with you and Rio. This is where she belongs. Are you going to give up Rio, too?"

Garrett turned from her and braced his hands on the railing. Clouds slid over the moon, engulfing the balcony in darkness.

Not able to stay away from him, she walked outside and placed her hand on his back. He tightened. "You are her father. Imagine packing her things and handing her over to them. People that didn't want her a month ago. People that don't want her brother. She's your daughter now. Do you think you could really just hand her over?"

He had a restlessness about him tonight. The ends of his hair stood up in different directions from his hands repetitively fussing with it. She loved how adorable it made him.

Not able to resist, she brushed it into place with her fingers, bringing her closer to him. The contact warmed her whole arm and traveled to her traitorous heart. Stepping back, she looked into the apartment. "Where's her sippy cup?"

"In the cabinet with the other cups. Why?" He followed her.

"If she has an ear infection, sucking on the bottle creates pressure. That was why she kept throwing it away. It hurt. We don't want her to get dehydrated, though. So when she wakes up, make sure she gets some water."

Turning, she had it in her hand, ready for him. "Are you over the delusion that giving her up is good for her?"

He grinned and nodded. The look made her want to cry. Why couldn't love be easy like it was in high school? "Your daughter is waiting for you, and I'm going back to my house. Good night, Garrett. I'll see you at seven."

One step at a time, she made it back to her room. The mountains of pillows and handmade quilts offered no comfort. She had lost her heart, and she doubted it would return unbroken.

Even if she gave in and accepted a lawman as her future, she didn't think his heart would be available.

As he filled the cup, he held it steady. That was an improvement. *Okay, God, You got me this far. What do I do now to keep them safe?*

Was he the best place for them? Shoulder leaning against the door, he paused. Rio's voice was low but clear. He was talking to his sister.

"I think it's going to be okay, Pilar. Our new daddy is nice and he doesn't yell or hit us, even when you cry a lot or when we mess up."

Every muscle tightened as he held himself still. The need to hit the man who caused all that pain was a waste of energy, but it still burned deep in his gut. Garrett heard a noise he couldn't identify.

"You like your room?" From the sound of his voice, Rio had moved.

Pilar answered with gurgling and the sweetest laughter that twisted his heart. How many of these late-night talks had happened when he thought they were sound asleep?

"Yeah, but it's for girls," Rio replied as if she had spoken in a clear language. "Maybe at your next birthday, if everything is still good, I'll stay in my bed. It's a race car, for a boy. Don't worry—I'll stay here as long as you need me. I promise not to leave you."

Garrett leaned the back of his head against the wall. Now he wanted to hug them close and cry over all the things he couldn't fix or wipe clean. Rio sounded like an old man, not a five-year-old. These were his children. His family. His responsibility to protect. His throat tightened. He could barely breathe.

Anjelica was right. He would never willingly turn either of these kids over to someone else. They were his. He was their father, and it was going to stay that way no matter what he had to do to make it happen.

He started forming a plan that would keep them all together. A plan to keep the kids safe. He hated that they might need to be protected from him. But they needed someone who could love them without hang-ups. Someone who would be steady when he fell apart. He imagined it would look better at court if he was married.

He softly knocked before going all the way in the

room. He didn't want to scare Rio. "How's our princess doing?"

His son had gone mute again. Well, he'd talk to him when he was ready.

Now that he had the beginnings of a plan, the ache in his belly eased. He would trust that God had brought the kids to him for a reason. And as soon as he got Anjelica alone, he'd talk to her about the plan. This could work.

Chapter Twelve

Leaving the doctor's office, Garrett knew more about nebulizers than he did his own truck engine. Pilar breathed with ease now, and that was all that mattered. An antibiotic for the ear infection and a sucker for her brave brother made everyone better.

In Anjelica's house, they settled the kids in the playroom for their naps so he could head into work. This was the perfect time to talk to her about his plan. So why was he nervous? It was simple, and he couldn't imagine her not going along.

Then again, he didn't have a great track record in understanding women. Jake would be a good one to talk to first. See what he thought. He took another drink of coffee as Anjelica walked into the room. He needed to talk to her and stop putting it off.

"They're doing great. Fell asleep right away." For the trip to Kerrville today, she wore her hair in a ponytail.

"Before I head to work, there's something I want to talk to you about." He rubbed his jaw. "Want to sit in the living room?"

Her eyebrows wrinkled. "Sure. Is something wrong?"

He waited for her to sit on the chair with the chicken pillow. Chickens—he never understood that. Glancing up, he realized she was staring at him, waiting.

"I'm worried I can't be here for the kids the way they need me." He paused, not sure what words to use to make her understand how important this was to him and the future of his family.

She tilted her head as if not understanding his words. "You've done a great job helping the kids feel safe." Standing, she left the chicken chair and sat next to him. "You were in a war zone—the things that happened, I can't even imagine. I've done some research and I think you need to find another vet, one you can talk to."

Keeping his face relaxed, he tried to hide the frustration at her suggestion. "Torres already suggested Reeves. I don't really see how that'll help." He stood and paced a few times before stopping at the window. "You've seen two episodes I've had where I lost track of reality. I can control it. I have for the last five years."

He moved to the bookshelf full of photos of her life. He wanted those kinds of roots for his little family. How much to tell her? Knots tightened in his gut when he even thought of what happened all those years ago. At times it seemed like yesterday. "I have a very important question to ask you. There's... I need you to know what happened so there aren't any misunderstandings."

She joined him, but when she reached out to touch his arm, he stepped away.

He never talked about what happened. There was no point. Not even to the required therapist. He told them just enough so they thought he felt a normal amount of guilt in order to get a clean bill of health.

"In Afghanistan one of our jobs was basically public relations. Establishing trust with people in the area. One of the things we started doing was playing soccer with the local kids."

He paced behind the sofa, watching his boots cover the area rug as he went back and forth. A cold sweat coated his tight skin. She didn't need to know everything. Just enough so she would understand why the kids couldn't count on him 100 percent of the time.

"I actually enjoyed that part. It was like a little piece of home. Kicking the ball around with the kids. One boy I got closer to. He was about ten. I shared the candy my sister would send me. Somewhere along the way, he became mine. We both had a single mom and a sister to protect, being the only male in our families."

Interlocking his fingers behind his head, he sat down again and arched his back until he saw the ceiling. "Early one morning, I was running late to the field. A couple of the other guys were already there. The wind was sweeping sand across the flat landscape. I saw..."

He hadn't spoken the boy's name since giving the initial reports. Everything inside twisted at the memory of the tracks of his tears on dust-covered cheeks.

"As soon as I saw him, I knew something was wrong."

He licked his lips. He had worked so hard to shut down these images, locking them in a box and burying the incident so deep it wouldn't impede his life in Texas.

"Garrett?" So soft, her voice lashed at the fog that started to creep through his brain, the fingers of hopelessness reaching to control him. She moved to sit next to him, her hands clasped in her lap. "It's all right."

"No, it's not. They had gotten to him. Probably

threatened his family." He should have known. Should have warned the kid. Done something to protect him.

He clenched his fists. The tension caused his arms to shake. "I knew. In my gut I knew what was about to happen, and I just stood there."

Warm skin intertwined with his. He took a deep breath and focused on her touch. She anchored him back down into the living room in Clear Water, Texas.

"He stood on the far side of the field. Kids ran around him, laughing as their loose shirts flapped in the wind. A few of the other guys that played with the kids were there."

He tried to swallow, but his throat tightened. Dry, no moisture. The kid needed him, and he had just stood there. Frozen.

Her hand squeezed his wrist. He took a chance to look at her. He found her gaze searching his face. "It wasn't your fault."

"I just stood there and did nothing when the device went off."

"For how long?"

"What?"

"From the time you got there to the time it… How long were you there? What could you have done?" Tears hovered on her bottom lashes. Her lips drew taut. "It's unimaginable. But how could you have changed what happened? How does it make you less of a father? That's what this is about, right? You explaining why you can't be the perfect father."

There was no way she would ever understand, and that was okay. She was protected from that kind of evil. "I should've known he'd be marked by the men hiding behind legitimate business. He was mine and they used him."

"I still don't understand how you could have changed that day."

"When the… I should have—" he pushed the hair back from his forehead and closed his eyes "—protected him. He was mine. Killed on my watch. Along with two other kids and a marine. A buddy of mine lost his arm. I didn't even have a scratch. I just stood there on the other side of the field."

"So what could you have done? Run across the field and disabled the bomb?"

He sighed and stood. He needed space. This was why he never bothered to talk about it. "You don't get it. I failed to protect them. I could've at least run to him and wrapped him up against me. Used my body to absorb the explosion. The other marine would've made it home. Boys would've seen their next birthdays. He wouldn't have died standing alone and scared."

"And you would have died. It's tragic what happened, and horrible. But if you weren't here, what would have happened to Rio and Pilar? They are safe and together because you are here, protecting them."

"That's not the point." He heard her move. She followed him to the window.

"You're right—it's not fair. The things that happen, why they happen, don't make sense. You can't focus on one part without looking at the big picture."

His jaw started to hurt.

"What you saw was horrific. Your strength amazes me."

Her hand rested on his shoulder blade. He stiffened, fighting the urge to turn and wrap himself in her warmth. He had been so cold for so long.

"I'm not strong." He stepped away from her and leaned against the frame of the window seat, trying to look casual. "You're the hero. The one with the real strength. You've kept your faith and your smile through the loss of your husband and baby."

Not able to resist any longer, he reached out and touched her wet cheek with the back of his knuckles. "You, Anjelica Ortega-Garza, are the hero. That's why..."

Long, restless steps took him away from her and back to the sofa. Once again sitting, he gestured for her to join him on the couch. She moved to the red chicken chair instead.

"Okay. There's a reason I wanted to tell you this. It wasn't about getting your sympathy, but for you to understand my limits and why the proposal I'm about to give you is so important to Rio and Pilar. I need you to know why I can't do this alone."

She sat forward, her elbows resting on her knees. "You're not alone."

"But I need a permanent safeguard for the kids." He feared she didn't understand what he was trying to tell her. "Sometimes I see Rio and all I see is...the boy I lost. I want to set up a safety net."

"You have me and all the Ortegas."

"Right, but you're just the nanny, the hired help. I know you're more than that, but in a court of law, that's all they'll see. A single bachelor. If... When I get custody, you'll have no legal rights." He rubbed his palms against his eye sockets. *Just say it. It's a good plan.*

Leaning forward, he looked her straight in the eyes.

"I want us to get married. It will give us an edge over a single grandmother Then you can adopt them and they'll have you as their legal parent. You'll be their mother."

Her mouth open and her eyes wide, she recoiled as if a scorpion had fallen from the ceiling.

Give her time to process. He licked his lips again.

Like a spring, she popped up. She moved around and put the chair between them, looking at him as if…as if he had gone crazy.

"Did you just ask me to marry you so I can be the mother of your children?"

He wasn't feeling good about the tone of her voice. "Yes, it's the surest way I can think of to provide them with everything they need. Unconditional love and security. We'd all live here in this house. Children need those things, especially Rio and Pilar. They need you."

"You want us to get married so that I can be a legal guardian of your children and provide the love that you can't give them? Because you want them to live in my home?"

"It's not that I don't love them. I just can't love them the way you can. You do love them, don't you?" Standing, he went around the overstuffed chair and stopped in front of her. He had to get her to understand. "This is a perfect solution for the kids. It's not all an act for your job, is it?"

"Garrett… I do love them." She touched his face. Tears hung on her eyelashes. "You're such an incredible man. You never hesitated to bring two children into your life once you knew they needed you."

Her gaze roamed over his face as if looking for something she'd lost. "That might be the biggest problem. I could easily love you. My heart would be wrapped up in you so fast…but you don't want my heart, do you? You just want me to love your children." She stepped back and shook her head. "I can't be in that kind of marriage. It would destroy me."

Heat burned his gut. He had to fix this. He had to make her stay. "I can't be a father without you."

"You want to love everyone at arm's length because it's safer for you."

Now there was a hint of anger in her voice. Somehow he'd messed this all up and needed to fix it. "It's not about me."

"Yes, this is all about you. How *you* might fail them. How *you* can't love them enough. How *you* can't be the perfect father. Guess what—humans make mistakes. None of us are perfect, not a single one of us. It can't be an excuse to stop trying. To stop giving. Your kids deserve all of you."

She crossed her arms around her waist. A sob broke up her breathing. "Whoever your wife will be deserves all of you. Not a watered-down shadow of the man you're afraid of being."

The tears fell freely now. "You have to figure out how to let people in and trust them with your broken parts, or you'll never be whole enough to love someone."

"You want me to say I love you? Should I have brought flowers and gotten on one knee? That's what I did for Viviana. Would that make all the ugliness better?"

Restless, he started pacing behind the sofa. Each step full of the anger at all the people he had loved. "My mother loved my father. She did everything to keep him. She also spent hours crying. I loved Viviana with every fiber of my being and told her that every time we were together. I gave her everything I had, and look where that got us. A mess with a little boy who didn't trust the world enough to speak."

He stopped and glared at Anjelica. She wanted something that didn't exist. "What I'm offering you is respect and friendship. I could say the words if it'll make you feel better. But we both know they don't mean anything."

Her eyes were now red and puffy as she wiped at the tears. He stood, feet planted. He would not give in to her. That was what he always did with his mother and Viviana. "I won't let you manipulate me with tears."

A rough laugh sounded from her soft lips. "Oh, Garrett. I hate that I'm crying right now." She wiped her hand on her jeans. "Believe me, if I could, I would dry them up and walk out. I would, but I can't. I also can't make you feel something you don't. I do love your children."

Her hand motioned toward the nursery. "They own my heart as if I'd given birth to them myself, but I will not marry you just to be their mother. You have been through some inhumane events. Please talk to someone about it. Someone who will understand everything you've been through."

"I don't need to talk to anyone." He crossed his arms over his chest.

"There's nothing wrong with asking for help! I spent many hours talking and listening in a grief group."

That sounded worse than his nightmares. He looked at the pictures on the shelf behind her. "There are parts of me so broken I can't give you the kind of marriage you want. I think there might be a war in me I can't win."

"I believe that God has the ability to fix the most broken clay pot. If only we decide to give it to Him." Turning her back to him, she walked over to her books. "I understand broken. I've been there in my own way." Her fingertips brushed along the spines until she came to a black leather book.

With the book in hand, she stood a foot from him. He could smell sweet vanilla and gardens.

"Here, take this. I've marked passages that helped me. Without God, I don't think I could have gotten out of bed. Let alone love again. I do see a marriage in my future, but it will be with two whole hearts that aren't afraid of scars and broken pieces."

His jaw ached with tension. "So why do you keep your scars covered? Are you ashamed of them?" As soon as he asked the question, he wanted to take it back.

The hurt in her eyes cut him. Her delicate hand went to the base of her throat, flattening the multicolored scarf she wore today. Her dark skin went a tint lighter.

Arm extended to her, he needed to take the pain away. The pain he had caused. She stepped out of his reach. "I'm sorry. That was a jerk thing to say." His arms ached to hold her. The years living with Viviana had taught him how words could hurt. He didn't want to be that person. "I'm sorry."

"No, you're right. I still have broken parts and fears I don't want to face. Life is not easy." She pulled the scarf off and wrapped it around her hand. "The scar is from the car accident that caused the death of my baby girl."

He couldn't stand it, being so far away from her after he was the one who caused her suffering. As gently as he could, he pulled her to the couch. She wouldn't look at him, but she followed.

"You don't owe me anything. It was none of my business to begin with, and I'm truly sorry for what I said. If there was a way to take it back, I would."

"I know." She shrugged. "As many times as I've asked for forgiveness, you'd think I'd be over it by now, but you're right. There's a part of me that hangs on to the guilt. They delivered the news about Steve. I shouldn't have been driving, but nothing would stop me. I'll probably never get completely over it."

Slowly, Anjelica rose and walked over to the picture of her late husband. "I promised Steve I would take care of our baby girl and made him promise not to play the hero. He pledged to come back home to us. We both failed."

She stood silent for a while before turning back to him. Maybe this was it—she would see how life was too short and she would change her mind about his proposal.

"Everyone kept telling me he died a hero. How I should be so proud of him." Her mouth was firm, all tenderness gone. Golden eyes now clear of tears, she stood straight, her chin up. "To tell the truth, I was angry. Another reason a marriage between us would never work. I can't live with another hero. A man that rushes into danger with a gun strapped to his body."

She shook. "Your guilt is you didn't react fast enough. That you didn't die that day and others did." A lopsided pull of her lips that formed a warped illusion of a smile became the saddest expression. "I can't sit at home wondering whose life you might save at the risk of your own. That sounds really selfish of me, but I can't do that again. We each have broken parts." She played with the edge of her scarf. "I realize it's so much easier to say 'hand it over to God' than to actually hand everything over. Yes, there are bits and pieces of me that clutter the floor, but I know my limits." A sigh heavy with sadness left her lips. "Marriage to a lawman that won't even love me? That's a line I cannot cross, not even for those precious babies."

There was a new weight on her shoulders he feared he had placed there.

She shrugged. "Maybe Steve didn't love me enough to play it safe, but he did love me completely while I had him. I deserve that kind of love, and so do your kids."

Picking up her sweater on the back of the chair, she looked at the pictures on her shelf. "I'm tired. I think I'll take a nap while Rio and Pilar are asleep. I'll have them up in your apartment with dinner ready when you get home. As soon as you get in, I'm leaving. I think I'm going to stay with my mom for a little bit. I need some clear boundaries."

Acid burned his stomach. "Don't worry about dinner. I can make it. Do what you need to. Will you be here for breakfast in the morning?"

She shook her head. "I'll be here right before you leave for your shift in the afternoon. I think our morning cups of coffee need to stop."

He wanted to yell and throw something. Instead of guaranteeing she would always be here for the kids, he'd pushed her away. He had to make her stay, but he didn't know how.

Maybe he did need to talk to someone. He looked at the Bible she had given him. Pink flags of paper stuck out. She was so different from his mother and Viviana that he didn't know what to say or do to make it right.

"All right." He wanted to tell her no, that he needed

her as much as the kids did, but she made it clear. A personal relationship would not work between them. Why couldn't she just let things stay the same? Teeth clenched, he fought the longing to reach out to her. Why did she want love to complicate their relationship?

She glanced at the clock. "It's time for you to leave if you're going to get to work on time."

With a nod, he turned and headed out the door. Making sure the screen door didn't slam, he eased it closed. He stood on the other side and watched her disappear into her bedroom.

The Bible she gave him was still in his hand. She claimed he would find answers in this leather-bound book. The plan had been to move into the future together, but now it was even more insecure.

He'd thought his proposal would be a win for both of them. Well, for him, anyway. All she would be getting in the trade was a messed-up husband who couldn't love her and two kids who weren't hers. She was smart to run, but it didn't mean he had to like it.

Anjelica buried her head in her pillow to muffle any sound and sobbed. Her whole body shook.

Without meaning to, Garrett had ripped her heart out.

She was in danger of losing her resolve to stay away from heroes. Telling him she could easily fall in love with him was a lie.

Without a doubt, she already loved him. In so many ways this feeling was deeper than the easy friendly first love she'd had for Steve. They had grown up together. They were friends years before they dated.

Garrett made her feel things in a new way, and that made him even more dangerous. He was so intense.

Raising her head, she pulled the tissues from her nightstand and attempted to clean her cheeks.

Her phone vibrated. Ignoring it, she covered her face with a pillow. If it was Garrett, she might give in and ask him to come back. It had been so tempting to say yes. To be his wife and a mother to two little ones who needed her.

In her core, the truth burned. If she stepped in and took care of everyone, he would never trust himself to be the father she knew he already was. Those babies would never fully know how much he loved them, because he was too afraid to believe it. He didn't know how strong he really was in his weakness.

But if she did say yes, they would be hers for real and she would be there for them every "good morning" and every story time.

She sat on the edge of her bed and looked out the window, where a giant oak tree had stood for a hundred years. Its wide base twisted and turned as it reached up and out, growing stronger through the storms.

Not able to resist, she gave her phone a sideways glance. "Unknown." Curious, she picked it up and read the text.

Hi. It's Dane Valdez. New coach. Alex's dad. He's been asking when he can meet up with Rio and play. He says Coco is missing y'all.

The new coach and his son had been at church. He seemed like a nice guy with a nice job. Was Garrett right that Coach Valdez would ask her out if given the opportunity? He fit the bill for what she thought she wanted, but her heart was not in it. She feared it had already found a home.

There had to be a way she could be there for Rio and Pilar without losing herself in the bigger-than-life hero Garrett Kincaid.

All right, the pity party had to be over. With her grandmother's Bible in hand, she turned to familiar pages and prayed.

Chapter Thirteen

Opening the refrigerator, Garrett tried to decide if he
needed milk for cereal or if he'd go for a full plate of
eggs and bacon. Anjelica believed the day didn't start
if you didn't have bacon.

This would be their first morning without her.

Cereal had less risk involved. Man, he couldn't even
commit to a breakfast. "Rio, do we go with cereal or
eggs and bacon?"

He glanced over to the door and found his son staring out the window toward the big house.

"Sorry, little man, but Anjelica won't be joining us
this morning."

Rio turned and glared at him. Going back to standing watch, he pressed his hands against the window.
"She's gone like Mommy?"

His heart dropped as he stopped what he was doing
to go to Rio and take him in his arms, pressing his lips
against the messy hair. "No, no. She's fine. Don't worry.
She'll be back later this afternoon. Whenever I go to
work, she'll be here for you." Rio turned his back to him,
as if ignoring his words would make his nanny appear.

"Hey, so what is it, cold or hot?"

Rio shook his head.

Garrett went ahead and scrambled some eggs. He almost burned the bacon, but everyone ate without complaint.

Pilar actually smiled and giggled. Rio ate in silence, glancing to the door.

Anger simmered as Garrett replayed their discussion. Anjelica said he didn't love them, or her, enough. He couldn't imagine loving them more. That was why he wanted to provide them with security only she could bring to them.

Washing the plates in the sink, he scrubbed a little harder than necessary. Done with that chore, he turned and looked at the kids. His skin felt too tight.

Normally when he got like this, he'd go for a run, but he didn't have a stroller that carried both kids. He needed something more physical than his music.

Both of the kids were playing in the middle of the living room. Rio stacked blocks and Pilar knocked them over. Their laughter over the simple action tugged at him.

He needed something to knock over. Glancing out the window, the pile of wood from the fallen trees gave him an idea.

"Come on, guys. We're going outside to split some wood." He gathered up Pilar and bundled the toys in the blanket. "We need some fresh air."

With everyone settled a safe distance away, next to the garden, Garrett attacked the wood with the ax. Between each hit, he glanced at his children. One of Anjelica's bunnies was checking out Rio. Garrett paused to make sure the boy was gentle. A goat came to the edge of the fence and tried to get their attention. The heaviness on his chest lightened.

Each swing carried less anger. *God, You brought me to this point.* Whack. *You put Anjelica in my path.* Whack. *How do I fix it?* Whack.

If he could get Anjelica on his team, everything else would fall into place. If he had a complete family to offer them, the courts wouldn't take Pilar.

His arms and shoulders burned. Never before had he seen such a clear vision of what he wanted his future to look like. Years ago he had wanted a perfect family.

He'd done everything in his power to make Viviana fit into that image. It hadn't been real. Then in Afghanistan, he failed to protect... Sayid. There, he'd said the boy's name.

He was not strong enough. Whack.

This time, he saw Rio jump, moving closer to his sister as she let the goat nibble on her fingers.

He was an idiot. Got a kid who watched his mother be beaten, sure take him outside and swing an ax around. What was he thinking? Another reason he couldn't be trusted. What if he had?

Garrett leaned the ax against the tree stump and walked over to the kids. Going down to the ground, he rested his arm over his knee. "You okay, little man?"

His son kept his gaze down as he pulled the floppy-eared bunny into his lap. Selena raised her head and looked at Garrett. Reaching across Rio, he scratched her under her chin.

"Are you still worried about Anjelica coming back?" Garrett waited. Rio had gone mute again. He sighed in frustration and raised his hand to push his hair back but stopped midway when the boy flinched.

Slowly, he put his arm down. "Rio, I'm not going to hit you. I told you that and I always keep my promises. Have I lied to you yet?"

He kept his head down, and the curly hair bounced with each shake. "But you're angry." Rio's words were so low Garrett had to strain to make each one out.

A short snort escaped. "You're one smart kid. I thought I hid it well. But yes, I'm angry. There was something I wanted and I didn't get it. That's why I came outside to chop wood."

Needing to touch Rio, he brushed the wild curls back. Haircut next day off. "We all get angry. It's a normal emotion. It's not the anger that's bad—it's what we do with that anger that can hurt others or ourselves. If we hold it inside, it'll burn a hole in our gut, or we'll explode and hurt those around us."

Rio petted the rabbit, which appeared to have gone to sleep. His eyes, too old for a five-year-old, made Garrett want to weep. "James yelled and threw things when he got angry."

His arms longed to pull his son into his lap. He had so many hurts and injustices to fix. "Rio, listen to me." He waited for the boy to look at him. "I promise to never hit you, and if I start yelling, you can ask me to stop. No matter what you do, no matter how big your mistake or accident is, I will love you. I might get mad and there will be consequences, but everything I do is for you. So you can grow into the best man possible."

"Will I be like you?"

"You'll be Rio Kincaid." He smiled and ruffled the mop of hair. "A better version of me."

"Pilar's dad said I was a waste of no-good space and I should crawl into a hole and die. He didn't like my voice."

Oh, Viviana, why? No longer able to keep space between them, he pulled Rio against him. "The best day of my life was the day I found out about you. Then I saw you. You were so brave, protecting your sister. I love you, Rio, and I'm so proud you're my son. You're a gift from God, and just because James was too…angry about life to see it, does not make it less true. Do you understand?"

Against his heart, he felt the slight nod. He didn't have the words to explain to his son how important he was to him. "You're mine, Rio, and I'm yours. God gave us to each other, and we have to be grateful every day for that." He swallowed emotions so strong they hurt. "It's okay to get angry. You just have to find good ways to get it out."

"Like chopping wood?"

He laughed. "Yeah, but you have to be taller than the ax before you swing it. I do have an idea, though." At that moment Pilar slowly fell to her side. "Oh, look, we bored her to sleep."

Rio giggled. "She's too little to get angry. She just sleeps, plays and eats."

Scooping up his daughter and cradling her in one arm, he took a moment to look at her tiny soft features. There was no way he was giving her up. She was as much his as Rio was. "Let's put her in the playpen, and I'll get the things we need to let go of our anger."

It took them a while, and putting water in balloons was harder than it looked. But he had Rio laughing, so the task was worth the humiliation and soaked clothes.

He tossed a water-filled balloon in the air. "Now, the thing is, you throw the balloon as hard as you can against the garden fence. You can roar like a lion if you want. With each throw, you get rid of an angry thought. Ready?"

He handed his son a balloon. "Don't hold back. Give it everything you got."

Rio tossed the red balloon just like Garrett had done. He narrowed his eyes and set his jaw, pulling his arm, and let a loud bellow out that bounced off the hills as he threw the balloon.

The pile of balloons got shorter and the garden fence was dripping with water. Rio's laughter was the best. The therapist had him drawing out his feelings, but sometimes a boy just needed to be physical.

They both turned at the sound of a vehicle pulling into the drive.

Rio took off running. "Anjelica!"

Garrett stayed close. It was too early to be Anjelica, but maybe she had changed her mind. As they rounded the corner, Rio stopped midstride. In order not to run over him, Garrett braced the little shoulder and jumped to the side.

An unfamiliar gray Civic pulled up to the house.

Rio slid behind him and grabbed his leg. "Is she here to take me?

A tall willowy woman stepped out and pushed her long red hair over her shoulder. Her name cut into his throat. Gloria, his mother, had shown up. Even at the age of fifty, she had the lost-princess look down pat.

She gave him a nervous wave, her pink lips forming a stiff smile.

"It's okay, Rio. The lady is my mother." He took Rio's hand and met Gloria Kincaid halfway across the yard.

Her hands interlocked in front of her. "Garrett. Surprise." She opened her palms before crossing them over her middle again. Her green-gray eyes, the same he saw in the mirror and in the sadness of his son's gaze, glanced down at Rio. His son was hiding behind him again.

With tears threating to spill over her lashes, she glanced between them. Rio stared at her with open wonder.

The minute he saw the picture of Rio, he'd recognized the eye color all three of them shared. It had been a bit eerie. What startled him now was what else his son and mother shared. In their eyes there was the same "I've seen too much, felt too much, loved too much" depth.

"She's your mom?" his son whispered.

Garrett picked him up and held him on his hip. "Hi, Mom. Yes, this is your grandmother."

Gloria covered her mouth and gave a sound that might have been a laugh or a gasp. Wiping her eyes, she gave Rio a smile. "You look so much like your dad when he was a little boy. You're so beautiful. Can I hug you?" She took a step forward.

Rio burrowed deeper against his chest, turning his face away from her.

"That's okay. You don't have to hug me. I can't believe I have a grandson. How about you call me GiGi. That sounds fun, doesn't it?"

"Mom, you have a granddaughter, too. I'm going to court to adopt his sister." He put his hand over Rio's ear and waited for her to say something. When she nodded and smiled, relief loosened his shoulders. "Why don't we go around back? She's asleep in her playpen. Don't want her to wake up alone."

"Pilar, right?" Her light laughter followed him. "When

you jump into being a father, you don't hold anything back."

"They're great kids."

"Oh, I brought something for you. Let me get it from the car and I'll join you."

After checking on Pilar, they settled into the double rocker and waited.

"Your mom's pretty."

Before Garrett replied, Gloria walked around the corner with a purple flower-printed box. He frowned. He remembered that box always being in a closet wherever they lived at the time.

"Why, thank you, Rio. That's the cutest name." She set the box on the wicker table and went straight to Pilar. Rio slid down and stood next to the playpen with Selena.

"Your sister is just about the most precious thing I've ever seen. I can't wait to hold her when she wakes up." She turned back to Garrett. "I can see why you lost your heart to her. She looks just like her mamma."

A deep breath in relaxed his muscles. It was a good thing he spent his anger earlier today.

"Mom. Why are you here? On the phone the other day you suggested I let the state take care of the kids."

She bit her bottom lip and rubbed her hand on the front of her long skirt. "I was wrong. I just know the pain… That's not why I'm here. I brought the box that has all your school stuff. There are pictures of you and Viviana. I thought Rio would like to see you and his mother together. Children need to know there were happy times."

He raised one disbelieving eyebrow at her but didn't say anything.

She glanced at Rio before leaning toward Garrett. "You know I worried Viviana would hurt you again. She loved trouble, and you loved getting her out of it." She reached for his hand, and her long fingers intertwined with his. "I don't know how it all ended, but I do know it was not a lack of trying on your part."

He glanced at her hand. "Mom? What's with the ring?"

Her face lit up. "Oh, um, Hank asked me to marry him. I'll tell you all about him later. Today is about you, Rio and Pilar. Garrett, I'm so sorry for not being a better mother."

"Mom—"

She lifted another picture out. "There are a few of your father, too." Twisting around, she talked to Rio. "Your grandfather was such a good-looking man. Just like you and your daddy."

"I thought you had destroyed everything that had to do with Dad."

She passed the photo to Garrett, then started digging into the box again. "Not everything. Sometimes I worry that my anger might have destroyed parts of you."

Okay, now he was officially freaking out. "Mom, what's going on? Are you sick?" This was the kind of thing that people did when they found out they were dying. "You don't have cancer, do you?"

Her hearty laughter surprised him. Rio left his sister and crawled up in Garrett's lap.

Gloria patted Rio on the leg, and her laughter trailed off, leaving a soft smile. The one Garrett lived for as a kid. "No. What I have is a grandson I want to know. And a granddaughter. I also have a fiancé saying I need to unpack my past and move forward with a clean vision of what I want for the future." She pulled the box into her lap. "I want my family to be happy and know that, despite my mess-ups as a mom, they can count on me."

"You didn't mess up. Since my own very short journey of being a single father began, I've thought of you several times. You did an amazing job with us. As kids, we didn't appreciate the sacrifices."

He opened his palm and wrapped his fingers around hers when she accepted his invitation to join them. He pulled her in next to him on the double rocker. With Rio wedged in on one side, his mother reached across and brushed the curls out of the boy's face.

"He looks so much like you it hurts. Now I'm crying for real." Using the tips of her fingers, she wiped under her eyes. "Is my mascara running?"

"Does my hair make you sad, GiGi?" Rio had the side of his face pressed against Garrett's chest, but he hadn't moved away from her touch this time.

"No, sweetheart. It just makes me think of your dad when he was little. I'm so proud of him, and you make me think of all the time that has gone by and how grown-up he is now. A father to his own son and daughter. Sometimes mammas make a mess out of raising up their babies, but it doesn't mean they don't love them."

"Mom, you did a great job. We always had a safe place and something to eat. You taught us to stand on our own, to be independent. Why all this…?"

Tears welled up in her eyes, hanging heavy on her lashes. "How did you end up becoming such a good man?"

The sound of a vehicle pulling into the front drive interrupted any words he was going to say. Rio had drifted off to sleep on his shoulder, but now he had his head up and was looking at Garrett.

He nodded. "My guess is it's Anjelica's truck, but I'm not sure. Come on—let's check it out."

"I'll stay here and watch Pilar." His mom lifted the lid of the box. "Is Anjelica the one helping with the kids?"

He nodded. "She's also my landlord."

This time, instead of stopping at the corner of the house, Rio picked up speed and launched himself at Anjelica. "I missed you so much!"

Her eyes went wide and she stared at Garrett. "Rio, honey, I love you. But don't worry if I'm not around for every breakfast." She wrapped her arms around him. He clung to her like a koala on a tree. With her arms holding him against her heart, she looked at Garrett. "Is everything all right?" Her gaze darted to the new car.

Garrett wanted to point out that she could be, maybe even should be, Rio's mother, but now was not the time for that discussion.

"Yolanda called and said Maria saw a strange car pull into the drive and stay." Worry clouded her eyes. "Does it have to do with the case?"

"It's my GiGi," Rio whispered as if unsure if it was good news or not.

"My mother arrived unannounced. She's on the back porch."

Anjelica swallowed and forced a smile. His mother had arrived. He wouldn't be needing her anymore. *Okay, Anjelica, this is not about you.*

"That's great, Garrett."

"God's timing, right? See, I've been reading the

Bible you gave me. Since you want more space, my mother can watch the kids."

She pressed her lips to Rio's forehead. Eyes closed, she roped in her emotions. "So is she staying?" Being replaced so easily hurt, but what else could she do?

"Yes, but I don't know for how long. She said she's here to help and—" he winked at Rio "—she wants to get to know her grandchildren."

Rio nodded. "I'm her first grandson, and Pilar is her first granddaughter. She said Daddy jumped in fast."

It was the first time she'd heard Rio call Garrett Daddy. Her gaze rushed to Garrett. She saw a sense of wonder fall across his face. He blinked hard a couple of times.

"Yep. That I did. Best day of my life, bringing you and your sister home."

With a big smile and a vigorous nod that caused his curls to bounce, he hugged Anjelica's neck. "Daddy and I were throwing away our anger."

She sent Garrett a questioning look. What had they been up to? "Rio's a fountain of words." She pulled him close in a tight hug. "I love the sound of your voice."

"Daddy said you did. He said he did, too, and that I shouldn't hide it."

Oh, great. She was going to meet Garrett's mom crying. "Well, he's right. Want to introduce me to your GiGi?"

He wiggled down and took her hand. With his other one, he reached for Garrett, weaving his small fingers with his father's strong ones.

With them joined as one, the little boy pulled them forward. She didn't dare look at Garrett, worried he'd see the weakness in her eyes. Her throat burned.

On the back porch, Selena sat tall on the top step, standing guard. Her tail thumped against the boards when she saw them.

A storybook princess stood and smiled at her. Garrett's mother looked as if she had stepped out of a fairy tale. Anjelica wasn't sure why, but she'd pictured her as more of a worn-out biker chick.

"Hello." She approached them with her hand out. "I'm Garrett's mother. Gloria."

"Mom, this is Anjelica Ortega-Garza. She's been helping with Rio and Pilar. I really couldn't have done it without her. This is her house. We live in the apartment above the garage."

"Oh, this house is perfect. I always dreamed of having wraparound porches."

"I tried trading houses with him, but he can be a bit stubborn when it comes to letting people help."

Rio looked in the box. Holding a picture in both hands, he brought it close to his face. "It's Mommy. She looks like a princess." An edge of confusion lined his low voice. "Is that you with my mommy?"

Gloria moved to sit on the padded bench. "They're at prom. Your parents were friends since they were ten years old. Her family lived next door in one of the apartments we moved to." She dug in the box and found another picture. "Here they are at their first middle-school dance. Your mother was a very pretty girl. You can see where your sister gets that dark curly hair."

"Daddy's so little. He's shorter than Mommy."

Garrett sat on the other side and took the picture. "I told you I was a scrawny kid. I didn't start growing until I was sixteen."

"And then he didn't stop. He was so hungry all the

time. I'd feed him a full meal and twenty minutes later he wanted to know what was for dinner." She laughed and smirked at Garrett. "Paybacks are coming your way."

Anjelica stayed at the bottom of the steps. She wanted to be part of that family, but they weren't hers. She had told him no. "Hey, guys. Let me take a picture of you, and then I'll be going back to town."

"Oh, I would love that." Gloria scooted closer to Rio and reached behind him to put her hand on Garrett's shoulder.

Rio tucked his chin and gave her a tentative smile.

After a few pictures, Garrett stood. "Can I talk to you before you leave?"

"Sure." Nerves knotted her stomach. She gave Garrett's mother a hug as she handed back her phone. "It was a pleasure meeting you, and I have a room upstairs for you to use."

"Is that all right with your husband?"

"There's no husband."

"Oh? You live in this big house all by yourself?"

"Mother. Don't. She doesn't date men with guns." Garrett placed his hand on the small of Anjelica's back and gently ushered her away. "Thanks for offering my mom a room."

Being alone with him was not good for her. She didn't want to hear any bad news. "What happened with Rio? He's talking, I mean really talking."

"He was worried when you didn't join us for breakfast."

"Oh, Garrett." She stopped as they passed the corner of the house. Next to the tree that shaded the old nursery. "I'm so sorry. I never meant to upset him."

"I know. We worked it out. What really bothered him was my anger. I thought I hid it, but apparently not. I was chopping wood and he wasn't sure what to do. We ended up talking about anger and how to handle it so we don't hurt the people we love or ourselves." After explaining his unexpected therapy, he grinned at her. "I never dreamed my five-year-old son would be teaching me about life." Garrett put his hands in the front pockets of his jeans.

"Throwing water balloons and roaring like lions sounds like it worked."

He nodded and looked toward the front gate. "We have the court date in three days. Are you still going with us?"

"I would love to. If it's all right with you."

His gaze stayed on the horizon. She wished she knew what he was thinking. Guessing would be dangerous. The urge to trace her fingertips along the edge of his gorgeous jawline until the hard muscles relaxed was difficult to fight. Twisting the ends of her scarf kept her hands distracted, but not much would help her heart. "Is that what you wanted to talk about?"

"Anjelica, I need to apologize."

"No. Please don't."

He turned his gaze to her. The green-gray of his eyes looked alive. "I broke what we had and I want to fix it." One step and he was close enough to kiss her.

Her heart slammed against its cage as if to reach out to him, wanting to touch him. She wasn't sure she could refuse him again.

"Yes. You're more than the nanny. There is something between us, but I'm so messed up I don't know how to handle this—" he waved his hand "—thing between us. I've never been in a normal relationship. I've never been with someone that didn't need me to save them."

He reached down and took her hand in his. "With my inappropriate proposal, I drove you away instead of making us closer." His other hand went to her chin. "Please let me fix it. I'm not sure how, but I want to fix what I broke."

Biting the inside of her cheek, she prayed. *Please don't let me cry.* "What do you want from me?"

"I want you to give us a chance to get to know each other as two adults. Would you go on a date with me? Just the two of us. I'll get a babysitter, maybe my mom."

She couldn't help but laugh. "I think we've gone about this the wrong way. First there were children, then you ask me to marry you. Now you're asking me on a date?"

"I told you I wasn't good at this relationship stuff. I was married to a woman that thought it was okay to date other people. I had a father that did the same to my mom. So this whole attempt at a normal relationship is new, and I might make some mistakes."

With the most earnest expression she'd ever seen, he took her other hand. She tried not to laugh, she really did. Biting down on her lip didn't hide it from him, though.

"Are you laughing at me?" His left eyebrow arched.

Shaking her head, she took a deep breath and gained some control. It would kill her to hurt his feelings, especially since he guarded them so well.

A lopsided grin pulled on the corner of his lips, causing her favorite dimple to make an appearance.

She caressed the sweet line on his cheek. Anticipation of a kiss started to burn.

Instead he moved back. "I concede."

Disappointment should not have been her reaction. Wanting kisses from him after turning down his proposal would just confuse them more.

His gaze searched her face. "Can I kiss you?"

Every muscle in her body tightened. If she didn't respond, would that be a yes? She stood still and waited.

"I'll take that as a yes." Those beautiful eyes of his closed as his lips made contact with hers.

Melting into him sounded like a good option.

Strong hands full of warmth cupped her jaw as he gently explored the corner of her mouth. He broke contact first, taking her scarf with him.

"Hey, that's mine." She reached for it.

With a quick move, he kissed the scar next to her ear. "You can get it back Thursday at seven when I pick you up for our date." Mischief danced as the green became intense in his eyes. "You're so beautiful you don't need it."

With one last grin, he turned and headed back to his mother and kids.

"I never said yes!" she yelled after him.

Waving her scarf like a flag won in combat, Garrett turned and had the gall to laugh. "Oh yes, you did. Sweetheart, I might have had my doubts earlier, but after that kiss? You said a whole lot, and yes to Thursday night was just the beginning." He continued to walk backward until he reached the corner of the house. Tossing his chin up, he winked, turned and disappeared behind the wall.

Hands crossed over her chest. Fingers wrapped

around the thin straps of her sundress. The cool breeze brushed her exposed skin. She tried to remember the last time she'd been outside without one of her scarves.

Tears moistened her lashes and burned her eyes. It had been about the same time she lost the only person who knew her enough to know what her kiss meant.

Steve had teased her that they had been together so long they could read each other's minds.

All the way back to preschool, when he had publicly claimed her as his wife. The wedding ceremony had taken place in the house center. Her cousin Diego had married them. The baby dolls and stuffed animals had witnessed the whole event. Steve had worn a fireman's hat, and she'd worn the lace veil from the dress-up box.

Her fingers became numb as her nails cut into the flesh of her palms. She'd never dreamed that kind of friendship—that kind of love—could be hers again.

Relaxing her fingers, she took a deep breath. Her house was just like the play center at the preschool. She went through the motions of pretending to have a life.

She had the nerve to tell Garrett he needed to open up and love the children up close.

She bowed her head and the tears fell hard. *God, forgive me for my self-righteous attitude. Thank You for opening my heart to see the truth of the walls I built to keep people out.*

Something brushed her leg. Opening her eyes, she found Selena sitting at her feet. The dog looked up with compassion in her blue and brown eyes.

Anjelica went to her knees and buried her face in the soft fur. "You're always taking care of the family, aren't you, girl?"

Anjelica's tears wet Selena's coat. Her sobs were soft as the tears released the truth of her own lies.

A wet nose pressed up against her neck. "Thank you, Selena." She stood. "Go watch over the family. I'll be back at dinnertime."

With one last pat to Selena, she moved to her car. God had given her a gift in Steve, and now it appeared she had gotten another. A whole family this time.

Was she brave enough to take a chance and love again?

Garrett stood at the nursery window. His stomach in a knot. He had made her cry. He thought of going out there. But afraid of making it worse, he hid inside behind the curtain like a coward. So the dog was a better person than he was.

He'd so missed the mark on that one. When he left her, he'd felt better than he had in…well, forever. That perfect kiss, apparently not so perfect for her. What had he done wrong now?

Idiot, he had taken her scarf thinking it would show her how beautiful she was to him. Well, that backfired. He needed a manual. Maybe he could ask his mom, but she and Anjelica seemed so different.

"Garrett, is everything okay?" His mother stood beside him, looking out the window. "You seemed very happy after your talk with Anjelica. What's wrong now?"

"I think I messed up." Her old Ford truck vanished over the hill, out of his sight. Turning to his mother, he smiled. "I'm really glad you're here, Mom." He glanced around her shoulder. "Rio fell asleep?"

"Before I got to the third page." She laid her hand on his arm. "Now it's just the two of us. Let's talk."

They settled on the sofa with the box of memories between them. "You need to stop thanking me for being here. I should've dropped everything and been on your doorstep the minute you called me." She closed the lid and ran her hand over the top. "I should've loved you more than I resented Viviana. But tell me about Anjelica. Are you dating?"

He snorted. Tilting his head back on the sofa, he closed his eyes. "I actually asked her to marry me. She said no. So today I asked her on a date. Come to think of it, I didn't ask her. I told her I would pick her up Thursday at seven. I was trying to fix everything, but I think I might've made it worse."

He didn't know what he expected, but gut-busting laughter was not it. "Oh, sweetheart, you are so messed up." She leaned toward him. "Tell me, how did you propose?"

He groaned. "I told her marriage between us would be good for the kids because she loved them better than I could. Her home would be a good place to raise them. Then I followed up by telling her I couldn't love her the way she wanted."

"And she told you no? Shocking." She gave him a teasing wink.

"One thing you did well as a mom was make us laugh at ourselves. There wasn't any problem too big."

"Yeah, well, I would have never gotten out of bed if I let the problems keep me down. A good sense of humor and God will get you far, or at least keep you from crying all the time." She patted his arm. "And what is this about you not loving people enough? Where did that hogwash come from? That's not even true. You might pretend to be a big bad loner, but you're not. The very core of you is the faithful protector. You were made to be a father and husband. You're lying to yourself, and her, if you say you can't love completely."

"I'm starting to think that might be true."

"Believe me, I know the difference. So what are you going to do about it?"

"First I want to focus on the court date we have coming up. I need to make sure I get guardianship of Pilar. Then I'll figure out what to do with Anjelica. I need to get myself straightened out before I can offer her more." He would talk to Jake about seeing that therapist. "What about you, Mom? Who is this Hank person you've spoken of?" He used his deep manly voice, and it made her laugh. He had lived for her laughter when he was small. A mom's laughter made the world a better place.

"I actually met him at a singles' party at the new church I'm attending. He's one of the youth directors. His wife died a few years back. He has three grown children and a grandchild. He's encouraged me to stop hating and blaming your father by forgiving him, even though he didn't ask for it. Or even deserve it. I'm taking back my life. I'm taking back my happy. I'm not letting other people hold my heart hostage anymore." She cupped his face. "How can I hate a man that gave me two amazing children?"

"We get the amazing part from you."

"See, you always say the right thing. You need to be a husband to a woman that will love you back. Your Anjelica seems very solid and family oriented, and she would be blessed to have you."

He sighed. If it were only that easy. "You hungry? I can heat up some soup Anjelica made from scratch."

"She cooks, too! Are you sure she's human?"

He chuckled. "Sometimes I wonder." *Okay, God. I need a plan. Your plan. Show me the way.* Si Dios quiere.

Chapter Fourteen

Garrett tried to set Rio down next to the toy train. Their day in court had arrived, and their case had finally been called up. He smiled at Rio. "Come on, little man. I always wanted a train when I was a kid." He pushed it down the tracks and made train noises.

Rio wouldn't let go of his arm. "I want to stay with you."

"I need you to stay here with Pilar. Babies aren't allowed in the courtroom."

One of the women with a ruffled apron joined them. "Are you Rio? I'm Colleen. I'll be here with you and your sister until your daddy can come back. Pilar is playing with a truck. Do you want to join her?"

Large eyes full of a fear that twisted Garrett's gut looked up at him. "You're coming back? They're not going to take us away?"

"I promise. You're my son. They can't take you from me."

"Are they going to take Pilar?" With his face buried in Garrett's jacket, the words came out muffled.

What did he say without lying? "We're going to talk

to the judge. Pilar's grandmother wants to spend time with her, too."

Rio pulled back and looked at Garrett. "I can talk to the judge. You said I should use my words to get what I want." Tears formed in his eyes.

Pressing his lips to the top of the curly hair, Garrett glanced at Anjelica in desperation. Pilar was pushing a truck along as she crawled behind it.

The urge to grab them and not look back sounded good right about now. Now it was clear why some parents ran with their kids.

Colleen put her hands under Rio's arms and pulled him toward her. "Come on, Rio. The faster your dad goes, the faster he'll be back."

Garrett pulled his arm out of Rio's grasp. His son started crying. *God help me—I can't do this.*

A warm touch grounded him. He turned and found Anjelica.

"We'll be back, Rio." Her hand slid down to Garrett's and she intertwined her fingers with his. With a squeeze of his hand, she leaned in close to his ear. "Smile at him and walk out the door like you know you're coming back."

With a smile, he winked at Rio and did as she said. He stepped into the hallway with all the confidence that he'd be back to take his family home, his whole family.

Once they got past the door, he leaned against the wall to slow his pulse and gain some form of control over his emotions. He had to appear calm and confident going into the courtroom, even if he needed to fake it.

Anjelica stopped next to him. "That was hard, but the longer you stood there, the more uncertain he would have become."

He sighed. "I know. The fear of disappointing him took over." A halfhearted grin pulled at his mouth. "For a moment, I thought I could grab them and run. What am I going to do if the judge gives Pilar to the grandmother?"

"We'll fight it. You can also make sure Rio gets to visit with her. But I just know you'll get her. I can't imagine the judge separating them."

He nodded. Sometimes he wished he had her optimism, but he knew the realities of life. Life was not fair, and the good guy didn't always win.

He wasn't even the good guy. "Thank you for being here. I meant to bring your scarf to you today. I shouldn't have taken it from you."

Her delicate shoulders shrugged and a sweet look of understanding he didn't deserve settled on her face. "If I wanted it back, I could have gotten it. I know where you live. I'll get it from you Thursday when you pick me up. Where are we going?"

"Are you sure you want to go out with me? I didn't really ask you and…" He didn't want her to know he had seen her cry afterward. "I didn't really ask."

"Oh, if you changed your mind—"

"No, I still want to go with you if you want to go. There's a place on the river in Kerrville that plays live jazz on their patio Thursday nights."

"Sounds lovely."

"Okay. Good."

His mother walked down the corridor. "Sharon said they're ready." She gave him a tentative smile. With her hair up, she looked too young to be his mother. Taking his hand, she gave him a reassuring smile. "Do you want to have a quick prayer before we go?"

He nodded. Anjelica moved in closer and took his other hand.

He opened his heart to God's will as he regulated his breathing. "Lord, please cover the courtroom with Your presence. Wrap Rio and Pilar so tightly in Your love that they'll always know You. Grant wisdom on the judge, and give me peace for Your will."

Both women squeezed his hands. He leaned over and kissed his mother on the cheek. "Thank you for being here."

"I should have been here sooner."

"You're here now. Come on—let's get this settled and hopefully have everyone home in time for dinner."

Walking into the courtroom, he stopped at the sight that greeted him. In the benches were Anjelica's parents, a few sisters and her grandparents. That didn't surprise him as much as the other couples who now stood to greet him. The sheriff, Jake Torres, and his wife, Vickie, were with Pastor John and his fiancée, Anjelica's cousin Lorrie Ann. Maggie and Yolanda, along with a few other Ortegas, filled the room. A couple of people from the church joined the group as they surrounded him.

His chest burned as if someone had punched him. They were here to support him. To help him keep his family together.

He tried swallowing, but his throat was too dry. He thought about something as they each shook his hand and encouraged him. He knew the community was tight and supportive, but somehow he'd missed the memo that he was a member of the community himself. This wasn't just for Anjelica; they were here for him, Rio and Pilar.

Smiling, he nodded and patted each handshake with his left hand on top of his right. Anjelica hugged people, tears sitting softly on her eyelashes. Instead of making her look weak, they showed how strong she was.

Anjelica had the sense to introduce his mother to everyone. Looking over, he saw Cecilia Barrow, Pilar's grandmother, sitting with a teenage girl. He thought it could be one of the granddaughters she was raising, but he wasn't sure.

The CPS caseworker was talking to her. No matter how many deep breaths he took, the knot in his stomach pulled tighter.

The judge entered the room and everyone got in place. After calling the court to order, she asked the child advocacy and CPS workers to approach the bench.

Everyone took a seat and waited for the judge's decision. She scanned the larger audience behind Garrett and Anjelica.

She looked down at her paper. "For me, when family comes into court wanting to keep a grandchild, it is an easy decision when that grandparent has a good record and has shown commitment to other grandchildren she has taken custody of. This has a little bit of a complication because the child in question also has a brother that has a father. Overall, I do believe blood relations are the best place for a child to feel like they belong."

Garrett was going to be sick. He wanted to stand and yell no.

Pilar's grandmother stood. "I'm sorry to interrupt, Your Honor, but is there a way I may speak to Mr. Kincaid alone before going any further?"

The judge raised an eyebrow. "I will let you ask him

here. I would prefer to do this quickly. Will you and Mr. Kincaid please approach the bench?"

Reaching for Anjelica's hand, he looked back in surprise when she didn't follow. She shook her head, and he let her go. He wanted her by his side, but she didn't have legal rights to be there. There were a few times in his life he'd been this scared, and they had always ended in disaster.

He glanced at Cecilia before turning to the judge. With no clue what she was up to, he couldn't even begin to sort his emotions.

"What did you want to ask Officer Kincaid?"

The older woman who was already raising her other grandchildren looked up at him. Her dark hair streaked with silver was pulled into a tight neat bun. "I was just told you had already had a lawyer put the money for both children into a trust fund you can't touch. Is that correct?"

That took him by surprise. Whatever he'd thought she might want to know, that was not it. Was she mad she couldn't get to the money?

"Yes. It can be used for college at any time, but if they don't go to college, then they'll get their portion when they're twenty-five. Do you have a problem with that? I worked it out with the CPS workers and the lawyers."

The wrinkles at the corners of her eyes elongated with her smile. "No, the reason I stepped in and filed for custody of baby Pilar was to protect her from being used for any money she might get."

"I don't need the money, and truthfully, I wouldn't want it either way."

She nodded and turned back to the judge. "I'm sorry,

but I would like to withdraw my claim of custody to Pilar. I would like visitations but not guardianship."

"This hearing was for guardianship." Impatience clipped the judge's words. "You can work out visitation between the two of you."

Stunned, Garrett was afraid of falling. His legs had disappeared from under him. She had withdrawn her claim. Pilar was his, for now.

"Yes!" He blinked back the burn in his eyes. "Yes, you can visit Pilar." He turned. Anjelica stood.

Even across the room, she helped him keep his feet in place. The judge might frown on him running from the room to get his children. His children. He bit down hard on the inside of his cheek. He had to keep it under control. There were still a few months before he could adopt her.

Dismissed by the judge, he went straight to Anjelica. He felt light as a helium balloon, and Anjelica's hand was the string that kept him earthbound.

With her hand in his, he faced all the people who had come to support him. Everyone had questions in their eyes. They hadn't heard the exchange from the front of the court. He smiled the first real smile all day.

"She dropped the claim. Pilar's mine. We're taking her home." Cheers erupted. Hugs and pats on the back made him feel like a new father who had just been told his baby had arrived healthy in the hospital. Standing to the side was his mother. Tears ran down her cheeks. Leaving the boisterous crowd, he went to her.

"We won."

With a napkin, she wiped under her eyes. "I'm so proud of you, Garrett. And I think, as a mother, Viviana is very happy about this outcome."

"I hope so. Come on—I want to tell Rio."

With his arm around his mother's slender waist, they went through the sea of people and to the door. Cecilia stood there.

"You have a lot of friends and family that are happy for you. That's good to see. I just wanted to make sure you were serious about me being able to visit her."

"I never meant to keep her away from you. You're more than welcome to visit. Do you want to see her now?"

Dark eyes lit up. "Can I? Thank you."

"Hello, I'm Garrett's mother. I just want you to know, from one grandmother to another, that Pilar is well loved. Thank you for letting him keep the children together."

The older woman looked over to the bench where her other granddaughter sat staring at a phone with earbuds blocking out the world. "I'm getting too old to raise kids." She looked through the window where the children played. "He wasn't always bad. Drugs eat the core of a person and gut them, taking control. I thought with Viviana and Pilar things were getting better. I prayed so hard. Then he lost his job. He cut me off, not allowing me to come over or see the kids. I feared he had gotten back into that world."

She turned her head and wiped at the tears. "Sorry. I just never dreamed it would end like this. At one time, he was a good boy. I want Pilar to know that about her father."

Garrett put a hand on her shoulder. "You can share the good parts with her. As they get older, there will be a lot of tough questions to answer. I'm glad you want to stay in her life. I think that'll help them sort through it. Let's go see them."

His mother, Pilar's grandmother and Anjelica joined him as he crossed the threshold to his children.

Rio stood when they walked into the playroom. Panic screamed from his eyes as he stood in front of his sister. Going to one knee in front of his son, Garrett laid a hand on one small shoulder. Rio's back was stiff as he glared at Pilar's grandmother. The little guy was ready to fight for his sister.

"Relax. She just came in to see Pilar. The judge agreed that the best place for you and Pilar to live was with me."

The eyes that looked so much like his own darted to him. "And Anjelica?"

"She'll still be in the big house." The only thing left now was to settle the role she played in their lives.

"Hello, Rio. Do you remember me? I'm Grandma CeCe."

"Grandmas are good to have, right?" He glanced over at Anjelica and Garrett's mother.

Anjelica joined him on the floor. "Oh yes. The more grandmothers, the better."

After a nod from Rio, Cecilia moved around to Pilar. "Oh, sweet girl."

While Cecilia talked to Pilar, Garrett pulled Rio into his arms. He wanted to absorb the scent and feel of his son. The day could have been devastating, but it wasn't. He was now one step closer to officially being their father. They were his children.

Not that long ago, he thought his plan in life was to build a cabin and live alone. Jake had made a joke about plans that he now understood.

A greater life waited for him, one he hadn't even known he wanted. Eyes closed, he pressed his lips against the soft curly hair of his son.

When he lifted his head, Anjelica was there, tears in her eyes and joy on her face. "You did it. They're coming home."

"I'm so ready to get out of here. We need to celebrate."

Colleen brought the diaper bag to them. "Congratulations. Some families are just meant to be together."

"Rio, go with Anjelica. I'll get your sister."

After one last kiss from Grandma CeCe, Garrett took Pilar. The urge to squeeze her riveted his muscles. Taking a deep breath, he relaxed his arms. The baby shampoo Anjelica had bought for her smelled of comfort and love. She was his. Oh man. If he didn't get a grip, he'd be crying in front of people.

His mother held out a cup of coffee. "Here, I know you didn't want any before the hearing, but you deserve it now."

"Thanks."

Diaper bag over his shoulder, his daughter in one arm and coffee in his hand, he followed Anjelica out of the courthouse. A new adventure waited. Now if he could just convince Anjelica to join him, life would be perfect.

A flash of heat rushed his body. A cold sweat covered his skin. Taking a sip of coffee, he mentally grounded himself. Just because life was good didn't mean something bad was about to happen.

Pilar touched his face with her now-chubby fingers. "Dada."

Anjelica gasped. "Did she just call you Dada?"

His mother clapped. "She did. Are these her first words?" She pulled her phone out. "Dada. See if you can get her to say it again."

"Mom, really?"

"Oh, don't play Mr. Tough Guy. We know you better and I saw you almost tear up. This is big. You will thank me for recording it. She'll be grown up and having her own family before you know what's happening."

"Mom. She's not even a year yet."

Pilar patted his face to get his attention. "Dada. Dada."

Ugh. His mom was right—he wanted to cry. He hated emotion. "I'm right here, baby girl."

"I can say *Daddy*, too. I'm a big boy, so I know how to say it right."

Standing at the car door, Garrett laughed. "Yes, and it takes time to learn how to say words. I remember someone not using his words not that long ago."

Anjelica opened the door and got Rio in his car seat. "Yep, words have power. We're proud of both of you."

"Dada! Dada!" Pilar giggled. "Dada! Dada!" She smiled as everyone told her how smart she was. "Dada!"

His heart officially belonged to her. No one had ever told him how a single word would change his life.

"I think this deserves ice cream. My treat." His mom climbed into the backseat between the car seats.

He couldn't help but smile. "Some of my favorite memories were you taking us to get ice cream when we had good grades or you got a new job."

"I wish I could have done more."

He gave his mom the best father look he could manage. He'd have to practice. "You raised some pretty good kids, Mom."

"Yes, I did."

Closing the door, he pressed all of his weight into his hands. Leaning hard against the car. The smell of rain hung in the air. Fresh and clean, washing away the dust. He had a new plan. Now, how to go about making it happen without messing everything up?

Getting in the car, he was greeted with "Dada! Dada!"

Everyone laughed as Pilar gave him a huge grin, kicking her feet. "Dada! Dada!"

Anjelica winked at him. "I think we might have created a monster."

"She's our monster now."

Chapter Fifteen

Three weeks had passed since the first date with Anjelica. He'd managed to get one more date in and several family excursions.

Garrett heaved a huge sigh of relief in the empty room. All the family noise outside was muffled. The church had been standing-room only for the Easter service, and now it seemed as if everyone had followed them home.

His guess? They picked up a few strays along the way. Anjelica had even invited Cecilia for the festivities, and Pilar's grandmother brought three of her older grandkids.

When he planned for a family Easter-egg hunt and dinner, he had foolishly imagined her parents and his kids. Maybe a few aunts and uncles and her favorite cousins. A perfect time to propose. But now it was a whole town event.

He hadn't been near this nervous when he asked Viviana to marry him. Then again, he had been naive and full of the fantasy of marriage.

Harsh reality replaced fantasies. The pendulum

swung back. He'd gone from thinking marriage would fix him, to thinking marriage was a death trap, to thinking marriage would fix his children. Now he settled somewhere in the middle.

Taking the ring out of his pocket, he wondered if it was too soon. He was ready to completely commit, but would she believe him?

She had turned him down once for every right reason. His hand shook a little when he placed the ring on the shelf above Steve's flag and picture.

"Well, I'm gonna try and get it right this time. Any suggestions? You loved the girl she was, and I hope she lets me love the woman she's become." Could he compete with a childhood love?

"Garrett?"

He jumped at the sound of his mother's voice.

"Who are you talking to?"

"Is it weird that I'm talking to her husband?"

She came over and rested her cheek on his upper arm as she looked up at the pictures. "No. You're both marines. You've seen the same things, loved the same girl. You have a great deal in common." She reached up and kissed him on the cheek. "Oh, Garrett! Is that box what I think it is?"

He nodded. "Somewhere in my addled brain, I thought today would be a great time to ask her. A grand romantic gesture in front of her family. I planned to hide it in an Easter egg with her name on it. Now it sounds lame. What if one of the kids finds it?" He went to the window and peeked through the curtains. The front was packed with cars and trucks. "I also don't want her to feel trapped. If I ask her in front of everyone…well, that might not end up well."

He put his left arm around his mother as he ran his other hand through his hair. "I want to make it special. Let her know how important she is to me. I don't know if this is good enough." He looked back at the picture. All the memories she must have made with Steve were everywhere. In the house, in town, at the church. How did he even begin to find a place in her life?

"Are you worried you haven't dated long enough?"

He snorted. "That's one concern that never occurred to me. I know her. We've shared as many breakfasts, lunches and dinners as a married couple. When you pace the floor at three in the morning soothing a sick child together, you know that person in a deeper way than if you'd met for a year's worth of dates. I know her. But what if she knows me too well? What if I'm not enough for her to get over her fear of how I make a living?"

"Oh, sweetheart, you're more than enough."

"You're my mom. Your opinion doesn't count."

"You do what you feel is right, but promise me you won't let fear be the thing that stops you." She patted his chest. "Don't hide in here for too long, or Buela will come looking for you. The kids are about to hit the pi-ñata. Anjelica sent me in to get more tea. She said it was on the stove."

"I'll help you. Last thing I want is Buela hunting me down."

They took the fresh-brewed tea to the beverage table, and his mom helped him pour it into a giant orange dispenser. Scanning the backyard, he found Anjelica bouncing Pilar on her hip while she talked to Vickie, the sheriff's wife.

Her one free hand was waving about as she explained

something. Her shoulders were bare except for the straps of the sundress she wore. He liked to think he had helped her feel more confident in some way.

Kids ran around. People talked and laughed. Someone was playing a guitar. A few of the men were stringing up a colorful star piñata, with the ribbon getting tangled in the wind. This was home.

His eyes went back to Anjelica. She was home.

A bump to the shoulder took him out of his own thoughts. Sheriff Torres stood there with a plateful of desserts. "You know you can go talk to her. You don't have to stare at her like a lovesick boy at a middle-school dance." He popped a lemon square in his mouth.

Garrett snorted. "I thought you already had dessert."

With a shrug, he glanced over to his wife and Anjelica. "Have to try everything to make sure no one's feelings get hurt. It's a sacrifice, but someone has to make sure it's done." He swung his gaze back to Garrett. "Speaking of sacrifice. How's family life treating you?"

Garrett found Rio running with several children. He laughed as a little mop of a dog jumped after him. Looked like Coach Valdez and his son had been invited, too. "Better than I thought."

"Yeah, it can take some getting used to. Still having good and bad days with Vickie's kids living with me." He laughed. "Vickie assures me it's normal. I wouldn't trade it for the world, though. Have you been seeing Reeves like I suggested?"

Nodding, Garrett kept an eye on Rio as the children ran behind the garden and around the Esperanza bush.

"Actually, it's helped a great deal. Thank you. I feel

more grounded than I have since getting back to the States."

"Yeah, he's a good guy. Let me know if you need anything. I'm always available. I'm a good wingman, too. Just sayin'. Don't wait too long. I wasted ten years afraid to just ask." With a smirk on his face, his gaze darted from Anjelica back to Garrett. Vickie waved at them. "Duty calls. Catch you later."

"Later."

Vickie's daughter ran to Torres and jumped into his arms. Holding the girl, he spoke with the women for a while before taking off on a mission to hang the donkey piñata for the smaller kids.

He could stand here all day and watch Anjelica in action. She brought order to chaos and made it seem easy. Glancing over her shoulder, she caught him staring at her.

Great, he did look like that awkward middle-school kid. With a nod, he turned to take the large pot back to the kitchen.

Today was not the right time. He needed to wait, but the question was when. Rushing something this big was not good. He'd done that with Viviana. But waiting too long could waste time, like Torres said.

What if she found someone else who didn't carry a gun for a living? Like the coach. With a grunt, he opened the screen door.

Maybe it was a test. If he really loved her, he'd give up law enforcement. He washed the pot and put it away, then stood in the middle of the kitchen.

He couldn't imagine doing anything else. Rubbing his temple, he took a deep breath. This was too complicated. What was wrong with wanting a simple life?

Then again, if he had stayed away from Viviana when he returned home, he wouldn't have Rio or Pilar. Now he was talking himself in circles. How could you regret a life that also brought you blessings?

Looking into the living room, he saw the ring on the high shelf. He needed to put it away for now.

Anjelica nodded at something Vickie said, but her attention stayed on the back door. Garrett hadn't smiled back at her when she caught him staring.

The last two days, he seemed distracted. She bit down on the inside of her cheek. What was wrong, and why was he not talking to her?

"Then a lion jumped from the stage and bit his head off."

She turned back to Vickie and blinked a couple of times. "What?"

"Oh, that you heard. So where did you go while Pilar and I had a talk?" She smiled at the little girl and tickled her tummy.

Pilar giggled and grabbed Anjelica's hair and pulled her close, slobbering on her cheek. "Oh, Anjelica. She's giving you kisses! She looks at you like you're her mamma."

Anjelica hugged her close. "Oh, baby girl, I love you, too." She glanced back at Vickie. "Enough of this mamma talk."

"Oh, give me a break. You take care of her. You practically live in the same house. You are basically her mamma. The only one she has or knows. The way her daddy has been looking at you, I say he wouldn't mind her calling you Mamma."

"We're just friends."

Vickie's eyebrow went high. "Is that what the kids are calling it these days? I thought you had gone on some real dates."

Shaking her head, she cupped Pilar's sweet face and kissed her dark curls. "We have, but I just don't think I can go down that road again."

"What road is that? Love? I think it might be too late."

Anjelica shook her head. "I married one man who had a hero complex. I can't sit at home and wait, praying he comes home." She looked at Vickie. "How do you not go crazy every time Jake goes to work?"

"First I pray every day to keep him protected." Vickie tilted her head. "But I don't get why you compare Steve to Garrett. I remember Steve pushing the edge all the time. He would rush headlong without thinking. Remember the time he jumped from one truck to another while they were going, like, eighty miles an hour? How many cars did he total?" She rolled her eyes. "That boy was downright crazy. I always thought you were the only reason he didn't get himself killed early on."

Anjelica blinked to keep tears from falling. Vickie laid a hand on her upper arm.

"I'm sorry. My mouth gets me in trouble all the time. I didn't mean to upset you. That was just stupid of me."

"No. I'm okay. I never really thought about it like that before. I loved Steve, but I spent a great deal of time waiting for him to grow up."

"He was a great kid. Biggest heart in the world, and he loved you. He also liked playing the hero, but not the way Jake and Garrett do. Garrett is smart. Jake's impressed with him. He considers the situation and takes charge. If that's the reason you're not sure, girl, you need to let that go." She looked back to the porch. "You have a great man there, and if I'm reading it right, he's in love with you."

"I don't know. The last few days he's been acting weird."

Vickie snorted. "Yeah! You're giving the poor guy every mixed message there is. Poor boys. We drive them crazy, but between you and me. I think they kinda like it." She reached for Pilar. "Let me take this little bit, and you go talk to your man. You're not wearing your scarves anymore—I'm guessing that has something to do with him. Put all the worries in God's hands and go."

Garrett was still in the house. She scanned the yard full of family and friends and realized he was alone inside. Maybe this was too much for him.

She was used to all the people all the time, but he was so private.

"Go. Stop overthinking it and go." Vickie waved her on.

"Okay, okay."

With a deep breath, her shoulders back, she walked forward. Why was she so nervous? Silence met her in the kitchen. "Garrett?"

"Anjelica? Do you need something?" His deep voice came from the living room.

They met at the archway as she moved into the living room and he walked into the kitchen.

He braced his hands on her arms so as not to run her over. "Everyone okay?"

"Yes. I just thought we could talk."

His eyebrows crunched down. "Now? Don't you have a few hundred guests outside?"

She bumped her fist against his upper arm. An upper arm that looked really good in the short-sleeved polo he wore. With a sigh, she looked up at his face. "Not that many. Is it making you nervous? I can ask them to leave. We've already done the Easter-egg hunt, and everyone's eaten."

With a grin on those perfect lips, he stepped back. Well, she couldn't trust herself to look at his face, either, without getting distracted. She'd always had a thing for jaws. Strong jaws and dimples. Like the long dimple on the side of… Ugh. *Focus, Anjelica.*

Now he had one eyebrow cocked, waiting for her to speak. Vickie was right. Garrett never rushed anything. Well, other than marriage. He'd rushed it with Viviana and tried with her.

Stepping into him, she cupped his face with her hands. Confusion clouded his expression. New stubble edged his jaw. His eyes searched her face.

Lifting her face, she pressed her lips to his. He closed his eyes. The muscles under her hand relaxed. Slowly, he joined the kiss, following her lead. She moved closer, wanting to sink into him and take him all in, his textures, his scent.

Fingers slid from his jaw to the pulse at the base of his neck.

Placing his hands on the backs of her arms, he pulled back. "Wow."

She was officially out of her mind. He had to think she was crazy. He was waiting for her to say something, but her brain knocked around her skull without a single idea. "Hi."

Really? That was all she had.

His lips moved to a wide-open smile. "Hi to you, too."

"I've really enjoyed these last three weeks with the kids."

"And the kids enjoy being with you."

She wrapped her arms around her middle and looked to the backyard. She'd never worried about her words with Steve.

Garrett looked relaxed with his hands in the front pockets of his jeans. An encouraging smile didn't really help her feel better.

"You know Steve was the only boy I ever dated, and we knew each other from the time we could walk. So this whole relationship thing is new to me, too."

"Ha. A normal relationship with a well-adjusted, strong woman is completely new territory for me. I…" He glanced over his shoulder into the living room. Coming back to her, he ran his hand through his hair, causing it to stand up on the side.

Not able to resist, she moved toward him and smoothed out the strays. "What is it?"

"Nothing. So you left the party to hunt me down and kiss me?"

She had to laugh. "You make me sound so…forward. The kiss was unexpected, but I hope it got the message across." Hand flat on his chest, she felt his heart beat. It seemed to pick up the pace. "I want to spend more time with you. Not because of the kids, but because I love you." There, she'd said it, and the house didn't fall down. Garrett was still standing, too. His face scrunched in a frown.

Okay, not the reaction she'd hoped for.

She looked for a way out. How did you make a graceful exit after saying those words? In one long step, he had his hands on her shoulders, anchoring her in place. No escaping now.

"You weren't supposed to say it first."

"What? It's a contest?"

He chuckled. "No. I've been debating for a week now, but worried I'd say it too soon. I really messed up last time, and I need to get this right.

"Last time? You've never said—" She covered her mouth when she realized he was talking about his marriage proposal. "The proposal? That was you saying you loved me?"

"Not very well." Holding his palm up, he waited for her to take his offer. "Come with me. I want to show you something."

They joined hands, and his thumb caressed the back of her hand. So much bigger than hers, his fingers engulfed her hand, making her feel safe and cherished.

She followed him out the kitchen door and up the stairs to his apartment. Now she was curious. What could be in the apartment she had not seen before?

In his living room, he dropped her hand. "Wait here." He disappeared into his room. Nerves started twisting as she tried to imagine what he wanted to show her.

Joining her, he held a boot box. Okay, so it wasn't a ring. Balancing the box with one hand, he lifted the lid. He pulled out a string? He stopped and looked at her. Uncertainty suddenly appeared on his face.

"What is it? You're killing me."

"I know we both have broken pieces, but I hope together we can make a family. I love you and can't imagine anyone else. I don't want anyone else."

With a lopsided grin, he lowered the box. Hanging from the string was her broken wind chime that had been destroyed in the storm.

Her hand covered her mouth. The one she had made when she was expecting Esperanza. She thought she'd lost it forever. Now he offered it back to her.

It was cracked and skewed, but he had glued the parts together. A few were missing, but it was beautiful. She wanted to cry.

Carefully, he put it back in the box. "I'm sorry. I didn't mean—"

Just like Rio, she launched herself at him. His arms came around her as he staggered back. His laughter rumbled from his chest.

"So you like it?"

"It's the nicest, best gift anyone has ever given me." Giving him some space, she stepped back and wiped her face.

"I had a whole speech to go with it. I know this might be too soon, but we've been through so much and I can't imagine more time will change anything for me." He took a knee in front of her and pulled a small box out of his pocket. "I know I'm not the easiest man to get along with, but I want to be there for you. You know me in ways no one else ever even tried to know me." He took a solitaire out of its velvet box. "Anjelica Ortega-Garza, will you accept all my broken parts and add Kincaid to your name?"

"Are you willing to take on the Ortega family and all that means?"

His dimples came out in full force. "Yes. I almost love them as much as I love you."

"Then yes! Garrett River Kincaid, I would be proud to marry you and be your wife."

Somehow his grin grew wider and he slipped the ring on her finger. It was a touch too big. His smile disappeared. "We'll have to get it sized, or you can pick another one."

Holding her hand up, she admired the swirl and twist of the gold band surrounding the simple classic diamond. "It's perfect." She took a deep breath and wrapped her arms around his neck. "I love you."

He glanced at the door. "We should go tell Rio and your family."

She let go of his neck and took his hand. She just wanted to stay there and absorb this moment with him. The love and happiness so complete it made her aware how empty she'd been before, going through the motions of living.

"Thank you, Garrett. For not giving up on me. I was so afraid of taking back my own happiness."

Cupping her face, he leaned in and kissed her. "Thank you."

With a nod, she turned to the door to make the announcement that would send her life in a new direction. A direction filled with love and laughter, even during the rough times.

Anjelica's hand in his, Garrett wanted to jump down the steps. Colorful confetti coated the yard. The *cascarones* wars must have broken out.

Many of the people turned and stared at them. Garrett was sure he had an expression on his face that gave them away. He scanned the yard for Rio.

From a group of children, his son ran toward him with one hand tucked behind his back. "Daddy, I have a secret."

Garrett leaned down, and Rio broke the confetti egg over his head. The boy laughed out loud, arching his whole body backward. "I got you, Daddy!"

"You did." Garrett shook his head and the colored paper flew around them.

"I have a secret, too. You wanna know what I did today?"

Rio looked at his hands with suspicion before getting closer. "What is it?"

He held out his hand to Anjelica. "I asked Anjelica to be my wife and your mother."

The little boy's eyes went wider as his gaze darted to Anjelica. He pressed his body against Garrett's side. "What did she say?" He whispered it, but the crowd had gotten quiet and it carried across the yard. It seemed as if the whole town waited for the answer.

Anjelica came down to Rio's eye level. "I said yes. Once we get married, we'll all live here together."

He whooped loud and jumped up. Before Garrett knew what had happened, they were surrounded. He picked Rio up so the crowd wouldn't overwhelm him.

This was his family. Every single person here was now a part of his future. He thought about the cabin he had planned. And didn't feel a twinge of regret or longing about it.

As people gathered and congratulated them, he kept his attention on Anjelica. Someone handed Pilar to her. They were so beautiful.

Parts of him might be forever broken, but the best

parts now belonged to her. God really did answer prayers not even prayed for. He'd sent Garrett his very own hero, and now she was going to be his wife. He wanted to laugh and dance. God was good. Life was good. Love was his.

* * * * *

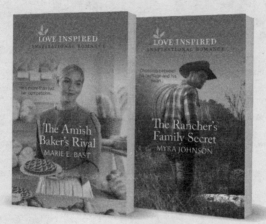